# PRODUCT OF THE STREET

## UNION CITY BOOK 2

**E. BOWSER**

# CONTENTS

# Acknowledgments

I WOULD LOVE TO HEAR FROM YOU, SO PLEASE CONSIDER JOINING THE **PRODUCT OF THE STREET BOOK GROUP ON FACEBOOK!**

I WANT TO THANK GOD FOR LETTING ME BE ABLE TO WRITE THE STORIES THAT I LOVE. I ALSO WANT TO THANK MY MOTHER AND THE LOVE OF MY LIFE FOR PUTTING UP WITH ME. I WOULD LIKE TO THANK SALLIE FOR STAYING UP WITH ME AND ENCOURAGING ME TO WRITE SOMETHING DIFFERENT. I WOULD ALSO LIKE TO THANK MY EDITOR JOI MINER FOR HELPING TO MAKE MY BOOK THE BEST IT CAN BE! BIG THANK YOU TO MY ARC READING TEAM! ALSO, THANK YOU TO SINFUL SECRETS WITH A DEADLY BITE GROUP, WHO ALWAYS HAS MY BACK WHENEVER I RELEASE, EVEN WHEN IT ISN'T PARANORMAL.

To all of you who have supported me through my writing career, just know that I appreciate it. That is what keeps me writing.

HTTPS://WWW.FACEBOOK.COM/GROUP

**TRIGGER/CONTENT WARNING**

*THIS BOOK CONTAINS **EXPLICIT** SEXUAL SCENES, HARD KINK/FETISH CONTENT, EXPLICIT LANGUAGE, **GRAPHIC** VIOLENCE, DRUG USE, AN INSINUATION OF RAPE, ORGANIZED CRIME, STALKING, OBSESSIVE, POSSESSIVE, KIDNAPPING, VOYEURISM, EXHIBITIONISM, HOPLOPHILE, MASK FETISH, FINDOM, PREGNANCY, AND PREGNANCY LOSS. THIS IS A SERIES! **IT IS INTENDED FOR ADULTS.***

*Dear Readers,*

*Product of the Street is a series that will span at least five books. My epilogues are not used to give you a happily-ever-after ending. They are used to progress the story's plot and develop characters in this universe. Product of the Street is a series; every character will still be a part of the storyline, and you will always see how their relationships progress. Those of you that have read my paranormal series already know. Once this series concludes, you will have an epilogue telling the futures of each character. I hope you stick along*

*for the ride and know that just because the story moves on does not mean it is the end of the story for your favorite character.*
*Thank you,*
*E. Bowser*

**Exhibitionist**- an exhibitionist is a person who becomes sexually aroused by being observed naked or engaging in sexual acts. This thrill can be achieved through fantasy or by performing these acts in front of people or in public.

**Voyeurism**- the practice of gaining sexual pleasure from watching others naked or engaged in sexual activity.

**Hoplophile**- someone with an irrational love of, or fetish for, weaponry (especially firearms).

**Mask fetishism**- is persons who want to see another person wearing a mask or taking off a mask. The mask may be a Halloween mask, a surgical mask, a ski mask, a ninja mask, a gas mask, a latex mask, or any other mask.

**Financial domination** (also known as '**findom**')- is a fetish lifestyle activity in which a submissive is required to give gifts or money to a dominant.

**Antisocial personality disorder**- A personality disorder characterized by a persistent disregard for the rights of other people. Failing to comply with laws and social customs, and irresponsible and reckless behavior.

**Psychopath**- A person affected by a chronic mental disorder with abnormal or violent social behavior.

**Sociopath**- A person with a personality disorder manifests in extreme antisocial attitudes and behavior and a lack of conscience.

**Shared psychotic disorder**- is a rare disorder characterized by sharing a delusion among two or more people in a close relationship.

## PROLOGUE

# Ian Nevin 'Rogue' Lawe

## *"She can ride my face until her cum is dripping down my throat."*

That thought repeated in my mind when her face graced my screen. Watching Shantel's every movement was foreplay. The thought of her body moving beneath me clouded my every thought whenever I saw Shantel Waters. When she spoke, all I could think about was her mouth wrapped around my dick. Her movements and authoritative nature were all foreplay to me because they showed how capable she would handle my brand of fucking. How would she respond if I asked her to tie me down and cover my face until she dripped cum down my throat? Even though I knew Lennox made it clear for her to stay away from me, Shantel's willingness to try to follow up about me had my dick rock hard.

I watched as she directed people and dealt with the authorities around *MYTH*. I stopped myself from grinding my teeth because I didn't know this shit was going down. I should have had the intel about this attack, but all it showed me was more people were at play than I initially thought. I folded my arms across my chest as the drone followed Shantel's movements in the parking lot area. She had a ton of clean-up from last night's events with the shooting. I watched her whip her arm out, cutting off whatever the detective said. Her stance seemed to mirror my own, making me smile as she stood her ground. They wanted to know who else was in the VIP section, and Shantel had given them all she was willing without lying.

Lennox and the crew left in time so they wouldn't be popping up all over the news regarding the shootout. It wasn't a secret that U.C.K. owned the club, but there was no evidence that they had been in attendance. Shantel had pushed everything away from them and onto the Del Mar crew. That seemed to satisfy the local police, but not the government types. I wasn't worried about them getting into any lower floors because Lennox, Hendrix, Fransisco, and Lakyn had that shit on lock. I let a smile cross my face as I rubbed my fingers over my goatee.

"Sir, I think you should look at this," Lex stated. I pulled my attention away from the one woman with a chokehold on my dick. I hadn't tasted it, but her scent still clouded my senses.

"What is it?" I said, turning to face my right hand. Lexington smoothed a palm over his buzz cut with a grin as he held out a tablet.

"I managed to get the footage inside the club when the attack went down. That one right there is a wild card, Boss. Be careful," he smirked while tipping his head at the screen showing a close-up of Shantel.

"Let me worry about the wild card, Lex, and you figure out how we didn't see this shit coming. You know I don't deal well with being in the fucking dark," I gritted, taking the tablet out of his hand and pressing play.

"I got you, Boss. Brick is gathering the information as we speak and will have something for you at the briefing," Lex stated.

I waved him away to concentrate on what he meant by wild card. I knew that the members of the U.C.K. crew were ruthless, but did that also extend to the women? They always seemed protected and never really needed to lift a finger, but something told me they could be just as hardcore as the men.

I sat behind the massive black desk facing the screen to still watch Shantel in real-time. I looked down at the tablet just as Shantel came into view. Her white pants suit clung to her body like a second skin. My eyes narrowed as Shantel stopped in the corridor where I first spoke to her face-to-face. Two men stood before the elevators, their backs facing away from the opening leading to the club. They kept checking over their shoulders but missed when Shantel appeared. They were dressed like the rest of the security team that worked for the club. Shantel must have noticed something off because she already had something in her hand when she approached the two men. The flashing lights made whatever she held glint, and I knew it was a blade.

The two men fully turned to face her when she was a few feet away, and I watched her lips move. '*Why are you both over here? This isn't your position.*' The taller man smirked at her, but before he could speak, her hand moved, slashing across his throat just as the other man reached for his weapon. Blood sprayed, and splashes hit her white suit jacket, but it didn't stop her. She brought her arm down, but the man had already pulled out his gun. Shantel was too close, and he could only use the gun to knock the blade out of her hand. I frowned when he grabbed the side of her head and slammed it against the elevator. If this nigga weren't dead, he would be by the end of the day. My brows rose, and I sat back in my leather chair as Shantel got a heeled foot up, pushed herself off the elevator, and slammed her head back into the man's face.

The music from the club turned into gunfire at that moment. The man stumbled back, giving Shantel time to spin around and drop to her knees. She reached for something on her leg and tossed it at the man. The slim blade hit him in the side of his neck, and Shantel was already on the move before I could blink. She reached for the blade and stabbed the bigger man repeatedly as blood squirted from the wounds on his neck. My hands tightened around the tablet, and I could hear the casing of the tablet groan from how tightly I held it. Two other men approached the corner of the hall, aiming weapons in her direction.

"Behind you," I shouted.

I bit down on my words because she couldn't hear me, and I knew she had to survive it. Shantel looked up in time to spin the man's body around to use as a shield. She gripped the hand that still held the gun and aimed. Shots were fired back and forth. I saw a man drop, but I held my breath as the bullets hit the body she was using as a shield. A tall, dark-skinned man came up behind the last shooter, stuck a gun to the back of his head, and fired. Shantel dropped the dead weight she held in her hands, and I wondered how she could hold up a dead body.

Shantel's once-white suit was covered in blood as she moved up to the man that took out the other shooter. He handed her a gun as she fixed her collar and began to speak into a watch on her wrist. *'Under attack. Shoot first and ask questions later. VIP is the priority.'* I watched as Shantel and the man that gave her the gun moved through the crowd, taking out whoever got in the way as she made it to the VIP section. I hit pause, and it stopped on blood-soaked Shantel looking up into the camera. It felt like she knew she was being watched. That's when I knew I had it all wrong. Everything that Shantel Jenson Waters did was nothing but foreplay to a man like me.

"Lex," I boomed. The surrounding team never stopped what they were doing, but I could feel all of them go on high alert at my tone. I sat the tablet down and unbuttoned my suit jacket.

"Yes, Boss," Lex answered.

"I want everything you can find on Shantel Waters."

"We have everything about her, sir."

"That is surface shit."

"There wasn't much more on her, *Rogue*," Lex stated.

"No. There is more to her than I read in that file, and I want to know what it is. Find it," I demanded.

Lex said nothing else and left to do what I asked. I looked at the live screen and saw Shantel staring into the distance. I was about to make it my business to know if she was thinking about me then. If she wasn't, I was going to make sure that changed.

## CHAPTER ONE

# LENNOX 'OZ' ANDERSON

I dialed Shandea four more times before I punched a wall. After these niggas told me that bullshit about me hiding the guns, I knew it was Xavier. I was hurt, and it hit me in the chest that my brother had betrayed me this way. I looked at my fist, but the pain and blood did nothing to calm my rage this time. The only thing that hurt worse was hearing that voicemail message of Dea telling me she was finished. I didn't know what she was thinking, but us being over would never be an option. The screaming from Cliff and the others had stopped. I turned to see Henny approaching us, but I turned around to look at Faxx. What in the fuck happened to make her leave a voicemail like that? I clicked into the app, pulled up her phone, and frowned at the location as it moved quickly.

"Oz, we find Dea, make sure she is safe, and then we go find this nigga, X," Henny said.

"Faxx and I can head over to Katrice's house and see if Ja bitch ass is hiding there while y'all get to Dea. This shit is getting hot, and they need to know what to look out for," Link said.

He tightened the restraints on the last two niggas. They twisted and pulled, trying to scream through the thick tape covering their mouths. I looked back at my phone and saw that it had stopped.

"First things is first, and that is getting Dea. Then we get X and take care of that situation. You and Faxx can—"

"It shows that she is at 348 Grand Course Ave. She's at the boutique," I stated, cutting Henny off.

It was only a few miles away. I had to get to her before anything happened. I started moving toward the door, and I could feel the others behind me. Dea knew better than to see her bitch ass cousin alone, but whatever happened must be fucking with her judgment. I didn't give a shit about what had her in her feelings. As long as we got to Dea before anyone else did, I could figure the rest of the shit out later. I didn't know what my brother wanted with her or how he knew Dea, but I had to dead this issue here and now. I was fucked up in the head, but X was on another playing field when he got a fixation on something or someone.

"Milo and Saint are on the way to the boutique. They are only a few minutes away," Faxx stated.

Henny beat me to the car and jumped in as I heard Faxx's cell ring.

"Milo? What? Who is there?" Faxx said. Henny started the car, and I was ready to move, but he hesitated.

"Nigga! Either drive or get the fuck out," I stated. I could feel the panic and rage in my blood, like I knew something was wrong.

"Oz! Nigga, chill for a second. Something isn't right," Henny gritted. Faxx leaned into the window, and I could see in his flat black eyes that whatever he knew wasn't good.

"She isn't there. Her phone and purse were in the parking lot, and it looked like the store was closed."

My mind ran wild with possibilities, but I knew. I knew my brother had something to do with this shit. I didn't realize I was hitting the dashboard until I heard Henny's voice shouting to calm down and think. How the fuck was I supposed to think when my world was burning to the fucking ground?!

"Oz! Nigga, we will find her! Her phone can't be the only way," Henny stated. That's when it clicked in my head about her necklace.

"Fuck! Link I need—"

I didn't need to finish the sentence before he stuck his laptop through the window. It took seconds for me to gather the information I needed to get the latitude and longitude of where Shandea could be. "He took her. He fucking took her!"

I looked at the address of the house that we grew up in before our mother was killed. He took her to the house we said we would never step foot into again. That house was where our mother was murdered, and he took Dea there.

"Where are we going?" Henny asked.

"3677 Canton Ave in South Griffin," I answered.

I could feel the car moving but couldn't see where we were through the red haze. I knew Henny would get me where I needed to be without me paying attention. Scenario after scenario played through my head at what the fuck X could be doing to Dea. He was crazy but couldn't be crazy enough to hurt her. Why in the hell would he want Dea? He knew what she meant to me. I made it clear that she would be my wife. So why would he do this? I balled my hands into fists because if anything happened to her because of him, I would have to kill my brother.

I clenched my teeth together at the thought. Even though Xavier was a fuck up at times, he was still my little brother and my twin. Whatever went down would be my fault. It was my fault for not preparing Dea better for this lifestyle. I didn't tell her who she should stay away from because I thought I could keep her safe at a distance. If she knew about our enemies, she might have thought twice about running out on her own over stupid shit. I didn't know what had happened, and it didn't matter. My heart was pounding out of my chest because I could feel that something was wrong. I knew we would walk into some fuck shit, and I didn't know what I would do. How could I take out the only blood family I had left? I could hear myself panting heavily and feel the sweat dripping down my face. I wanted to be wrong, but I knew that I wasn't. I dialed his number, and it kept going to voicemail.

"Faxx! Make sure your niggas are on Tali and Crescent's asses," Henny gritted.

"It's done," Faxx said over the speaker. I was trying to determine what was happening and why X wanted Dea. It made little sense, and his anger toward me made no fucking sense.

"They have them in sight now. Milo and Saint are heading over to the bitch Katrice's house," Faxx grunted.

He was serious for once, but I knew he understood the gravity of this situation. They all understood what was happening, so it was no surprise to learn that Faxx and Link were behind us. I looked at the laptop and assured myself that she hadn't moved. We were close, but it felt like we were going ten miles per hour.

"Henny," I gritted.

"Not far, Oz. We will be there in two minutes," he said.

Henny took a turn, almost putting us on two wheels. We ran a red light and nearly missed a tractor trailer that pulled out slowly into the right lane. Henny swerved, and we went up on the sidewalk for a minute until we passed by the truck, then he made a hard left turn. My old neighborhood came into view, bringing back memories I would rather forget.

The two-story house sat at the end of the cul-de-sac. My door was open before the squealing of Henny's tires stopped. I ran toward the rundown house and kicked the door open. The house smelled like it hadn't been opened in years. Thick cords ran the length of the floor leading into the kitchen. The peeling yellow paint and the broken white cabinets hung loosely. It was in stark contrast to the brand-new refrigerator and stove. The thick cables ran under a door I knew led to the house's basement. On the outside, it didn't look like it could be this large, but there were three rooms, a kitchen, and another living room. The basement was always off-limits to us when we were young, but now I knew what it was used for. I swung open the door just as a scream rang in my ears.

"Oz!" I heard Henny, but I couldn't stop or acknowledge him. I knew it was Dea screaming at the end of the hall. The door was closed, but I raised my foot and kicked the hinges. The door slammed open, and I saw a blinding haze of red. X stood over Dea, shouting as she lay there with blood covering her thighs. I didn't realize I hadn't stopped moving until I had Xavier slammed into the wall. I heard his head crack from the impact, but I needed more than that from him. My mind shifted on its own, and I was on the bed trying to figure out what the fuck happened. Why was she bleeding? What the fuck did he do? When I threw him into the wall, his pants were around his ankles, but he wasn't my concern. Yet. I knew the others would make sure his ass wouldn't move.

"Shandea! Dea!" I shook her shoulder. I checked her pulse and could barely find one. I screamed her name again while pushing back at someone trying to pull me away from her body. "Dea! Sweetness! Shandea, wake up," I roared.

"Oz! Nigga, move!" Henny's voice finally filtered through the rage and panic, but I still couldn't pull myself away from her. I felt arms wrap around my shoulders, pulling me back forcibly.

"Get the fuck off of me!"

"Let me check her, Lennox! Tighten up, my nigga! She isn't dead but she's losing a lot of blood."

My eyes turned to look at X as he faced off with Link.

"What the fuck did you do?" I grunted. In one movement, I broke through the hold Faxx had on me and pushed past Link. My fist went into X's ribs just as I grabbed the Glock Link was holding and slammed it into his face.

"I didn't do shit to her! Why the fuck does it matter what I do with possessions," Xavier wheezed. Blood streamed from his nose and from the large gash to his forehead.

"Faxx! We need to get her to the Clinic ASAP!"

"What the fuck you say, nigga?" I said, turning on Henny. He wasn't looking at me because his focus was on Shandea. He used the blankets to wrap her body up before he answered me.

"Not that *Clinic*, my nigga. Get your mind clear so we can handle this shit, and you can be there when Dea wakes up. She will need you once she finds out," Henny stated. He handed Dea to Faxx, which caused me to snap back into reality as his words circled my mind.

"Give her to me. I will take her where she needs to go," I said, turning away from my brother. I barely noticed that the entire time I spoke to Henny, I used the Glock to hit him repeatedly until he collapsed to the floor.

"Oz! You need to handle this so that when she wakes up, it is done. You need to get your mind right to be there for Dea. If this is what I believe it is, she will wake up and discover she has lost her baby. Your baby," Henny stated. Faxx was already out of the door. I didn't see Link move, but I knew he was with Faxx, leaving Henny, X, and me in this room. This muthafucka took Dea to the same room we found our mother dismembered. He was a sick piece of shit, and now–

"What the fuck did you just say?" I blinked. I tried catching Henny's words, but it kept starting and stopping before the last five words could repeat. "That...that isn't possible...she...don't fuck with me, Hendrix." The bass in my voice seemed to vibrate the walls and caused X to stir.

"Ahhh, fuck, ah," Xavier moaned on the floor.

"Oz," Henny grumbled. I held up a hand, stopping him from saying another motherfucking word. I turned back to my brother, my fucking twin, to whom I gave everything, and felt nothing but hate.

"I should have killed you back at the shop!" I raised my booted foot and came down on his ribs. I reached down and pulled him to his feet. Blood poured from his mouth as he tried and failed to speak. His face no longer looked like mine, with both eyes swollen and a busted lip. I slammed him against the wall. "Why! Why the fuck would you do this!? You took her and then killed my fucking seed," I seethed. X coughed and spat blood out of his mouth as he began to chuckle.

"Not so...not so untouchable, are you?"

I raised the Glock and pointed it at his head.

"Why?" I was shaking with pain and anger. Half of my mind was here in this moment, witnessing my own brother betray me, and the other was en route with Dea.

"Because the great and powerful Oz can't have everything he fucking wants. You got the club, the money, my bitch! It was always you! Everything about you! Jakobe might lie about a lot of shit, but he was right about one thing. You're a pussy, and you will lose everything."

I started to laugh at the fucking idiot. I felt like I couldn't breathe as Dea got further away, but how could I look her in the eye and tell her that he still lived after what he'd done? I knew X would do it again if he had the chance. I couldn't cover for his crazy ass, not this time.

"You had everything I had, Xavier. You wanted nothing. Everything I had, you had. You've never wanted for a fucking thing," I gritted. I pressed the barrel of the gun harder into his forehead.

"Look at you. You can't even follow through. Give me a chance, and I wouldn't hesitate to put a bullet through your fucking head.

"You hate me like that, nigga?"

"Naw, never that. How do you hate someone you never loved in the first place? Let's be honest, Oz, we don't know what that even means," Xavier laughed. "If you think you won't hurt her as I have, you're delusional. You're just as fucking crazy as I am," he coughed. My hand shook because despite what he said, I loved my brother. But I knew he couldn't live. My trigger finger flexed, and I closed my eyes.

"That is where you got the shit fucked up, X. Your brother is nothing like you and never has been. He isn't a pussy because he doesn't want to kill his own brother. It just means he has a small conscience. It's too fucking bad that I don't," Henny scoffed. The silenced gunshot seemed loud, like a thunderclap, to me. Brain matter exited from the side of X's head, and I watched as the light in his surprised eyes faded. I released his shirt and let his body fall to the blood-covered floor. I didn't realize I still clutched the gun until Henny took it from my grasp.

"You killed my brother."

"No. Your three brothers are still here. Just because you shared blood doesn't mean shit. Let the cleaners burn this place to the ground. We need to get moving."

I swallowed as I stared down at the one person who should have been by my side through every fucking thing in life. Instead, he wanted to end my life and take what I worked for, for himself. I knew Henny was right, and it wasn't like we all hadn't thought it before. I didn't think he would go this far or target his craziness toward me. That was my fuck up, and it was something I wouldn't repeat. Whatever was fucking wrong with Xavier had to have come from that bastard's gene pool. Still, I wouldn't leave him here, but he didn't deserve a marked grave either.

"Don't leave his body—"

"It's already done. Now we need to move and get to Dea. I already ordered things to be in place. All she is going to need right now is you. We will deal with his burial later when we deal with that nigga, Jakobe."

"You know this nigga gassed him up."

"I am sure he had a hand in it, and we will find out how much," Henny said.

"Let's move. I won't trust anyone else with her care," I said. I turned away from my twin, knowing this would be the last time I saw his face. Henny waited long enough, allowing me to take this nigga out, but I couldn't.

"We might be fucked in the head, Oz, but there are limits we all have. I'll carry this burden because you are my brother, and this is one thing you don't need to see in your nightmares."

Nothing else needed to be said as we rushed out of the rundown house. Faxx's people were already here waiting for us to leave. As soon as my foot hit the pavement, all of my thoughts went exactly where they needed to be, and that was with Dea. I knew fucking well X hadn't acted on his own, and it wasn't all Ja, either. Everyone who directly or indirectly had something to do with us losing a child would die. My butcher block was going to be used well very soon.

"There is no way X did all this on his own. This Shandea situation was all him. But the club, I don't believe it," I gritted. Did my telling him about Dea and my plans for her push him over the edge? Did he want to hurt her because he knew it would hurt me?

"We both know that there are more people at play. His hate toward you was fostered. He was manipulated, but this shit with Dea was all him. There was no saving him this time around, Oz," Henny stated.

I turned to look out of the window, knowing damn well he was right. Jakobe and whoever else used my brother to get to me would never leave Union City alive once I found them.

We made it to the Women's Center long after Faxx and Link. I was out of the car before that shit stopped. The center wasn't open yet, so no one was at the desk to tell me where I needed to go. I guess I was lucky because

I knew I was covered in blood on some level. None of it was mine but a mixture of Shandea's and Xavier's fluids.

"This way," Henny shouted. He was already moving through a set of double doors, and I rushed through them to see Faxx and Link standing next to two large doors.

"Where the fuck is she?" I demanded. Both looked up, but Henny said nothing as he pushed past them and through the doors that said "Staff Only". I tried following, but Faxx and Link grabbed me. I tried to fight through these niggas, but Faxx had his biceps wrapped firmly around my neck, and Link had one of my arms pushed behind my back. "Let me fucking go!"

"Just! Just fucking wait! Wait a fucking second, Oz! Let Henny assess her and do what he needs to do. You can't go in there right now. Look at yourself, nigga!" Link ordered. "When she wakes up, she doesn't need to see you looking like this, my nigga. You need to get your shit right and change before anything else," Faxx grunted. I fought some more, managing to get my arm free. I reached around to toss Faxx's big ass across the fucking floor.

"Oz! Do you want Dea to see you covered in fucking blood? Is that what you want her to see when she opens her eyes?"

Link's words cut me deep, and I knew that was his intention. I couldn't let Dea see me this way, but I knew I had to be beside her when she found out. I closed my eyes as a feeling I had never thought of ripped through my body. Overwhelming sadness, guilt, and fear clawed a hole into my chest. Sadness and guilt were feelings I could deal with, but fear was something I had never felt in my life. I knew what I felt because it had been the only emotion I could never mimic. Who would I fear when I was the one who put fear into others? Now I knew what true fear was if what Henny said about her being pregnant was true. What if losing this baby means I lost Dea as well?

I took Link and Faxx's advice to change out of my clothes. I pulled on a pair of navy blue scrubs and texted Shantel so she could be on guard. I debated calling Tali but decided to wait until I knew exactly what to tell her. My phone buzzed with an incoming text.

**Sam:** *The cookout is over.*
**Wiz:** *Are the leftovers put on ice?*
**Sam:** *Safely stored.*
**Wiz:** *Bet. Finish assisting Shantel with clean up.*
**Sam:** *I should be there.*
**Wiz:** *Faxx is here.*
**Sam:** *So, enough tools to take down a small city. I got it.*

I stuck the phone in the small pocket of the scrub pants and exited the locker room. Faxx stood there with a black plastic bag held out. I didn't know if X had anything else up his sleeve, but I wanted more eyes on Shantel and my club. I tossed my clothes inside the bag and kept walking.

"You still have eyes on Tali?"

"Don't ask stupid questions. And yes, they have been doubled."

I nodded before I rounded the corner and saw Henny and Link beside the "Staff Only" doors. Henny looked up just as Link turned and walked away. I frowned at the pace he was moving while typing a message frantically.

"What the fuck is happening?"

"Dea is fine. Let's go back," Henny answered. He knew what I was asking but excluded me from everything else. I followed him through the doors and made an immediate right. The fresh paint and sterile smell would be a scent I would never forget.

"Okay, she is fine, but...did she lose our baby? What the hell did he do to make her miscarry?"

I needed the answers now to process the loss, so I was there to help Dea through it as well. Henny pushed open a white door, and I saw Dea in a hospital bed with an I.V., and fluids hooked up. When we walked inside, an older nurse with navy blue scrubs checked her vitals. Her eyes widened for a second before she finished what she was doing. As soon as the door shut, I moved to Dea's side. She was still sleeping, and even I knew this wasn't exactly normal. A light purple bruise had formed across her cheek. I could tell that her right eye would swell and bruise as well. I clenched my teeth together. "Henny?"

"First, it never got that far. There was no evidence of rape or force other than the kidnapping."

"Thank—"

"I was able to stop the bleeding, but the stress of what was happening had already done the damage. Just by looking Dea over, she put up a fight. Also, knowing she shouldn't even be able to carry a baby, it was too much for her body to handle."

My fist clenched at my side, but I kept a hand on Dea's forehead. We may never get the chance for a child again, and I would have to be the one to tell her.

"Fuck. Fuck. Fuck. Fuck," I grumbled under my breath.

"I needed you to hear that and to understand how quickly things can go wrong. No stress, plenty of rest, and healthy eating will be best for Dea now."

I slowly opened my eyes and turned to look at Henny. He stood at a computer typing and reading over a chart.

"What the fuck are you talking about?"

Henny closed the chart and then looked away from the monitor. His eyes traced over Dea like he was analyzing something before looking back at me.

"Shandea lost one baby. The other one—"

"The other one? Other what?"

"Let me fucking finish, nigga. Shandea was pregnant with twins, so knowing her history, she must stay overnight and have weekly visits unless her OB-GYN says differently. I can refer you both to the best–"

"Nigga, do you think I will trust another doctor with my child or their mother? You must've lost your damn mind. Whatever care she needs, I think you can handle it."

"Oz, this is not my field of expertise. She needs someone who does this and only this, not me," Henny frowned.

"Hendrix, let's not sit here and act like you don't know your way around a pussy."

"Nigga! Seriously, it is a hell of a lot more than that," he chuckled. "She needs to be under the care of a specialist."

"So you are going to look me in the eye and tell me you won't care for my wife," I asked. The pain of losing a child sat heavily on my chest, and I would *not* add to this shit.

"Lennox, I will make sure she sees the best. We know the best, Oz, and you know that. I will personally keep up with her care, and if I see anything wrong, I'll take over. But you got to trust me on this one. The first thing is helping her through what just happened. We got her back, but let's be real, Oz, shit is just getting started."

I stared at him for a long moment knowing every word he spoke was the truth. We did know the best. I gave a quick nod just as Dea began to move.

"Sweetness," I whispered. Dea groaned and twisted beneath the sheets before opening her eyes. I stared into her light brown gaze until she was fully awake. "Dea, everything is going to be fine."

Shandea blinked her good eye slowly before using her tongue to wet her lips. I could feel her body tensing up and see the panic written over her features.

"Don't touch me," she cried.

"Dea. Sweet–" I said again.

"No! Don't fucking touch me!"

## CHAPTER TWO

# HENDRIX 'HENNY' PHARMA

"Don't touch me! Don't fucking touch me!" I dropped the chart and moved to the bed to help Oz hold Dea.

"Sweetness, Sweetness! It's me! It's me! It's Lennox," Oz shouted.

"Lennox! Lennox!"

"I'm here! I'm here! It's me, Sweetness. It's Lennox! Look at me! Look at me!"

I held Shandea's arm down so she wouldn't rip out her I.V., while Oz held her shoulders.

"Dea baby. It's me. It's me. Look at me...look at me," Oz whispered.

Dea's fight-or-flight instincts began to calm the longer she stared into Oz's eyes. Dea stopped struggling, and I let her go immediately so she didn't feel trapped. I wanted to examine her while she was awake but knew it would need to wait. I tipped my head toward the door. Letting Oz know I would be outside. I knew Oz would want to give her the news alone and would let me know when they were ready. I grabbed her chart on my way out the door and mentally switched gears. I needed to know if they found this nigga Ja and I wanted to know more about the cousin. I stepped into the corridor just as Faxx rounded the corner with his phone to his ear. I crossed my arms as he stopped a few feet from me.

"Crescent, ain't nobody trying to kidnap your crazy ass. You and Tali stay in the damn truck! Keep running that mouth, and you will see what happens," Faxx gritted. "Why I always got to fuck with the psychos and shit?"

"Nigga, you know you don't fall far from that tree, right? And Crescent isn't crazy. She's just opinionated," I answered.

I wanted to laugh at this yellow ass nigga, but my blood was boiling about this shit. Faxx sucked his teeth and gave me a look like 'be fucking serious' before he schooled his expression and wiped a hand down his face. Crescent wasn't even here and was giving him a fit.

"Yeah, aight. If you say so. I already got word that nigga Ja was not there, but the cousin was home," Faxx scoffed.

"Make sure they keep her ass at the house. I think Shantel or Mala need to talk with her ass. Make sure she can't contact anyone."

We all knew that she was the reason X managed to get to Dea. But how long has this been a plan?

"I got you. I'll make sure they sit on her ass," Faxx scowled.

"Where in the hell are they taking us? What's going on?" Tali shouted. Faxx gave me a look, and I smirked when I saw Crescent's nails tapping the phone's screen, pointing at him.

"Nigga, I don't know who you think you are, but this shit here ain't going to fly. You are not my man, and I don't give a fuc–"

"Cent! Chill the fuck out. We can talk about what you do not understand when I see you in twenty minutes," Faxx swore, flexing his jaw before disconnecting the call. I shook my head as I made another call I wasn't expecting to make for another month. The phone rang twice before the call was picked up at the other end. Faxx turned away and went to the front to be there when Crescent and Tali arrived.

"Yes."

"Dr. McQueen," I answered.

"Dr. Pharma, I wasn't expecting to hear from you for a little while now. Have you reconsidered my counteroffer," Seyra asked.

"You know good, and well, I don't need money, Seyra. But I do need you to come earlier than expected."

Seyra blew out a frustrated breath. I could hear the irritation and resignation that she owed a debt that had to be paid. It wasn't like she had a bad deal at the end of the day—a full ride through the best schools and medical schools.

"How early?"

"Tomorrow early."

"What? There is no way I can do that. I just can't up and leave like this, Henny. I have deliveries, surgeries, and appointments until the end–"

"You are needed here, Dr. McQueen. There was an incident, and the only other person I trust to care for this patient is you. You work for a group so those patients can be absorbed."

"That isn't the point, Henny–"

"Seyra, for the inconvenience, you will find a bonus in your account. But this is not up for negotiation. This has nothing to do with our other business. This is more important," I said.

"What happened? Fuck the money, Henny. Did something happen to Link, Faxx, or Oz?"

"Indirectly, but yes. Call me when you land," I said before disconnecting. I texted Stephanie quickly to make arrangements for Seyra when the doors burst open. I saw Tali marching toward me, gray eyes blazing in anger. Every time I saw Tali, she instantly had my dick hard as fuck.

"Where in the hell is my sister? What the hell did you all do?" Tali snapped.

Faxx and Crescent came through the door next. Faxx had Crescent around the waist as he shrugged at me, pulling her in the opposite direction. I honestly didn't have time for this shit, but I knew Tali had every right to be mad as fuck. When she was close enough, I pulled her around the corner and away from any foot traffic.

"What the hell are you doing?"

"Tali, I am going to need you to calm down and chill out," I advised. There weren't many people here because we weren't officially open, but we didn't need anyone in our business. "I'm going to need you to lower your fucking voice, Thickness," I grimaced. I pushed Tali up against the wall and looked to see if anyone was coming by.

"What the fuck ever, Hendrix! What is—"

"Tali," I shouted. I stared into her eyes, and she closed her mouth, turning away from me. She took a breath before she turned back to face me. Tali narrowed her eyes at me. I saw the fear in them, and I wasn't sure if it was fear of me.

"I was taken off the unit by two huge ass dudes and dragged outside and into a truck. If Crescent wasn't already inside the truck, I would have thought I was being fucking kidnapped. Then I got here, and all Faxx would say was Henny will explain because it's about Dea. What the hell happened, and where is my sister, Dr. Pharma," Tali hissed. I stared into Tali's gray eyes and saw the held back tears, anger, and fear. I could see now that the fear wasn't of me, but of what might have happened to her sister. I placed both hands on the wall to cage her in, debating what to say. It couldn't be much because we were too exposed, but I had to tell her something.

"Dea...Dea was kidnapped—"

"What! Move! Move! Where the fuck is my sister?" Tali screamed. She pushed against my chest, trying to move me out of the way. "What the fuck did y'all get us into? This is why we left! This is why right here! Get out of my way, Henny," she advised. I caught her hands in one of mine and pushed her into the wall so she couldn't move. I pinned her arms to the side and leaned down to her ear. She bucked against me, and I knew she could feel my dick pressing against her thigh as I got closer.

"Listen to me, Tali. Dea is fine, and you need to calm the fuck down before you go in there and get her agitated. She doesn't need that shit right now."

"Is this because of the club shit or whatever the fuck y'all niggas got going on?" Tali shivered. All her movements weren't doing anything but making my dick harder, and now wasn't the time.

"This has nothing to do about the club shit. Not really. Did Dea ever tell you that Oz had a twin?"

Tali stopped twisting her wrists, and she jerked her head to the side with a frown. I waited because, depending on what she knew, this shit might be easier to tell.

"Yeah, Dea told me once before that he had a twin, and she felt stupid because when she went to class, Dea realized she knew him. She wondered why she never paid him any mind but was infatuated with Lenno—Yeah, Dea told me about him. But she didn't know him like that. She never really talked about him, but he was never a topic of conversation," Tali finished quickly. I raised a brow, because clearly, Oz wasn't the only one that was obsessed.

"Well, to make a long story short, that nigga had a thing for Dea. I didn't get the chance to ask him anything or how long he had it for Shandea, but it was him. He took Dea when she went to meet up with Katrice," I explained.

"What the fuck? Jesus, I need to see her. I need to see her now," she choked. I swallowed because that wasn't all, and I refused to let her go inside that room unprepared. Tonight conversations would need to be had, and Tali would need to understand that none of this changes shit about us.

"Wait, Thickness. I'm not finished," I sighed. I leaned back slightly, and she turned her face to mine, and her eyes roamed over me. It was like she was taking in every detail of my features, what I was wearing, and what I wasn't saying. She swallowed and narrowed her eyes at me.

"What? Just tell me, Hendrix," she whispered. It was like she knew whatever I would say would rip her heart out, and I knew it would. Tali and Dea are close as shit, and any loss Dea would feel, Tali would feel as well. I let her hands go and balled my hand into fists, resting them on the sides of her head. I reined in my anger at what the fuck this nigga did and replayed the moment I pulled the trigger. It seemed to calm me down enough to tell her about the baby.

"Dea was pregnant, and she lost one of the babies. She's–"

"Pregnant? No, no, that's impossible. She can't… she can't–" Tali trailed off, and the tears she was holding back slid down her cheeks, and I didn't think she noticed. I sucked in a breath and reached for her face, wiping them away.

"She is and is with Oz resting, but–"

"Wait. Wait, a minute. You said she lost *one* baby. Was she pregnant with twins? Oh my God. Oh my God, I can't believe this. What the fuck did he do to her? No…no, don't answer that. Is the other baby okay? Will it survive because she…she shouldn't–" Tali's voice stalled, and I pulled her into my chest. I stared out of the opening as her hot tears soaked my shirt.

"I examined and took care of her myself. We did everything that we could, but it was too late for one. The other one is doing well, but she will need time. She will need rest and no stress. I already called in for a specialist. She will be her only patient. Everything is taken care of, Thickness, but you need to pull it together before you go in there," I said.

Tali pulled away, and I stepped back to give her some space. She wiped at her face, ran a hand through her locs, and breathed heavily. Tali stopped in mid-motion and looked up at me with a frown. She cocked her head to the side.

"What?"

"What do you mean everything is taken care of?"

"I mean exactly what the fuck I said, Thickness. Everything is done. I have the doctor coming, Dea is resting, and the baby is safe. Everything is straight," I replied.

I checked my watch and knew I would need to wrap this shit up. I wanted to be sure Tali was with Dea. I would make sure that Dea and the baby were out of the woods, and then I needed to hit the fucking streets. Xavier did this shit on his own, but it was only to a certain extent. Jakobe hyped this nigga up on some bullshit with the club and the Dea situation. They hit the club, my fucking Veterinary Clinic, and now Dea.

"Even Oz's brother? Where the fuck is he?"

I snapped back to attention, and Tali stared up at me with her arms across her chest. I leaned my head to the side and studied her before I licked my lips.

"Tali, you understand who I am, right? If not everything, you have a good idea of who we are," I chuckled. I stepped forward, and she dropped her hands to her side as her eyes widened at my movement. Her back was against the wall again, and my hand to her neck. I tipped her chin up so she could see my eyes and know I meant what I was about to say. Tali bit down on her thick bottom lip and tried to nod her head. "Naw, I need you to use your words, Tali."

"Yes. I think I might know a little too much," she stated.

"Then that means, when I say it is taken care of, it means it's handled." I stepped closer and leaned down to kiss her lips. "I made sure his shit cracked, and no one is putting those pieces back together again. I don't fuck around when it comes to the very limited amount of people that I give a fuck about. So, remember that shit," I gritted. I held her marble-gray eyes as I caressed her neck until she let out the breath she was holding.

"I think I misspoke by saying I know a little too much, because I think it's definitely not enough," she said. I heard a door open, so I peeked and saw

Oz looking at his phone. My phone buzzed and knew it was him texting me. I looked back at Tali and could see the fear and curiosity in her gaze.

"Probably not enough, but all that will be fixed soon. The first thing is making sure Dea is good. We will monitor her overnight, and then she can go home once her new O.B. sees her in the morning. And we have some good news regarding your mother's treatment and surgery," I said to change the subject.

"What news? I didn't know they would try something else or if surgery was still viable," Tali said, frowning.

"Well, not every oncologist specializes in this particular type of cancer. One of the leading doctors is coming in to look at her case. I know you've heard about Dr. Tremont's advancements with this cancer and success with his surgical treatments. He will be here in the next week or two," I said. Her eyes bugged out of her head before she blinked them quickly.

"How...how...I mean...when did you−"

"You know I will make anything happen for you, Thickness. Now let's go," I said, stepping back.

I reached for her hand and pulled her out into the hall, looking down at her. But she wasn't paying attention, just staring into space. I knew that was a lot of information to take in all at once, but that wasn't even half of it. Oz's head snapped up, and I could see the rage in his eyes. Once he noticed Tali, he schooled his features, and his dark eyes lit up in their usual shade.

"Tali. I told Dea that I would get you here," he said. Tali blinked a few times before she looked up to see Oz. She glanced at me for a quick second before giving a small smile to Oz.

"Yeah, yeah, of course. Where is she?" she asked. She let go of my hand and walked faster toward Oz. He looked at me, and I knew he would need answers, preferably from someone on his butcher's table. That would kill two birds with one stone. It would get him the answers he needed and the release he needed at the same time.

"I'll check into a few things and make some calls. I'll come back and check on Dea in a few," I stated. Tali slowed down and looked over her shoulder at me. "It's all good, Thickness. Remember what I said. It's taken care of. Just take care of Shandea right now," I smiled. I waited as Oz told Tali where to go, and she disappeared through the double doors. Oz stared at the door briefly before looking back at me.

"Did they get his shit before they burned down the house? His phone or anything thing else that nigga had there," Oz grunted.

"Nigga, you don't need to ask. You know our people don't miss."

"If they don't miss, then how the fuck did he manage to get Shandea? How nigga?" he shouted.

"It was Xavier that we're talking about, Lennox. He knows our shit and how protection would've been laid out," I said.

"So you know what that means. Whatever the fuck he knew, no matter how fucking small it was, it means Jakobe now knows. But first thing is first. I will need to have a conversation with that bitch Katrice."

Oz was right, and I already had Link handle the situation. Once I confirmed that Dea was going to make it and the life of her child was ensured, all I could think about was how long had this nigga X had been talking with Ja. What other shit does he know? It wasn't like Xavier was on the inside of anything, but he knew the locations of a few bodies and the location of the *Clinic.*

"I got Link handling whatever needs to be moved, and Faxx is dealing with the Katrice situation. Not only do we need to deal with this shit, but I also need to deal with that hospital leak. I don't know what else this nigga got planned, but we need to secure our shit and check our people. I think these niggas might have forgotten who the fuck we are because we've been low. That shit is dead. Do you feel what I am saying?"

"You damn right this shit dead, my nigga. Once Dea is settled, we're going through all these niggas, and if we find anyone else fuckin' with that nigga, they'll be on the fucking table."

"Bet," I nodded because he was right. Some of these niggas would end up in Black Bay or would end up with a bomb shoved down their throats. I didn't know if these niggas thought they were seeing weakness because we were quiet, but that shit was about to end. If that was the case, it was mostly my fault because I wanted shit quiet while we built our empires. Fuck it.

"Did you know the woman in the picture?"

"Yes, and I have a meeting coming up with Pamela about the incident with Crescent. That actually lets me get closer to her without trying. We can handle all this shit. Be with Dea. We can get down to business once you get her home tomorrow. Seyra will be here in the morning, and Dea will be her only patient for now. Let us get the info we need to take care of this shit while you take care of your wife. I'll keep you in the loop."

Oz nodded, half listening, but I knew he heard me. He shook his head and checked his phone again, typing a quick text.

"Shantel is expecting a call, and the club is still locked down. Them niggas finally left my shit, but I know they're watching. They probably left behind some listening devices and shit. Like niggas are fucking stupid," Oz said, pocketing his phone. He looked up, and beyond the rage, I saw the devastation in his eyes. "She can barely fucking look at me, Henny. This nigga—"

"Won't be able to do anything else because he's done, my nigga. She knows you aren't him, Lennox, but she needs time. It's all fresh, so the best thing is to be there. Remember, she calmed down when she looked at you. We fucked up by not giving them the information they needed to move around safely in this city. We're not about to let it happen again," I squeezed his shoulder.

Oz ran a hand over his beard, and I saw him riding the edge. The lives he took earlier today weren't enough to cool that rage inside his ass. Whoever remained at the Butcher shop wasn't going out easy, even when they talked.

"You're right, but not right now," he sucked his teeth.

"Later. Be with your wife. Let us handle this other shit."

I watched Oz walk back through the doors before I headed in the other direction. Before we moved the *Clinic* to another location, I needed to purge my frustration. At least I had good news for Dea and Tali about their mother's treatment. I had to pull many strings to get one of the leading surgical oncologists to sign-on with Union Memorial. But I would do whatever was necessary to ensure she didn't think about leaving once these six months were up.

I checked on Dea one more time before I left because I needed to get back to the *Clinic* before Link had that shit shut down and closed up. I wanted to know who those other niggas were and why they were there. I didn't know any of them, and they weren't any of ours that decided to run with this nigga X. I had so much shit on my mind I had to reevaluate things and figure out where to start with this bullshit. We could get to work once we had everyone close to us safe. We needed to find this nigga Ja and put his ass down, because he wasn't the biggest threat any longer. Now that we knew all our businesses were being looked into, we had to focus on protecting that.

I pulled up to the *Clinic* and waited for the doors to open. It didn't happen as fast as it normally should, but within a few minutes, they started to rise. I pulled inside beside two trucks and noticed that a lot of our shit had been packed up, ready for transport. I got out of the car, noticing the only people there were those who stayed at the *Clinic*.

Not everyone in the crew knew where to find the *Clinic*, but everyone knew what it was about. People didn't know we had a dedicated crew working on this site. The men and women here had no dealing with anyone else that was down with U.C.K., and this was the reason why. These eight people were a part of Faxx's team. Their loyalty was to themselves and him. Since Lennox, Link, and I were an extension of Faxx, loyalty was extended to us.

They were with him when Faxx left the military and returned to Union City. We still didn't know real names, and whenever we asked Faxx's ass, he would change the subject. Link tried and failed to figure out who they were. I think he was still trying to this day. But at this point, I would trust them with my life and hadn't been disappointed. They were only called for special shit and seemed to like it whenever that type of work came up.

"Sorry about the wait, Henny. We are triple checking everyone before they can pull in here," Whisper said. Her quiet tone was always just loud enough to hear, but it was on the edge of being just a release of air.

"It's all good...how do you pronounce your name again?"

"Le chuchotement," she smirked. I repeated it twice in my head and shook it before slamming my door.

"Bitch, it still says Whisper in French," I said. Whisper lifted a crate, which looked like it was my weight, and smirked as she walked away. "Damn," I mumbled. I headed for the small office to get changed, but stopped.

"Where is Link?" I called over my shoulder.

"Link is giving the patients swimming lessons," she said before walking into one of the tractor trailers with open doors.

"Fuck," I gritted. I moved a little faster, made my way upstairs, and walked through the connecting door and into the *Clinic*.

"I said I don't know them niggas! We don't know them niggas! They just started shooting, and we didn't want to end up shot, my nigga. No. No. No–"

His 'no' was cut off when Link pushed his head back into the water. He looked up as I entered, and I looked at the others left.

"I don't think they have anything to do with X or Jakobe. They keep talking about some Roman nigga. But apparently, they don't know his last name," Link stated. I raised a brow at him because the nigga he casually held under the water was barely struggling. Link looked down and seemed almost surprised. "Oh shit," he chuckled. He pulled the dude out of the water, and the muted screams of the other two grew frantic.

"I guess you were too late. Where is your sling?" I asked and turned to the other two.

"It's fine. I needed to take a break from wearing it for a minute. Damn, you're right. I am too late. Damn, that's a waste. I wasn't even looking at him. I hate it when I have to do this indoors. It's never the same," he added.

"It's all good. You have a few left, and you can watch those unless you need to do something else," I said. I walked over to the tables and looked down at the niggas that were left. Link stood up, leaving the body on the floor, and pulled out his *heat*, tapping it on his leg.

"I've done all I can do right now. We need more answers to where the fuck this nigga Ja is hiding because that is exactly what his ass is doing. None of this shit is sitting right with me. Because why would X do that shit alone? Ja would know how Oz felt for Dea, and if X was riding with that nigga, then why wouldn't Ja be with him to set the trap to take us out? Jakobe knew we would come with Oz once we found Dea, so why weren't they waiting together?"

I didn't answer immediately but reached out and ripped the tape off the last two niggas' mouths.

"Listen, listen, man, I am not trying to fucking die! We saw some niggas go under some tables in the back and pull out some hammers. You know how tight that fuckin' security is in *MYTH*, and we didn't have shit! They started lettin' off, and Roman said to check under the tables, and it was mad shit under there. We weren't tryna get hit up, so we took that shit so we could get the fuck out. We only went to the VIP` because of Roman! He was told his bitch was at the club and went up to VIP before all this shit popped off. I don't fucking know a nigga named Ja or fucking X! We're not even from Union City! Nigga, we're from Clapton. We were only at the club for the fucking concert—"

I was already in this niggas face before he could finish. I didn't know I was rocking his jaw until I felt Link catch my arm. I only stopped because I wasn't sure if this nigga was using his fucked up arm to pull me off. I didn't know if it was Tali or Crescent he was talking about, but the shit sounded too personal. His bitch? The fuck? Link dropped my arm, and I clenched my fists to not rock this nigga to sleep.

"Ahh, fuck! What the fuck," he choked. Blood ran out the corner of his mouth as he rolled his head to the side. I stepped forward, smacking this nigga in the face until he focused.

"Who the fuck is Roman, and who the fuck is he looking for?"

Tali and Crescent were the only two brought into the VIP after that little fight. So which one was this nigga talking about?

"Ro—Roman wanted—"

"Shut the fuck up, Trig!"

Link casually stepped around me and shot the nigga in his shoulder. Trig's eyes bugged out as his boy screamed from the pain.

"What the fuck were you saying, Trevor?" Link said. Trevor's eyes grew wide, and he darted them to Link and back to me.

"How...how—"

Link looked at his watch, and I figured he was getting more information on these niggas.

"I know this nigga not asking questions before he answers mine. That's some disrespectful ass shit," I accused.

"That is some disrespectful shit. My mother and father would not approve of that behavior," Link sighed. He put the gun to the other man's uninjured shoulder and pulled the trigger.

"Ahhh! You bitc...you bitc–"

"No...no...no, I wasn't...all we wanted was to get Cent's bitch ass and leave, and that's it. That's all Roman wanted was his bitch. We ain't have shit to do with this war y'all got going on," Trevor sobbed. I heard something crash to the floor and looked over my shoulder. *SHIT.*

"Did he just fix his mouth to say a nigga named Roman was coming for Crescent? I'm glad I made it just in time because both these niggas are about to tell me everything they know about Roman and who he thinks his bitch is," Faxx demanded.

I sighed when I saw what he was holding in his hand. At least we would be done with this place when it blew up making clean-up easier.

## CHAPTER THREE

# JAKOBE 'JA' HOWARD

I held the phone in a death grip to my ear and the other hand on the steering wheel. It had been over a week since the club shit and the night Roe's bitch ass jumped into my shit. Nothing had been going right since that fucking night. It had to be them niggas fucking with me! Who else could do some shit like this with my money? But it was all good because if they could do this bitch shit, then so could I. When Katrice returned to the house, everything was confirmed that Xavier had taken Shandea. I almost killed that bitch for going to the bank first with that fucking money, but it was all good. I knew those niggas were at the *Clinic* and wouldn't know Dea was missing yet. I wanted Oz to kill his twin, but if I could take his ass out along with the rest of them, I was good with that. I could kill X myself before I got out of Union City. He wouldn't expect me to show up, so it would be an easy hit.

I left the house and hit up Rodney to give his ass the information on the *Clinic*. Rodney had better hurry and do whatever he needed before they left. After I hung up, I checked my accounts, and each was fucking empty.

"I need you to explain this shit again. Where the fuck is my money?" I roared into the phone. I turned onto Monroe Street and then made a series of turns until I ended up close to the *Clinic*. I wanted to see the shit go down, but now I couldn't give a fuck. If it was Link who fucked with my money, I would never get that shit back if he went down today.

"I'm sorry, Mr. Houser, but your account has been cleared per your instructions."

"I gave no instructions on moving my fucking money! Where was it moved to?" I shouted into the phone.

"Again, per your instruction, we cannot give out that information on the phone. As you requested, you must come into the bank yourself with the proper identification," the bank manager urged. I had to use this fake identity because the Cartel knew my other ones, and I couldn't take the chance.

"William, I did not move any of my fucking money! How can this be fucking possible?"

"Sir, this is all the information I can give you now. If you want more information, you must appear here at the bank or where you sent your money. Have a great day," William stated.

"Hello! Yo! What the—" I slammed my palms against the steering wheel repeatedly as I screamed. "AHHH! What the fuck! What the fuck! I'm going to kill these muthafuckas! I swear I am—"

I watched black SUVs roll by, followed by flashing lights without sirens. The niggas on the streets knew what it was about. I watched as people sitting on the stoops or outside stores stood up and walked inside. I turned around in my seat, grinding my teeth together, trying to figure out what the fuck I was going to do. Half of my fucking money was gone, and I needed that shit if I was going to disappear. I felt my phone vibrating, and I looked at the screen, cursing.

"Yo, what's good, Pops?"

"Don't fucking 'what's good' me, Jakobe. What fuck shit are you up to? Because a little birdy told me you about to dip off on some fuck shit."

"I don't know what you're fucking talkin' about, old man," I gritted, sucking my teeth.

"See, see. I would believe that shit if I didn't get a call from one of the Roja brothers about your little side jobs. What the fuck are you doing, Ja? Fuck it. It doesn't matter because I will be in Union City soon. I'll text you where to meet, and your bitch ass better not be late," Marvin hissed.

"I don't know what the fuc–"

**Boom. Boom. Boom.**

My words were cut short when a loud explosion shook the ground. "Oh shit!"

I dropped my phone as I stared at the flames licking the sky toward where the *Clinic* would be. I clenched my jaw, knowing if that shit went up like that, those niggas were long fucking gone. "Fuck! Fuck! Fuck!"

I didn't wait around to see what the fuck was happening. I already knew if that shit blew up, those niggas was ghost. If they were gone, my best bet would be to meet up with X and wait for them niggas to show up. I knew Xavier had some niggas that were down that could come so we could ambush them bitches, but when I pulled up to that piece of shit house, there was nothing left. Fire trucks and police cars lined the street as the firefighters fought the blaze of fire consuming Oz and Xavier's childhood home.

"Son of a bitch," I gritted. I punched my dashboard before reining in my anger because I had to think. I had no proof of either of these niggas being dead, so that meant I wouldn't get the other half of the money. And the money I did receive was fucking stolen. I had to get out of fucking dodge. But if this nigga was coming, I knew either Carmelo or Alejandro would be with him. I hadn't secured the streets or shut U.C.K. down. At this point, I didn't know if X was still alive, but since he hadn't reached out, I knew these niggas had him. I needed to regroup, hit up the Senator, and get the fuck out of Union City. It was impossible now to just bounce since these niggas stole my money. I had to complete the job if I would dip before my Pops and the Cartel showed up. I threw my car in reverse when my phone buzzed in my lap. I looked at the screen, and the number was unknown. I ignored it while making a U-turn, but it started up again.

"Yo!"

"What the fuck is going on, Ja? You set me up, nigga?" Rodney seethed.

"I don't know what the fuck you are talking about. I gave you the info, and the rest was up to you," I said. Fire trucks and ambulances went flying by me as I hit the corner. Going back to Katrice's house was a no-go because if they got X, then Oz had to know about the cousin.

"There was nothing in the fucking club! Nothing!"

"Did you search all the levels? Did you think the shit would be that easy, my nigga? You're the agent. Figure that shit out. Just make sure you got my end handled," I snapped. I still needed an out because, at the end of the day, Senator Morgan would fold if the Cartel got to him.

"I didn't fucking get anything."

"You're not looking hard enough, Roe."

"You need to tell that bitch Pamela to step up her game because the shit she brought me on the hospital ain't going to cut it," he seethed.

"That shit is between you and her ass. I just gave you an in because she owed me. You need more then you need to press her on that shit," I snapped.

"Naw nigga, not after this bullshit tip you gave me that damn near got me and my team blew the fuck up. If you think I would do shit for you, Jakobe, you trippin'. Make the call Ja, and give me something I can use. Or make it out of this country on your fucking own," Rodney cursed before disconnecting.

"Fuck! Fuck!" I roared in the car and pressed on the gas. I might not trust the information I got from X anymore, but I did know that Tali Ho was back in town. So, if I wanted my money and to get these niggas, I would have to take Henny's obsession. I unlocked my screen, went into my contacts, and hit a number without a name attached.

"Is it done?"

"One down and one to go, but this one isn't as easy to take out," I lied.

"You said you could take care of it. Did I get the wrong man to handle the job?"

"Senator Morgan, I got this shit over here. All I will need from you is a place to lay low. I will take out Lennox Anderson, but I will need my money in cash this time," I dictated.

"What? Are you fucking serious? That is a lot of money to put together and something that would cause attention," he gritted.

"Don't pretend you don't know how to get what you need, my nigga. This ain't your first time, and I am sure not the last," I chuckled. "So, do you have a spot or naw? Because now that Xavier is dead, Oz will be trying to figure out who did it, and it will all point back at you. You have a decision to make," I said. The line was quiet, and I knew this nigga was thinking up ways to fuck me over. But if he thought I didn't have some dirt on his ass, he was buggin'.

"You will have the other half of the payment when you bring me proof that Lennox is taken care of."

"Done," I smirked. I knew if I went to Henny, Oz would be right there beside this nigga. Every last one of them would go down before I left Union City for the last time.

"Here's the address."

I stuck the address in the GPS before disconnecting the call. I knew that if I wanted to back up some of this money, I would need to take it from the sale of the *Silk*. I knew that would bring more heat from the Cartel, but if I were already gone, it wouldn't matter. I just needed to make it look like U.C.K. were the ones that did the robbery.

## CHAPTER FOUR

## Tali Saunders

I sat next to Dea's bed while she slept. I followed Oz's directions, but it was still a larger-than-normal facility, but luckily a nurse was in the hall and pointed me to the door I needed. Every thought ran wild through my mind as I sat here staring into space while Oz spoke to Henny. I was still processing that Hendrix had managed to get Tre to come to Union City. I closed my eyes because I knew I couldn't avoid him if he treated my Mama. I just prayed that he let the past stay in the past, because I didn't need any of this shit right now.

I looked at Dea and felt a tear slip from my eye. I wiped it away quickly just in case she woke up. I didn't want her to see me being a mess. I wanted to know what had happened since Mama and I spoke with Dea. I blinked back the tears, trying not to think about the what ifs, because she was here and alive. I didn't know who to blame for the situation, because if Henny told me the truth, this had nothing to do with what happened at the club. But at the same time, it was still connected to them. Why would Oz's brother do some crazy shit like this?

I wiped the tear away that slid down my face. I knew I was more upset that I hadn't picked up when she called or had the chance to check my messages. Shandea was at work when I spoke to her, and I knew now for a fact that she had to have guards sitting on her. So what happened? I don't know why Dea would have felt the need to see that bitch Katrice alone in the first place. I frowned because no one else would've known where Dea would be going other than me. So how the fuck did Oz's brother know where to scoop her up? The door opened, and I looked at Oz, but he didn't see me at first. His usual cognac-colored eyes were dark. They were damn near black until he saw Dea lying in bed. His features smoothed out, and he blinked a few times before turning his attention to me.

"Was she awake when you came in?" Oz asked. He closed the door softly and moved to the other side of the bed. Dea shifted restlessly, but Oz touched her forehead when he sat down. He made sure not to touch anything bruised, and she calmed down, but didn't wake up.

"Yes, but only briefly before she fell back to sleep. What the hell happened, Oz?" I asked. I knew my eyes were hard, but he held them as his jaw flexed.

"Honestly, Tali, I don't know the full story. I only know that Dea left me some wild as fuck message, and the next thing I know, she was taken. I don't know what made her leave work early or decide to go to see Katrice alone," he grunted. I leaned back in my chair but didn't let her hand go as I stared at Oz, a sick feeling building in my gut.

"Does Katrice have anything to do with her being taken?" I asked as calmly as I could. I didn't want to reveal the rage that was building in my blood. Oz's eyes bounced between mine, and he tilted his head to the side. I felt like he was studying me like a bug, and I could feel the pressure in his stare sucking the air out of the room. Oz blinked, and the moment passed as he let out a breath.

"Dea was at the boutique when she was taken," he said.

"I am not going to act as if I know everything about y'all, Oz. But I think I have a pretty good idea of what you all are capable of. So, I know that you know if Katrice had something to do with my sister being kidnapped," I snapped.

My heart was pounding at the death stare he gave me, but I knew deep down that his anger wasn't directed toward me. The shit was still unnerving as fuck, and it caused me to shift in my seat. I held that stare because I wasn't about to back down. Hendrix said I needed to know more, and when it came to my sister, I wanted to know it all.

"Sis, I am unsure how much she was involved, but Katrice was down with the bullshit. It all happened outside of her store, and other shit we found out shows that she and my brother were having a relationship," he said. I leaned back, clenching my jaws tightly, trying not to flip the fuck out. That bitch stooped that fucking low that she would let her blood be kidnapped.

"Where is she?" I demanded. Oz raised a brow and sat back in his chair, staring at me. He took his hand away from Shandea's head and rubbed his beard with a smirk.

"I find it funny you aren't asking about my brother, Tali. You don't need to worry about offending me or asking me anything about him. But I can tell you I don't know why he would do this," Oz stated.

"The only reason I don't give a shit about that piece of trash is because I already know he is no longer a threat. But my cousin, yeah, she's still running free while my sister is lying here. We won't know anything until she wakes up and tells us what happened," I hissed. "So, do you know where that bitch is?"

"I will soon enough, and when I have her—"

"You are going to let me have a conversation with her," Dea said.

My head whipped toward my sister, and I was on my feet, hovering over her before I knew I was moving.

"Dea, oh shit, oh my God. Are you okay? You can't be scaring me like this," I rushed out. I kissed her where it looked like it wouldn't hurt, and she smiled. Her light brown eyes stared at me, but I could see the pain, hurt, devastation, and anger flaring in them. Oz moved, and Dea's good eye moved at the motion. The pain I saw was something else. She looked back at me and shook her head slightly.

"I will be fine, Tali. I promise I will be good when I can get the hell out of here," Dea whispered. "But you're right, Tali. Where the hell is Katrice?"

Oz stood up, picked up a pitcher, and filled a small cup with water.

"Sweetness, I will tell both of you once I know she is secured."

I felt like Oz was choosing his words about Katrice carefully. Did they kill her or have her already?

"Is it true that Xavier is...is−"

"You don't need to worry about him," Oz grumbled.

He placed the cup to Shandea's lips, and she took a sip with narrowed eyes. I looked at Oz and couldn't see a hint of remorse or if the knowledge that Henny killed his brother affected him. I blinked a few times as that knowledge settled in my mind. I know what he said to me, but my mind was more focused on getting to Dea. How did knowing that Henny has killed people affect me? I saw it at the club when the bullets were flying and how he didn't hesitate to take the shot. Who the fuck were we actually involved with? Was Crescent right that they were more than what we thought? I was more sure now that Cent was right than I was after the club situation.

"What do you mean, Lennox? Where is he? Because I can't−"

"Shandea, calm down, please," Oz said, looking at the monitors. I looked up, saw her pulse rate spiking, and touched her arm.

"He's right, Dea. Please calm down," I said softly. She looked at me and swallowed before settling back into the pillows.

"I want to press charges on him, Oz. I know he is your brother, but he's...he is sick. He is fucking insane and, and—"

"And he is dead. No charges, Sweetness. Xavier ain't never coming back," Oz stated.

His firm tone and dismissive attitude about his brother said all that was needed. He didn't want to talk about his death or what happened to him after the fact. Shandea put a hand to her stomach, and my gaze went to the motion. I looked at Oz, and he was staring at Dea. I wanted to ask her why she went to see Katrice on her own? What would make her make that decision like that? Doing something like that, knowing how those bitches got down, was unlike Shandea. I opened my mouth and then closed it because it was too soon.

"When are we leaving?" Dea asked.

"I can take you home tomorrow. Hendrix wants to monitor you and the baby overnight. We have an OB-GYN coming to see you in the morning. Then I can take you home," Oz said. Dea frowned slightly as she stared at her stomach, and I couldn't tell what she was thinking.

"Home? No, I will return to the apartment the agency set up for me. I don't have a place here," Dea said. I felt the energy in the room shift, and I swear that shit grew colder. I bit down on my tongue and refused to look at Oz.

"Shandea, I know we're going through some shit, but if you think you will not be at OUR home, you might need an MRI of the brain. Please don't play with me, Dea. Right now is not the time, and if you think I forgot about that little message you left me—"

Dea's head snapped up, and she glared at Oz with tears building in the corners.

"You really think I want to be around you right now? Your fucking lies got me in the position I am now!"

"What the fuck are you talking about?"

The monitor's beeping got louder to the point someone knocked on the door. The nurse that helped me in the hall stepped inside and moved over to the monitor.

"Ms. Saunders, your heart rate is up. Are you in pain?"

I could tell that Dea was in pain, but she smiled at the nurse.

"No, no, I'm fine. I just got a little overly excited. Thank you," she smiled. The nurse looked at Oz but quickly looked back at Dea.

"Okay. If you need me, just hit the red cross right here," she pointed. We all stayed silent until the nurse left. Before anyone said anything else, Oz went to the monitor and hit a few buttons. I raised my brows as he changed the parameters so it wouldn't begin setting off alarms.

"What the hell are you doing, Lennox," Dea scowled.

"I will put it back when we finish this conversation. I was willing to wait until we got home and had some privacy, but that shit was out the window. Are you blaming me for our child's death? Is that what you're doing, Shandea?"

I sucked in a breath because I could see the cold mask slipping over Oz's features, and it was one that I'd never seen when it came to Dea. Dea laughed bitterly and shook her head slightly.

"Wow, just fucking wow. Now you're playing the victim when you're the one that was doing some fuck shit. Not only did I get a bomb dropped on me, then my bitch ass cousin called, and I wasn't thinking straight. Not after I saw what the fuck I saw Lennox. I would have never left my job if…if…if—"

"If what?" I shouted. The room was tense as fuck, and I didn't know what Dea was talking about. Neither did Oz, apparently.

"The video of you fucking that bitch! You introduced me to her like shit was all good, but you were fucking her raw! Raw! Then had the nerve to turn around and act—"

"Dea, I don't know what the fuck you are talking about, but I am telling you right now, slow your roll. Pump your fucking brakes before you say some shit you will regret later," Oz urged.

"Nigga, I saw the video! I saw it, Oz! Two days before I returned to Union, you and that chick Nia were fucking! And you think I want to return to your place with a lying ass nigga like you? Naw, I can't. I need–"

The water pitcher hit the wall when the small bedside table flew across the room. I jumped, and Dea closed her mouth as Oz paced the room. His low chuckle had Dea and me looking at each other like 'what the fuck' before he turned around. Oz stalked back toward the bed, and Dea gripped the thin blanket tightly. He leaned down and kissed the top of Dea's head.

"I'm going to let you get some rest, Sweetness, and hopefully, you will think about the shit you're saying right now. Just remember everything isn't always what it seems, but the more important thing to remember is that you're not going anywhere. No. Where. Once I get you home tomorrow, we can talk about this further. I need to go handle some business right now," Oz intoned.

"Len–Lennox–"

"Naw, Dea. It's the wrong time to do this shit. I'll be back late tonight to make sure I am here in the morning when the doctor arrives. I love you," he said. He kissed her once more before leaving. There was no hint of color in his eyes, and he seemed to keep them downcast so Dea wouldn't notice. I waited for a few minutes before turning to look at Dea.

"Bissh, that nigga is fucking crazy," I whispered. Shandea said nothing, and I knew I needed to snap her out of it. I knew my sister, and she needed to get out whatever thoughts were in her head. I let out a breath and threw what would be my problem on the table. "Well, how do you think Henny will react when he realizes he hired a doctor I used to fuck?"

Shandea stared at me for a full minute before she burst out laughing.

"What the hell did you just say?" she asked, shaking her head. A smile played on her lips, but I could see the sadness in her eyes. She wasn't ready to talk yet.

"Dr. Ignacio Tremont will be joining Union Memorial. The only positive thing about that is he can treat Mama. He is one of the leading oncologists in her form of cancer, and Hendrix just told me he hired him," I sighed.

"I mean, that is a good thing for Mama. Things may move a little faster now, though, so we will need to be ready with the cost of it," Dea sighed.

"Yes, but we can deal with that when it comes," I said. Shandea looked at me and bit down on her lower lip.

"And you decided not to tell Henny that you knew the good doctor, and he was sort of kind of sub–"

"He was not a substitute for anyone. I thought in the beginning that we...that we were compatible. But...things just didn't work out that way," I said, sucking my teeth. Dea stared at me while I picked up the pitcher and the table Oz had knocked over. I returned to the bed, sat beside her, and crossed my legs. I picked at my scrubs pants for a second before looking at Dea. I sighed and shook my head with a laugh. "Okay, fine, Tre sort of reminded me of Henny in a way, but it wasn't the same. Yeah, yeah, I know it was only one night with the nigga, but the connection–"

I drifted off thinking about Tre's overpowering presence when I met him on my second travel nursing job. He came at me hard, and I felt some of the same energy Henny carried. And Tre was on some wild stuff, but he just never gave me that same feeling or made it seem comfortable. It was almost like I was judged even if he said nothing.

"So, when are you going to tell Henny?" Dea said when I was quiet for too long. I met her eyes and then looked away because I wasn't. At least not yet, with all that was happening at the moment. I think his earlier statement had me biting my tongue on the subject. *'I don't fuck around when it comes to the very limited amount of people that I give a fuck about. So, remember that shit,'* was a warning to me. I didn't know what that nigga might or might not do.

"I will tell him all that when it needs to come out. That isn't important right now. You are what I'm worried about the most. I know you may not want to talk about it, but you need to, sis, and you also need to hear congratulations," I said softly. I wanted to cry at the tears in Dea's eyes, but I had to be strong. I had to let her see that I could carry her weight no matter what.

"I know I should be happy about this baby, but...how? One is already gone, Tali. I shouldn't be able to carry it at all. What if...what if I lose this one as well? What if–"

"We can't deal in what ifs, Shandea. Hendrix told me that he checked you out himself and that you and the baby are healthy. I know this will be a difficult pregnancy, but we can get through this shit. All of it. Because you deserve to have this baby," I choked. A tear slid down her cheek, and she tried to wipe it away. Dea smiled, but I could tell it was still forced.

"That isn't my only worry, though. What if the baby...what if it ends up like them," she whispered. I frowned and leaned forward, trying to understand what she was saying.

"Like who, sis?"

"Lennox or Xavier! They are fucking insane, and I don't mean just regular crazy. I'm talking about certifiably, clinically insane. Tali, this nigga kidnapped me because, in his head, we had an entire relationship I didn't know about. Who does shit like that?"

"You love Oz, and you will love that baby, Dea."

"Why are you taking his side?"

"I'm not. I'm just pointing out the truth. If I lie to you or let you spin some crazy shit, then I'm not helping you. And because I know how much you love Oz. I know how long you've been in love with his crazy ass," I replied.

"Of course, I love Lennox. But how...how can I look at him without seeing...seeing his brother! What did I do to lead him on?" She agonized. Dea slammed her fists onto the bed and pushed the back of her head into the pillow. She looked up at the ceiling and closed her eyes.

"What? How could you think you did something? You said that you didn't even talk to him like that," I retorted. "And I don't think Oz is anything like his brother. That is on an entirely diff—"

"Did you or did you not just see what I just saw? Who in the hell acts that way? Like the flip of a switch, he was manic and then controlled. Lennox all but said I couldn't go anywhere, Tali," Dea shrieked.

She threw up her hand and then dropped it when the I.V. pulled. I knew what she was saying, and I didn't like the fact that I could see both sides of the situation. Why would Oz let her out of his sight after what happened? Then I understood why she wouldn't want to be around him and her fear for her baby. I swallowed and sighed long, knowing she wouldn't like what I said.

"Shandea, after what just happened, Oz is right. You can't go back to that apartment. Yes, his brother can't come back...but we can't forget about the club and what happened—"

"Tali, he was fucking another bitch right before I returned to Union. Raw! Then had the nerve to introduce me to the girl like shit was cool. I'm not even mad that he had sex with her. It was the lies he told me while..." she shook her head. "He told me that he doesn't fuck other women raw or like he does me, but two days before I arrived, that's what he was doing. I trusted him with my body, Tali! How do I know how many others before me he was knockin' down raw doggin' it?" she shouted.

"Is that what happened? Is that the reason why you went to meet Katrice alone? Because clearly, you weren't thinking. Why would you go see that hoe on your own like that?" I asked. I changed the subject slightly because I could see her heart rate spiking, and I wanted her to focus on someone else.

"Ohh, oh, that bitch! She knew! She knew Tali, and she fucking helped his ass," she shouted. Changing the topic didn't help because her heart rate kept increasing.

"Dea, I need you to calm down. Deep breath and just tell me what happened. You can't be getting your pressure up like this," I said. I stood and checked the monitor. I adjusted the parameters to what they should be while Dea took a few calming breaths.

"I'm sorry," she whispered.

"Nothing to be sorry for, baby. What you went through is traumatic, and you deserve to be pissed off. But I think you should remember what Oz said. Shit isn't always what it seems. Where did the video come from?" I asked. There was a knock at the door, and I got up and opened it to see Crescent. I stepped back, and she rushed inside, looking Dea over. Cent turned to me, and her right eye had a tick.

"Where is the bitch Katrice?" Crescent demanded.

"Cent, I'm fine. I'm good, just come and sit with me. Please," Dea said. Crescent stared at me for a minute before turning to Dea. I sat back down as Crescent moved around the room, moving things into place and helping Dea reposition in the bed. She sat in the chair Oz sat in and let out a long breath.

"What the fuck happened?"

Dea looked at me, and I raised a brow for her to continue.

"Well, I got an email from Sincere and opened it. It was a video with Lennox and this chick named Nia when I did. They were fucking, and I mean going at it hard. At first, I was like, what the fuck? But when I checked the date, that's when my world flipped. I was already feeling like shit, then to see that after this nigga fucked me while telling me he never fuck another raw because it was for me! Then I saw it with my own eyes, and it was only a few days before I returned to Union City. I intentionally looked for the date because I couldn't fault him for having sex with others. But the date of it and he knew that I was coming and his intentions toward me. Then Oz has the nerve to put a ring on my finger, which he planned to do before I came back here. He knew that I was coming, and he...it was the lie, not the sex," she exclaimed. I looked at Cent, and she stared at Dea.

"Listen, full disclosure. I was standing outside of the door when you were screaming. I didn't want just to burst in, but at the same time, I wanna know what exactly happened," she said.

"Which part did you hear?" Dea asked.

"I came in on insane," Crescent smirked. "But, going back to what you said, Dea. You opened an email from that nigga at the club that night. From the little I know from you about that dude, how trustworthy is he? We live in the age of technology," Crescent shrugged. Dea narrowed her eyes and looked between us before leaning her head into the pillow.

"I can agree, but he still fucked ole girl," Dea said. "I...I'm unsure if I can just excuse that shit," she sighed.

"But you excused other men doing you dirty?" I pointed out. We wouldn't discuss the Roe relationship or the one she had with that Del Mar dude. Shandea glared at me, and I raised my brows because she knew I was right.

"And, is that supposed to make that shit right?"

"No, no, I didn't say it made it right. I'm just saying before you go through this 'I'm leaving' bullcrap while pregnant like some Tubi Movie drama, maybe you should see what he says about it and get all the facts."

Dea glared at me, but I could tell she was thinking about my words and figuring out the best way to argue her point.

"Also, you seemed to excuse him killing niggas as well," Crescent mumbled. I pressed my lips together because she had a point. I understood why

Dea was pissed, I did. But at the same time, she needed to get answers. If it was one thing I knew, it was that Oz wouldn't lie about it, whether it would hurt her feelings or not.

"That...that is...different. Aww, hell, I can't even sell that to myself. Still, his lies are a problem I refuse to put up with. As you said, I let shit slide with other men, and look where it got me," she sighed. I leaned forward, taking Dea's hand and lacing our fingers together. I got it, but we both knew Oz was no 'other' man.

"Let's table this because that can be handled later. Tell us what happened because, let's be honest, that's the real reason you are trying to pull away from Lennox. That other shit can be addressed, especially knowing that where the information came from is questionable. But what just happened to you is a totally different story," I said. Dea squeezed my hand and then started when Katrice called her earlier today.

"You got to be fucking with me," Crescent said.

"No, I told Lennox that his brother had this entire relationship in his head for years. Even when I left for six years, we were on a break in his head. He was crazy as shit, and I never knew how he felt all this time. I didn't know shit about him really or knew he liked me like that."

"Well, we don't need to worry about his ass anymore," I said.

"That's going to need to be unpacked. But my question is, where is your bitch ass cousin?" Crescent ranted.

"That's what I want to know. That bitch helped him. She set it all up. But how did she not know his obsession with me?" Dea asked. "I know we all never been on the same page, but we are fucking family. How could she help him do some shit like that? She didn't know if he would kill me or what," Dea fumed.

"And she didn't care either way. So, when I find her and beat her until the white meat show, I won't give a fuck either," I said.

"Well, I hope you both realize that Katrice ain't going to make it out of this city. She fucked with a U.C.K. nigga's woman. If they took out his brother just like that, what the hell do you think will happen when they catch her?" Cent asked.

I looked at Dea, and she stared at me for a long minute. I found that I honestly didn't care, and that knowledge scared me. Messing with these men brought out a side of Dea and me that neither of us had ever seen, because I could tell she didn't care either.

"Honestly, Crescent, I want to get to her ass first," Dea gritted.

"Mmm, I think I like this side of Shandea," Crescent laughed.

"When do you want to tell Mama?" I asked. Shandea looked at me with wide eyes like she hadn't considered it.

"I...I don't know. Do you think it's a good time to do it? Maybe I will wait until...until I'm certain I can carry it to term. I don't want to add any more stress on her right now," she said.

"It's your choice, but I agree with you," I said. I could see the thought of having a baby was taking root in her head. She smiled when she closed her eyes, and I looked up at Crescent. She mouthed that it would be okay, and I just nodded because I knew it would. That seemed to break the tense moment, and Dea shook her head as she rubbed at her stomach.

I planned to ask Crescent more about her past because she hadn't blinked once with all this crazy ass shit. And I wanted to know where the hell Faxx dragged her off to and what she had going on with his sexy ass. First, I had to be sure my sister got all the care she would need after this mess. But I knew Oz would ensure she did.

I let Dea get everything off her chest, and I could tell that it was no longer the video that really bothered her, but the fact that it was Oz's twin. How could she look at the same face as the person who kidnapped and tried to rape her? I took out my phone and looked for a therapist because she would need one, whether or not she thought so. Hearing everything she went through broke my heart, but it filled me with so much rage my hand shook slightly. I would kill Katrice and Yasmin's trifling asses if I found out she had anything to do with it. I knew what was happening with Oz and Dea would work itself out. If she decided she didn't want to stay, I would help her figure out how to get out of dodge. It just wouldn't be that easy, and she knew that. As I scrolled through the list of doctors, a message came from a number without a name. I hit the notification and gripped the phone tightly as I read it.

**Unknown:** *You could have told me about your mother, Tali. I wanted to let you know I took the job for you.*

## CHAPTER FIVE

# Lennox 'Oz' Anderson

I was walking and had no idea where the fuck I was going. I was so heated. I didn't realize I was standing in the parking lot until someone cleared their throat. I spun around to see Sam watching me calmly.

"You good?" Sam asked. He looked down at my balled fists and then back to my face. His dark brown eyes stared at me with a detached flat glare.

"I thought I told you to stick to Shantel's ass," I reprimanded.

"You did, but Faxx pulled me off of that and told me to come here because he had to leave. Damari is there watching her without her knowledge because she made it very clear she doesn't need a bodyguard," Sam chuckled.

Damari was a good fit because she wouldn't think that he would be there to guard her. It also worked because I needed Sam to run down some shit for me, and I needed to release some of this tension. There was only one fucking video Dea could be talking about, but that was done before I even knew Shandea existed.

"Bet. I need you to get into Dea's email and find out what video was sent to her."

"Personal or work email?" Sam asked. He took out his phone and began typing, but I wasn't sure which one. It couldn't be her work email because it wasn't known to others outside the company. It was more likely to be her personal email.

"Personal. If you can't find anything, then check her work email," I said. I looked around for my truck and realized it was back at the *Clinic*. I needed to go back there and change, get my shit, and head to the *Shop*. There were questions I still needed to ask the niggas who betrayed us for money.

"My Suburban is over there, Wiz. Where to first?" Sam asked.

He turned away, and I followed him to his SUV as my blood started to pump. My mind was all over the place. My twin brother was killed by a man I considered my brother. My unborn baby never had the chance to be born was sending me spiraling Now my wife wanted to fucking leave me! If Dea thought that shit was any kind of option, she was losing her fucking mind. Once she stepped through that door in *MYTH,* there was no going back. She knew that, I told her as much, and she agreed. I needed to refocus my shit before I lost it.

"The *Clinic*," I replied. Sam stopped at the back of his truck and looked over his shoulder.

"No one called you?"

"What the fuck are you talking about? What happened?" My first thought was Henny, Link, or Faxx getting hit if Ja had the location. Fuck! I should've been there or–

"Henny ordered a complete dismantle, and a new location is being secured and set up as we speak but–"

"Nigga, but what? What the fuck is going on?" I asked. I reached into my pocket and pulled out my phone. I didn't have any calls, alerts, or messages from any of them.

"The *Clinic* blew up. From the quick explanation I received from Faxx, he overheard something about his woman, and things went left."

"His woman? What woman?"

"Crescent, I believe. Let's get in the truck, Wiz. I don't like you being out in the open," Sam stated.

He opened the passenger side back door, and I climbed into the truck. What the fuck could Faxx have overheard that bad that he would blow up a building in the middle of downtown? Sam climbed into the front seat and looked at me in the rearview mirror. I looked to my left and saw a change of clothes and shoes. Sam must have known what I would need to do because there was a suit I would need for later, and a long-sleeved black tee shirt, and black tactical pants with boots that I wore to the *Shop*.

"So, this thing he got for Dea and Tali's friend is serious?"

"He has begun construction on his home to accommodate her hobby."

I didn't even want to know what the fuck crazy ass shit he was up to. He just met the girl, but I couldn't say a fucking thing with the way I acted about mine.

"What did someone say to make Faxx resort to his bombs?"

"I have no idea. But that isn't everything. Before the walls came tumbling down, I received a call from my contact that we would be raided. I called to tell Link, and that's when I found out what was happening. But I also discovered that the lead agent on it is Rodney Gates," Sam laughed. He started the engine and put the truck in drive.

"I knew that nigga smelled funny. He would've taken that ass whooping and then went on to be the enemy," I chuckled. I knew there was always a reason I didn't fuck with that nigga. He was on some vendetta shit, but I knew it wasn't all about that night he hit Dea.

"Not all of us smell funny, my nigga," Sam refuted. I laughed, which sounded slightly unhinged, meaning my psycho tendencies were showing. That was the real reason I had to step away from Dea for a moment.

"Samier, I didn't say all, my nigga. I wasn't trying to hurt your feelings and shit," I said. I reached out for the tee shirt. "Take me to the *Shop*."

"Fuck you, nigga. I told you about calling me that," he sucked his teeth. "I don't give a shit anyway. The best thing I did was quit because them niggas are dirtier than the shit we do. Plus, y'all pay better," he said.

I changed and tossed the scrubs in the third-row seats. The fact that Sam used to be a Union City detective for over ten years worked in our favor on so many levels. There were many niggas on the team who didn't trust Sam. All that shit was dead when Faxx just started giving niggas headshots that talked back to Sam or were disrespectful toward him. Faxx didn't bring on Cliff, but he was one of the men that came up as we did, so his betrayal hit home. Now I was questioning the rest of the men that worked for me. I was sure they knew that loyalty would be in question after the hit on the club. For their sake, I hoped they all passed Shantel's little interrogation, or they would be next up in the *Shop*.

"I never asked what happened to mak−"

"Sometimes the ones that are supposed to have your back are the ones who are trying to stab you in the back," Sam imparted. I leaned back in the leather seat and stared into the rearview mirror studying him for a second before he looked up. "Oz, you know I hate it when you do that. It's like a knife to the jugular when you stare like that," he attested. I blinked and turned to look out the window at the heavy traffic. "Yeah, you must purge some of that crazy before returning to Dea. We will be at the *Shop* in twenty minutes."

I said nothing else and pulled out my phone to text Henny. I was sure they would all come for the show once they knew I was heading to the *Shop*.

We pulled up in the back of a shopping center that I owned. This property was the first piece of real estate I purchased when I gained access to the money my mother left me. I think that was also a reason why Xavier had a problem with me, because my mother left everything to me. She knew, just as I did, that X wouldn't have been able to handle that type of money. And she also knew that I would take care of my brother. Had my mother known he didn't have it all back then? She had to know, even if she never told me about it. She knew about me, and even helped me learn to manage it. It was always 'Lennox. You must care for your little brother. Lennox, watch out for your younger brother. He isn't like you,' but I didn't understand it until she died. In my head, this nigga and I were twins and just alike. That shit changed when we met Henny and his brother, though.

"Oz, I still find this shit a little fucked up that you have the *Shop* beneath *FANCY PLANTS*. A vegan restaurant, my nigga," Sam said. He exited the truck, and I followed, shaking my head.

"Be honest, would you ever think a place called the *Butcher Shop* would be anywhere near a Vegan establishment? I know people talk about it. The 'authorities' have heard of it but wouldn't think to look here. Plus, it isn't in my name. It's the perfect cover. Am I right, or am I wrong?"

My mood was lifting slightly because I was getting closer to the release needed to get back to Shandea. We had to iron a few things out, and I needed to make sure she understood the life she chose.

"You are not wrong. I can honestly say when I first came, I was shocked. And no cop or any government agency would look at this place twice. The shit is just fucked up," he said.

"Did you make the call?"

"It's clear," he said, opening the back door.

We would have entered the kitchen if I didn't have it refigured to be a small storage room. If anyone did come looking, they would find nothing but a secondary storage room. I waited until Sam closed and locked the door before I reached behind the shelving and pressed my palm against the wall. I was always amazed at the shit Link could come up with when the door opened. The door was made to look to be a part of the gray wall, and I knew when it closed, no one else would be able to tell the difference. The cold air hit my face as I entered the space and continued forward until I reached a set of stairs leading downward.

"What else did you find about Roe?" I asked. I hit the bottom landing, and the eight bodies of my people sat tied to the chairs lined up against the wall. I clapped my hands together, causing the ones who were asleep to be startled awake. Bloodshot eyes met mine as they looked from Sam to me.

"He left Union City State, went to Westmont, and finished two years of college. He changed his business major to criminal justice. He earned a few more degrees before dropping off the grid for a bit and reappearing four years later. He rose the ranks in Piedmont and quickly became a detective, and not soon after, he became a DEA Agent. I'll have more personal information tomorrow. From what I'm told, it's good shit, but I have no idea what led him back to Union City," Sam stated.

All while he was talking, I was walking back and forth in front of these niggas, trying to decide who to take out first. I could hear their mumbles or screams behind the tape, but I stopped in front of one I thought wouldn't make it. I stood looking down at Haze, and a slow smile spread across my face. The fear I saw had me glad I let Henny come and perform that surgery on his ass. Now he was well enough to answer a few more questions.

"Just keep me informed on whatever else you find on him."

"Got it, Boss."

I stared at Haze momentarily, making him more uncomfortable by the minute.

"Haze, I am so glad you survived," I said. I ripped the tape from his mouth, and he grimaced at the pain.

"Fuck! You know I'm not–"

Haze's words were cut off as I rocked his jaw. His head snapped to the side, and blood leaked out of his mouth. He spit the blood onto the floor before he raised his head to face me.

I could feel my heart pounding in my chest as excitement filled my veins. I knew if anyone out of the eight men here would know something, it would be Haze. Haze was the one who secured the upper levels and had to get the codes for the elevators from Cliff. He knew more if Cliff trusted him enough to secure that position. He might have played that role of not knowing anything that night at the club, but after I calmed down, I was more clear-minded. Haze had the information about Jakobe, but I knew getting it out of him wouldn't be easy. Haze knew how I got down, to a certain extent. Yeah, I could have Henny whip up some shit, but this was one of my niggas. I wanted to do this shit my way. I knew he was thinking, why should he say anything when I would kill his ass anyway. But there were so many other things that could happen before death.

I heard the scrape of a metal chair dragging across the floor. I looked behind me and saw Sam stepping back, leaving the chair for me to sit in. I sat, leaned over, placed my elbows on my knees, and smiled.

"I don't think I asked this nigga a question yet. Did I Sam, because I'm not sure? They say I'm not right in the head," I smirked.

"Naw, you good Wiz because I didn't hear you ask him anything. Maybe we both are crazy," Sam chuckled.

"I thought so. Now let's have a conversation, Haze. Can we do that?"

"You can talk all you want to. We already know that we're not getting out of this bitch alive," he sneered.

"Oh, oh shit, that's...that's what y'all think? Damn, you all really must think I am a fucked-up person. All of you have been with me from the jump, so why would I do you like that? I mean, punishment needs to happen. But dying...that's extreme," I said, tilting my head. "I mean, all of you did this for money. But I know for a fact I pay all of you enough money for shit like this not to happen, so it had to be more than that. Hell, Sam, don't I pay you enough?"

"Sure do, Boss."

"Why the fuck do you trust that nigga? He the enemy," Haze snarled.

"Oh, you are lucky Faxx isn't here," I chuckled.

His eyes went wide before they started to dart around the room. I smacked him in the face to refocus his attention. He brought his eyes back to me and glared at me. I could feel his cold, calculating gaze, trying to figure out what I would do or ask. He was hard to read, and I knew I would have to tread carefully if I wanted to get any information from him. Killing the others would loosen his lips like it did those other niggas, but I wanted them to believe they had a chance of getting out of here.

"So, Haze," I began, my voice calm and measured. "I understand that you have some information that could be useful to me. Don't give me that 'I don't know' or 'fuck you' bullshit. If Cliff trusted you to handle the upstairs situation, then I am sure you were with him when he met up with Ja."

Haze simply smirked at me, his eyes narrowing slightly. "And why should I tell you anything?" he said, his voice dripping with sarcasm. I leaned forward, my tone becoming more assertive.

"Because if you don't, you're going to spend a lot of time in a very small, uncomfortable room, wishing you could die while I come to remove pieces of your body each day."

Haze's smirk faded slightly, and I saw a glimmer of fear in his eyes. But he quickly composed himself. He licked his dried and cracked lips while he cleared his throat.

"You think you can scare me, Oz?" he said, his voice low and menacing. "I've been through worse than anything you could throw at me. You know how life is in Union City. It's every man for himself out in these streets," he scoffed.

"So that's what this is about. You thought if you could take us out, it was your turn to rule some shit? Is that what Jakobe promised you?"

I knew I had to be careful. Haze was seasoned in these streets and wouldn't give up information easily. But in the end, I would get whatever information he held close to his chest out of him.

"Look, Haze," I said, my voice becoming more conciliatory. "We both know that Jakobe was on some fuck shit back then and still is today. I just don't understand how you could fall for his bullshit. It's in your best interest to cooperate and tell me what you fucking know before my patience wears out."

Haze snorted derisively. "You're not giving me much incentive here, Oz. See, you ain't going to do anything but kill us. So why should I tell you anything? I'm not going down like no snitch ass nigga."

I took a deep breath, trying to keep my face from showing how happy I was that he was playing hard. "Fine. Let's cut to the chase. Where is Jakobe hiding?" I asked.

I stood up, and Sam moved the chair out of the way. I might tell certain people to bring my enemies here, but they were never around when shit went down. The only people that knew what happened in this room were Henny, Faxx, Link, Shantel, and Sam. Not even Mala had seen what I did in this room, but I was sure Shantel told her about it or told her that she didn't want to know. I moved over to the far wall and put a code into a keypad. A part of the wall dropped open, lowering into a table that held all my tools. I looked over my shoulder and saw that every eye looked my way. I knew the moment they could fully see all of my tools. I looked over at Haze. His expression didn't change, but I could see a flicker of panic in his eyes.

"You...you...you think I'm just going to give him up like that?"

"Sam, this nigga stuttering and shit! You, you, you...nigga really?" I laughed.

"I don't know, Boss, I might stutter at seeing some of that shit, too," Sam chuckled. I heard him opening things and knew he was preparing my table. I looked over my tools, choosing what to use before turning around. I saw the black leather apron waiting for me and the black gloves.

"Do you have my beard cover? You know I don't like shit in my beard," I said. Sam shook his head and pulled out the hair and beard coverings.

"You a bougie ass nigga," Sam laughed. But I didn't miss the fact he put one on himself. I raised a brow.

"This is a first," I said, looking at him.

"I can't sit this one out. This shit got past me too, and I don't like that shit."

I didn't say another word as I tied my apron and then moved over to one of the men in the chairs.

"I think you're right, Sam. It is a little fucked up that I chop up meat under a vegan shop. Maybe I will move it and make this into a coffee shop or something," I said.

I smirked at the muffled screams as Sam cut the zip ties holding this little nigga named Von down, and we dragged his ass to the Butcher block table.

I had hoped that Haze wouldn't cooperate, and it seemed I would get what I wanted. I knew they were all weak, but everyone got their second wind once the toys came out. Von struggled all the way until the moment his limbs were strapped down to the table. I didn't remove the tape over his mouth yet, but his eyes pleaded with me not to kill him.

"Fuck you, Oz! Why should I say shit to you about anything? I don't give a fuck about these niggas! I ain't snitching for no one," Haze roared behind me. I raised my brows at Von, and the wild look in his eyes screamed at me in panic for his life.

"Damn, niggas ain't shit these days. I still don't know why he believes I will kill them?"

Sam chuckled while he finished securing Von's legs to the table. I looked at the monitor on the wall showing the busy restaurant upstairs and the back of the building.

"There are things worse than death," Sam said. Sam stood back against the wall and crossed his arms over his chest. I laughed, reached down, and ripped the tape away from Von's mouth.

"Ahh! Ahh! Ahh! Wiz, Wiz, Wiz, listen man. Listen, I have no idea what's happening. I don't even know why I am here. I would never do anything to fuck you over. Come on, you know me. You know my mama and my sister," Von cried.

"You're right, Von. I do know your mama and your baby sister. Just like I know they don't fuck with you like that. Maybe after this shit, you can do something to be a better son and brother."

"I will! I will, man. I swear I will. Just don't kill me. I will tell you what I know," Von promised.

"You don't need to beg for your life because I already said I am not going to kill you or them," I said, tipping my head to the others. "I just need someone to incentivize Haze to want to speak. Now he has said that he doesn't give a shit about any of y'all."

"And I don't! Kill that snitchin' ass nigga. We're going to die anyway. I don't give a fuck what you are saying," Haze shouted. I kept my eyes on Von.

"So, since he isn't going to tell me shit, I will ask you," I said, my voice taking on a more conversational tone. "What do you know about Jakobe's plans? Is there anything we should be aware of?"

I glanced at Haze, and his eyes narrowed. I could see a hint of suspicion in his gaze, but I smiled.

"How would I know? I don't know him," Von stated. His eyes bounced everywhere when I moved away. I knew he was trying to see where I was going, but he couldn't move. I went to my table and looked over my tools. I picked up my butcher knife and touched its tip before I looked at the others. They stared at me, and I moved over to them and stood before them. I ripped the tape from another one of their mouths.

"Oh shit, oh shit, oh shit!"

"Shhh, it's okay. We're all family here, right? Don't I treat y'all like we family?"

"Von! Tell him whatever you know, man. You put me on," he gritted. I turned away from him and returned to the table as Sam stepped forward. I leaned over Von, trying to project an air of sincerity in my voice.

"If you brought that nigga in, who brought you in to betray me?"

"Haze! It was Haze."

"Snitch ass nigga," Haze cursed.

"Okay, is Jakobe planning something else we need to be prepared for," I asked. Von's eyes widened, and he licked his bleeding, cracked lips.

"I...I...I don't know. I don't know. I don't even know that nigga."

I shrugged and raised my knife to eye level before I brought it down.

"Oh shit!" Haze and the other nigga screamed before the pain registered for Von.

"Ahh! Ahh, I don't know. I don't know!" Von screamed. Sam was next to me with a blow torch sealing the wound where I cut off Von's ring and pinky fingers. "I don't know this nigga Jakobe! I don't fucking know him," he screamed. Sam pulled away, grabbing Von's two fingers in the process. He walked over to the nigga that I took the tape off his mouth and shoved the pinky finger inside. Sam slapped his hand over his mouth and nose as the dude struggled.

"Swallow or suffocate. Your choice," he lamented. I waited, and it didn't take long for the nigga to decide to swallow. Sam moved his hand, and the nigga gasped for air and started to gag, but Sam already covered his mouth with a fresh piece of tape. Von's cries were pushed to the background, and Haze's shouts of us being sick were like listening to white noise.

"Well, since we all see where this is going, let's not waste any more time," I said and turned back to face Von.

By the time I was done, Von had lost both hands and all his toes. I was taking his right foot when the door opened, and Faxx, Henny, and Link stepped inside. The mumbled screams of the other niggas seemed to get louder than the gagging Haze was doing.

"Damn, Oz, just kill the nigga," Faxx said. He looked at Von before walking over to the far wall, posting up. Von was no longer screaming, but he wasn't dead. I told him I wouldn't kill him and meant that shit. I couldn't say the same about everyone else. I didn't lie, though, because when he died, the life insurance policy I had on this nigga would give a better life to his peoples. At least they would believe he died being a better son and brother.

"Naw, I told them we don't kill family over a misunderstanding. All we need to know is where the fuck is Jakobe's bitch ass," I stated. Von lost his foot, but Sam ensured he would live before he could bleed out. I dropped my saw on the table next to my knife and turned to look at Haze. "See, he isn't dead. Von has endured his punishment, and now he gets to rest."

"Rest? That nigga passed the fuck out," Henny chuckled. "But he ain't dead, so that's saying a lot," Henny shrugged.

Haze looked at me for a long moment as if trying to decide whether or not he would make it out alive or fucked up like Von. Would he choose to die quickly or prolong the suffering I had in store if he kept fucking with me? Finally, he spoke.

"Okay, okay, I'll tell you what I know. But you have to promise me something in return."

I raised an eyebrow, intrigued. "This nigga really negotiating and shit."

Link came over and showed me something on his tablet before moving away. He screwed his face up at me, and I looked down at myself. I was covered in blood, but the rage I felt before I got here had simmered until I saw that shit. Sam must have shot Link a text about the Dea situation because Link had her email pulled up. I saw who it was from and the video she was talking about. I didn't understand at first where Shandea had gotten her timeframe for this video, but looking at the date, I could understand her being upset. What I couldn't get past was her not giving me the benefit of the doubt no matter what she saw. That was something we would need to get straight because I have never lied to her about any fucking thing, and I wouldn't start. Then he swiped left, and I read an encrypted email from the Governor to his friend and donor, Alex Tilderman, about finding Nia and taking her out. I felt my teeth grinding together as I looked at Haze again in irritation. He saw the pain he would feel in my eyes if he didn't cut his bullshit. "What the fuck do you want?"

Haze leaned forward, his voice dropping to a murmur. "You have to promise to protect my daughter and her mother. It ain't Ja that I am worried about. It's the nigga he was with when Cliff and I went to meet with this nigga."

I nodded, understanding the gravity of his request. I was going to be a father now, so I got it, but his family ain't got shit to do with me. Once he was dead, her best bet will be to take that money from his policy and move the fuck out of Union City. I felt my brothers in the room, but they all were silent and waiting. "Speak nigga! I'm losing the patience I gained from chopping this nigga the fuck up! Now, if you don't want to know what ole boy over here tastes like, I think you should speak the fuck up. You had all that mouth earlier, my nigga," I exploded.

"Yo, this nigga wildin'," Faxx laughed.

Haze looked at the eyes of the other men in the room. Two of them were actually dead from vomiting because they choked on it, but the others just shook their heads trying to warn this nigga.

"Jakobe has been meeting in what looks like an abandoned warehouse on the city's outskirts. He's been using it as a base of operations, and it's where he creates *Silk*."

"Where the fuck is this warehouse," Henny demanded.

"I don't know! I don't know how—"

His words were cut off when Henny moved forward and slammed a fist into his stomach.

"I don't know how to tell you where it is! I can show you," Haze choked. He gasped for breath as Henny stared down at him.

"Aight, then you going to show us where it is tonight," Henny ordered.

"He...he won't...he only goes there on Friday. I'll show you where it is but...but...I ain't going in there. You might kill me, but that niggas connections would fuck up my entire family's lives. The nigga is connected."

"The fact that you believe we won't is laughable," Henny glared.

"I...I...I'm not saying," Haze stammered.

"Are you talking about the Cartel?" Link said, snapping his fingers in his face.

"Yeah, them niggas too, but they weren't there this time. Jakobe is good with that Senator nigga. Cliff might not know who the fuck he was, but I recognized him. It was Kenneth Morgan," he rasped. Henny turned to look at me, and I felt my jaw clench tight as fuck at that name. I felt a sense of burning hot rage wash over me. Why was Jakobe meeting with the nigga that I believed was my father? The man that killed my mother and left her body parts for Xavier and me to find.

"Sam, take care of this nigga Von and get this shit cleaned up. Take them niggas to the farm and leave the others for later. Make sure we get Haze cleaned up and ready to go before Friday," I said.

"I'll take care of it, Boss. Anything else?" Sam asked.

"Yeah, I want you and Damari to head up to the house where Nia is staying and keep an eye on her. I'll bring you up to speed once you get there," I stated.

"Oz, I can't leave and–"

"Sam!" My shout bounced off the walls, and Faxx touched my shoulder.

"It's all good, Sam. I'll handle getting him covered," Faxx stated.

"Alright, Wiz, I got it handled," Sam grumbled.

"I will call you once I have all the information. Make sure you leave once this shit is done."

I knew Sam was mad as fuck about being stuck on babysitting duty, but he and Damari were the only ones I trusted right now with Nia's life. It wasn't like any of us could stay there with her right now. Henny faced me, and I knew he could see the murder in my gaze. He rubbed his goatee and shook his head.

"Why would Morgan be meeting with Ja personally? *Silk* ain't that damn important for him to put himself in a position to get caught up."

"Nope, it isn't, but maybe he thinks he found a nigga that could finish what he started," I gritted.

"What?"

"Killing the bastard children of the woman he murdered. Then there is the fact that the Cartel believes they can just post up in this city. What kind of deal is Morgan working on for them? Finding out Ja knows us or me was a bonus." I looked at Haze for a moment. "That information might have saved your life, my nigga."

"Then, there's something else y'all niggas should know. Jakobe told X to let the Del Mar niggas know if they get hemmed up to make a deal. He told X to give them all the information he could about the lower levels of *MYTH*," Haze said quickly. I looked at Henny because there was only one nigga that got locked up from that crew, and it was Yung D-Mar.

"It will be handled," Henny said, pulling out his phone.

## CHAPTER SIX

## SHANDEA 'DEA' SAUNDERS

I stared out the window, wishing Dr. McQueen said I could return to work tomorrow. I didn't want to be stuck in the house with Lennox and hoped his ass had things to do. I sighed because I knew he would bring up the sex video, and I just didn't care any longer. He did what he did and lied about it like the rest of these niggas. The real reason was that I couldn't look at him without seeing his brother, and it's fucking with me. I pressed a hand to my stomach, still unable to believe I was carrying a child. Dr. McQueen was wonderful, and I was happy that she also confirmed that everything looked good so far. I was doubly glad when she entered the room and saw that she was an African American woman, around my age or slightly older. She immediately made me feel comfortable and didn't dismiss any of my large or small concerns. I sighed again and rubbed my arms as we pulled into the underground garage of the tower.

"Shandea, how about you say whatever it is that you need to say instead of sighing every five seconds? Nothing will get figured out unless you open your mouth," Lennox said.

I turned slowly to look at him like he was crazy. It had been less than thirty hours since everything went down. I'd noticed that he looked at my finger occasionally and knew he wanted to say something about that, but he didn't. What the fuck did he want me to say that I hadn't already said? He knew that I knew what the hell he did and that his fucking brother kidnapped me, causing me to lose my child.

"I lost a baby, Lennox. I think I have a right to sigh whenever I feel like it," I stated as soon as he put the truck in park. I reached down for my purse and pulled at the handle to exit the truck. The doors were locked, and when I went to unlock them, Lennox locked them again. "What the fuck, Lennox? Let me out," I said, facing him. His eyes were on me when I faced him. His brows were furrowed, and his jaw clenched telling me he was holding back.

"Dea, I am going to say this shit one time, and I hope you take a second to understand the shit you are saying. *WE* lost a baby. Not just you but *WE*. Don't think I'm not fucking sick over this shit or that I don't feel like this all falls on me, because I do. I know what happened and take responsibility for it because I should've been there faster. I should've ensured you were protected more and told you about other shit happening because you would've thought twice before leaving that day. But don't sit as if you are the only one that is hurting. My pain just isn't visible," he insisted.

Lennox opened his door and got out of the truck, leaving me to sit there staring at the space he just occupied. I didn't realize he had opened my door until I felt his hand on my arm, helping me out of his Navigator. I felt like a bitch for not thinking about how Lennox felt about the baby. I closed my eyes as he guided me toward the elevators that would take us to our home. I knew I was only thinking of myself and had good reason to think of myself, but I also knew that wasn't fair. I knew Lennox, and I was letting shit that other men had done to me fuel my anger instead of figuring out Sincere's endgame.

It still nagged at me because, any way you looked at it, he had sex with the girl. But that didn't excuse how I treated him because he also lost a child. I stepped onto the elevator and watched Lennox enter the penthouse code. The doors closed, and I saw my reflection. I wanted to scream and cry all over again at what Xavier did to me. Then it hit me that not only had he lost a child, but he lost his twin brother. Fuck. And from what Tali said, Henny took him out, but Lennox was there when it happened.

"I'm not excusing everything we need to discuss, but I am truly sorry, Lennox. I know you are feeling what I am feeling about the loss of our child. I never wanted to make you feel as if your feelings weren't as valid," I apologized.

I didn't have it in me yet to say anything about his brother because it was just too fresh for me. He didn't say anything, and the doors opened to our floor. He held the elevator doors open, and I exited. I waited while he unlocked the door, and we stepped inside. My stomach growled as I dropped my purse on the small table beside the door.

"What do you want to eat?"

"I don't know. All I really want is some honeydew melon and peanut butter," I said. I moved over to the couch and sat down, hating the tension I was feeling between us. I reached up and probed around my eye, now glad Dr. McQueen gave me some time off. I couldn't go back to work looking how I was looking. I sighed and then looked up to see Lennox staring at me like I was crazy. "What?"

"Honeydew melon and peanut butter?"

"It's good, Lennox. You just haven't tried it," I laughed. "Hell, anything with peanut butter at this point. You know what sounds good?"

"I don't know if I want to know," Lennox said. He tugged at his tie as he entered his office and returned with his laptop. Lennox placed it on the long media console and opened it. "What sounds good, Dea? I'll get you some fruit and shit delivered if that's what you want to snack on, but you need to eat something while we have this conversation," Lennox stated. I watched as he connected the laptop and TV together with the Bluetooth and realized that we never really watched the big ass thing.

"I don't know what I want, but it needs to have something to do with peanut butter. And some pork!"

Lennox turned around to look at me at my outburst, but the more I talked about it, the more that shit sounded good. His face was hilarious, though, and I laughed when he put his phone to his ear.

"Henny, I think something is wrong."

"Oh, my God! Nothing is wrong with me," I laughed. My smile was hurting my face, but I couldn't help it.

"She wants some weird ass shit, nigga."

I cackled and shook my head at this fool because how did he not know what this was?

"Cravings? That's disgusting, but I got you. She better start craving this dick because all this weird ass shit she is saying is nasty as fuck. Just come check her out, just in case you get a chance. Nigga, for real," Lennox gritted. "Hello! Yo!"

He glared at me as I fell over on the couch, shaking my head. Lennox ended the call with Henny and called someone else. I heard him speaking to the chef about food as he walked away. I knew if he told him what I had a taste for, Chef Remington would whip up some good food for me. Lennox came back into the living room and gone was the suit. All he had on was a pair of dark gray sweatpants and socks as he went to the laptop. He hit a few buttons and then came to sit next to me on the couch.

"You are wild as hell," I laughed. Laughing felt good, but I knew my little happiness wouldn't last. I looked over Lennox's body, itching to touch his tattoos and resting my head on his chest. What actually happened was that it brought a flashback to Xavier, but I could see the tatts were different in that flashback. Not only different, but X didn't have as many as Lennox. I stared at Lennox, noticing some slight differences in him that you wouldn't see unless you were looking. I think that was what made me mad at myself because, from the jump, I should have fucking known that it wasn't him.

"I'm not wild. I'm saying if I wake up and you're eating some cucumbers and peanut butter at two in the morning. I'm going to throw up," he smirked.

"You only going to throw up because you don't like cucumbers! But that does sound good," I said as my stomach growled. Lennox had a small smile on his face, but it dropped off when he took a breath.

"Shandea, I know what you saw and what you think you know."

"It's not what I think I know, Lennox. It's what I know. I heard you while we were at the women's center, but I failed to see how I got it messed up. You lied to me when it was unnecessary. If this was any other nigga and I told you this, you would tell me to leave him alone. So why is it different because it's you? If it's about the baby, I would never keep you from your child, and you know that," I assured.

"You're right. That's exactly what I would tell you to do, but let's get one thing straight, Sweetness. I am not any of those other niggas or any nigga out here. You know damn well, or at least I thought you did, that I have never and will not lie to you. But I feel you. I thought you trusted me more, but I got it. One thing for sure, though, is that no matter how you feel about any situation, argument, or disagreement that we have, US," he said, pointing between him and me, "will never be done. So, seeing my child or being around my child will never be a problem because my wife will be exactly where I am. I get that some shit was used against us, putting you in a situation I wish I could erase. To ensure something like this doesn't happen again, I will lay all this shit out on the table. Because at the end of this conversation, whether you are mad or not, that ring better sit on your left ring finger."

I sucked in a breath and held it while staring at Lennox. I knew I would need to tell him it wasn't all about the video, but that had to be put to bed. I didn't think he could clean anything up about him fucking that chick raw two days before I came here. I knew that Lennox was possessive and obsessive, but he had to be fucking kidding. I bit back on that response because I knew Lennox, and looking into his eyes, I knew he was dead ass serious.

"You can not make me marry you, Lennox. It doesn't work that way," I said.

Everything else I thought about saying, I kept that shit to myself for now. Lennox chuckled before turning back to the TV and picking up the remote. I turned to look at the screen, and my eyes bugged out of my damn head. This nigga had the fucking video pulled up of him and this girl for me to watch again on this eighty-five-inch television! My body began to shake, and I felt his large hand land on my leg, squeezing my thigh tightly.

"Get the fuck off me, Oz," I hissed.

He raised a brow at me using his nickname, but pressed play. The sounds of moans and skin-on-skin played in the surround sound system like we were on a fucking movie set. I refused to look at the shit and turned my head away, crossing my arms. I would've tried to get up, but I knew his ass wasn't about to let me move.

"Look at it, Dea. This is the same video that was sent to your email," he insisted. His finger gripped my chin, and I turned my head to face the screen.

"Get the fuck off me! Why would you even do some ignorant shit like this?" I pushed at his hand and then tried to stand up. He caught my wrists in one of his large hands and pulled me back down on the couch. I felt his hand at my waist as he lifted me and sat me in his lap. "Lennox! Get the fuck off me! Let me go now," I shouted. I was not about to look at him fucking someone else. I knew I should've figured out how not to come back here.

"Look at the damn screen, Dea! Look at it and tell me what the hell you see," he said apologetically. I turned sharply toward the TV, and saw it was a split screen of the same video. I stared at it, hating what I saw as bile rose in my throat. "You can call me a murderer, a pimp, a blackmailer, and even a psychopath, but nobody can call me a liar. I let you get away with saying that shit a few times now, but that shit is done."

"Whatever. Let me go," I said quietly.

"You're not looking, Shandea," he stated. Lennox picked up the remote and muted it. "Just look at it. Really look at it. Fuck the sex part, because we will not sit here and act like neither of us wasn't fucking other people beforehand."

He held me still, and I looked at the TV to get it over with. As soon as his ass let me go, I was out. Fuck this! I would stay at my Mama's house until my job could find me another place to stay. My gaze narrowed at the screen because, looking at both videos, something wasn't right. The one on the right showed something entirely different from the one on the left. I could tell the one on the left was the one from my email.

"How...this isn't...what the fuck is this?" I asked.

"One is the original video, and the other is a deep fake with some mediocre-ass artificial intelligence bullshit. They changed enough of it without making it look like anything was wrong. The only reason I know shit is off is because I was there."

I tried moving again, but he tightened his hold on me. There was a knock at the door, but Lennox didn't move.

"Might be one of your bitches at the door," I said.

"Fuck that door. Look at the damn TV and tell me what you see that is different," he ordered. The one he said was the original also had another dude in the video, but I didn't know who he was. He reminded me of

Henny, but I knew it wasn't him. But what was interesting was I could clearly see that Lennox was wearing a condom.

"How do I know this isn't the one that was photoshopped or a deep fake or whatever," I said. "Either way, the shit happened when you claimed you planned for us to be together."

Lennox laughed. It wasn't a real laugh, but one of irritation.

"These bitch ass niggas really did a job on you, Shandea. I've been the one to never lie to you and always been there for you. But you can't take my word for this shit. You can see that video is fake as fuck, Sweetness. That's all, and that's it," he said.

"Okay. Fine, it's fake, and you didn't lie about fucking bitches raw. Okay, cool. I don't give a fuck anymore, Lennox. After all that has happened, this isn't even important," I said. I was trying not to freak the fuck out by him still holding me, and I think he realized it because I was shaking so badly.

"I'm sorry, Sweetness. I just want you to see what people will do to fuck with us. What can happen if you can't see through shit like this? What can happen if you don't trust me," he indicated. "This was recorded a year before I even met you. You know the business that I'm in, Dea. How do you think it got started? That was the launching point to pull people in, but it never went further than that between Nia and me because it was just business. I wanted the money coming from every end. I didn't know that I would become the owner of *MYTH* at that time. I was going to create my own version of *MYTH*. This one video gave me a platform, and I expanded on that. Just to show you how old it is, the other dude in the video is Malcolm. That is Henny's brother, who died six years ago. As a matter of fact, he died the night I came back to find you had left," he disclosed. I looked at the TV again and then back to Lennox.

"How? Why would he...when did...wait. When was the last time you and she had sex?"

"The only feelings I have for Nia are nothing more than platonic ones. You should know me better than that, Dea. That night was the last and first time I ever slept with that girl, and trust me, neither one of us wants to repeat it," Lennox gritted.

"How in the hell did Sincere get it?"

"Get it? Anyone with a subscription back then could have gotten it. It was online, so anyone could have seen it or downloaded it. If I'm honest, different clips of that night could still be found, but it's all old footage. I built my money back in college making flicks. That's how I knew so many men and women who were ready to take it to the next level when I took ownership of *MYTH*. They were already working for me."

"I thought U.C.K. sold drugs back then."

"We dabbled in that, but it wasn't our end game. It was just a way to keep control over our territory. But it was always understood we would have our hands in everything. So, of course, sex was another venture, and I took that on to mold it into what I wanted. I wanted to sell sex, but I wanted to sell it as a dream. That's how I got the idea for what I turned *MYTH* into," he explained.

"Is that video still out there? Are there other videos of you?"

I scrunched my nose up at that knowledge, trying to figure out how I didn't know he was doing some porn shit.

"It was a one-time thing, Dea, so don't sit there and think I'm out there like that because I'm not. I already had the footage pulled from our subscription service and scrubbed online as much as possible. It will no longer be offered anywhere."

His knowing exactly what I was thinking said how much he knew me. It made sense that Sincere recognized him because he had a stripper and porn addiction.

"Okay. But look at it from my point of view, Lennox. How do you think I would feel or react whether I know you or not? Do you see how that shit could hurt? Look at it. After all, you were saying to me, and then I saw this. Come on," I gestured.

"I get that, but your first thought was to run when you said you wouldn't do that. As soon as some shit went down, your ass was ready to call shit quits and run. I told you that wasn't going to happen, Dea. If some shit like this happens again, you talk to me. You come at me and get the truth, because you know damn well I ain't going to lie about shit. Especially not to you." I didn't say anything because he was right. I was done, and I was going to leave. "I know what happened is fucking with you, and it should. We will get through it together, and I will do whatever it takes to ensure it doesn't happen again."

Lennox stood up and went to the door, and I sat there watching the video replay and noticed the dates at the bottom. *Shit.* Lennox returned and sat on the couch with a bag containing the fruit and peanut butter I requested. I sat back on the cushions, thinking about what I just found out and what else I didn't know.

"When you're right, you're right. I was going to run, and honestly, the thought was still in my head to run. But all of that is just baffling, and I still feel as though you should've told me about her. You introduced me to the girl like it was all good. I'm not saying it had to be right then and there, but maybe if you had told me, a lot of this may have been avoided. And if I had stopped to think first, I wouldn't have just run out like that. Even if I didn't know about the Xavier mess, I should've thought twice after the club scene."

"We both did some things wrong, but you should know I wouldn't do no shit like that to you."

"You say I should know you, but I really don't know you like I thought I did. Not all of you, Lennox. So how about we start there," I said. Lennox picked up the remote and cut the TV off before looking at me. He leaned his head to the side, studying me for a full minute.

"You're right. Let me start with who my mother was and how she died. My mother was a high-class escort, and the nigga that killed her was her client. At least, that is what she said in a video recording she left to me in case something happened to her. All I have left of my mother is that video and the fifty million dollars I inherited when I turned twenty-eight. Well, I received twenty million at twenty-eight, and I will get the remaining when I turn thirty-five."

"What? What did you just say..." I was speechless as I stared at him. All this time, I thought his money came from everything else he did. So, what was he worth now? "A life insurance policy or something?"

"No. It was set up as a trust. She didn't have a life insurance policy."

"Where in the hell did she get that type of money? She couldn't have been getting that type of money escorting. Ain't no way," I said.

"No. I'm unsure, and I have no way of finding out. I had Link look into it, and I asked the old owner of *MYTH,* but he didn't know she had that kind of money. I don't know," he frowned.

I could see how talking about his mother affected him. Lennox wasn't over the death of his mother, and now his brother was dead. He had no family left, so to speak, and here I was talking about leaving and shit. I closed my eyes and winced slightly at the pain.

"What do you know about her client?" I really wanted to know if he found him and took his ass out. Lennox opened the bag, took out the fruit, and placed it on the table.

"The only thing I know for sure is that he is my father."

Another knock was at the door, and Lennox stood up to answer it. I got up and went into the kitchen for a knife and plate. I returned and picked through the fruit, grabbing what I wanted before opening the peanut butter jar. I used the butter knife to scoop out the peanut butter and put it on the saucer plate when Lennox returned with a large bag. The smells coming from it had me licking my lips, but I wanted the fruit more now.

"We can eat later since you're eating that weird ass shit right now," he said. Lennox took the bag into the kitchen, and I took a bite of the fruit I had been craving. Lennox came around the corner holding a box, and my heart picked up momentarily, slamming against my chest. One second, I saw Xavier coming at me. The next, it was Lennox. I knew that Tali was right and that I would need to talk with someone about this because there was no way I could live like this. It seemed like the only thing that was helping was this conversation, and now that it seemed like I was about to get answers from Lennox. Hopefully, it would keep my mind clear of what happened. "You good, Sweetness?"

"Yeah, yeah, I'm fine."

Lennox stared at me for a minute longer and narrowed his eyes.

"Remember you said that we should see a therapist together?"

"Yes."

"I'm going to make an appointment tomorrow with one I trust. Someone you can speak to freely. How about we both have a couple's session, and you can do a private one," he asked. I nodded because it was a damn good idea.

"Make the appointment," I smiled.

"Say less. I got this after my mother was found murdered," he said, sitting beside me. I inched closer to him, wanting to feel his heat and, on some level, needing to be close to him. I hated the involuntary tremors occasionally, but I figured they would pass. The shit was still fresh. He pulled out an old, single-player DVD player.

"Damn."

"Shut up. I have it backed up, but this is all I have left that my mother had touched. Everything else was either stolen, sold, or destroyed when she died."

I reached out and placed a hand on his leg as he got that old ass shit started. I took another bite of the fruit and leaned forward to look in the box. A framed picture of his mother was in the box, and I reached inside to see it better.

"This is her?" I asked softly.

"Yeah."

"Why don't you keep it out? She's beautiful," I said. I looked closer at the picture and frowned slightly. "Dr. McQueen favors her except for the eyes," I noted. His mother had the same cognac-colored eyes as he did. "What was her name?" I asked as I pulled the frame out of the box.

"Soleil Anderson. I guess they do favor a little. I never really noticed. I never took her photo out of the box," he said, clearing his throat.

"That's pretty. Sun. I like it, but yeah, they do," I said, sticking the rest of the honeydew in my mouth. Dr. McQueen was thicker, though. His mother had a more slim, petite figure. When I pulled out the frame, there was a piece of paper stuck to the back of it. "Did you know there was a letter in here," I said. I pulled the paper from the back of it and saw that there was an envelope stuck to the frame. Lennox leaned over with a frown, looking at the aged envelope.

"Naw. Like I said, I never took out the picture. I don't know what the fuck that shit is," he said. "Open it and read it," he said, pointing to it with his chin. I wiped my hand on a napkin, carefully opened the small envelope, and pulled out a handwritten letter.

"Okay, it says—"

**DEAR SONNY,**
**AS WE DISCUSSED WHEN I FOUND YOU, THEY WILL BE CARED FOR NO MATTER WHAT HAPPENS. I WILL FOREVER AND ALWAYS WATCH OVER THEM.**
**IAN L.**

"Let me see that," Lennox said. I handed him the letter, and he was on his feet instantly. Lennox had his phone to his ear with an angry look crossing his face. "Link, I need you to come and run some fucking prints for me. It's about that nigga Ian."

Lennox turned back to look at me, and I raised my brows at him.

"I take it you know who that is?"

Lennox rubbed a hand down his face as he let out a slow, measured breath. I could tell this letter just opened up more shit for him.

"I'm not sure, but if it's the same Ian I'm thinking, this nigga knows more than what he is letting on. Are you ready for your nasty ass peanut butter and pork sandwich while I tell you what you need to know to keep your ass safe?"

Lennox tried to smirk at me, but I could see his mind was everywhere else but here. His description of the food made me sure that Chef Remington whipped up something tasty. If I was truly going to give this relationship everything, I needed to know all he could tell me.

"You get the food, and I will start the video," I said, concluding that I wasn't going anywhere.

CHAPTER SEVEN

## TALI SAUNDERS

It had been a week since Shandea was discharged to go home. Things had been quiet, but for Dea, she'd been losing her damn mind. So after Crescent finished working, Cent and I would go and chill with her for a while. I had been checking in on her, but I'd been too tired going between work and caring for Mama to stay long with Dea. I stood in the bathroom mirror, staring at myself while rubbing the mango scented body cream into my skin. My mind was a thousand miles away thinking about all the shit that was told to Dea, Crescent, and myself about what exactly Henny, Oz, Faxx, and Link were into. The only one of the three of us that wasn't terrified for our lives, was Crescent. That girl was holding back some secrets, but I felt it was more like trauma.

At least now that I knew to stay the fuck away from Jakobe was a thing, I figured that I should have told Henny earlier on that I ran into him when leaving Katrice's boutique. When he heard that news, he was not happy at all, and I swore if he could have lifted the marble island, that shit would have gone out of the window. I just didn't know it was so important at the time. This is where more communication was key. Then there was the fact that Tre was coming here. I didn't know how that shit would go down, and it had my nerves bad as fuck.

I had no reason for them to be because it wasn't like I was in a relationship with either of them. Henny and I were in a situationship. The only claim I felt he was concerned about was my pussy and nothing else. I knew he cared for me, but it wasn't the same as Dea and Oz. Just as Crescent and I predicted, Dea was staying exactly where she was, even though she said she did not want to see, speak, or ever meet the chick in-person that was in the video. I didn't know if she and Oz agreed about it because when Shandea said it, Oz never agreed with her.

I needed to mentally prepare myself to support Hendrix today because he wanted me to sit in on the surgery that would reverse the damage that had been done to cause Sanchez to go blind. Hendrix was nervous about it, but I'd stayed up late with him as he reviewed every pro and con until he finally concluded that it could be done. I told him I would be there watching, and it calmed him down. I got his anxiety about it, because this was one of his friends he was operating on, which was never a good idea, but he didn't trust anyone else to perform it.

I had received texts from Tre asking if we could catch up once he got into town, but I still hadn't replied. That situation felt dangerous, and I didn't want any part of it. Tre was an outstanding doctor and a good man at times, when his ego didn't get in the way. I just had too much shit going on, and now I had to be in on this review board meeting because of the fight with Pamela and Crescent. At least, that would be tomorrow. I didn't want to be worried about Tre's dumb ass saying anything or doing something that would set Henny off, but I knew Tre. He always felt like he was entitled to everything and everyone. That was one of many reasons we didn't work out, but the main reason was that he couldn't seem to hold back his critical judgments on the shit I liked. He had no problem giving it to me, but I knew it was a power trip for him. After the fact, I would feel his disapproval about what got me off, like I was wrong to have these feelings.

"What are you thinking so hard about?"

Henny's deep rumble pulled me out of my thoughts, and I blinked. He stood behind me, staring at me in the mirror while holding the ends of his black and gray striped tie. I wasn't about to say shit about Tre right now, so I steered the conversation to something safe that would give me a better understanding of Hendrix.

"How do you do it?" I asked. I turned around, causing him to take a step back while he looked down at me. I brushed his hands away and began to fix his tie for him.

"Do what, Thickness?" he asked.

"Wear so many hats? Which one is the real you? Is it the doctor, the multiple business owner, the U.C.K. nigga, the kill–"

Henny caught my hands just as I smoothed down his tie and forced them down to my sides. He stepped closer, and I had to lean back to keep eye contact. Henny leaned down and kissed me slowly while keeping his eyes open, watching me. His kiss caused me to shiver as his tongue licked the roof of my mouth. He sucked on my tongue while his thumbs rubbed circles inside my wrists. I could feel how hard he was, but I knew we didn't have time and couldn't be late this morning. Hendrix pulled back, let my hands go to reach around me, and pick up his glasses.

"Why do I need to be just one of them? I'm Hendrix Pharma. I am all the personalities you listed, and probably more."

"Baby, you're so young to be doing all this shit. How? How can you keep it all straight? It has to be too much for one person to handle. Why can't you choose one or the other?"

Henny smirked at me while he adjusted his sexy-as-hell glasses before looking down at me. He leaned down, and I raised my head for his kiss, but he bit my lips instead.

"You better watch yourself calling me baby. You're going to have me thinking I am winning our bet," he whispered against my lips. He kissed me like he was taking away the slight pain from when he bit me.

"Ain't no way, boy," I smiled. I didn't even realize I had said that until he pointed it out. I needed to be more careful about what the hell I was saying. Hendrix smirked, but he pulled away, not believing my words.

"When I started down this path, I clarified that I wanted it all. I wanted to be on top of both worlds, and I've accomplished that. Now, I just need to keep it. If I'm being completely honest with you, Tali, if I didn't have all this to handle, I don't know how I would be able to contain my impulses. Everything I do is an outlet to help my brothers and me lead productive lives while satisfying the darker parts of our souls. So helping others in the process and rebuilding to make our community what it should be also help when those darker parts of me get...get out of hand."

All I was hearing was that if this became an actual relationship, I would need the number to Dea and Oz's therapist because, clearly, this nigga was crazy. But it didn't matter because I was gone once I finished with these six months, and by then, Mama would be on the mend. Now that Dea was staying in Union City, I wasn't too worried about Mama being here. Thinking of Mama had me thinking about them bitch ass cousins of mine, and I frowned.

"Well, if it works for you, I'm happy about it. Can I ask you if y'all found Katrice yet?"

Henny backed further away from me but pulled my hand so I would follow him back into the room. He let me go, and I moved over to the bed to start dressing so we could leave the house on time.

"We will get her, Thickness, but I want to talk to you about something. It's about your Mother," he sighed.

"What? What about my Mama?" I frowned. My heart beat rapidly like it would fly out of my chest.

"Calm down, Thickness, she's fine. It's just when I went back through her medical record, I looked over her labs."

"Okay," I hesitated. I was scared of what Henny would say, but I needed him to spit it out.

"They found high levels of lithium in her bloodstream."

"What! How...wait, what? There is no need for her to be taking lithium, nor is it one of her usual medications," I stated.

"I know, baby, but I believe the side effects of the lithium brought her to the hospital. From there, she was treated initially, but we also found cancer. Either way, we will figure it out. I will make it my business to figure out how it happened," Henny assured.

I could feel myself shaking at the knowledge and questioning what had happened these last few months. I knew I needed to let Dea know, but I didn't want her worrying.

"I'll take care of everything, Tali. All you need to do is focus on your Mama right now. Now hurry up so you have time to eat breakfast," he commanded. Henny left the room quickly, and I narrowed my eyes at him. I felt like he was either hiding that they had already found Katrice or they had killed her. Did he know something else about why Mama had a high amount of lithium in her blood? My jaw clenched because I wanted a piece of Katrice's ass if I was being real. But, now I was just more worried about Mama and didn't give a fuck if the bitch was dead or not. That thought had me looking at myself in the mirror because I must have gone completely insane that I couldn't find it in myself to care if the bitch was dead or alive.

I didn't have to work today but wanted to check on Mama and see what was up with Crescent before joining Henny for the surgery. I made my way to the floor after I had to convince Henny that he did not need me in his office. I knew what he wanted and told him if he did this surgery flawlessly, he could bend me over his desk later today. It wasn't like that shit was a hardship for me, but he took it a step further, telling me he would bend me over his desk after his meeting. But only if I was under it, giving him head until the meeting was concluded. I couldn't lie and say my pussy didn't clench, and my panties weren't soaked when he said it.

"Hey, girl! Don't go in there waking up Mrs. Naomi. I just got her bathed, and she is finally napping. She didn't have a good night last night, but I took care of it," Crescent said.

"Why? What happened last night? I didn't get a call," I rushed. Crescent finished entering her documentation before she turned around.

"She was just up stressing over meeting this new doctor and money. You know all the normal things. So she didn't get any rest last night, and the Tech neglected to tell the nurse about her pain."

"What!"

"Calm down, girl. I handled it."

"Handle it how?" I asked, skeptical. Cent didn't need to be in any more fights on the job. I don't think even Dr. Sexy could save her ass the next time.

"Chill out, Tali. You act like I dogged walked the girl or something," Crescent laughed. I raised my brows, and she laughed harder. Crescent slapped a hand over her mouth when people walked by, looking at us. I didn't think people recognized me because I wasn't in scrubs today and had my locs in a French braid.

"Anything is possible, bish," I laughed.

"Naw, she was a new Tech. I told her she needs to inform the nurse even if they don't ask for pain medicine, but they tell her their pain is over a five. I cussed the nurse out because it was documented as an eight, and she should have checked on her, but your Mama said she didn't come back in after evening meds," Crescent sneered.

"It was that bitch Stacey, wasn't it? You know she and Pam are tight like that. Who is in charge because–"

"Tali, Tali I handled it. When I came in, I spoke with the charge nurse and ensured she wouldn't be with Mrs. Naomi again. I also spoke to the director about it, and Stacey was pulled up last I checked. You know I don't play about Mrs. Naomi, girl," Crescent smiled. I closed my eyes, thanking God I didn't need to lose my job for whipping somebody's ass.

"I'm surprised at how well you handled that," I smiled.

"I'm not ghetto all the time. It was just that bitch Pam and her bullshit. I often let her slick-ass comments slide before I stomped her ass out. Now, are we still going over to see Dea later today? Faxx wants his hair braided, and I told his ass that Dea did mine, so he said he's stopping by," she rolled her eyes. I didn't know why she acted like she wasn't feeling his fine ass.

"Girl, stop acting like you don't like that boy."

"He's aight and everything, but he's crazy. I don't know if I can do it, and he has been asking me too many personal questions and shit. I don't have time for all that," she insisted.

I didn't care what shit she was talking about because anyone with eyes or even blind could tell they were feeling each other. I think soon I would need to dig into Crescent's shit. She was getting in deep just like us, but at times it was like she was holding back, almost like she was afraid of getting too close.

"Yeah, well, you're not far behind his ass, so it's a match made in heaven."

"You mean Hell!" Crescent laughed, and I couldn't help but shake my head at her craziness. "Anyway, girl, I saw your Mama's new doctor, and that man is fine as hell, girl. I think he's about to give Dr. Sexy a run for his money. I'm about to divorce Dr. Sexy, so I can get with this new one because chile, he looks like he's working with a mons–"

I knew Crescent saw my eyes get huge as Henny walked up behind her ass, running off at the mouth. My mind was stuck on the fact that Tre was already here, and my time to figure out how to tell Henny about him was up.

"Who are you divorcing, Cent? I know you're not talking about me," Hendrix asked.

His voice always made my nipples hard and had me pressing my thighs together.

"Ahh...hey, Dr. Sexy," Crescent smiled as she turned to face him. "Now you know you will always be my number one. Can't nobody replace you," she smiled. Hendrix smirked at her, and Crescent looked down like her ass was all shy and shit. Hendrix looked around for a second before leaning closer so only Crescent and I could hear him.

"You think that shit is funny, Cent. Now I think I should let Faxx know about that little crush you got. You might need a spanking. Both of y'all," he chuckled. Crescent's head shot up, and her eyes were wide at that threat, telling me all I needed to know.

"I didn't say a word," I said quickly.

"That's the problem, Tali. But it's all good," he laughed. His eyes roamed over me before returning to Crescent's wide-eyed stare.

"You wouldn't do that, Hendrix. You know that your boy is crazy, right? I don't want to have to shoot his ass," Crescent hissed. Hendrix smiled. I pressed my lips together because what did he mean by that's the problem? Did he know about Tre and me? I was trippin' because there was no way he could.

"If you know he is crazy, you better watch your words from now on because I won't always be there to save your ass. Now, go give Sanchez some love before his surgery," Hendrix ordered. Crescent glared at him but hugged Henny before running to the elevator to see Sanchez.

"Why are you messing with that girl? You know her ass is all talk and crazy as hell," I laughed.

"Because ain't nobody going to be replacing me. I'm the only Dr. Sexy she knows," he stated. The fact that this fool wasn't laughing or smiling was all I needed to know. He was serious as fuck. A slow smile spread across his face.

"You're so wrong. What does Faxx have to say about that?"

"I don't give a fuck what he got to say. Crescent was my friend first, meaning Faxx can kiss my ass. And Dr. Tremont better stick to treating his patients."

I could see that he was joking with me and the stress hiding in the depths of his eyes. I could tell that it wasn't only the surgery that was bothering him, but now wasn't the time to ask about it. I knew that things in the street were heating up for him and the fact that Jakobe was still running loose in these streets aggravated him. He once confessed to me that he hated how long it took to get to Ja, but Ja was the only one now who knew their tactics. He would need to change how they moved when coming to Jakobe because he was one of them at one point. Henny hated the fact that he liked it. He was upset that he was enjoying the hunt for Ja because he felt it disrespected his brother's memory.

"Oh wow. You are such a hypocrite, and that's some childish junk right there," I smiled. Henny shrugged before looking at his watch.

"Let's go, Tali. We need to get scrubbed in," he said, turning away.

"Wait! What did you say? I can't be in there, Henny," I hissed. We stood at the employee elevators and waited.

"I need you in there with me, Thickness. This procedure is important, and you calm me. No one will even know who you are, so don't worry about it. I'll just let them know you will be observing. Have you thought more about joining the Women's Center team?"

I frowned because he knew damn well I was leaving Union City as soon as possible.

"Hendrix, you know that I—"

The elevator dinged, and he held a hand out for me to enter first.

"Don't even answer that question, Tali. I can see that you aren't addicted to me enough yet. I will reevaluate later," he stated. I kept my mouth closed because, truth be told, I was completely addicted to this man, which was why I needed to get the hell away. There was no denying our chemistry in bed, or even out of it. It was his way of life that shook me. I didn't know how Dea was willing to accept it. I could respect it and him for all of his accomplishments, but I didn't need to live it.

"I've always wanted to sit in on a major surgery."

Henny looked me over as the elevator descended and narrowed his eyes.

"I may have misspoken a minute ago."

"You don't need me in the room with you? I can—"

"No, I want you there, and it's a great experience. But I'm talking about you being addicted. I need you just as obsessed with me as I am with you. You aren't obsessed with me enough yet. That will need to change," he declared as the doors opened.

*Obsessed?* What does that even look like on a man like him?

The procedure was deemed a success, and the only thing to do now was wait until Sanchez was awake. We all knew it wouldn't be a quick fix and would take time, but we should know something once he opened his eyes. I changed into my outfit of a tight knee-length black pencil skirt and burgundy quarter-sleeved blouse with matching burgundy heels inside Henny's office bathroom so I didn't need to use the locker room. There were so many people in the operating room that I was barely noticed, but I could tell that Hendrix was hyper-aware that I was present. The entire time I stood there, the only thing that played on a loop in my mind was how he wanted me to be obsessed with him. Why? What did that shit even mean?

"Tali? Are you finished? I have a meeting in five minutes," Hendrix called out. I blinked, dropped my scrubs inside the basket, and grabbed my purse.

Now would be a good time to check on Mama and pray that I don't run into Tre until we sit down with everyone.

"Yup. Give me a second," I said. I checked myself in the mirror before opening the door and exiting. My heels sank into the plush carpet, making me wonder how it would feel against my skin. Like everything else he had, I could tell it was of the highest quality. Hendrix sat behind his massive desk, typing on his laptop before he glanced up at me. He closed it and moved it to the side before clasping his hands together. "I'm going to go and see Mama and then probably head over to Dea's once Crescent is off," I said. I stepped over toward him and leaned down to kiss him. As soon as I was close enough, his hand gripped my jaw, holding me in place. My brows rose at his fast movement. I licked my lips while he stared at them before his eyes found mine.

"Thickness, I'm not sure how you forgot what you said this morning, but I haven't. If I'm honest, that's what got me through the damn proce-dure. Thoughts of you under my desk with my dick in your mouth while I do business," he asserted. My eyes widened because I didn't think he would take me seriously, but I should've known better. I also should've known how my body would react to just thinking about doing something like that. I swallowed, and my breathing picked up as he stared me in the eyes.

"Who...who...I don't—"

"Thickness, let's not act like you don't want to do it. Your nipples are hard just thinking about it. All you need to do is make sure you do it quietly.

"It's not online?" I gasped. His fingers pinched my hardened nipple, and I felt my core clench. My mouth watered at the thought of taking him to the back of my throat. He was worried about me making noise when it should be him that was worried about himself.

"Nope."

**KNOCK KNOCK KNOCK**

My eyes moved to the door, and I could hear Ms. Stephanie telling Hendrix that his two-thirty had arrived. Hendrix looked at the flashing light on his phone and grimaced. She must've been calling but received no answer because he was messing with me. He raised a brow at me before letting my face go. He pushed away from his desk and waited to see what I would do. I returned to the bathroom, hung my purse behind the door, and kicked off my low heels before exiting.

"I can't believe you have me doing this," I whispered while crawling beneath his desk. Henny stood up and took off his suit jacket.

"You like it," he chuckled while unzipping his pants. He sat back down and scooted in close, effectively trapping and hiding me simultaneously. "Please show him in, Stephanie," he called out authoritatively. I reached for his dick and noticed he wasn't wearing the boxer briefs he had put on this morning. He purposely ensured I had easy access when he changed out of his scrubs. Henny's long thick dick throbbed in my hand, and I licked the tip, tasting his pre-cum. I wanted to moan, but the door opened at that moment.

"Dr. Tremont, thank you for taking this time out. I know you like to dive right into work," he stated.

"Come on, Hendrix, call me Ignacio," Tre said. I could tell they were shaking hands, and I froze at the bass in Tre's voice. Memories of us flashed through my mind of him groaning my name when we were together. I blinked fast, clearing my thoughts and wishing I'd asked whose meeting this was so I could escape. I could tell that Tre respected Henny because he corrected him about using his first name, but he didn't offer the use of Tre, which let me know he didn't like him. Only his close friends called him Tre, and others he deemed beneath him called him Dr. Tremont.

"Not a problem, Ignacio. Let's get down to business. I will make this as quick as possible," Hendrix said. I felt his hand wrap around the side of my neck just as he shoved my face forward.

My mouth wrapped around his dick, and his head hit the back of my throat from the force. I swallowed so that I wouldn't gag. Luckily, I didn't have much of a gag reflex because we surely would've been caught. And that wasn't how I would want to see Tre again after a year of no contact with me. A swooshing sound was in my ears as I zoned out, trying not to think about my ex sitting across from the man I was now fucking.

If I was honest, Tre was like a filler because I couldn't find the feeling Henny gave me anywhere else. Tre was the only one who came close, but it wasn't the same. I felt Henny's thumb rubbing my jaw, but I felt his grip on the side of my neck tighten as I pulled back. I let my tongue trace the vein on his dick before diving in, taking him deeply in my mouth. I had checked out of their conversation and focused on the knowledge that I could be caught and that someone else was in this room who knew me intimately enough to know exactly how Henny was feeling. I swallowed around his length and would have jumped when Henny's hand came down on his desk. I pulled back again, letting my tongue drag along his length, and smiled. I reached into his pants and gripped his length as I licked his tip, sucking in the head and letting my tongue make circles around it.

"Is everything okay? Did you have a hard case this morning?"

I almost choked because something was hard this morning, and it definitely was now.

"It was a very draining procedure, but you know how it goes. We power through it," he grunted. His dick jerked in my mouth, and his hand reached the back of my neck, holding me in place.

"I've already met with the patient, and her case intrigues me. I think we should start with a different treatment, but we should speak with her family first to explain the procedure. I want to be sure they know the risks," Tre said. Henny released my head, but I didn't immediately pull back. I slid my mouth off him, slowly dipping my tongue at the tip.

"Yes, I think that will work. This is your case, and we are happy to be the first to perform this procedure. I will let you get back to your day," Henny said quickly.

"Yes. I think I will. Your facility has the state-of-the-art equipment needed and will make things easier. And the large bonus for a two-year contract helped tremendously. This family must be special. But either way, I'm glad I chose to come here, Hendrix," Tre said.

"I do what I can to ensure all my patients and employees get the best treatments. Our community and families deserve that much," Henny stated through gritted teeth. I could hear Tre getting to his feet, and I heard more pleasantries before the door opened and closed. As soon as it did, I slurped his dick into my mouth again as he groaned. Henny threw his head back, but his eyes watched me through narrowed slits. I pulled back with a pop, and he pushed his chair backward.

"Stand up, Tali," Henny demanded. He held out a hand, and I took it. I was on my feet and turned around to face his desk instantly.

"Hendrix, the door...the door isn't locked," I whimpered.

"Then you better pray this pussy grips me so tight that I cum before someone else comes in here," he replied.

I heard his belt and felt his hands sliding up my knee-length skirt. My mind rushed with the knowledge anyone could walk in here at any moment. My thongs slid to the side, his thick fingers rubbing along my slit. I was already soaked for him. Hendrix knew what his words did to me by how he growled into my ear. Henny pressed me into the desk and leaned his massive body over me.

"Hendrix," I moaned. I felt the head of his dick press at my entrance for a quick second before he plunged inside. I would have screamed at the pleasure and pain, but his hand covered my mouth as he thrust deeply inside me.

"Shhhh...I'm going to need you to take this dick quietly, Tali. I still have another appointment today, and I'm sure they are waiting right outside that door," he whispered. Henny was pressed so tightly against me that every flex of his hips raised me onto my toes. "Can you do that for me, Thickness?"

My eyes rolled back in my head at his words, but I snapped to attention when his other hand went to my hip, holding me in place. His dick throbbed inside me, and all I needed was for him to move to give me the release I'd needed since this morning. "Tali?"

I nodded my head, saying anything he wanted to hear as long as he moved. He let my hip go and slipped his middle and pointer fingers into my mouth. "I want you to suck them like you sucked my dick."

I moaned, but I caught it before it got any louder. Henny began to move again and used his other hand to slam me back to his length. He rotated his hips, making sure he hit every spot in my pussy, and I felt my core clenching around him. I threw my ass back as much as possible, but my upper body was tight between him and the desk. The friction of the smooth, cold wood against my nipples had me hissing around his fingers. I could feel my juices running down my leg at how wet I was, and he bent his legs and stroked upward. I almost fucked up and screamed. I opened my mouth as pleasure consumed me as he hit my G-spot repeatedly. Henny covered my mouth with his own before a scream could rip from my throat, sucking my moans right out of me as I came hard. His fingers wrapped around my neck, pulling me off the desk as I panted. My legs were weak, but he held my waist to keep me up and pulled me down on his length.

"Hen—Hen...Hendrix," I moaned breathlessly. I felt him push himself deep into my core and felt his teeth clamp between my neck and shoulder as he came. Henny's ragged breaths blew heat onto my skin as he held me down on his length until his throbbing dick stopped jerking. I blinked once and then again when I felt his thick cum running out of me. "Hen...Henny, what in the hell did we just do?"

I felt his arms squeeze tightly around my waist before falling backward into his office chair.

"I'm just making sure your obsession with me starts today."

Oh no, this nigga did not. He was not about to 'Shandea' me!

"You better fucking get me a Plan B, Hendrix," I whispered-shouted. Henny chuckled lightly before kissing the side of my neck.

"Anything you say, Tali. I will write you a prescription. But just know I'm all the Plan B you need."

## CHAPTER EIGHT

# HENDRIX 'HENNY' PHARMA

Even though I had another meeting after Tali left my office, it wasn't with who she expected. I opened the door for her to leave, and Stephanie turned toward me with a raised brow. She looked at Tali and smiled like she knew what was up. Tali smiled and spoke, but looked everywhere except Stephanie's face until she heard Faxx's voice.

"How are you, Tali?" Faxx grinned. I knew neither could have heard us, but she didn't need to know that for sure. I knew that she might have been embarrassed, but she loved the thought they could've heard. I was sure Faxx assumed what was going on.

"Hey, Faxx," she smiled. She approached him, hugging him before looking him over. "Are you playing security guard today to spy on Crescent?"

"I actually had some work to do here today. But are you saying I should? What is she doing that I need to be spying on her? Is she talking to another nig–"

Tali laughed before pushing Faxx out of the way and waved over her shoulder. I could tell Tali wasn't taking Faxx seriously, but he wasn't joking. Now he would be all in Cent's personal space, just waiting for another man to approach her ass.

"Tali, I'll pick you up later," I said before she could escape. She almost tripped over her feet but looked back at me and then at Stephanie, who just kept typing on her computer. I knew her ass wasn't doing any kind of work but probably messaging Aunt Vanessa on today's events and telling her I was fucking someone else. It didn't matter because I would introduce them to each other soon enough.

"It's only across the street, Henny. If anything, I can get Crescent to–"

"Cent's car will be in the shop later," Faxx announced. Tali frowned at his words, probably thinking Crescent had said nothing like that.

"I'll be there later, Tali," I said again. She held my eyes briefly before darting her gaze around the waiting area.

"Whatever you say, Hendrix," she smiled. I watched as she walked away, but I could tell Faxx was irritated and plotting, so I turned toward him.

"You know Tali was fucking with you, right? Crescent isn't talking to anyone up in here, let alone you. She barely wants to speak to your crazy ass now," I laughed.

"We talk daily. Don't let Cent bullshit y'all into thinking she's brushing me off. We have a connection. I just need her to open up about this nigga Roman," Faxx sucked his teeth. I knew that was another reason he asked Tali if she was talking to anyone. We didn't know much about this Roman nigga, and it seems Crescent has been tight-lipped about him with Faxx.

"Hendrix, when will we all be meeting your new friend?" Stephanie smiled.

I knew she was asking for my Aunt, and I shook my head and turned to enter into my office.

"Tell Aunt Vanessa when she admits she's sleeping with Remington," I shot back. I heard Stephanie damn near fall out of her chair before Faxx shut the door, chuckling.

"Why are you fucking with Auntie?"

"She's always in my business. I don't know why she acts like we don't know about them, but that's another story. What have you found out?"

Faxx breathed deeply and smirked before crossing my office to sit on the couch.

"Is this clean?" he asked, but sat down, anyway. He already knew my office was clean by the smell of the products I used to wipe down my desk. I would have left it smelling like Tali's pussy, but I'll save all that for my home office.

"What have you found out?" I asked, while taking a seat behind my desk.

"For starters, the building Haze was talking about is legit. They're making and packing that shit, but I haven't seen Jakobe's bitch ass there. He didn't show up on Friday, but I overheard today that he's coming this week. He made a change, and it will be Thursday instead. It's hard to get closer to overhear shit or see shit inside of that place. And they have a no electronic rule once they enter through the gates. No one gets in there with any electronics. Not even a fucking pacemaker would make it through. Ja ain't taking no chances because he knows how Link gets down," Faxx stated.

It was only Monday, but I knew waiting would be best. Maybe Katrice could shed some light on what those niggas were doing. I think she's been sweating it out long enough and should be terrified enough to say everything she knew.

I wanted to interrogate her ass last week, but I knew Oz needed some time to be with Dea, and it worked out well enough to keep Yasmin on edge as well. She'd been walking around on pins and needles because she knew her sister was missing. I just wondered why she hadn't filed a missing person's report. That might actually be a good idea for Tali and Shandea to do so that no one suspected anything. I didn't want to keep brushing Tali off about her cousin, because I didn't want her getting involved if we had to lay her ass out. But ensuring they seemed like concerned family members would help them in the long run. Shantel had already agreed to get whatever information from her, so Katrice was hers for now.

"Then we need to move Thursday. That's the priority. We need to put this nigga down," I retorted. I'd confessed to Tali that I was getting a perverse pleasure from hunting this nigga because not many could elude us for this long. But now, knowing this nigga was that close to Tali and Dea had the muscles tightening in my neck. I leaned my neck from side-to-side and then frowned as Faxx leaned forward.

"There is one more thing. If Oz is right and Kenneth is his father, then how the fuck are we going to get Mala away from that family? His son Charles, the Deputy Mayor, and Oz's maybe stepbrother is her damn Fiancé. Since she's back in Union City, and once we know for sure, we can't let her stay with the dude," Faxx sighed. "I know she's in love and shit, but if we take out his daddy, we can't trust this nigga," Faxx stated.

I knew he was right, but we needed that concrete evidence. I would do whatever was needed to get my little cousin out of danger. After all this time with the man, though, he'd done nothing to hurt her. Just the opposite, in fact. He cared for her like a man should care for his woman, so there wasn't anything we could say about it yet.

"It's a problem we'll handle when we get there. I'll handle Mala. What's the other problem?" I asked, because I knew there was something else. Faxx was stalling, and whenever he had to say, I knew it would piss me the fuck off. "What?" I snapped.

He looked up at me and leaned back against the couch, shaking his head. He broke out in a full smile, making him look like a pretty boy who didn't get his hands dirty. Whoever thought that would be wrong, dead fucking wrong. And would find themselves buried alive in the woods some fucking where or blown to pieces like the last niggas.

"The texts haven't stopped and seem to have become more frequent. Daily, if I'm being real about it."

I felt my teeth grinding together at his words, and he watched me carefully, taking pleasure in how irritated and possessive I was getting. I forced myself to relax because, as far as I knew, Tali hadn't replied. Unless he was about to tell me that changed.

"Did she respond?"

"Why don't you just check her phone?"

"No," I answered. "Did she answer him back?"

"Well, if you aren't going to look at her phone, then have Link hack into it."

"Naw, I ain't doing all that. I only wanted tabs on him, so I can be sure he isn't going to be talking about the advancements we will be making here while he's on board."

"Then don't worry about the shit then, my nigga," Faxx smirked.

"Nigga! Don't fucking answer. Get the fuck out. I'll see your dumbass at the meeting tomorrow," I waved. I grabbed my laptop and opened it, pulling up my notes on Yasmin's treacherous ass. Faxx laughed his ass off until he got to the door.

"She ain't answer him, damn nigga. You got it bad for Tali thick ass," Faxx chuckled.

"Don't make me fuck you up, Fransisco."

"Damn, not the government name. You and Oz have a problem. Y'all niggas are crazy as shit and really should see someone about that problem," Faxx said. He opened the door, but I looked up with a smirk.

"Yo?"

Faxx turned back, trying to wipe the smile off his face as he looked at me.

"Crescent was talking about the good Doctor earlier. She was wondering if he was working with a monster and was considering finding out if it was true," I said straight-faced. Faxx's cold black eyes widened, but before he could say anything else, Yasmin was at the door with raised brows.

"Am I early?"

"No, Miss James, please come on inside. Mr. Wellington was just leaving. Thank you, Fransisco, for the heads up on the situation," I nodded.

His glare would have had a lesser man shitting himself, but it satisfied me. Now all I needed to do was get through Yasmin's bullshit and figure out how to get this listening device somewhere on her body without her knowing. I just wanted to finish all my shit so I could get Tali's ass home and find out what the fuck was up with her and Dr. Ignacio Tremont. She had plenty of time and opportunity to say something to me about him, but she chose not to. If she thought I was joking about that spanking, she was wrong. I felt my dick harden at the thought of smacking her round ass and had to adjust myself.

"Yasmin, is everything alright? You look...stressed," I asked. She blinked a few times before she gave me a fake ass smile.

"Yes, yes, I'm good Hendrix. Just...ahh...just family problems. How can I help you find this money you think is lost," she smiled.

"How about we sit on the couch and discuss it while having a drink?"

Yasmin raised a brow and licked her lips as she smiled.

"Okay. That sounds good, actually. Are you sure?" she asked while standing.

I stood up as she smoothed down her tan and cream skirt and pushed her chest out, showing her hard nipples against the thin material of her cream-colored silk shirt. Her eyes went immediately to my dick, and I knew she thought my dick was hard for her. Yasmin bit down on her lip and looked up to meet my eyes, raising her brows suggestively. Too bad for her, the drink was all her ass was getting, and maybe a small pinch to her neck.

"I mean, since we both will be leaving for the day after this meeting, I can't see why we can't. It looks like you might need it with...with your family problems," I smirked.

Yasmin barely felt the little pinch to her neck that installed Link's new technology inside her bloodstream. We would have a total of seventy-two hours to get the information until the miniature microchip would no longer transmit. This was just a tester because I knew Link was already working on the next generation.

"So, is this for me?" Yasmin asked. She tried to run her hand over my length, but I effectively pushed her hand away.

"Naw, it's not, and this," I gestured to myself, "isn't what you are here for," I said, standing.

Her mouth fell open as I reached out, picked up my drink, and took a sip.

"Hendrix, I don't understand why—"

"Miss James, how about we stick to why you're here so we both can get on with our day."

"Are you fucking someone else? Is this why you're acting like an ass-hole?"

"I think you forgot that what I do isn't any of your concern, so either you can drink your beverage and get this meeting started, or you can leave," I shrugged. I could see the disbelief in Yasmin's eyes at my dismissal. Her brown eyes narrowed, and I could see her wheels spinning on what this all meant. I held her gaze as her disbelief turned to anger and the realization that I was never fucking her again.

Once I finished dealing with Yasmin's bullshit, I took a quick shower and changed before leaving through the back entrance. I jumped in my SUV with the feeling that someone was watching me. I took out my phone, typed a quick message to the dealership owner where I purchased my Bentayga S, and told him I was on my way. He understood what that meant, but there would be a slight change because I would make two purchases. I knew he would have the latest model ready and was waiting when I arrived. My jaw flexed, and I turned my phone onto airplane mode so no one could reach me. I didn't trust my vehicle, and it was about time for me to trade this shit in for a newer year, anyway.

I made a series of turns, doubled back to the hospital before jumping on the I-85, and exiting onto Appleton before jumping back on the highway and going in the opposite direction. I looked into the mirror and noticed that the two cars that were following me were no longer visible. I pressed harder on the gas as I gripped my steering wheel tightly.

I would be late meeting Oz at the Veterinary Clinic, but I knew he would get the hint when my shit went straight to voicemail. About forty minutes later, I turned into the dealership and saw Shelton standing next to two Bentayga Speeds, one in burgundy and the other in a gun-metal gray with black chromed-out wheels. He gave me options but didn't know he had chosen the perfect colors because the burgundy perfectly suited Tali's espresso skin tone. So I knew this was the right move, because I didn't know if whoever was tracking me had done anything to her car. I wasn't about to take that chance. I grabbed everything I needed from my SUV and closed the door.

"It's wonderful to see you today, Dr. Pharma. Please take a look, and if you would like something different, we can accommodate you," Shelton said. His assistant stood exactly four paces behind him, waiting for whatever orders Shelton would give her.

"You have chosen exactly what I need, Shelton. I'll take both. Have the burgundy one delivered tomorrow to my address, and I will take this one tonight."

"Excellent choice, Doctor. Will anything need to be added special to your purchase? It comes fully loaded, of course, to your specifications," he smiled. I could see the dollar signs in his eyes.

"Nothing from you, but someone will be here tonight to add what I need to the vehicle. Please make sure there are no problems when Mr. Moore arrives."

"As always, it's no problem, and I'll have everything uploaded for you to E-Sign. It is always a pleasure to do business with you," Shelton grinned widely. He held out the key fob, and I grabbed it, wasting no time jumping in the SUV. I left the dealership without a backward glance and went to the Veterinary Clinic where I was meeting Oz. The exchange at the dealership didn't take long, but it was long enough that I dug into my pocket and powered up my other phone. Immediately it rang with a number without a name, but I knew it was Oz.

"I'll be there in a few."

"Why the fuck was your shit going to voicemail?"

Did this nigga think he was my fucking father or something? I stayed silent until he cursed under his breath. "Nigga, let's not forget mutha-fuckas is after us. I already lost one fucking brother," he snarled.

I eased up my grip on the steering wheel before I snapped the shit off, and I drove off the side of this fucking bridge. I rolled down the window and tossed my personal phone out of it before putting it back up. I didn't trust it not to be compromised, and I refused to take the chance. I would use our untraceable phone Link encrypted until I could pick up another one for my personal use.

"I think my truck was tampered with," I said. He was dead silent for a full minute. I would've thought he hung up, but I could still hear the beeping from our product being moved in the background.

"Is someone tailing you?"

"Naw, I lost them and the fucking car. I decided to upgrade today. Make sure you check over your shit. I know I'm being paranoid because no one should've been able to get inside our vehicles with the shit Link encoded into the systems, but I wasn't about to take the chance. I knew for sure that someone was watching me when I left the hospital, and I was damn certain I was being followed."

"Makes sense. I actually just traded both my cars in. I don't think Dea will realize it because I got the exact same thing. Did you hit up Link yet?"

"Naw, but I will once I get to the spot. I need him to give Tali's new shit a work over, and then he can do mine. I'll be there in less than five minutes," I stated.

I hung up the phone and stopped at a red light. My windows were slightly tinted, but not as much as I wanted them to be. I watched as bitch ass Rodney held a door open for Yasmin. They entered the Littman Hotel, but it wasn't surprising. Oz had said they were fucking when he saw them at his restaurant. But now that we knew what we knew, it was much more than that. It was all good because I got that listening device inside her body. Link worked magic with shit like this, and now we would know what the fuck Yasmin was telling this nigga. The light turned green, and I made my way onto Trade Street and pulled into a parking lot full of construction. I parked next to a large Lincoln Navigator that was so dark gray that it almost looked black. I knew it had to be Oz's new shit, and when he stepped out, it was confirmed. I jumped out, looking over at the construction, glad to see that no time was being wasted.

"Nigga, when you going to get something bigger? I don't know how you fold your big ass inside that tight ass shit," Oz chuckled. I didn't even look in his direction because fuck him.

"Ain't nobody big as fuck like you, nigga. I don't need to overcompensate for my shit."

Oz laughed, but I could tell it was forced, so I turned to look at him. "What is it? Do I need to kill someone else?" I asked. He didn't even look in my direction, but I saw his smirk.

"Nigga, that is not always the answer."

I said nothing and waited him out. "Most of the time, that is the answer, but you, not this time. I don't need Henny. I need Dr. Pharma," he said quietly. His voice would have been lost in the construction noise if I wasn't listening. Whatever was up, I knew I needed to figure the shit out before I went over the inventory here.

"Lennox, if this shit is about Dea eating weird ass shit, I will fuck you up. I told you—"

"Naw, naw, it ain't that. I got all that shit the first time you told me what it was. I still think that shit is nasty as fuck, but it is what it is. I will go and get her whatever she wants when it gets bad. But it's worse than that shit. Shandea, she...Dea fucking jumps every time I walk into the room. I could sit beside her and stand up, and she's jumping damn near to the ceiling. I know why. I do. But what the fuck do I do to fix this shit? Therapy is helping, and Dr. Mena is good. At least Faxx's bitch ass was good for something," he grunted.

"What did she say about it?"

"Whenever I try to bring the shit up, Dea will talk over me like she has no problem. Why the fuck wouldn't she want the doctor to know that shit? Doesn't she want help in dealing with that shit?"

"Have you asked her about it?"

"You're damn right I asked her ass. I spanked her ass about the shit too, but she says she can deal with it. It's almost like she doesn't want to seem weak or something. It's weird as fuck, and I need the shit to fucking stop," he sighed frustratedly.

I started walking toward the building and felt him beside me as we approached. I wasn't worried about the construction workers or them seeing us enter this building and where we went. Emerald Construction was just another of many businesses Oz owned and we co-owned. I stepped inside, hating to look at my brother's clinic, but I knew it would be restored to exactly what it had been before all this shit. We walked to the back, and I entered the office. I stood in front of a large painting of my father holding my brother in his arms, and I stood next to him with my mother beside me. I stared at my father and let the renal scan read my eyes until the door behind us opened. I turned away from the painting Aunt Vanessa painted for me as a gift the day I walked across the graduation stage for the last time.

"Oz, I can tell you that if Dea would stop trying to fix this problem and tell the therapist, all this shit could be avoided. I can tell you right now that Shandea is only trying so hard to handle this herself because she feels it shouldn't be happening. She knows you, and now that her mind is clear, she can see your differences that she didn't see that day when it was Xavier."

"You are saying all this to say what?"

Once we went down a flight of stairs, we came out into a large open area that looked like it could be a food warehouse or something. But instead of food, it was rows and rows of every drug sold on the market.

"I said all that to say, just announce yourself, my nigga. When you are about to get up, talk to her about something stupid before moving. Before you enter the room, call out her name and ask her a question. It will help trick her mind into seeing you before she sees you."

"Nigga what? What kind of quack-ass shit are you talking about? Are you a holistic doctor now or something? I thought you were about to get me some magical cure down here," Oz scoffed.

"Nigga shut the fuck up. I'm serious, Lennox. Do it. It will help, and I swear things will be so much easier. It won't be forever. Now, if we are done with your relationship problems, help me with that fucking count. Big Pharma will be back open next week, and business will be at capacity. People haven't been able to get what they need or have had to pay exorbitant prices," I said.

There wasn't anything else to say as we moved from row-to-row, taking in the count and speaking to the floor managers that made sure this place stayed in order and the numbers added up. Everyone knew the price if the numbers didn't match, and no one wanted those consequences.

"Hendrix," Gabriel called out with a wave. I looked up as he made his way toward me. I looked over the last stack before giving him my full attention.

"Gabe, what's good with you? What are you doing down here?" I asked.

He didn't need to do this work now that he was running the Veterinary Clinic. I tried to tell him he didn't need to worry about this part of the business anymore, but he would mutter about who else could keep this place in order, and he wasn't wrong. He and my brother had plans for this place, so he was the natural choice as the Vet once he finished school.

"Man, I can't stay home. I need something to do, but it won't last long. I think we will be opening soon," Gabe smiled.

"In another week or so, don't worry. Everything will be exactly like it was before," I said. Gabe smirked because I knew his OCD ass just as well as my brother. I knew if shit was out of place by an inch, someone could lose a fucking hand. I knew that if the place wasn't full of people and animals, Gabriel probably would have tried to take them niggas out. I looked around at the warehouse as evidence of his heavy-handed ways.

"Good. Good," he nodded before turning away. I didn't take offense to it because I knew he was only making small talk about ensuring everything would be returned exactly as it was before Jakobe did his bullshit. The only person who could handle his brand of crazy was his husband, Bryson, and that was on them.

"Oz, let's go. Everything is in order on my end and ready to go. I need to pick up another phone on the way back to the spot. Oh shit!" I said, snapping my fingers.

"What?"

"I saw that nigga Rodney and that bitch Yasmin going into the Littman on my way here. We can listen to what the fuck is going on once we get into the truck. You're driving. I'm going to text Link to come get mine," I stated.

We drove through Union City, listening to Yasmin damn near screaming at Rodney to find her fucking sister. She didn't know where she was and was probably missing because of the shit he had her doing. I smirked and turned my head to look out of the passenger window to see Jakobe coming out of an upscale restaurant with a large dark skin man with the same width in shoulders as Oz. "Nigga stop. Stop," I shouted, not caring if he held up the heavy traffic downtown.

"Nigga, what the fuck is the pro—" I knew Oz's words cut off because he saw what I was seeing standing a few lanes over from us.

Senator Morgan was looking down and rubbing at his eyes before standing up straight, blinking rapidly as a grimace formed on his face. I let the window down like I could get closer because his mismatched eyes were unmistakably one hundred percent like Xavier's when he blinked. The color of his eyes was the same placement and all. All of this happened in a split second as I reached for the heat I knew Oz kept in his glove compartment. He was already pulling out just as Jakobe turned toward us. I saw the whites of his eyes and the snarl of hatred that crossed his face as he reached for his shit. Jakobe and two other niggas with him pulled out guns and started firing toward us.

Ja pushed the Senator toward the ground but never stopped firing. Oz quickly swerved the huge truck to avoid the bullets and tried to speed away, but they were relentless. I leaned out the window, pointing and shooting, trying my best not to hit anyone in the way, but I knew Ja didn't give a shit. He never gave a shit about innocent people in the way. I leaned back, and I could hear bullets hitting the new truck. I knew now was the time to get this nigga because he fell right into our laps.

"Fuck this shit! I want both of them," I roared.

Excitement and adrenaline coursed through my veins as I tried to dodge the bullets and return fire. The streets were chaotic as people ran for cover, and I knew we had to act fast if I wanted to get these niggas. It had all been confirmed that Jakobe and that bitch ass nigga Kenneth were working together. Oz rolled up on the sidewalk, throwing the truck into park.

Before we stopped, I was already climbing over the driver's side when Oz got out.

Shots were still flying as people ran for cover. I tried to keep my cool and focus on taking out Jakobe, but I didn't want it by a bullet. I wanted to feel his blood in my hands and watch the life drain out of him as I slit his fucking throat open. He wanted to run with the Cartel. I would give him a death they dealt out on the daily. I knew we had to end this quickly before they got the upper hand or fled. Oz fired back at one of the others that was with him, but I could tell he was trying his best to make it to his father. He wanted the man that killed his mother and left him and his brother to fight on the streets for themselves.

"Where you at, Henny? Stop hiding, my nigga," Jakobe taunted. I wasn't listening to this nigga as I crept around the other side of the truck, aiming. I let off a shot, hitting the other nigga he was with in the neck.

"Shit!" I heard a shout over the screaming.

"Fuck this shit," Oz boomed before pushing away from the truck. His eyes were pitch black. Gone was the business owner, and what was left was a nigga that wielded a meat cleaver, that I had no clue where he got it. He ran into the street, and I followed because I would not let this nigga go out alone. My blood rushed, and I felt the rush when I saw Jakobe pulling at Kenneth. He saw us coming and raised his hand as he shouted, and Kenneth moved to lunge into a waiting vehicle.

*Pop Pop Pop*

I dodged the bullets, but not before I got my lick off and heard the scream that sent satisfaction through my veins.

"No! No!" Oz roared as he let off shot after shot until his clip ran empty. I was already on my feet and saw the large pool of blood in the street, but no Jakobe. I'd hit his bitch ass, but he managed to get away.

"Fuck! Fuck!" I heaved. I knew I was spiraling as my breaths picked up and the screaming around us faded.

"Henny! We need to move," I growled. His voice sounded like thunder in my ears. I almost turned and snapped at this nigga, but he was right. We needed to get out of here and call Link and Faxx. We would need Link to scrub all the cameras in this fucking area and check to see if he could figure out where the black Mercedes van went.

"It was him, Hendrix! It was him, and he knew who I was," Oz roared. "I saw the recognition in his eyes, Henny," Oz thundered. We went back to the truck, but with the bullet holes and the way other cars were around us, there was no way we would get out of there.

"We need to move. Fuck the truck for now. We can take care of it later," I said as the sirens grew louder. I put my gun away, and Oz did the same. He looked at his cleaver before wiping it off quickly and dropping it to the ground as we blended into the chaos on the street.

## CHAPTER NINE

## CRESCENT 'CENT' JOHNSON

T ali and my time with Dea were interrupted by Faxx showing up with his sexy-ass friend Link to really get his damn head braided. Tali was in the middle of telling us how Dr. Sexy fucked her brains out in his office, but what happened before that was what sent us into hysterics and me into shock. I couldn't believe she also had sex with that fine ass doctor that just came on board. I shared her concern with telling Henny about him, but her best bet was to get that shit over with ASAP. It wasn't anything that he could do about her past, and as long as she didn't give Dr. Tremont any indication that she wanted to rekindle a relationship with him, then it should be all good. That was, as long as he didn't say or do anything fucking stupid.

I watched as Faxx leaned his head on Dea's lap with a smirk while she stared at her sister to answer her question. Tali was re-twisting Link's long ass locs while he stared at his phone, ignoring all of us.

"Tali!" Dea shouted. I looked over at Tali because I wanted to know as well. It was not out of the realm that Henny would try to get that girl pregnant. He was crazy enough to do some wild ass shit like that, but I also knew that he wouldn't try to force some shit on her that she didn't want.

"I got the prescription, and apparently, I have an appointment to ensure I wouldn't need it again. Or at least until I am ready to make the right choice and just accept that it will happen," Tali bit out.

I bit down on my lip as I texted Gigi, regretting that I had given her my information. It wasn't a big deal because I knew if she was lying about not fucking with Roman anymore that they couldn't get anything from this number. It was prepaid and held no attachment to me. Therefore, Roman wouldn't be able to find me. I just prayed that he didn't think to look for me in Union City. It would be hard for him to roll up in this territory because it belonged to them. It belonged to U.C.K. Even though I was cool with them, it didn't mean they would want to go to war for some chick they didn't know like that. Dr. Sexy and I were cool as shit, but these were the type of niggas that didn't mess around or forgive when it came to disloyalty. And they would probably see me doing some shit that I did as disloyal and not ask no questions about why I did what I did.

How would they feel knowing I had stolen over half a million dollars from this nigga Roman? They would no longer trust me, was the one thing I knew for sure. They probably wouldn't even want to hear me out if I tried to explain because their first thoughts would be, whether I was trying to do the same to them?

"I still think you need to say something before we have a run-in. I mean, it's not like you—" Shandea bit off her words, leaving them hanging for us to read between the lines. Tali sighed loudly, like I should've been doing.

I was trying to ignore Francisco's ass because this nigga had my car towed, talking about he heard some ticking noises and it should be checked out. I swear I was about to shoot his ass, but I felt like he probably would like that shit. I wasn't trying to lead his crazy ass on, even though I had to confess to loving our late-night conversations. Faxx was different when we talked alone. Most of the time, I could forget about his psycho tendencies. Especially when he talked about his daughter. It was almost like he was a completely different person when it was just us together. But lately, he'd been really trying to push into my life as if it was a done deal and he was my man, which he was not. I refused to be with another nigga who thought they could use their money to make me comply with their will or were so overbearing that I got lost in them. I wasn't about to repeat the same mistakes, and honestly didn't want to bring my problems to his doorstep.

"Yeah, I know, and I am," Tali confirmed with a nod. Faxx moved, and my eyes went to him when he sat up to crack his neck.

"Did you fall asleep, Faxx? I told you that you could sit in the chair and I could stand," Dea said.

"No, I didn't fall asleep. I just needed to stretch a little bit. I'm cool with sitting on the floor, Dea. You need to be comfortable and shouldn't be on your feet for that long," Faxx chided.

"He's right," Link said without looking up.

"Fine, fine, whatever. I'm almost done, anyway. I just have two more left, and then you're all good," Dea smiled. I looked her over, and I could see the light bruises on her face were finally healing up. Tali told me she was speaking with someone, and I was so happy about that because it was absolutely needed.

"Dea, can I have this mango? I'm hungry as shit, and Cent act like she doesn't ever want to feed me," Faxx accused. I opened my mouth to tell his ass to cook for himself if it was about food, but I knew differently. Fransisco wasn't talking about food, but Dea began to laugh along with Tali.

"Oh no, that is just sad. Cent, you could feed that boy. That's not right," Dea reprimanded.

"Right, that's messed up, Crescent. After all he does for you and stuff. He takes your car to the shop, and I know he's the one that brings you those bomb-ass lunches and shit. You could at least cook him something to eat," Tali said.

"You can have the mango, Faxx. Did you want some peanut butter on it?" Dea laughed.

"Ewww," we all said at once, and Dea started to laugh.

Faxx sat back down, never taking his eyes off me as I glared at his bitch ass. He reached out for the mango while also reaching for the knife I knew he kept strapped to his leg. My eyes darted to Dea and Tali. Tali had a furrow on her brow as she watched him, and Dea stared at him in the large mirror across from them. We all watched as he cut the mango in half and sat the other half on the table before him.

"Yo, let me get the other half. I'm starving right now. We should've ordered something from Emerald," Link said. That was the first time he looked away from his phone or put it down. Faxx sucked his teeth but handed him the other half.

"This will hold me over until we finish," Faxx said. He held eye contact with me, and I swallowed. All three of us watched as he picked up the plump, yellow fruit, and I smelled its sweet aroma from where I was sitting. I glanced at Link as his nostrils flared at the ripe mango like it was more than just a piece of fruit to eat.

"What's happening?" Tali whispered. I knew she was asking because of how the room's energy changed. You could feel the sexual charge in the air when Faxx licked his lips.

I stared at Faxx as the juice from the mango already began to dribble down his fingers as he took his first bite. The flesh looked firm yet yielded to him, with just the right amount of pressure from his teeth.

"Good God, this can't be legal," Dea gasped.

Faxx's eyes stayed on mine, and I felt my heart kick to a rhythm I knew was dangerous as fuck. As he chewed, Faxx growled slightly as the flavor exploded in his mouth. I wondered if it was the perfect balance of sweetness and tartness with a hint of tanginess. I swallowed hard because that was his exact words on how he thought my pussy tasted. Faxx closed his eyes and savored the taste of the juice, coating his tongue with a grunt.

"This is porn. This is fucking porn," Tali mumbled. It caused me to glance at Link, but he was focused on taking his next bite and then another, each bite dragging out a groan of satisfaction. His long tongue seemed to swipe up the juices from the fruit.

"Would I be wrong if I said my nipples were hard?" I said, turning my gaze back to Faxx when he chuckled.

As he continued to eat, I couldn't help but marvel at how he placed the entire mango over his tongue to suck the fruit into his mouth. All I could hear were the words he whispered into my ear the night I watched Dr. Sexy fuck Tali against the VIP glass. *I bet the flesh of your pussy is like eating a mango. I know it's silky-smooth, and your juices are creamier, and will satisfy me.'* We all watched as they sucked out every last drop of juice from the fruit, relishing the burst of flavor with each bite they took. I didn't think Link was doing it on purpose because he wasn't even looking at us, but this nigga Faxx knew what he was doing.

I heard a door opening, but I couldn't look away as Faxx licked his fingers, savoring the last remnants of the sweet, sticky juice. By the way, he licked his lips, I could tell the taste lingered in his mouth, and he felt a sense of contentment as he watched me damn near hyperventilate.

"Jesus, I don't know if I should offer them another one to get another show or what?" Dea wheezed.

"What the fuck are you offering, Shandea? And Faxx, if you don't get your big ass from between my wife's legs, I will shoot you in the face," Oz shouted.

"Lennox!" Dea shook her head.

"Nigga, she just doing my hair with your jealous ass," Faxx laughed. I blinked and looked up as Henny, Oz, and two other women stood in the room with us. Henny was staring at Tali's ass just as Link slurped the rest of the mango into his mouth. Tali's eyes snagged on how Link licked the juice off his thumb before she blinked fast, looking up to see Henny.

"Ahh, damn, shit," she mumbled. "Ahh, I'm ahh, I'm all done, Link," Tali stammered before looking away. Dea quickly finished Faxx's last braid, but I noticed her full glare on Oz before looking at the one woman none of us knew. I just hoped it wasn't that chick Nia because this was about to get awkward. I looked Oz and Henny over and frowned.

"What in the hell happened to y'all?" I asked. It was like a splash of cold water thrown on all three of us because Dea turned around fully. Her light brown eyes got huge, but I couldn't miss the quick looks she kept throwing at the other girl. I knew the tall, brown-skinned woman from the club was Shantel, but I didn't recognize the other, brown-skinned woman with them.

"Yeah, what is going on?" Tali frowned at Henny.

"They are okay, ladies. I'm just glad we were close to downtown," the woman said, setting her purse on the table.

She looked at Link momentarily, and I saw her lick her lips quickly before turning away. She kicked off her shoes as Hendrix nodded at Link and Faxx. They both stood up without another word, and I could see from the serious expressions on their faces some shit had just gone down. Shantel followed the crew down the hall just as Dea got herself worked up because Oz hadn't said shit, and I was really starting to think this was the girl.

Dea's face screwed up at the woman kicking off her shoes and going over to the kitchen like she owned the place. I looked at Tali, but she was already approaching Dea as she stood up.

"What the hell? I know I'm not trippin', and this nigga is doing this shit again? Because whatever fucking happened to have him looking like that might have been the safer option than coming back here," Dea said. The woman came out of the kitchen with a bottle of water to her lips and a frown on her face. I heard hard footsteps coming back toward us and knew Oz would be in the lead.

"Oh, God. I hope you don't think I'm sleeping with Oz. Ewww, no, you can have that shit and don't even ask me about Henny because he's my cousin. Yuck! And I am Mala since neither of them thought introducing me would be a good idea," Mala frowned.

"Shandea, I know damn well you not out here trippin' and jumping to conclusions?"

"I know damn well you are not walking in here with someone I don't know after everything that went down. We spoke about things like this, Lennox. Not to mention you didn't even introduce the girl. She had to introduce herself," she snapped. Tali looked at me and shrugged because, clearly, Dea was still working through some things. Everything wasn't all peachy, and I could fully understand that. But I could tell some serious shit had happened. For Hendrix to say nothing to Tali or me said a lot. Link came up beside me and grabbed his jacket from the back of my chair.

"Oh, my bad, Link," I said, standing up and moving to the side.

"You good, Cent. And I want to know who the fuck would want to fuck Mala in the first place. Don't anybody with their right mind wants to deal with that stank ass attitude," Link sucked his teeth. Mala capped her water bottle before slamming it on the dining table. She crossed her arms over her chest as everyone else returned to the living room.

"Kyte, I wouldn't fuck you if you were the last nigga on this earth," Mala spat.

"I told you to stop calling me that, and if you were the last woman on this earth, I would probably drown myself just to get away from you," he chuckled and dodged the water bottle she threw at him.

"Fuck you, Kyte," Mala huffed.

*Why in the hell does she keep calling him Kyte? I guess it's an inside joke.*

But the way Link was muggin' her when she used it made it seem like he didn't think it was funny. Shantel shook her head at the scene just as Oz approached Dea. He kissed her forehead, but my body became alert as hands slid around my waist. Faxx gripped my curves in his large hands before moving them up my sides. I felt his hard chest against my back and smelled his unique scent of leather and gunmetal.

"I'll come back to pick you up since your car won't be ready until Thursday. Just so you know, every time the juice of the mango hit my tongue, I imagined it was the juices from your pussy. Are you going to let me taste it, Cent?" Faxx murmured into my ear. My entire body shivered as his fingers rubbed circles on my bare arms.

"Will you still want to if I demand that you make me cum three times in a row with your mouth alone, and if you can't, you lose access to this good pussy?" I whispered with a laugh.

I loved fucking with him because I knew he thought, with his pretty boy looks, he could get whatever and who he wanted. Though, thoughts like that went away when you stared into his dark gaze and saw the hint of crazy that lived in the depths of his eyes that was barely contained. I hoped he was getting frustrated by me not giving in to him, and he would just leave me alone. His dark chuckle seemed to vibrate my skin as he pressed a kiss to my neck. He always held me like I belonged to him or something. I felt myself losing will power when it came to him, and it scared the fuck out of me. Fucking with Faxx, a U.C.K. nigga, was like playing with a live bomb. I didn't want to end up blown to pieces if and when he rejected me.

"I will let you hold my Glock to my head while I eat that tight pussy until all your demands are met. Don't fuck with me, Crescent," Faxx gritted.

He licked my ear before smacking my ass. I felt him step back and walk around me, leaving me fucking speechless.

CHAPTER TEN

## SHANDEA 'DEA' SAUNDERS

I wouldn't lie and say I didn't think that woman was another one of the long line of bitches he'd probably fucked. I knew I had to rein that shit in, though, because more often than not, I would probably end up being wrong. It wasn't so much me thinking it was another one like Nia, but the fact I didn't know her and she was in my space. We spoke about that and how I needed to know the people around me, or that were coming into what was supposed to be our home. But I knew I had to chill the hell out because I could clearly see something was happening.

I was just so tired all the freaking time and sick of being in the damn house. At least I didn't really get morning sickness all like that, but the fucking smells. I hated the smell of sweat and smoke! When Lennox lit a cigar in his office, I almost threw one of the potted plants at his face. But I also smelled his cigar case, almost tasting their flavors. Pregnancy was weird as fuck, but now that it's settled in my mind, I was happy as shit. Now, whatever was going on was trying to bulldoze its way into my happiness.

"Sweetness, we can talk about all this shit later. I need to handle some shit right now, but I get it. No need to get upset," Lennox ordered. The firm kiss on my forehead told me his mind was elsewhere. I didn't say anything and just nodded at him, letting him know that I understood and that he didn't need to worry about me. I could tell he had enough on his mind without having to be worried about my personal shit.

"It's all good, Lennox. I get it. Just fix it, please," I said softly.

I stepped back and only noticed that he had changed out of the rumpled and torn Bespoke navy blue suit I had laid out this morning. Now he was wearing a long sleeve black t-shirt and black pants. His gold grills flashed when he looked away from me and grimaced. He looked back down at me, and I held his eyes.

"Nothing will touch you or our baby, Shandea. We're handling it. Don't wait up, Sweetness. I will probably be back late," he said, stepping away. "Shantel, I need you to figure out how to get my truck from downtown and have another one delivered by tomorrow," he demanded. Shantel rolled her eyes as she typed furiously on her smartphone. Her face told me she wanted to tell him he was late, but she just nodded.

"I got you, Boss," she said.

I watched as Lennox, Faxx, Henny, and Link all moved silently out the door with a look that would send chills over a person if they saw their dead-eyed expressions. But that was only because they didn't know them.

"Well, thank God they're gone," Shantel said, pocketing her phone. I turned to face her before shaking my head and cleaning up the hair supplies on the table. "Shandea, I have a little surprise for you, but if you want it, we need to leave now," Shantel said cryptically.

Now I didn't know her all like that, but I'd been talking to her a lot lately since the shit happened with Xavier. She told me something like that happened to her, so she wanted to let me know that I could talk to her because she would understand how I was feeling. I appreciated that. But what could she have for me?

"A surprise? Why do we need to leave for me to get it?" I asked, confused.

"Because it's at the farm," Shantel stated. She looked at her slim diamond studded watch before looking back up into my eyes.

"You're taking me to a farm? You do realize how that shit sounds, right?" I said.

"What farm?" Mala asked.

I knew I might have come off as kind of harsh toward her, but I hoped she could forgive me. I wasn't about to explain why I reacted that way, but I was sure Shantel would probably fill her in if she hadn't already. Looking at her, I can tell that she is related to Henny. They had some of the same features. You could see them clearly when they stood together.

"Oh, girl, you have been out of the loop too long. Listen, we need to go. Do you want your surprise or not?" Shantel shrugged.

"Fuck it. I'm so tired of sitting around. I love Lennox, but he's trying to keep me wrapped up. What about those guards?" I said. I looked at Tali, but she seemed to be engrossed in her phone, and I hoped that if it was Tre, her ass didn't answer. That would be all we needed, an insane Dr. Pharma running around in these streets. Tali looked up at that moment, almost like the conversation had just caught up with her.

"A farm? And yes, Shandea, he should keep your ass bubble wrapped," she squinted.

"Yes, yes, a farm, and don't worry about the guards. I know we have a short window of time to get to my Range and get the hell on the road. My time is winding down, and I need to finish what I've already started at the farm. So, are y'all coming?" I stared at Tali and then looked at Crescent, who grabbed her purse.

"I'm intrigued. I feel like this is about to be a good time," Crescent giggled. I smiled and turned my gaze to my little sister.

"Fine, fine, let's go. I'll already be in enough trouble as it is, so I might as well live it up tonight," she grumbled.

"Well, I just want to see this farm you're discussing. The only person who even talked about buying a farm is Kyt–" Mala shut her mouth. "I know you're not taking me to this nigga's house?"

"Girl, he won't be there now. Let's go," Shantel directed.

She spun on her heels and marched to the door. I was in my dark green Terry Cropped hoodie, so I went to the coat closet and grabbed my black leather jacket. Crescent and Tali were behind me as we followed the two women out of the house.

I was pleasantly surprised at how easily Shantel got around the guards, and I wondered how we all would pay for that shit later. Yeah, I knew shit was going down, and it was for my protection, but I didn't think Shantel was anything to play with. When overhearing her and Lennox speaking, she was just as dangerous as them, if not more so, because she looked helpless until you stared into her dark brown eyes. I could see the pain hidden deep in them when she came to me and told me that she understood how I felt.

We all piled into her Range Rover and headed out of Union City. Mala sat up front, but about thirty minutes into the trip, she turned around to face us.

"So Tali, you and my cousin, huh? How did you meet him?" She smiled. I smirked because Tali bit her lip before smirking.

"I actually met him about six years ago, but I went away to college. When I came back, I ran into him at the hospital," she explained. That was the easiest and least scandalous way she could have worded it. Crescent snorted because she now knew the entire story. I told her about the whole scream platinum thing before Link and Faxx rolled up and crashed our little talk session.

"It was probably some freaky shit because that sounds way too normal for his crazy ass. I don't want to know if it is. I'll keep that meeting in my head just like that," Mala laughed. She pushed a long Goddess loc over her ear, and I saw the huge ass diamond that sat on her ring finger.

"Beautiful ring," I said when the laughter died down. Mala looked at her hand momentarily before turning to face me with a small smile.

"Thanks. It is beautiful," she said. I swear I saw a quick flash of regret, disgust, or sadness when she looked at it, but it was gone in a moment. She smiled at me as she put her hand on her lap. Mala reached up and turned the radio up slightly, and the song by Yung D-Mar had just finished playing brought back memories of that night at the club.

*"This is JBL Hot 97.4 out of Union City! This is Dj Hyper-X, and that was Yung D-Mar's latest hit and maybe his last, according to sources that say it's not looking good for the Del Mar rapper. But in other news, it looks like the Union City Butcher has struck again! If you don't know by now, let me tell you what happened a few hours ago. A major shootout went down in the middle of downtown, not far from your very own Hot 97.4 building. Now we all know guns are not the Butcher's style, but sources close to me said a cleaver was found on the scene of this mess. Some people were hurt, but no casualties have been reported. Union City Memorial Hospital has committed to ensuring all involved will be well cared for. But if anyone knows or sees anything, use your best judgment because I wouldn't want the Butcher of Union City coming for me! Especially now if he's using guns to make noise. In other news—"*

Mala cut the radio back down and looked toward Shantel, who gripped the steering wheel tighter.

I looked at Tali and Cent. They both looked at me, and Cent raised her brows at me like it couldn't be a coincidence. I opened my mouth to ask one of them upfront when Mala turned to face us with a smile. Her brown eyes landed on me.

"Congratulations to you, Dea. Lennox told me about the baby when we scooped them up from downtown. Are you excited?"

I blinked a few times, and my hands went directly to my stomach. The cleaver comment stuck in my mind, and I remembered hearing Lennox telling Sam he wanted those who betrayed him down at the *Shop*. But could he have meant the *Butcher Shop*, or am I reaching? I shook my head, remembering that Mala was asking me a question.

"I...I think I'm getting there. It's still all new to me, but I'm happy," I said. We made a turn, and that's when I noticed we'd left the highway and were on a dark road.

"Where in the hell are you taking us, Shantel?" Tali asked, looking around.

"Hell yeah, because if I wanted to get murdered, I could've stayed in Union City and just walked the block," Crescent said, holding up her phone. "There's no signal," she said, tapping the screen.

"Calm down, y'all damn. There will not be a signal now that we're here," Shantel laughed. I turned to look forward and saw nothing but endless land with a few large buildings. But nothing compared to the large farmhouse that covered the ground. The long porch wrapped around the entire house, and I wished it was still daytime so I could see it better.

"Oh damn. Who lives like this? This shit is nice-nice. Like big money rancher style nice," Crescent noted. She was right because this house was beautiful in the dark. I would love to see it when the sun rose. The house was lit up inside, but Shantel pulled the Range behind the house and stopped in front of a large, dark red building that I thought was a barn.

"Okay, let's go," she said, hopping out of the truck. I opened my door and climbed out, unsure if I really wanted her surprise. I had nothing against animals, but I didn't want to take care of any. I hoped she wasn't trying to surprise me with a support horse or something.

"Shantel, what is this?" I asked, but she was already moving to the large doors. I followed her as Crescent, Tali, and Mala looked around like something would jump out at them at any moment. Shantel scanned her palm on a pad placed into the wall, and I heard a clicking sound before she pushed the door open. I stepped inside after her and stopped when she stood there facing me. She waited until we were inside the building, and the door was closed before she unlocked the next door, leading us inside a large room with stables.

"I hope you like it and consider this my early wedding, baby shower, and Christmas gift," Shantel exclaimed as she pushed open a stall door. I stopped and gasped when I saw Katrice screaming at me behind a ball gag.

I stepped closer as Katrice screamed behind the gag, tears sliding down her cheeks. I felt it when the others stepped into the space, and I heard the gasps of surprise.

"Oh, they got this bitch," Crescent laughed. She folded her arms across her chest, raising her large breasts. I could tell she was waiting on the word to fuck Katrice up by the tapping of her nails on her arm. Tali pushed between us, and I saw the rage and anger flashing in her gray eyes when she got a good look at who was sitting there.

"How long have they had this bitch?" Tali shouted. I didn't give a shit about how long, I just wanted to know why Lennox hadn't told me. I knew he was trying to protect me, but I needed this. Beating her motherfuckin' ass would be therapeutic for my healing process. Katrice struggled against the ropes that held her in place. I stepped forward and walked around her, eyeing her and loving the fear that was in her gaze. She was tied in a Boxtie style, and her ankles were cuffed to thick hooks on the floor.

I only knew about this rope tie style because I wanted to try something like that. Whoever tied her up like this did it expertly.

"I think it's about time you get some answers from your cousin Dea. I need you all to understand how we get down, and when I say we, I mean all of us. We do not take disloyalty lightly and especially when it comes to family. We also don't like when people fuck with the flow of our money. I was put in charge of this bitch and to find out everything she knows about anything she knows. If the three of you are coming into our world, I need to know how deep you are willing to go," Shantel stated. She stood up straighter and fixed her black suit jacket before wiping imaginary lent off her dark gray dress pants.

Before I could say anything, Tali stepped forward and slapped the shit out of Katrice. She grabbed her tangled weave and damn near ripped the glued lace front off her head.

"My sister and your cousin could have died, you fucking bitch!"

Tali punched Katrice so hard that it echoed throughout the building and caused me to jump. I snapped out of whatever state I was in and moved to pull Tali away. Crescent was standing there glaring at Katrice, and I knew I had to take control.

"Tali! Tali! Tali, chill the fuck out. I'm good and here," I said, holding her. I looked at Shantel and saw the approval in her gaze. Mala stood there nodding like Tali wasn't about to beat this girl to death.

"I want to talk to her! Let me talk to her," I said to Shantel. Tali finally settled down when she heard my words and turned to look at me.

"She can't get out of this, Dea. I could have lost you, and we already lost the–"

"It's all good, Tali. I know what you're feeling, but something tells me more is at stake. Am I right, Shantel?"

I didn't take my eyes off Katrice as Shantel moved forward. I saw the fear in Katrice's eyes when Shantel came close. That told me it wasn't the first time she'd seen Shantel. What happened between the two before today?

Shantel removed the ball gag from her mouth, and Katrice coughed while sucking in much-needed air. I walked around Katrice in the dimly lit stall. When she saw me step into this stall, the surprise on her face told me everything. Katrice was *not* expecting me to be alive. She knew exactly what type of man Xavier was and served me up without a second thought. My heart was pounding with nervous anticipation of what she would say. But I also felt rage running through my veins at what she did and what she made me lose. This was my chance to find out the truth about my so-called sister Yasmin and whatever else their trifling asses had done.

"What the fuck is wrong with y'all?" Katrice screamed. The hit from Tali was already leaving a bruise across her face, but she needed more than that. Shantel stepped forward almost lightning fast, slapping Katrice across her face, and snapped her fingers.

"Shut the fuck up! You put yourself in this position being a grimy, dirty ass bitch. Now you came here for the part you played in Dea's kidnapping, but it seems like you might know a little more information. Information we can use, and I want it. I want all of it, and what you don't know, your bitch ass will find out," Shantel demanded.

"I don't know who the fuck you are or how they got you to do this, but you will regret this shit. My sister will–"

Crescent and Tali moved at the same time.

"No! If you hit her too hard, we won't hear what she has to say. We can't be killing too many brain cells," I said, looking at Shantel.

"I'm not helping or telling y'all bitches shit!"

Mala pushed off the wall, and it was like looking at a different person.

"You fucked with U.C.K. when you fucked with Shandea, and you're riding with that nigga Ja. So if you don't fucking talk, I can't see why we need your stank ass around here," she snapped. "So sit here and shut the fuck up until someone asks you a fucking question," Mala seethed. Mala mushed Katrice hard on the forehead before stepping away. I could tell it was more going on than just her involvement, which must've been why Lennox wouldn't tell me if they had her or not. I approached the chair where Katrice was bound. Her eyes were darting nervously around the room.

"Ask your questions, Shantel, but I must get my answers when you're done. Then I want to make sure she feels the pain I felt when I was told I lost my baby," I whispered. Shantel stared at me momentarily, and I could see the understanding in her brown eyes. I felt Tali come up beside me. She wrapped an arm around my waist and glared down at Katrice. "Well, let's get started. Katrice!" Shantel shouted as she snapped her fingers twice. Katrice turned to face her and pressed her lips together. "I need to know what you know about Yasmin's involvement in the hospital embezzlement," Shantel said calmly.

Katrice shifted uncomfortably in her chair, her eyes flickering with uncertainty.

"I don't know anything about that," she said, her voice shaking slightly. One slap and another so quick I didn't see it happen, but I heard it echo. We all knew she was lying. I knew Katrice and Yasmin talked constantly, and I was sure Yasmin ran her mouth about something like this. When it came to money, these bitches were ten toes down. "Why would I know if my sister knows anything about an embezzlement?"

Shantel slapped her twice and then moved so close to her face that I knew Katrice could feel her breath on her skin.

"I need to know what she's planning to do with the money she stole and how she's going to make it look like Dr. Hendrix Pharma is responsible."

Katrice's eyes widened in shock, and so did mine. I looked at Tali, and the hate she had a moment ago was overshadowed by blinding rage. I could tell Shantel had hit a nerve, and I could see the cracks starting to form. She was sweating and cold because she shivered uncontrollably, and her eyes couldn't meet anyone. Katrice tried to move, but the ropes would get tighter each time.

"I don't know anything about that," she stammered.

Shantel leaned in closer, her voice low and urgent, before she snapped her fingers twice in a row three times. I frowned because I did know why she kept doing that. "Katrice, I need you to tell me the truth. I know that Yasmin has been giving false information to agents working on the case, and I want to know who it is and who else is helping her steal from the hospital."

Katrice hesitated momentarily, her eyes darting around the room as if searching for an escape. But then she slowly began to blink as she stared forward.

"Okay," she said, her voice barely above a whisper. "Yasmin told me that she would transfer the money to our offshore account and then plant evidence to make it look like Dr. Pharma was responsible. She said that it would be easy and that she would get away with it. She also is helping Rodney plant evidence in the hospital that he is purchasing his medications under false licenses and forges signatures to receive more shares of control substances than other hospitals. Rodney wants to take everything from them and you," Katrice said, looking in my direction.

Shantel looked at Mala, and a silent message passed between the two women. But all I could do was stare at the blurry eyes of my cousin. I didn't know what Shantel had done, but there was no more struggling, lying, or antics coming out of her mouth. All the lies and bullshit for what? Why do all of this shit for money? Yasmin and Katrice were both smart and beautiful women who could get all this shit on their own. Why steal and deceive and be so conniving like this? I moved closer, wanting the answers and wanting the truth.

"Why? Why would you let that nigga take me? What have I ever done to you to make you turn your back on your family," I shouted. Katrice gave a slow blink before raising her eyes to meet mine.

"Exist. Neither of you should have ever existed. Everything you have, we should have had. You stole it from us, so why not help my mother steal it all back?" Katrice said monotone.

I felt a wave of anger and sadness wash over me. My sister and my cousin were stealing from a hospital and their family. Not to mention trying to frame an innocent man for their bullshit. Knowing Rodney was involved wasn't a surprise to me, but I wasn't worried. He would get his in the end too.

"Bring her out of whatever the hell you did. I need her to hear this and feel this pain," I said, my voice hoarse with emotion.

"I got you. All I ask is you don't kill her. I will need her later," Shantel said, stepping before Katrice. Shantel clapped twice and snapped her fingers, and Katrice blinked at her with a sneer.

"Fuck y'all!" Katrice snarled. Shantel pulled out a long knife, and Katrice started to scream, but all Shantel did was cut the ropes.

"You've done the right thing by telling me the truth. Now you will use your trifling ass ways to serve me," Shantel said. Shantel jumped back as Katrice stood up and tried to grab onto her. She must have forgotten about her legs because she doesn't get far. Katrice fell over onto the floor, and it was on. Crescent moved first, using the pointed toe of her boot to kick the bitch in the stomach.

"Ah, Ahh, get this crazy bitch," Katrice screamed. Shantel tossed the key in front of her to unlock herself while Tali pulled Crescent off her. I waited until she released her ankles and stood before my fist flew into her face. I just kept hitting and hitting until I felt hard arms grab my waist as shouting filled my ears. All I saw was blood as Katrice spit blood onto the ground.

"Shandea! What the fuck are you doing?" Lennox roared.

"Let that bitch go! Let her go, and I can finish what that nigga couldn't," Katrice shrieked.

"Let me go, Henny! Fuck you, bitch," Tali screamed, and I heard flesh meet flesh before more shouting.

"Tali, you're a dumb bitch. You're letting that nigga hold you while he's been fucking Yasmin. You just like your nasty ass Mama, aren't you? Fucking your sister's, man bitch," Katrice hissed.

"I'm going to kill this bitc—"

Things went silent once Lennox went through the door, and it closed behind us. I didn't even realize that I was crying or why I was crying so hard. All of this, everything I went through, was for nothing. It was all about jealousy and fucking money.

"Dea, Sweetness, what the hell were you thinking?" Lennox asked once he had me away from the building. He pressed me up against a big ass black pickup truck. Lennox was also dressed in black, making it hard to see him in the darkness. I felt his arms on the side of me as he caged me in and waited for me to speak. I opened my mouth, and nothing came out. I tried again, and I broke.

"We lost our child because of people who hate us for no fucking reason. Katrice and I didn't get along like that, but doing something like this and having no remorse is sickening. X wasn't the only one who played a part in my losing my child because she helped him. I wanted to kill her, Lennox, and you should have let me," I exploded. I pushed at his hard chest, but he didn't move. Lennox leaned closer to me, and I felt his lips press against my skin.

"By the time our child is born and you are healed, we should have gotten every use out of her. When the day comes that she is no longer needed, you can walk into that room and put a bullet in her head."

I looked up, trying to see his face in the darkness, but it was hard. All I could see was the flash of gold when he spoke. His hand found my face, and I reached up to hold it.

"What if I decided to use a cleaver?"

## CHAPTER ELEVEN

# Fransisco 'Faxx' Wellington

I wiped the water from my face as I stepped out of the shower. The events last night were wild as fuck, and I didn't think I would see Ms. Dea monkey-stomping the shit out of her cousin like that. If Oz hadn't pulled her away and Henny hadn't dragged Tali out of the barn, that girl would be useless to us. It would be another week before we could return her to her life until her time was finished. No way she would live past her use if I was going by the look in Oz's eyes when Link wheeled her out of the barn and to the storage area that was set up as a mini-clinic to get her cleaned up.

"Papi, are we getting breakfast, or are you cooking?" Francesca asked.

I leaned on the counter and stared at myself in the mirror. How the fuck did I manage to slip up and fuck that bitch again? I wanted more kids, but not with that bitch of a baby momma I had. I looked at the closed door, knowing what she wanted, and that wasn't food on the go.

"Papi will make you something to eat. Can you go and get ready for school, and we can sit down and eat together."

"Thank you, Papi," Francesca squealed. I looked down at my phone and saw I missed a call from Link. I grabbed my phone and left for the bedroom to get ready. I looked at my empty bed and mentally calculated how long it would take to have Crescent in it.

"Three weeks give or take," I said to myself.

"What nigga?" Link said. I looked down at my phone, forgetting I had called this nigga.

"Just giving myself a goal. What's good?"

"How's my niece?"

"I found another one of her dolls stuck in the oven when I came home last night," I answered.

I normally didn't need to get all decked out and shit, but today it was needed. I had to be my security firm's head in a few meetings today. I hated owning shit, but at the end of the day, I hated working for someone else more.

"Did the doll do something bad?"

I pulled on my white dress shirt and looked down at the phone like it would explode.

"You know, I didn't think to ask her that. Good idea," I answered.

"I know. But anyway, I received all the information on this Ian nigga this morning. We need to meet up before handling anything else. I already spoke to Oz and Henny. I will be by there to scoop you up. Crescent called and asked me for a ride."

I stopped mid-motion at my future wife's name until Link laughed. "This nigga right here. That girl ain't call me," Link chuckled.

"Keep fucking with me, and I will blow up your houseboat," I threatened.

"Naw, but seriously, I'll be on my way, and we can drop my niece off at school and then meet at the new *Clinic*."

I didn't know why I was letting this nigga get to me. I knew he was picking me up because that was where Crescent's new car was after I had everything that needed to be installed loaded up. I already made plans to pick her up after we finished with all the bullshit.

"Bet."

I ended the call and grabbed my jacket before exiting my room. I went by my daughter's room and saw her looking at herself in the mirror. I stopped and stared at her for a moment. It had been six years, and she already acted like she's sixteen. I watched as she blew kisses at herself in the mirror and then rolled her eyes before getting into a fighting stance.

"Papi, do I really have to wear pink? It's so girly," she sighed. I smirked at her before walking away without answering. Francesca knew it's exactly what she would wear because she couldn't go to school in all-black tactical gear. "Papi?"

"Let's go, Cece. Uncle Link will be here soon," I called back. I heard her little foot stomp, but her footsteps behind me told me she understood the assignment. Act normal, live normal, and people would leave you the fuck alone. "Cece, why was the baby in the oven last night?"

"Because."

"Because why?"

"Because she said she thought you were stupid for building a room for that girl. And I said nobody calls my Papi stupid. Then I said she had to be punished," she shrugged. I took out everything to make her a quick breakfast while making a mental note to make an appointment with our therapist.

"Well, it doesn't matter what others say about me. You shouldn't put your doll in the oven. Just put her away inside her house."

"Like you told mommy to go to her house and never come back?"

"Exactly," I said. I put her pancakes, eggs, and turkey bacon before her, sat down, and waited for Link.

Cece ate the last piece of her turkey bacon just as Link texted he was outside. I stood up, and she rushed to her feet. "Don't forget your book bag, little girl. And don't forget you're staying with your mommy this week, so she will pick you up after school."

"Ahhh, man, I hate staying with her. She doesn't even know how to cook. Why can't I just stay with Popop and Mimi?" Cece whined. I would always be grateful to Link's parents for caring for Cece when I had to do business. Shit, we were all glad that they basically treated us all like we were their sons and daughters. When Cece was born, it was never a question regarding care, because Mrs. Laverne was at my apartment the day I brought Francesca home. I learned how to care for her because of Mama Laverne, but I knew how to be a father because of Mr. Elijah.

"It's only one week out of the month. Give Mimi and Popop a break and man up. Let's go."

"Fine! I can't wait to meet your girlfriend. She will help me. I hear her telling you what to do all the time," Cece said. She grabbed her bag and ran to the door. She was out of it in a second, and Link had her in his arms when I walked outside.

"Good morning, Mr. Wellington."

"Good morning, Fred," I waved.

The older man was my closest neighbor, even though I only saw him whenever he was on his golf cart looking for his missing golf balls. My neighbors and I were so far apart that you wouldn't think I had any. Still, I didn't want to have to see anyone or any of them looking at my property.

"Bring your white picket fence ass on before we're late. I thought you were getting a privacy fence?" Link said, climbing into the truck.

"Shut the fuck up, and I am. They will be installing it this week. Just get in and fucking drive," I gritted.

*BE NORMAL, ACT NORMAL, AND EVERYONE WILL LEAVE YOU THE FUCK ALONE.*

After dropping Francesca off at school, we made our way downtown and over the Eastend bridge, where there was nothing but warehouses.

"You know your daughter is a psychopath, right?"

"This has been established already. Why are we revisiting this shit?"

"Because she asked me if I could set up a video feed on her tablet so she can watch her new mommy while she works," Link said. I slowly turned my head toward him and could tell he wasn't joking. *What in the fuck is happening? How did I pass this shit down? Why wasn't therapy helping like they all said it would if caught at a young age?*

"What did you say?"

"I told her that once she meets her, she can ask if that would be okay. Crescent is just as crazy as the two of y'all, so she might think it's cute."

"Nigga, next time, just say no."

"Cece already likes her, and she hasn't met Cent yet. That's a good thing. I don't know how Tyenika will feel about it," Link said. I sucked my teeth because not only did that bitch catch me slipping six years ago after Malcom died, but she got my ass again a few months ago when I blacked out. I had to get that shit under control because she noticed how off I was when dropping off Cece. I was pissed and needed a distraction from knowing that someone had been fucking with my weapons shipments, costing me a few million. Tyenika liked to push me until I damn near snapped, then sucking the fuck out of my dick. So mistake number two was catching up with me now that her bitch ass claimed she was pregnant.

"Fuck Tye. She knows I don't fuck with her like that, and if this child turns out to be mine, then I will take custody of that one, too. I might be fucked in the head, but that bitch isn't raising my children."

"I think once Sanchez is finished with his recovery for his eyes, he is going for sole custody of Kaleb. I think that was the only thing that was stopping him. I don't know how y'all both got caught in that bitch's web, but she's lucky that she's my niece's mother, or I would have tossed her ignorant ass into Blackbay."

I knew he wasn't lying because he and Tye hated each other on sight. I had no idea that she and Sanchez had a child when I met her because I didn't know the nigga until Link brought him to the club. When he started complaining about his son's mother, the shit sounded familiar. I knew her son but nothing about his father, and I didn't ask. Before she even had my daughter, I knew what she was about and treated her accordingly.

Finding out how she took custody of Kaleb and had Sanchez pay bank in child support had me moving differently. My lawyers were on deck before my baby came into this world. She knew what was up and signed those papers giving over custody to my daughter as soon as she was born. That week once a month was a courtesy and because I wanted my daughter to know her mother, even if she was a bitch. It was all good as long as my baby didn't come home and tell me no bullshit.

"I told him Kaleb could stay with me until he had shit straightened out. Tye wouldn't even try and open her mouth about it," I said.

"You know how Sanchez is. He wants to do the shit himself, but I'm sure things would be different if she mistreated the boy. At least she ain't that fucking stupid. So," Link let the word drift off as we pulled up to massive doors.

"So what?"

"Do you think it's yours? Tell her to get one of those DNA tests. It can be done safely," Link shrugged.

"Fuck no, I don't think it's mine. I just don't get that feeling. It's different this time. It isn't the same feeling I had when she told me about Francesca. This bitch is up to something, and if she thinks she will pull one over on me, she's trippin'. I don't know her angle yet because she doesn't want to have it done. She cites statistics and shit about it and then tries to throw a guilt trip at me. It is what it is. I can't say for sure it isn't mine, so until the baby is born, I will make sure she is straight," I grunted.

"What about Crescent? Does she know about your baby momma drama?"

"Why are you in my fucking business regarding Cent?"

"Nigga, you wildin'. I don't see Crescent dealing with that shit."

I looked at Link, who shrugged as he parked the truck next to Oz's new shit.

"Honestly, she's the one who advised me not to push the DNA shit and to let it play out. She said it would all come out when the baby is born, and at least I will show Cece that even though her mother is a bitch, I still respect her because that is her mother. Then she said if the baby is mine, I will be in a prime position to take that baby before she starts any bullshit," I laughed.

"Crescent is on point. I can't believe she's cool with it."

"That's what I said, and she was like, why shouldn't she be? I'm not her man, and she doesn't fuck with light-skin ass niggas."

I got out of the truck while his ass laughed, mentally preparing myself for whatever bullshit we would need to handle today. I waited for Link and followed him to where we were all supposed to be meeting. I wanted to look around and get to know this building, but I wouldn't have time. I didn't see any of my people, but I could sense their presence and feel their eyes on us as we moved.

"It's about fucking time. What the fuck did you find out, Link?" Oz asked. He rubbed a hand through his beard and checked his watch. I sat down at the large table, and Henny looked up when Link turned on the large monitors.

"First off, the letter you found had fingerprints on it, but it didn't come back as anyone dead or alive. After entering in the information, when I went back to it, the shit didn't exist anymore. So I went in another direction and began to study the handwriting. I developed a forgery program about eight years ago, but it's better and more accurate now. This is what took so long because I had to dig deep. I went so far that it went back years, and the only match I could come up with was a high school thesis paper about the endurance of physical pain and how to overcome it."

"That's a little fucked up," Henny chuckled. I sat forward, more interested, and actually thinking of telling Link to send me a copy of the work.

"No, what's fucked up is that this was the only match for the handwriting in that note. Even when I ran the paper through it, nothing else came back. It's almost like this person is a ghost or something. No name was attached to this paper, but I contacted the teacher that uploaded this paper to a study. And do you know that he gave me a name because he said the child was so unforgettable that you wish you could forget him," Link said. He tossed three file folders to the table, and I grabbed them. I opened it up, frowned, and almost choked when I stared at the picture.

"That's the nigga that was in my club."

"Ian Nevin Morgan is the name of the student that wrote the thesis at Milton Union Prep and who we know as also Ian Nevin Lawe. The very same person we want to get into business with," Link stated. His hands were on his hips as he stared at Oz, who glared at the picture, and I didn't think they knew who the fuck this was. I knew who it was the moment I saw the picture. This was Rogue. This was....oh shit.

"I'm guessing you couldn't find anything else about him or where he is. Wait, let me take it a step further that the only reason you even got as far as you did is that someone let you," I said, staring at Link. His black eyes turned to me, pinning me in my seat and causing me to laugh as I closed the file.

"When I left Professor Mckenna's home, I had a nagging feeling in the back of my mind, so I turned back around and went straight back to his house. I never left the road leading away from his home, so I know I didn't pass anyone else, but when I got back there, no one was there. The entire house was empty when I broke in, and the old man and his dogs were gone."

"What the fuck do you know, Faxx?" Henny asked. He leaned back in his chair, rubbing his eyes. I looked around at all three of them and smirked.

"I know I want his fucking autograph because he is who all of us on my team want to be. The only thing I do know is that this nigga wanted us to know who he is because there is no way we would find anything on Rogue. If I'm right, and I think I am right, this nigga is CIA or used to be," I shrugged. Link turned to the large screen and typed something on his watch, and all we saw was the sky.

"Well, I found him. And he should be coming into view in 5, 4, 3, 2, now."

I leaned forward as two men came into view, walking through a parking lot. They were talking as they walked toward a large building. It was him, and I was shocked that Link managed to get this close. The two men stopped, and Ian turned around and looked up directly into the camera. A patch covered one of his eyes, but his dark brown eye stared into the camera as a smile formed across his face. Rogue winked before everything went to static. Maybe I should start wearing an eye patch.

"How the fuck did he know my drone was there. No one should–"

"Don't get bent out of shape about it, Link. Nothing is wrong with any of your shit," I said. I turned to look at Henny, but he was watching Oz. I looked at Oz and saw that he was about to lose his fucking mind.

"First, I don't think you all are realizing something. I found that note with my mother's things, and we all know who my bastard of a father is for sure now. So, do any of you believe his last name being Morgan is a coincidence?"

I could feel Crescent staring a hole into the side of my face as I pulled into the parking garage at the hospital.

"Where the fuck is my car, Faxx?" she asked for the tenth time in the forty-five minutes it took to get to Union Memorial.

"From what I am told, it needs some engine work, so it will be a little longer. So, this will be your rental until then," I smirked.

Crescent narrowed her eyes at me before she rolled them. She knew that I was lying, and I didn't give a fuck. She needed something more reliable than that piece of shit Honda, and I needed to be sure I could find her if need be. Those niggas that were at the *Clinic* had a lot and nothing at all to say about this nigga Roman. All I knew was he now knew the city Crescent was in and that they were told to bring her to him by any means necessary. I wasn't feeling that shit, none of us were, but at least this wasn't an immediate threat. From what I could tell, no one knew where Crescent lived, worked, or attended school. They probably would've never found her if she weren't in the club that night because they knew not to pull any shit in Union City.

"You can keep it. I'll find a ride home or ask Dr. Sexy to take me," she said, opening the door. I watched her thick ass climb out of the car and smiled. I climbed my tall ass out of the Audi RS 7 and jogged to catch up with her. I didn't see the problem. It wasn't like the car was outrageously expensive or over the top. I held my tongue on her last remark that she thought somebody else would take her home. I didn't give a fuck if it was Henny. She had a car, and she was going to fucking use it. Like that shit or not.

We entered the hospital's main lobby, and I nodded at the security guards on duty. I reached out and grabbed the bag Crescent was holding, and I knew she would have fought me if people weren't around. When Crescent came out dressed in a black and light gray geometric high-neck bodycon dress that hugged all her curves, I thought I would need to murder the niggas standing on the corner next to her apartment building for staring too fucking hard. I didn't know what she was trying to prove to Pamela and this bullshit mediation meeting with her attorney and the hospital's representation, but she almost got fucked against the car. Crescent gave me a tight smile as she pushed her braids over her shoulder before stabbing the up button to the elevator.

"I don't even have a lawyer. I know this bitch will try and do everything to have me fired, at the very least. I'm actually surprised that she hasn't pressed charges," she sneered. The doors opened, and we stepped inside. I hit the button for the third floor where the business conference rooms were located. "Why are you going anyway? Don't you need to guard something?" She raised a brow. I stared at our reflections in the metal of the elevator doors. I could see her head facing me and her eyes roaming my body up and down.

"I am guarding something. Who do you think requested to have the head of security at the meeting? Apparently, I need to guard Pamela from you," I said as the doors opened.

"I know you're fucking lying," Crescent laughed, but I wasn't. They did request security to be in the meeting, but I took it upon myself to take this one. We walked down the hall toward the conference room where this meeting would occur.

"Nope. So don't even look at her when it starts. Just let the hospital lawyer and Hendrix handle it. Just sit there and look sexy," I said, opening the doors.

Crescent opened her mouth to say something but stopped when she saw Tali and Henny sitting at the table. Justice, our lawyer, sat next to Hendrix, looking through a folder. Crescent moved by me and took the seat next to Tali. She was biting her glossed lip, and I could tell she was actually nervous. I didn't know why she was nervous because she knew damn well we wouldn't let shit happen to her or her position at the hospital. I sat next to Crescent when the doors opened again, and Pamela, Yasmin, and her lawyer walked inside. I saw the flex in Henny's jaw when Yasmin entered the room, and Tali's marble gray eyes darkened when she saw her sister-cousin.

Yasmin raised a brow but quickly moved around the table and sat beside Justice. Pamela smiled at Cent like she had shit in the bag, but Crescent studied her nails, not giving her the time of day. Henny cleared his throat, and Justice closed her folder and raised her head. She took off her glasses and leaned back in the chair, crossing her legs as she stared at the lawyer that came with Pamela. The man sat down and threw a folder on the table. He folded his hands and looked directly at Crescent. I almost pulled my Glock out and shot him in the face, but then Henny would say I was overreacting. Justice smiled and then sat forward, her brown eyes flashing.

"So, why are we here today, Kevin?" she asked. Kevin smirked like he'd already won when this shit was dead in the water. We already knew Pamela was bluffing with this shit, but it did make it easier to keep a closer eye on her ass.

"We are here because my client feels as though her safety at this facility is in question. We are also here because my client has lost wages from being unable to work due to employee Crescent Johnson's vendetta against my client. But we are willing to put all of this to bed and not move forward in suing the hospital for having an unsafe environment and mental damages."

"And to make this go away, what will we need to do to make this happen?" Justice asked.

"All my client wants is her back wages paid and the firing of Miss Johnson," Kevin retorted.

I zoned out as they went back and forth with each other. I heard Tali giving her side of the story of the events. Pamela also had signed statements from others that witnessed the events. Crescent's leg bounced under the table, and I reached under it to grip her thigh tight. She stopped moving, and I rubbed her leg while they dealt with this shit. I could tell she was biting down on her tongue and trying her best to stay quiet.

"Well, we are fully prepared to let Mrs. Drake go and pay for her medical expenses. From what is gathered here, she seems to be the perpetrator in this situation. We have valid accusations of her targeting Miss Johnson for months. So, I see no need to do anything you have asked. I think we are done here," Justice said.

"Wait! Wait, please. Dr. Pharma, this is not how I wanted any of this to go. I have been a valuable company employee and don't want this. I would be fine if we no longer worked together on the same floor. Crescent is a float, so I think that is possible," Pamela said quickly. Henny sat back in his chair, nodding at her like this nigga didn't already have a job in mind for the nurse. He wanted her close, but not too close, because he wanted to know what information she was handing over and who put her up to it. He didn't want her anywhere near Tali or Crescent, and the position he would give her would be an illusion that she'd been promoted.

"You have been a dedicated nurse, and I honestly wouldn't want to lose either of my valuable employees. If we can put all of this to bed today, I think I have a solution that will benefit everyone."

"Yes, yes, anything," Pamela said.

"Pam. You really need to let me handle this," Kevin gritted.

"No. I am about to lose my job messing with you, and I can't afford...just shut up, please," she finished. Pamela looked at Henny like a lifeline, but I could see Cent glaring daggers at Henny.

"I would like you to come and work at the Women's Center with a new nursing director that has just signed on. It's a slight pay raise, and they are eight-hour shifts. If that sounds good, you can speak with HR to handle everything else."

"Yes. I'd love to."

If I wasn't holding Crescent down, she would have reached across Tali's body and punched Henny for keeping this bitch on the job. I knew she had no idea Pamela was into some shit, and sometimes things like this were necessary. I heard chairs moving and people moving around the room. I tore my gaze away from Crescent, knowing my obsession with her was worsening. I looked up and saw Yasmin look back at Tali.

"Tali, have you or Shandea heard from Katrice? I haven't spoken to her in a few days," Yasmin asked. Tali raised a brow and tried to hide the barely concealed sneer on her face.

"Why would I know where that bitch is? Why would I care unless she runs with the money she owes my Mama?"

"It's a damn simple yes or no question. Regardless of what's going on, we are family," Yasmin sucked her teeth.

"I haven't seen her," Tali gritted.

"What about Dea? Katrice said she was meeting up with her last week and then..."

"We haven't heard from or seen your sister, Yasmin," Tali snapped. Yasmin glared at her, shaking her head before closing the door behind her. Everyone except Tali, Crescent, Henny, and me were gone now. "Fuck her," Tali mumbled.

"Yes, fuck that bitch. Now, what the fuck, Dr. Sexy? Why did you give this bitch a new job and better pay?"

"I want to know why Yasmin's ass was here in the first place," Tali muttered.

Henny stood up and came to the back of Crescent's chair. He leaned down, hugging her from behind. She put her hand on his forearm, and I glared at it. Henny smirked at me before kissing her on the cheek. "Stop playing Dr. Sexy and answer me, because this is bullshit," Crescent laughed.

"Cent, don't be mad at Dr. Sexy," he smirked at me. I did pull out my Glock this time and sat it on the table. The door opened at that moment, revealing Oz and Dea. Oz raised a brow as he pulled Dea inside before locking the door.

"What the hell is going on in here?" Dea laughed.

"Henny about to catch a bullet. At least we are already in a hospital," I answered. Henny laughed but pulled away from Crescent.

"Yasmin was here for the show because when it deals with the hospital and having to pay money, it's her job. And I kept Pamela because keeping your enemies closer is better."

"After what Katrice said that bitch tried to do to my Mama—"

"Tali, I told you it would all be handled. Yasmin will get what's coming to her," Henny assured. Tali looked at Henny and bit down on her tongue before she nodded. I could see the hurt in her eyes, and I was sure it was over what Katrice had said about him and Yasmin. Henny would need to handle that shit quickly before that hurt turned into hate.

Crescent looked up at him, still unhappy with what he was saying but rolled her eyes.

"See, this why you might be getting replaced, Dr. Sexy. I'm going to see Mrs. Naomi and hopefully run into her NEW doctor," Crescent said, pushing her chair back. Tali was already standing and moving to hug Dea, and Henny was picking up his folders. He burst out laughing and looked at me.

"See. I told you, Faxx," he smiled. I saw Crescent's eyes get huge before she turned to face me. I was tapping my Glock on the table as my gaze locked onto her.

"Faxx, it's not—"

I let my Glock go and reached inside my suit jacket. I pulled out on Crescent and shot her in the arm. Tali and Dea screamed, and Crescent narrowed her eyes at me while rubbing her arm. The paint smeared on her fingertips, but I knew that shit stung.

"Why in the hell would you do some crazy ass shit like that?" she screamed.

"Would you rather a body on your hands, Cent? You keep fucking playing with me. I let that shit go when Henny told me about this doctor the first time, but then you say the shit out of your mouth in front of me.

You needed punishment for that, and you got it, but I'm done. I shouldn't even fuck with you no more because clearly–"

"Ahh! Ahh shit, Cent," I roared, holding my chest.

"Shit! What the fuck? How the hell did she get that shit in here?" Henny said, snatching the gun out of Crescent's hand.

"Faxx, what kind of slow ass reaction time was that?" Oz stated.

I rubbed at the spot the rubber bullet hit, and it stung like a bitch, but I was proud of the placement of the shot. The shit did knock my ass out of the chair, but I wasn't worried because I knew I could have dodged it. Crescent glared at me, and I smiled at her, licking my bottom lip. My dick was hard as fuck, and when her eyes darted down, her breath hitched.

"The shot was punishment enough without you saying that shit, Faxx," she muttered. Her eyes grew wider as I stood up from the floor.

"Jesus, look at...damn. What kind of freaky ass shit is this?" Tali asked no one.

"Fransisco, what are you doing? Punishment was handed out, and now we are even," she gasped. Cent was on her feet and moving backward, looking around.

"Don't look for help now," Henny grunted. I didn't give a shit about who else was in the room. Crescent knew what the fuck she was doing, and she knew what that type of shit would do to me. She laughed slightly, but I moved, scooping her up before she could run around the table.

"Fransisco!" Crescent stammered as her curvy body moved against me, only making my dick harder.

"Henny," I said, holding out my hand. I didn't need to say what I wanted because he knew. I felt the metal of the gun in my hand.

"Fransisco, what the hell are you doing?" Cent panted. I laid her on the table and held her down with a hand between those large breasts. I used my knees to knock her legs apart so I could stand between her thick thighs. I moved my Glock out of the way before putting her smaller gun on the table. I felt her nails digging into my wrist, but I kept doing what I was doing. Her eyes were large, but the lust swirling in her brown gaze had my dick harder. I reached under her dress and pushed it up her thighs, not giving a shit who was still in the room.

"I am so glad these rooms are soundproof," Henny mumbled.

"That's all you got to say? He got my friend laid out like a steak dinner right now after she shot him," Tali shrieked.

"I think she about to be breakfast, lunch, and dinner at this point," Dea rasped.

I ignored all of them while I pushed Cent's tight dress up, reached up, and ripped her thin ass thong off. I rubbed a hand over her curves and her stomach. I gripped the sides, and she moaned.

"Open your eyes, Crescent. Do you remember what I told you?"

"You said a lot," she panted. I ran a finger down her slit, loving that she was wet as fuck for me.

"I will let you hold my Glock to my head while I eat that tight pussy until all your demands are met. Only I am sure you will be shaking so badly you might pull the trigger, so let's use your gun. Let's see how many times I can make this pretty pussy cum for me," I said, getting to my knees. I picked up the gun and put it in her hand. She was shaking, but I pointed it to my head before I took a long slow lick. My wide tongue parted her folds and showed me her clit.

"Oh fuck," Crescent moaned.

"Oh, my God. He is eating her just like he was eating that mango," Dea whispered.

I chuckled, and the vibrations had Crescent twitching. I pulled back slightly and licked her juices from my lips.

"Open your eyes, Cent," I ordered. Her brown eyes snapped open, and she stared down at me while biting the corner of her bottom lip. "I want you to watch me while I eat this pussy because my face will be the last one you will ever see between these thighs. I told you once, Crescent, don't play with me," I assured. The gun with the rubber bullets shook in her hand as I leaned in, sucking her clit into my mouth.

# CHAPTER TWELVE

## TALI SAUNDERS

I cut my eyes to Dea and knew my expression mirrored hers. Her mouth was hanging open, and her pupils were dilated. I could feel my palms beginning to sweat as my heart raced while watching this scene. I wonder if Crescent felt this sensation in the VIP room that night.

"Yup, just like that fucking mango. What if her finger slips?" Dea whispered. I felt a hand circle around my waist as Henny pulled my back flush to his body. His scent teased my nose, making me slicker than I was a few seconds ago. I was horny as fuck now, and I wished I would've let him fuck me last night, but I was too pissed off.

"Keep your eyes on me, Cent," Faxx demanded. He slapped her pussy, and Crescent jumped but let out a long moan when his tongue licked her from bottom to top. The slurping noises as he sucked her clit had me pressing my thighs together.

"Got damn," I whispered, then felt a slap on my thigh. I felt Henny's goatee against my ear as he leaned down. His unique smell seemed to wrap around my senses, wreaking havoc with my body.

"You like to watch now? Too bad it's not enough time for me to bend you over this table and pull your locs so you can watch to see if she cums or if the gun goes bang," he chuckled, slapping my thigh along with the word bang. I bit down hard on my lip, cursing myself for unconsciously rubbing my ass on his dick. I heard a moan, and I turned slightly and saw Oz's hand sliding down Dea's shirt.

"I am so glad the doctor just said we can resume regularly scheduled programming. Faxx, make Crescent turn this way," Oz said. My eyes got huge, and I turned to see Faxx take the gun out of Cent's, shaking hand while his other hand slid up her body and gripped her chin.

"Eyes open, Crescent," he commanded. He turned Crescent's head to the side, forcing her to face our way. He stuck two fingers in her mouth just as she screamed. Pleasure filled her heavy-lidded gaze as she came hard. Crescent held Faxx's head down, and I knew if his hair was out, she might have ripped that pretty ass shit out. Oz had moved Dea to the table, and I knew I had to get the fuck out of there before it went further.

"Look at your friend, Sweetness. See how she took her punishment and then got rewarded? I will reward this pussy later when I let you ride my face."

"Lennox, stop playing. I need to cum," Dea groaned.

"Naw, naw, I don't know if I should let you, Dea. You like to watch other niggas eating mangos and shit," Oz laughed.

Faxx and Henny started to chuckle at his words, confirming Faxx knew exactly what his ass was doing. All of them were crazy as hell, and they were pulling us into their madness. When Henny came inside Dea's house behind Oz, and he saw us staring at Link and Faxx fucking those mangos up, I was waiting for him to call me on it. I was waiting for his disapproval of liking what I saw and getting horny from it. I knew I wouldn't act on it, but Tre all but made it seem like if he wasn't there, I was cheating or some shit. So I automatically applied that knowledge to our situation. I never understood why Tre acted that way because nothing was happening, but it was deemed cheating if I enjoyed watching others. But he had no problem letting others watch what he wanted to do to me. I should've known not to compare them. I shook my head when Crescent cried out, and Faxx growled when she wrapped her legs around his head.

"I think this is our cue to get to work, Thickness," Henny whispered against my ear. Henny was right because although I wouldn't mind watching Cent and Faxx, seeing my sister get it in was another story. That was my hard no. I felt his hand on the back of my neck, but my gaze got stuck when Faxx raised Crescent's butt off the table while his tongue fucked her core.

"I think I just came," I whispered. I had no clue when Henny opened the door or how he slipped us both out until the door was shut in my face.

I moved away from Henny and shivered at the difference in temperature in the hallway. Was it this cold in the conference room, or was it because that shit was just so hot I didn't feel the chill?

"You good, Ms. Saunders?" Henny asked. I looked up, and his honey eyes were smiling at me, but his face was neutral. A few people were walking by, and now I was glad he had these rooms soundproofed, too, because ain't no way no one would've heard Crescent scream.

"Ye-yes, Dr. Pharma. Is that all you needed from me today?" I asked. I knew my breathing was slightly off, but it began to even out. I looked at my watch, seeing that I had another hour before I needed to get the report.

"If I need anything else today, I will let you know," he smiled.

He adjusted his glasses before tipping his chin toward the back elevators. I turned around and started walking to the staff elevators, trying to get my mind back into work mode. I felt my phone buzz in my pocket, but I didn't take it out to check it. Tre hadn't stopped texting me, and it was so bad I had Shandea set up the meeting with him and the other doctors on our mother's case. I hit the up arrow and turned to the side to look at Henny.

"I'm going to visit with Mama for a few before I start my shift. I think I will also have lunch with her today," I said.

"I have a few meetings today, but I want to make you dinner tonight. I know your meeting with your mother's new doctor is coming up. I thought we could go over the new treatment plan, so you're ready if you have questions," Henny offered. The doors opened, and I stepped inside. I turned around as he stepped on. I moved closer to him, and he grabbed my hand.

"Yes. I think that would be good. I need to talk to you about something as well. I also want to thank you for everything you've done to help my mother. I know you would've paid for it, but it would've felt wrong to me. I don't know why, so don't ask. But she was accepted to all of the programs you suggested, so it worked out," I said.

I stood on my toes quickly and kissed him before we got to my floor. I was still aggravated and hurt about this Yasmin situation because, once he knew that those bitches were related to us, he should have said something. I wasn't about to sit here and act like he would have known any of my family. But once he figured the shit out, he should've told me. The only problem with that was now, with this Tre shit, I felt like a hypocrite.

"I told you I will do whatever it takes for the people I care about, but you're welcome," he said, searching my eyes. "I know we have shit to discuss, and we can do that before I leave late tonight. Also, before you go home, I think you should file a missing person's report for your cousin. It's a shame she's missing in action," he said. I frowned as the elevator slowed but didn't question it because this wasn't the place or the time. I tried hiding my feelings about the Yasmin situation but knowing Hendrix, I was sure that he picked up on it. I also thought that step with a missing person report was a good idea.

"Okay. I will take care of it when I leave for the day. I'll see you later," I said as the doors opened.

"I hope you tell your mother I said hello. It's probably time that she meets the new man in your life. Especially before you end up pregnant," he chuckled.

I spun around just as the doors slid closed, but I didn't miss the flash of his white teeth. I finally realized that I wasn't breathing and sucked in air as I stormed away from the elevators. I must've dragged in too much because I started to choke and cough. I knew he was fucking with me. Why in the hell would he say some shit like that, knowing damn well he prescribed for me to get Plan B so I wouldn't get pregnant. When I went to the pharmacy, I didn't know that working for Union, we didn't need to pay the over-the-counter price if we had a prescription. While waiting, I began to second guess my decision to take the damn thing. I wondered if he knew that I hadn't taken it. I'd stared at the pills in the bathroom for about an hour. I knew how these types of drugs affected a woman's body, just like birth control. That was the reason that I never wanted to use it.

Now that I feel like this nigga might be actively trying to get me pregnant, it just might be a thought. We weren't in a normal relationship. Or was I just telling myself that? I tried calming myself down because I knew that I wasn't ovulating. Or was I? No, no, I wasn't. I turned the corner to get to my mother's room, still coughing and barely able to catch my breath. He was fucking with me, because there was no way Hendrix would want something like that. Not right now, and definitely not with me. This entire situation we found ourselves in was all about sex and nothing more. Hot as fuck, curl your damn toes sex, but that was it.

"Tali. Tali, are you alright, Squishy?" Tre's deep voice said behind me.

The nickname he used for me sounded like a punch in the gut. I remember he would squeeze me tight, telling me how much he loved how I felt in his arms. I felt his warm hand on the small of my back and the other under my chin. He raised my head to look into his dark brown gaze that was so intense and full of heat that I felt it burn between us. My eyes traced the lines of his handsome face, landing on his thick lickable lips that I spent too much time doing just that to. His smooth brown skin was still flawless, and his thick brows drew down the longer I stared at him. The only change I saw in him was his clean-shaven face, which only showed off his angular jawline. Tre was always toned, but now he was slightly more muscled in the chest by how his dress shirt stretched across it. The man was finer than fine, and the slow smile crossing his face told me I was looking too damn long. I opened my mouth and covered it before coughing again when I breathed. The scent of his cologne hung between us, and the sweet but spicy smell brought back memories of him and me at Club *Deviant*.

Along with those memories came the ones he threw in my face that we could never be serious. How could he marry or let anyone know about our relationship when I was basically for the streets? None of that shit was true, but it was almost like putting me down made him feel better about the shit that he liked to do.

I pulled my chin away and stepped forward to get out of his hold as I covered my mouth.

"Sorry, sorry. I'm fine, Dr. Tremont. Tha—thank you for asking," I said, clearing my throat. He frowned at me as he leaned his head to the side.

"It's Tre. It's always been Tre to you, Tali," he frowned. I cleared my throat again and swallowed, wishing I had some damn water right now. "Come here, Tali. Let me take a look at you. Are you sure you're okay?" Tre asked. He stepped forward, and I stepped back, looking toward my mother's hospital room door. He followed my line of sight, and before I could say anything, he stepped forward and pushed open her door. I had to step backward inside the room or risk him rubbing against me. I looked behind me, expecting to see my mother, but the room was empty.

"Where—"

"They came to get your mother for a few tests I ordered this morning. She will be gone for a few hours and probably will be exhausted when she returns. Now come here, Squish, and let me examine you. You have been coughing for a few minutes. So much so that you didn't even notice I was behind you," Tre said. He pulled over a chair and pushed on my shoulders for me to have a seat.

"Tre, I said I was fine," I attested. "I just swallowed my saliva, and it went down the wrong tube," I argued. I tried standing, but he kept his hands on my shoulders.

"So, you're saying that you were aspirating. That is even more reason for me to check you out, or you could just admit that you've been avoiding me," he accused.

"There isn't a need for me to avoid you, Tre. I think everything was said the night I left," I asserted. My comeback was less impactful when I started to clear my throat again. I coughed slightly to clear it faster and prove to his ass that I was fine.

"You do not sound fine to me, Tali. Let me check you out. It will be over with before you know it. I think we can discuss anything else after I ensure you are okay. Is it wrong that I want to make sure you're good? I do care about you, Tali, whether you want to believe it or not."

"Fine, just...fine," I said. I just wanted him to check me out so he could step the fuck back. I knew if I didn't allow him to check me over, he would just continue to harp on it and probably follow me up to the main nurses' station. I didn't need anyone in my business like that. Tre didn't say anything, but instead brought his hand to my throat. He raised my chin and checked my lymph nodes to ensure they weren't swollen. His firm fingers felt along my neck and around the back of it. He turned away, and I thought he was finished, but he returned with something he grabbed out of the supply cabinet. I cocked my head to the side at the tongue depressor and his small flashlight in his other hand.

"Really, Tre?"

"Just humor me, Tali. You know how I am. If I am going to do something, I want to do it correctly. Now open your mouth for me and stick out your tongue," he smirked. I stared at him, and his smile grew wider. I caught myself before I laughed. I knew he was being serious, but we always joked about how some things said in the medical field were dirty as hell, and this was at the top. "The faster you do it, the faster it will be over," he chuckled. I opened my mouth and stuck out my tongue, and he placed the tongue depressor on my tongue. Tre shined the light in the back of my throat, but he pulled back and looked at me.

"What?" I laughed.

"You know what? Stick your tongue out for me again, Tali," he asked. I sighed but did what he asked while he chuckled slightly. "Now, I need you to gag for me," he urged. "Come on, Tali, gag for me."

I jumped when the door slammed open, and I thought it would be the morning nurse or tech coming into the room. Tre pulled back, and I turned my head, seeing Henny standing in the doorway. My heart about damn near leaped from my chest, and I pushed the chair back and stood up. His honey-colored eyes flashed dangerously behind his glasses. I looked down and saw his hand clenched tightly into a fist.

"Dr. Pharma? What is the problem? Is this how you enter all your patients' rooms?" Tre scoffed.

"Did I hire you to harass my employees sexually? Is that what's going on in here? Because I clearly do not see your patient in this room, Dr. Tremont," Henny challenged. Oh shit. Oh shit, oh shit, I need to end this mess right now.

"Tali, is he harassing you?" Henny asked. His glare never left Tre, but I could tell by his posture that he was ready to beat the brakes off Tre, ruining my career and ending his in this hospital. I refused to let anything like that happen to him. I don't know what Henny was thinking, but this confrontation did not need to go on any longer.

"Harassing? Are you insane? Tali, am I harassing you? And honestly, whatever Ms. Saunders and I are discussing or doing is not your concern. Are you worried about all your employees like this? You know all of them by name," Tre questioned. Henny stepped forward, and I snapped out of shock at seeing him. Why was he up here?

"Dr. Pharma, I'm fine. Dr. Tremont was not harassing me. I was coughing, and he kindly offered to evaluate me. That's it. Did you need something?" I asked. I stood before him, hoping he would look down at me. He never took his eyes off Tre, and I turned to look back at Tre, whose gaze narrowed on Henny. What in the fuck was happening?

"Tali, there isn't a need to explain yourself. I am sure Dr. Pharma misunderstood what he may have heard," Tre smirked. That smirk did it, and I felt Henny move forward, but my hands came up to his chest.

"Dr. Pharma! Did you need me for something," I said loudly to get his attention. Henny looked down at me, and I saw murder in his eyes. I knew Tre could handle himself, but against Henny, I think not. Tre was liable to end up on a fucking surgical table being dissected fucking with Henny.

"Yes! Actually, yes, I do. I visited my patient Mr. Smith, and he asked for his nurse. I didn't know I would run into you here, but your name is on his board for this morning," he gritted. I knew that Henny was talking about Sanchez, but I had no clue why he was on this floor. It was probably on purpose because Crescent and I both worked on this unit.

"Yes. Yes, I told Mr. Smith he would be first on my list."

I turned around to see Tre eyeing me with a frown, but it smoothed out when I faced him.

"Dr. Tremont, it was good to see you again, and thank you for taking on my mother's case. I am sure I will see you in the family meeting when discussing my mother's treatment plan," I said, gesturing around the empty room. Tre nodded, and I turned around, only for Henny to take my arm.

He pulled me out of the room and down the hall. I frantically looked to see if anyone noticed us, but most were engrossed in charting or giving report.

"I think you got me fucked up, Tali," Henny grunted. He turned a corner to the last room that was at the back of the floor. It was normally a negative pressure room, but I guessed this was where Sanchez stayed. We went through the first set of doors, and they closed behind us. I pulled my arm away and glared at him.

"I got you fucked up? Are you fucking serious right now? If you would have gone at him, for no reason, I might add, he could have had your job, Hendrix. He is a very respected Doctor, and I know you know that. I know him, and he would have gone to the board because he's petty like that," I hissed. Henny stepped forward, crowding my space, and my back hit the wall.

"You think I give a fuck about this job, Tali? Do you think I would give a fuck if that bitch ass nigga went to the board when I am the fucking board," he seethed. I knew my eyes were wide at what he was saying, and I wondered if he was saying what I thought he was saying. "Why the fuck was he touching you like he knows you or something? Is there anything you need to say? You fucking this nigga?"

I didn't know where my sudden anger came from, but I pushed him back. I pushed him again before punching him in his chest.

"Fuck you. If I were fucking him, it wouldn't be your business, Hendrix. We aren't in a relationship. We are in the middle of a bet! And it isn't like you can say a fucking thing, because how the fuck do I know if you're not going down to the next floor and fucking my cousin?"

"Sister."

"What the fuck ever, Hendrix. Sister don't make the shit any better," I cried. I was getting so mad I felt tears in my eyes.

"I haven't fucked Yasmin in months. I didn't know you were related or knew each other. But you knew when this nigga got here that he would seek you out. All those texts, phone calls, and shit, and you never thought to say, let me tell Henny about this shit." I knew my eyes were huge, but the knowledge that this nigga had my phone bugged or whatever had me seeing red. "Nope. Slow your fucking roll, Thickness. I never went through your phone or messages. His is the one that we go through, for obvious reasons."

"Then you know that–"

"Yes, I know you never answered any calls or texted back. I didn't ask about it because I figured you would tell me," he shrugged. I turned my head and looked out of the small window, seeing the outer area beginning to get busier.

"Come on," I said. I pushed him back and pulled him into the connecting room. I opened the door, and Sanchez rose, looking at the door. He used his call bell to turn his TV down as we entered.

"Tali? Henny? What the hell is going on?"

"Hey Sanchez, sorry, we just need privacy for a minute," I said, turning around.

"I was going to tell you, Henny. I was going to tell you tonight, actually. I wasn't expecting to see him today or just now," I stated. His jaw flexed, and he stepped forward, putting his hand on the base of my throat.

"Do you remember that little display downstairs earlier, Thickness?"

I frowned, trying to figure out where he was going with this. Then the entire scene with Crescent snapped to the forefront of my mind, and I swallowed.

"Ye-yes, I do."

"Then you remember that sometimes you need to take the punishment. You shouldn't have let that nigga put his hands on you, Tali. You let him touch the body that is clearly mine, Tali, and now I need to erase that shit before I am forced to erase his ass, and believe me, nothing will be left."

I began to pant at the heat in his eyes and hated myself because his words had me wet as shit. Sanchez was quiet as fuck, but I knew he was watching this shit play out.

"I don't want to get shot, Henny."

Henny chuckled as he rubbed my neck, and then he smiled.

"The only shot you're getting, Tali, is my cum down your throat."

I was drenched and couldn't help but lick my lips at his words.

"What about your punishment? I wasn't the only one in the wrong," I panted. His other hand caressed my face as his eyes narrowed.

"Whatever you come up with as a punishment, I won't protest it. But right now, I need to erase this nigga smell off of you."

"Fine."

"Now shut up and do this one thing for me."

"Wh-what's that, Henny?"

"Gag for me."

"What?" I asked incredulously. I almost choked again, but he reached up as Sanchez threw something. I saw it was a pillow, and he dropped it to my feet before he slowly pushed me to my knees. I watched as he unzipped his pants, and saliva pooled in my mouth as his hard dick appeared. I felt the head of his dick on my lips, and I opened my mouth eagerly, ready to taste him.

"GAG. FOR. ME."

His voice was a rumble as he pushed his dick to the back of my throat.

"Ahhh, shit. Here we fucking go again," Sanchez chuckled.

## CHAPTER THIRTEEN

# HENDRIX 'HENNY' PHARMA

E ven though my dick was in Tali's mouth, I was still mad as fuck. I heard what this nigga said, and even if it wasn't what it appeared, I could see in his eyes he wanted her. Ignacio was going to be a problem, and he was a problem I couldn't just dispose of because he served a purpose. If it wasn't for this nigga and his expertise in the form of cancer Tali's mother had, I would've kidnapped his ass and taken him to the *Clinic*. It took everything inside me not to pull the scalpel out of my pocket and slice his jugular open.

"Fuck," I moaned. I held Tali's head down and felt her swallowing around me as she gagged on my dick. The slurping noises from her made my dick get harder than it was when I watched her sink to her knees. I was already rock hard when I realized she was worried more about me losing my job than anything else. I let her head go, and she pulled back slowly, using her tongue to trace the vein on my length. I opened my eyes and saw Sanchez's hand over his face, shaking his head and laughing to himself.

"You can see this shit, my nigga?" I felt Tali stiffen momentarily, and I wrapped my fist in her long locs. I was glad I had informed the director of this floor that Tali and Crescent would be Sanchez's nurse and Tech when they were working, and he would be their only patient. I did it under the guise that he needed one-on-one care.

"I can, and now I wish I couldn't because...fuck!"

I chuckled as I moved my hips so Tali could continue. She must have forgotten that Sanchez may be able to see now. Tali's talented tongue licked the tip before she moved to my balls. Tali moved back to my length and sucked me in so slowly that I thought I would bust right there. The visual of her thick lips wrapped around me and her gray eyes looking into mine had my shit jumping. All thoughts in my head went blank when she wrapped her small hand around me and began to stroke as she slurped faster on my length.

"Look at you. Let me hear you gag on it, Tali," I gritted. I felt the head hitting the back of her throat repeatedly. On the next stroke, I gripped her locs tight and used my other hand to control her face. I began to fuck her face hard and fast as saliva leaked from the corner of her lips. She gagged hard, and I pulled back.

"It's all good, my nigga. She likes to be watched. You know that," I said before I pulled Tali to her feet. She moaned in displeasure as she wiped her mouth.

"Hendrix, I wasn't−"

"Stand up, Thickness," I demanded. My pants were still around my hips as I spun her around to face Sanchez. His brows were raised as he shook his head. He turned the volume up on the TV and leaned back.

"Y'all both like to live dangerously," he cleared his throat. I slid my hand down her scrub pants and into her panties, feeling her soaked pussy. Tali moaned, and I let my other hand travel across the skin of her stomach and up to her soft breast. I pinched her hardened nipple over her bra, and she moaned again, closing her eyes. "Nope, keep your eyes open. Sanchez said he's going to watch you cum," I smirked.

"Oh shit, fuck Hendrix," she whispered.

"I shouldn't let him because I know you like that shit. I shouldn't, because you let another nigga touch you," I chastised.

"Henny, I didn't—"

"Naw, Thickness, I saw it, and he's lucky I didn't cut his throat right there. And you're lucky that I love you enough to give you what you need to cum. But if that shit happens again, Tali, I'm not going to give a fuck who it is. And then I won't let you cum for a week."

"Oh my God," Tali whispered.

I had Tali facing Sanchez, who slowly looked up at me, and I didn't know why. It wasn't like he didn't know how I got down or been there when shit happened. I replayed my words and realized I said love. It was true, and it slightly surprised me that it came out so naturally. Sanchez raised a brow at me before leaning back against his pillows. I pushed Tali's pants and panties down to her ankles, then helped her step out of them. Saying the word love didn't bother me because I knew that shit six years ago. It just wasn't our time. So, if she thought this was all just a bet, she had another thing coming.

"I can't wait to get discharged," Sanchez grunted.

I chuckled and stepped back to pull the recliner chair before Tali. I locked it before I moved around it. I sat down, and Tali's thick ass was facing me. I smacked it as I used my knees to widen her stance.

"Sit on my dick, Thickness," I commanded. My hands were already around her waist, pulling her to my length that stood straight up like it knew what was coming. I had one hand around her waist and the other wrapped around her neck as she slowly lowered her wet pussy onto me. I groaned, and she groaned simultaneously as she fully sat on me. I let her get used to every inch until it was too hard not to move.

"Hendrix," she moaned. I saw her eyes blink rapidly, and her head fell back.

"I thought you liked being watched. How do you know if he's looking if your eyes are closed?"

I waited until her gray eyes opened and saw the pleasure and lust clouded in the depths. But I saw something else. Something that wasn't there earlier, and I had a feeling whatever dealing she had with Tremont had her feeling insecure or some shit. It was almost like she didn't want to let go or was now afraid to let go. "You know what, Thickness, why don't you tell me what you want? Because you were watching awfully hard downstairs, I'm starting to think you like that shit as well. You can tell me anything, Tali," I whispered in her ear. I felt her shiver, and I rotated my hips while pushing her hips down. Her thick ass slapped against my abs, and I knew I would need to change once we were done.

"I...I don't—"

I squeezed her throat and leaned her back against my chest. I bit down on her ear before I sucked her lobe into my mouth.

"I'm not that nigga, Thickness. Say it," I commanded. I let the hand on her waist move around until my finger stroked her clit. "You want to watch?"

Tali's eyes were on me, but I saw when they slid over to Sanchez.

"Oh shit. I guess that is the closest you will ever get to another threesome again, so why not? Ask him. Tell him what you want," I said. Sanchez must have heard me, because he frowned and rubbed his eyes before catching himself. I stopped moving, and Tali groaned. "Go ahead and ask. He is just as much as a freak as the rest of us," I said. Tali swallowed, and I could tell she thought this would come back to bite her in the ass. What the fuck kind of bullshit was that nigga on? If she wanted to be watched or wanted to watch, there was nothing wrong with the shit. I only drew the line at another man touching her. That would never happen again.

"Sanchez, I want to watch you cum. I want to see you stroke your dick and cum when I do," she gasped like she couldn't believe the words that came out of her mouth. I looked at Sanchez, and to his credit, he didn't say a word. I started to move again and buried my face in her neck. "Oh, my God. Oh shit," Tali moaned.

I fought not to laugh and just smiled when her core clenched around me. I scooted down slightly so I could widen my legs. I pushed Tali forward a little, but my hand around her throat kept her looking forward. Tali's pussy tightened around my dick as if her life depended on it. I could feel her walls tightening as she bounced her ass harder when I thrust upward.

"Fuck Thickness. Throw that ass back, Tali," I grunted.

"Hendrix, shit Hendrix, shit," she moaned. The noises her pussy was making from the suction it had on my dick almost had me cumming. "I'm going to cum, Hendrix. Please," Tali cried. I let her hair go to hold her down on my length. "No, no, please," she panted.

"Fuck!" I heard Sanchez, but I was focused on Tali and ensuring her thick ass wouldn't cum yet. I wasn't ready for her to get hers after that bullshit. She needed to know that shit wouldn't fly, and I had to ensure she understood that no other nigga would be deep in this pussy. She belonged to me, and her pussy walls had formed to my dick.

"Don't you dare cum, Thickness! You don't deserve to yet after hiding that nigga been contacting you from me."

"I don't think I can...I wasn't hiding—" Tali's eyes rolled back as I slowed and circled my hips before stopping abruptly, touching her clit with my thumb. She vibrated on my lap. Tali moaned loudly because I didn't give her what she wanted.

"Keep your eyes open. You asked for what you wanted, and you got it. Now, do you, sexy," I said.

"Hendrix, let me come, please," she begged.

"Naw, not yet. How would you cum when you asked Sanchez to do it with you? That's selfish, Tali. You about to nut, Sanchez?"

"Nope. I'm still working on my hand-eye coordination," he chuckled. I laughed as Tali groaned.

"Y'all are on some shit. Please, Henny," she whined. I removed my thumb from her clit and pushed her forward more. I let my fingers slide through her locs again and raised her head. I used my other hand to direct her hips to raise and slam her back down.

"No, I don't always give you what you want when you want it, Thickness, but I give you what you need, and right now, you need to take this dick."

Her expression was priceless. I laughed. She looked like she wanted to scream or cry, but Tali ground down on me as her sheath squeezed tight around me. "Damn, Tali. Ride me, baby."

Tali was so wet I could feel her juices soaking into my pants as she rode me reverse style. She was grinding down on me before she rotated her hips and bounced her pussy on my dick faster. I knew she was chasing her orgasm, and I let her, while I watched her ass bounce on me. I felt my balls drawing up as Tali's breaths became labored, and I couldn't take the shit anymore. I let her go and raised her from my lap. Before she could protest, I stood up and moved around the chair, taking her with me as my back hit the wall. I gripped her around her waist and lifted her. I managed to get each leg over my arms and lowered her back down hard. I let the wall hold me up as I began to fuck her like she wanted.

"You better keep your head up and eyes open, Tali, if you want to cum," I gritted.

"Fuck. Fuck. Fuck me, Henny. Oh God, right there. Harder, harder, please," she moaned. I bit down on my tongue as I watched the blissed-out expression on her face.

Her eyes rolled back, and she threw her head backward, arching her back. Tali's breasts were covered, and I wished I had removed her shirt. I wanted to see her nipples pebble as her climax got closer. I was in the frame of mind to say fuck the rest of the day and take her ass home and fuck her until she couldn't walk.

I slid my dick in and out of her pussy rapidly as she liked it, dragging a deep moan from the back of her throat.

"Oh, Hendrix, fuck," she cried.

She reached back, wrapping her arm around my neck and pulling my head closer. Her soft lips pressed against mine, and she opened for me. I sucked her tongue into my mouth, and she moaned. I kept my eyes on her and couldn't help chuckling when her gray eyes opened and slid to where Sanchez was. Her core clamped tightly, realizing again that he was watching and doing exactly what she asked. I felt it around my dick and saw it in her eyes. Tali pulled away from my mouth when I let one of her legs get lower than the other. It gave me a different angle, but I never slowed my pace. I hit her G-spot, and she cried. Her moaning and whispering, '*Oh my God, Hendrix! Daddy, please. Just let me cum, please,*' just made me go harder. The wetness from her pussy slid down her thighs and onto my hand. I wanted to suck my fingers, throw her ass on that bed, and stick my tongue between her slit, but I knew that would need to wait. Tali looked like she was in her element, and I knew I would be taking her ass back to *MYTH,* but this time to the lower levels. Just thinking about it had me pulling her body tighter to me as I circled my hips, pushing deeper into her pussy.

"I need to cum, Hendrix," she panted.

"Then cum Tali," I whispered against her neck. Tali groaned, and my dick throbbed in her as she came with full force around me.

"Fuck! Shit, shit." I heard Sanchez, but then I heard a door close. I opened my eyes and saw that he had gone into the bathroom. I couldn't help the laugh that escaped as Tali pulsated around me as her cream covered my dick. I never stopped fucking her through her orgasm and waited until she released all she held back.

"Pretty. You look so beautiful when you cum for me, Thickness," I praised. She panted heavily, and I could feel my own orgasm building, but I still needed to do something. I loved cumming in her heated core but needed her mouth today.

"Henny," she said, sounding drugged. I lowered her feet to the floor and turned her to face me. Her gray eyes found mine, and her mouth was slightly parted. Perfect.

"Get on your knees, Tali," I ordered. She blinked but didn't hesitate to drop down and reach for me. My hands dug into her hair as she swallowed my dick to the back of her throat. I threw my head back at the sensation when I heard a door open. I opened my eyes, expecting to see Sanchez, but Dr. Ignacio Tremont stood in the doorway with hate burning in his eyes. The sucking noise and moans from Tali made me smile. I thrust forward and held her head to the base of my dick as cum shot down her throat.

"Gag for me, Tali. Swallow it all for me, baby. Sensational."

After giving Tali what she clearly needed, I had to get her to go to my office and get scrubs. There was no way I could walk out of Sanchez's room covered in her juices without what went down becoming obvious. If we hadn't been so far in the back, we would have been heard, but I didn't give a fuck. It was enough that this nigga dared to walk in this room looking for her that had me tight as fuck. What the hell did he think this shit was? Because I didn't bring this nigga here to pursue what was mine.

As I headed toward Blackbay, where Link's casino was located, I pushed those thoughts out of my head. My thought of canceling everything for the day had happened, just not why I wanted it to happen. I had already contacted Faxx and Oz to meet me there. I didn't know what was happening, but I felt like it had something to do with this nigga Jakobe. I know good and well I shot this nigga, but he wasn't dead. The night we went back out on the street, I made that shit known we wanted his ass, and any muthafucka in Union City that was helping this nigga would die beside him. We wasted no time that night going into old clubs, bars, and homes Jakobe frequented. I didn't give a fuck about who was there or what they didn't know. By the time we left those places, they all knew the consequences of fucking with U.C.K., and they all knew if Ja showed his face, it would be in their best interest to shoot first and ask questions later.

I pulled into the parking garage and into the private parking area. Like at Emerald, the valet quickly approached my truck to park it. I stepped out and nodded to the young woman on duty.

"Should I keep it close, Henny?" she asked.

"Yeah, ma. Keep it nearby," I said, handing her the fob. I walked directly to the elevator that I knew would lead me straight to the floor where Link's office was located. The doors closed, and I stared at my reflection in the glass. I rubbed my tongue over my bottom grill, wishing I had the taste of Tali on my tongue instead of this toothpaste. The doors opened, and I stepped off, moving with purpose toward the large black doors at the end of the hall. They opened, and I saw Oz standing there as he cracked his neck. I walked in, and he closed the door behind me. Link sat behind his desk on his tablet and laptop. Faxx stood at the window, speaking urgently into his phone.

"What the fuck is so important?" I asked. Oz came over and sat in the leather chair in front of Link's desk. I looked over at Faxx, who finished his phone call, and saw his dead-eyed stare that meant somebody was about to die. I took the other seat in front of the desk and waited until Link finished what he was doing.

"Faxx, what is up with you?" I asked. I could tell Link probably hadn't even noticed us yet, and it would be nothing we could do until he did.

"This nigga Roman is using back channels to find Crescent. I was alerted to a contract out for her kidnapping on the dark web. When I checked into it, I confirmed it was legit," Faxx bit out. "I had it removed, but I had to put more men around her apartment and the hospital. At least until I can get her ass moved into my house. Then it won't be so bad," he gritted. I had opened my mouth but closed it as he explained what he was doing about the shit. Whoever this Roman was needed to be dealt with.

"Who the fuck is this nigga, and when are we taking his ass out? As a matter of fact, you need to make Crescent tell you who the fuck it is, or I will," I gritted. After tonight I knew Faxx was about to double down on finding out who this nigga Roman really was and why he wanted Crescent so badly. Once we took care of Ja, I would be right there with him. Niggas really thought they could operate in our city. They were about to fuck around and find out why that shit ain't smart at all.

"Nigga, like I told y'all niggas before, leave everything about Crescent to me. Stay the fuck away from her. I got this shit handled. Worry about your own shit," Faxx grunted. Oz laughed, but I could tell he was itching to return to Dea. I didn't know what he would do when she had to return to work or, more like, wanted to return to work.

"Faxx, you know we love Cent thicker than a biscuit ass," Oz smirked.

"I don't know why any of y'all are fucking with me about this knowing damn well I will fucking shoot you," he boomed. We all turned to Link when we heard him close his laptop. He leaned back in his chair and stared at the wall behind us. Oz turned around and looked at the wall to see if something was there before looking back his way.

"What the fuck is this nigga looking at?" he said to no one. I stared at Link because I knew his mind was working, but I didn't know on what. Then his black gaze shifted like he just realized we all were sitting there waiting for his ass.

"We have three problems, and two of them we need to take care of tonight," he stated.

"No, we have one. We need to handle Ja because his bitch ass will be where the *Silk* is tonight for sure," I retorted.

"Yes, that is one of the problems."

"And the other?" Oz asked as my frown deepened.

"Second is the shipment that supplies Big Pharma has been targeted for a hijacking. It will be hit tonight, and I know Jakobe has a hand in that. He's trying to keep us distracted," Link responded. My anger and irritation grew to new levels at this nigga's audacity like he wasn't the one in the wrong.

"How the fuck does he know about it?"

"I don't think he did it on his own. I think this came down from the Cartel. Someone in the warehouses where our drugs are held has been talking, but luckily there is surveillance all over our trucks. They are being followed and have been for a few days now. Tonight will be the best moment to make a move because they will be on trucking roads," he explained.

"Fuck," I roared. I clamped my mouth shut and reined in my anger on the bullshit. I had to keep a level head about it, or I couldn't think all this shit through thoroughly as I knew it would need to. "And the third problem," I gritted. Link turned his head and leveled his gaze on Oz. I didn't have to look to see Oz go on alert as he sat forward.

"I received an alert about Alex Tilderman. He has come into possession of some footage that he will use to try to blackmail you," Link sighed.

"What? What the fuck can this bitch have on me? All the shit we have on this nasty bastard, and he's what? Going to try to use my club or something?"

"I sent the video to your email, but you better talk to Nia's ass. Alex now knows that the Governor isn't the father of her child. Either way, it isn't stopping the threat to her life and anyone close to her," Link sucked his teeth.

"What the fuck do you mean not his kid? I mean, I guess it's possible she was fucking someone else, but this was her play. Why the fuck didn't she give me a heads-up about this shit?"

Link looked at Faxx, then back to Oz, and pressed his lips together. "What the fuck are you not saying, my nigga?" Oz demanded. I raised a brow. I wanted to know this shit as well because anything that could fuck shit up for us is a problem. If the kid wasn't Wes's child, that was fine. It's whatever but keeping us in the dark about it was another thing.

"I think it would be best if you look at that shit for yourself, but I will say I don't think Wes bitch ass knows anything about this. I think Alex is acting for himself because he probably feels the Governor is on his way out the door."

"Fuck! Is this some shit I need to be worried about at this moment? Am I going to have to kill the real father or something?"

"Naw, naw, it's...naw. This can be put on hold for now. We need to focus on this shipment and the warehouse," Link chuckled. Oz narrowed his eyes at Link, but we both knew that if he said it could wait, it could wait. I could feel the aggravation leaking from Oz at the knowledge Nia was fucking up the plans he had set in motion, but it would wait for now.

"Alright, then it will hold. The solution is simple. Oz and I will hit the warehouse and get Jakobe, and whoever else is with his ass, and you and Faxx will take the truck. We do this right and do it simultaneously," I said, looking between them. I felt my palm itching to wrap around that niggas throat, and I could visualize sending his severed head back to his father.

"Bet." They each nodded as Link hit a button on his desk. We turned around to face a large screen so we could view each area to formulate every single contingency plan we could come up with.

"Two in the morning, it's a go. I want to hit them hard and leave no witnesses," I said, looking at all of them.

"Did I tell y'all I think Dea wants to use a cleaver on Katrice?" Oz asked.

I looked at Lennox like he had lost his mind because this nigga was smiling like that shit was a good thing. I opened my mouth to say something, then thought better of it. Because what if it was a good thing? Had we corrupted them so badly that our crazy was rubbing off onto them? I knew

Tali wasn't far behind if Dea could even think about doing something like that. Maybe we should have left them alone instead of pulling them into our world, but it was too late for Tali when she stepped back into Union City. Now I would need to ensure Tali understood that this bet shit was over. If she didn't catch onto it earlier, she would before I left out for the night. Tali belonged here in Union City with her family. But most of all, she belonged with me.

# CHAPTER FOURTEEN

## TALI SAUNDERS

I felt like everyone on the unit could tell I was just bustin' it open when I left Sanchez's room. But I knew it was all in my imagination, just like the fact Hendrix said he loved me. If anything, he was in love with having sex with me and the knowledge that I didn't flinch at the public sex he liked to have. Once I finished my shift and returned home, I pulled up to my assigned parking space, but a sexy-as-hell burgundy Bentley SUV was in my spot. I started to get pissed the hell off until my eyes widened at the license plate.

*PLATINUM18*

I forgot to breathe until a tap at my window snapped me out of it. I looked up and saw Milo signaling for me to put my car in park. I was simply told I should gather everything I wanted out of my car and put it in the new one so he could take it.

*What. The. Fuck.*

I didn't know if this gift of a luxury vehicle was because he thought he loved me or just another way to control the situation. Just like fucking after he saw me with Tre was another form of his controlling nature. I shook my head, thinking about the after of that crazy ass situation. I had to bring Henny's scrubs because his clothes were covered in my cum. When I came back to the room, I could barely look at Sanchez. I mumbled a quick 'Let me clock in and check in at the nurse's station' before I damn near ran out of the room. I knew Henny would question me about it later, but it wasn't the reason he was probably thinking. It wasn't so much having sex in front of Sanchez because it wasn't the first time. It was mainly old insecurities rearing their heads. I tried brushing it off and continued going about my day, but I knew I was walking funny by the way Crescent frowned at me every time we made a move. I could barely look at her or Sanchez when we did his medications. I knew I would need to tell him it wasn't about him.

It was like I was waiting for the other shoe to drop and for Henny to ask me about the Sanchez situation. Why the fuck would I ask Sanchez to do that shit? I should've just let it have been enough that he was watching, but Henny made me feel so comfortable. The words just fell from my lips, and when Sanchez said nothing and just stood up while watching me, I almost swallowed my tongue. I saw the slight furrow of his brows after he took his eyes away from Henny, like asking for permission or something. I wondered just how well he was seeing, but when I did the test on him per Henny's instructions, it confirmed his vision was sixty-two percent better than when he awoke from surgery. So, knowing that, I knew damn well he was watching and could see us just fine. But when he pulled out his thick dick and stroked it, I felt my core clench so tight around Henny I thought I was snapping him in half.

Sanchez was so fucking thick I didn't know how this nigga wasn't tipping over. He had to be about eight inches, but this niggas dick was about as thick as a fucking twelve-ounce can of soda.

Then I spent most of my time hiding in Mama's room so Crescent couldn't grill me about why I was acting weird. That was easily done, though, because she seemed preoccupied with her own thoughts.

"Fuck," I groaned. Just thinking about how he stroked his length and then nutted when I came had my knees weak as fuck.

"Tali? My bad, Thickness, my meeting ran late. I know I said I wanted to cook, but I brought something from Emerald," Henny apologized. When he texted and said he would bring some food for us and would be late, I knew I needed to do something to occupy my thoughts. I sighed and finished the last layer of fruit on my *Berry Tres Leches Cake*. At least my ass got the baking gene from Mama, because I couldn't cook. The only dish I could make was spaghetti. Shandea managed to get the cooking and baking down, but it was all good because she would make me whatever I wanted. Hendrix knew his way around a kitchen, and I figured his ass could've been a damn chef if he wasn't a doctor. Bags of delicious-smelling food sat on the counter on the other side of the cake. I felt his hands on my hips and his lips on the side of my neck.

"That cake looks good as shit. I guess this is why you said no dessert," he whispered along my skin. Henny was hard as he pressed up against me, and my head fell back on his chest. When he started to push up his tee shirt that I was wearing, I turned my head to face him. Henny pulled back, and I caught sight of his platinum grills flashing when he licked his lips. He leaned down and kissed me before pulling away. I frowned because he wasn't dressed as Hendrix, so I knew the meeting was different.

"Everything okay?"

"Yeah, it's all good. Just a lot of shit happening as usual, but nothing to worry about. We have it handled," he said. He looked at the cake again, and I reached out, taking one of the raspberries and dipping it into the whipped cream frosting that was left in the bowl. I held it out for him to eat it, and he smiled, flashing his teeth at me.

"I think y'all have some kind of sick fascination with fruit all of a sudden," he claimed.

I bit my lips and pulled my hand back because I wasn't even thinking about that shit. I didn't move in time because he caught my wrist. He leaned down to take it into his mouth. I raised my brows, trying not to laugh because when he's right, he's right. After seeing that display the other day, I wanted to see what would happen. At least, that is what I told myself. I really wanted to know his reaction. Would he say anything about it? Would he say I was wrong in watching them? I picked up a plump, juicy strawberry, its glossy red surface glistening as I covered it in a thick layer of creamy frosting. I knew just how sweet the frosting was, but it was like it was calling out to him, enticing him to take a bite.

"Maybe. I mean, I'm not asking for a competition or anything," I shrugged.

I really wanted to see what he would do. I held it out briefly before he leaned forward again, holding my eyes as he sank his teeth into the strawberry. The juice from the flesh burst open, flooding his mouth with a burst of tangy sweetness I knew because I had tried them before I started the cake. The frosting on top added a rich, creamy note that complemented the fruit perfectly, and I heard the rumble in his chest. Henny closed his eyes and savored the taste, letting the flavors dance across his tongue while licking the juice from his lips. He leaned in again, eating the rest of the strawberry from my hand. His lips wrapped around my fingers, and he sucked them into his mouth.

"Oh fuck," I whispered.

My other hand gripped the counter as I watched him lick the juice between my fingers. He let my fingers slide out his mouth and then caged me against the counter. He dropped his head, and I wasted no time opening my mouth. He kissed me, and the combination of the tart, juicy strawberry and the sweet, velvety frosting was pure bliss. I couldn't help but marvel at the texture of the frosting on his tongue as it danced with mine. His kiss was slow, smooth, and silky, with just the right amount of pressure. The sweetness of the strawberry was perfectly balanced, not overly sugary but just enough to enhance the natural sweetness, making his kiss feel like a fucking meal. I was wet as hell and could feel my heart beating out of my chest, but I was still sore from earlier today. It still didn't stop me from wanting whatever he was willing to put down.

Henny pulled back, and I followed his movement. He chuckled and shook his head at me before kissing my forehead.

"I think that little box needs a rest, Thickness," he licked his bottom lip.

"You are not wrong," I laughed.

"It is good, though. The perfect combination of sweet, creamy, and juicy. Just like your pussy," he gritted. "Go sit down so we can eat before I fuck you on this island," he insisted. I saw the bulge in his pants and knew he wasn't playing.

"I mean..."

"Tali!"

"Okay, okay, I'll get the plates," I snorted.

I sat down at the table, and he took out the food. My stomach rumbled at the scent. Henny fixed our plates, and I waited until he sat down before eating. I had a lot on my mind and a ton of shit I wanted to say but didn't know where to start. I was looking at my food, but I knew damn well he was staring at me while he chewed. This nigga was waiting me out. He was going to make me start the conversation first, and I knew the reason why. He wanted to see where my head was because I wanted the same thing. *What is this that we are doing? What does he want out of all of this?* I sat my fork down and picked up the glass of white wine I had poured when I started to bake the cake.

"Okay. So, I can tell you don't know what to say. I was giving you time to speak on whatever you wanted, but since you're so quiet, I will start," he smirked. He wiped his mouth and picked up his glass of *Henny,* taking it to the head. I almost spit out my wine because he called me out on my shit. I licked my lips and opened my mouth, but he beat me to it. "How about we start easy? Did you like your car?"

My eyes widened because, out of all the things, I did not expect him to bring that up. But since we were on it, I wanted to know what he was thinking. There was no way I could accept that car. I make good money, but there was no way I could afford that car payment.

"It's beautiful, but what the hell were you thinking getting me that thing? There is no way I can afford that payment, especially if we will be helping Mama if anything else comes up," I said. I sat my glass down on the table. Henny sat back in the chair, squinting at me before running a hand over his goatee.

"So you're telling me that you don't like it. We can choose another," he said. Henny picked up his fork and put a piece of steak in his mouth.

"That is not what I said. I love the car. I do, but..."

"But what?"

"Why? Why do you feel the need to do this? Let's be honest, Henny, this is a sexual thing, and once it's over, it's over. What do you even know about me for real?" I laughed. It wasn't one of hilarity but resignation.

"What do you mean what do I know? Since you've been back here, you have been with me. I know your passions, business mind, and what you want to achieve. The only thing I want to do is foster that, and I will. Trust me. I saw that when I met you from day one. I have a sense like that, and it never steers me wrong. I know that you can't cook, you like to read health journals instead of watching TV, and you hate the unfairness of the health care system. Just like me. I also know that you want to work for a women's center that is centered around helping women find natural ways to balance their bodies. While also giving them the care they need and a safe space, especially for black women, to speak about their health problems and be listened to. You didn't need to write that thesis paper on women of color and healthcare, but you did it anyway. It was very insightful, just like I knew it would be. I also knew when I wrote that prescription, you wouldn't put that into your body," he stated.

I was too stunned to speak, so I sipped my wine again before licking my lips. He raised a brow at me, and I cleared my throat.

"How? How do you know all that?"

"Because I care enough to learn those things. I see in you who I wanted to become before my mother died. I saw a smart young black person that wanted to make a difference. I saw your determination and stance about what you wanted in life. I had that Women's Center built for you. And no, I didn't know when you would return, but I knew once shit was in place, I would follow that feeling and come get your ass. Believe me. It wouldn't have taken much because Oz spoke to Dea every day. So all your accomplishments, goals, and ideas were proudly told to us by Dea. A lot has happened in six years, but my feelings about you never changed."

I stared at him because first, that is some stalker ass shit, but at the same time, WHAT! He built me a center, and I knew that had to be years in the making. I sighed again and leaned back in my chair.

"I will not deny what you're saying because I also felt it that night. As a matter of fact, I ran from it. I couldn't have you holding me back. Your presence even now feels larger than life, and six years ago, I needed to find myself. Only, I continued looking for someone like you. I searched for that same feeling. Except that when you looked at me, touched me, I already knew, but I wasn't ready then," I sighed.

"You're ready now, though."

"I...I don't know. Knowing I was just here for a bet was different, but all this....it's a lot to take in. Even the car! How am I going to afford that because I refuse to leach off you, Henny?" I pursed my lips.

"Okay. Okay, we will not act like I don't have the money to purchase a vehicle outright. What we also aren't going to do is act as though you're stupid, Tali."

"Nigga what?"

"Nigga what? What do you mean? I know you heard me when I said I was on the board. I know you heard me say I take care of the people I care about, and I know you heard me when I said I loved you. We not about to play games, Tali," he challenged. My eyes widened, and his brows raised. That car question was a fucking setup if I'd ever seen one, and I walked right into it. I cleared my throat and picked up my wine, taking another sip.

"First off, I'm not acting any kind of way. Yes, I heard you when you said all those things, and yes, I know you have money. But that money ain't mine. So what would I look like presuming something? And when you say you are on the board, what does that mean exactly? You got the board in hand or—"

"It means exactly what the hell I said. Between me and the others, we are the board. Union is my fucking hospital, just like the city."

I stared at him for a long moment as things seemed to connect in my head. I knew who he was and what he was. I heard Crescent say they are U.C.K. They are the Union City Kings. They are on top, but I didn't think that meant...

"Those programs Dea and I signed Mama up for," I trailed off.

"Are real programs I put in place for people needing help. The people of this City deserve just as much care as everyone else. Yes, I make money off the legal and illegal side of it, but so what. It helps others, and it lines my pockets. Just because I can get the hospital a huge tax write-off doesn't mean anything other than I play the game everyone else does. You have to play the game to get ahead, Tali. As for your mother, yes, she was accepted, but I paid all that shit myself because she is family. Point blank, period. The house situation was handled as well. Oz bought the bank that owned the loan for her house and that bitches boutique."

"What?" All the information he just dropped rolled around in my head, repeating itself as my eyes bugged out. I knew I had to talk to Dea because there was no way she knew this and didn't tell me.

"I get it. Y'all want to feel as though you don't need to rely on us, and you probably would've figured it all out on your own, but–"

"But! But what? You and Oz just decided all this for us? Where we live. What car will we drive, and what bills will we pay? That is heavy-handed, Hendrix."

I knew I wasn't upset about what they did because it said a lot. It said a lot without him even needing to say I love you. I was mad because...

"And where you work. You're damn right. We are heavy-handed. We need to be to get shit done. You are staring at me with your mouth open because you can't even come up with a reason as to why you are mad. Your man is taking care of you. That's all you need to worry about," he smirked.

"What the fuck you say?"

Henny pushed away from the table, and I could see his slight struggle at not clearing and cleaning the table. I don't know why that had me trying to hold back a laugh, but I failed and slapped a hand to my mouth.

"Shut up. You know I have OCD issues. NOW, get up."

Henny pulled me to my feet and then sat in my chair, pulling me down to sit on his lap.

"Let me ask you this one thing," I said. I stared into his eyes, ensuring I held eye contact with him so I knew if he was lying.

"What the fuck is wrong with you all? Seriously, do you even know what love is? Can you even feel that, or is this more of an obsession for you? I need to know because I feel like there is so much more that I'll be finding out, and I won't lie, I am scared as shit. Yes, you shot people in the club, but that was self-defense. Even when you admitted to taking out X, I understood why. But what I saw on your face when you entered my mother's hospital room looked terrifying. I thought you would kill Tre right there before my eyes," I finished.

"Because I was going to kill him right there in front of you. If you hadn't gotten in my space, I was about two seconds from cutting his throat in that room. I don't know what you and that nigga had going on, but I will give you another warning, Tali. If you let him touch you again, I will fucking cut his hands off and have his organs donated. No one will ever find a trace of that nigga. As for what is wrong with us, it isn't anything that we cannot control. And do I know what love is? I do. Have I felt it other than for my family? Nope. How do I know that what I said was true is the fact I knew you were different when I put you in my bed six years ago," he explained. "I'm saying all this, but you still haven't said anything. How the fuck do I know what you feel? Do I care if you say it back? No, I don't."

"What! You make no sense, Hendrix. How the hell do you not care if I reciprocate your feelings?"

"Because you say it in your sleep every night. You've said I love you, Hendrix, in your sleep every night when you roll onto my chest."

I sat there staring at him, trying to remember what I had said. Did I feel it? Yes, but I never said the shit out loud because I would run. There was no way I could have stayed here knowing this would end eventually, and my feelings would've been caught up.

"You're making that shit up," I laughed.

"Tali, you can't tell me you don't feel that shit when I am deep in that pussy. I make sure you stare at me when I push in so deep I make your back bow and your legs shake. I ensured we connected on a deeper level the moment I brought you home. I told you I wanted you obsessed with me, and I meant that shit. Your soul is tied to me, Thickness. Look in my eyes and tell me I'm lying," he ordered, but I couldn't. "I want you to understand that doesn't mean I am not possessive and obsessed with you because I am. So do me a favor and stay the fuck away from that nigga. I want to ensure your Mama has the best, but I will find someone else if I have to. I don't give a fuck what it will cost," he demanded.

"Don't kill him, Hendrix," I said quickly. The words felt clumsy on my tongue, and I couldn't believe I was having this conversation.

"Are you trying to protect this nigga," he grimaced. His hand came up, squeezing my face but not hurting me as he looked for something in my gaze.

"No. No, I'm not. I just don't think he is worth it."

Henny grunted and let my face go, but his hand only slid to my throat.

"You seem to be taking this a little too well. Am I going to leave tonight and only find that you packed your shit and ran?"

I laughed because he was right. I was taking it too well. I wasn't, really. I was just processing all of it.

"Run where, Henny? From what I can tell, even if I called my job and requested another assignment, it wouldn't happen. Not to mention where would I go when you have niggas following me around and shit? I think running is long out of the picture now. It's just I think I need to process all of this in my own time. But, regarding...regarding what you said about handling, it will need more explaining," I said. Henny looked away, and I thought that would finally make him close down on me. He was never a talker anyway or gave up information about himself like that, but I needed to know. I could see the same signs in him as Dea said she saw in Oz. He was clearly insane, and I clearly liked the shit. What did that say about me? But just how crazy were they? Seeing Katrice kidnapped and tied up in a fucking barn should tell me what I needed to know, but I could sense there was more. And that was what I needed to know because if I was going to stay, I needed to know all of Hendrix Pharma. Not just what he wanted me to know until it blew up in my face.

"I think the handling part will need to be shown. It just won't be right now, but I will. I honestly don't want you even dealing with that side of me. I want you in the hospital, doing what you got a degree for, and not worried about my shit."

"I will do what I want to do, Henny. But I refuse to walk around blindly. If this between us is serious, I need to know who I'm letting into my body, mind, and heart. I need to know every side of you. I need to see all the personalities I know you have," I stated. "This won't work otherwise."

Henny was quiet for so long that I moved to get up to clean off the table.

"Naw, sit your ass right here. I hear what you say, Tali. But I will warn you, once you see it, ain't no turning back. Dea made that choice with less time. I am giving you time. Think about everything we've talked about and then make a decision. I'll let you go if you decide it might be too much," he proposed.

"See, that was the first lie you told me. I don't believe you would let me go," I stated. Henny pulled me closer by my throat and kept his eyes on me as he licked my lips. I could feel his dick hard as hell beneath me, and I knew my pussy was dripping at his actions.

"That's because you're as smart as I always believed you were. I let you walk out of my life once, and I'll be damned if I let you do it again. I'll burn this fucking city to the ground until I find you and bring you back. You are mine, Thickness."

"Just like you are mine, Hendrix," I panted.

"I don't see a problem with that."

"So you're not Yasmin's?"

"Fuck Yasmin. If I had known you were related to her, I would have never fucked that girl. She doesn't and has never meant shit to me. I'll kill her."

"What?" I squeaked.

"Shut up and feed me my dessert," he chuckled before pushing my plate to the side and placing me on the table. His tee shirt rose up around my hips as my ass met the glass table. Henny spread my legs apart, quickly removing the small piece of fabric covering my core. He pulled his chair close to the table and whispered, *'Good food, good meat, good God, now I'm going to eat'* before his tongue traveled from my ass to my clit.

"Oh my God, you are crazy," I moaned as my eyes rolled to the back of my head. I still couldn't forget the psychotic look in his eyes when he said, *I'll kill her* because I didn't think this nigga was lying. Yasmin was family, but if she had anything to do with what happened to Dea, I would take her out myself. The sad part was knowing this bitch was trying to take Hendrix down when he had done so much for Union City. Even if she had nothing to do with what Katrice's ignorant ass did to Dea, she was fucking with Henny, and I knew I couldn't stand for that shit, either.

Henny's hand snaked up my body, pushing my chest down so I could lie flat on the table. He sat at the edge of the chair as he tongue fucked my entrance.

"Shit, Hendrix, please, don't stop," I moaned. Henny's tongue made circles around my clit before he sucked the pearl into his mouth. He pulled away, making me groan at the loss of the heat of his mouth.

"I told you that you tasted like the strawberry juices and frosting. Fuck, the smell of you is about to make me cum," Hendrix growled.

My quick disappointment was replaced by instant pleasure when his long wide tongue swiped up my slit. My core clenched, screaming to be filled with his finger, tongue, or his dick. At this point, I didn't care which. Henny sucked my clit into his heated mouth, and his tongue worked on that bundle of nerves causing me to squirm. I felt his hands on my thighs as he opened me up further, growling into my pussy. The vibration made me reach out for his head and hold his face down as I rode his tongue. Henny feasted on me like the dinner he called me. I shifted, trying to move away from his mouth as I shook from the pleasure running up and down my spine.

"Oh shit, I'm going to cum, baby. Fuck," I moaned. His hands slid up my thighs, and I felt them clamp down on my hips to prevent me from running.

"Don't fucking run, Tali. Didn't I say this is my pussy," he grunted. I opened my eyes and looked down at him. He held my gaze while lowering his mouth back between my legs. His tongue slipped into my center as deep as he could go. I moaned so loud that I knew if someone was standing outside of the door, they heard me.

"Oh fuck!" I screamed. I felt his grip loosen, and his hand left my hip. I felt his fingers trailing against my skin and up my inner thighs. Henny leaned back and began playing with my folds while watching. A finger pressed against my entrance, and he licked his thick lips. "Yes, please, baby. Please, Hendrix," I cried. Henny's finger slipped inside me and twisted upward directly on my G-spot while wiggling. He leaned forward and bit down on my clit. "Ahh," I screamed before he sucked it lightly into his mouth. He fucked me with his fingers while circling my clit softly like he was making love to it. He pulled back slightly, but I could feel his breath against my pussy as he panted. A third finger slid inside me, and he began to pump faster as the pressure built.

"Say it, Tali. Tell me," he demanded. I was screaming already as my orgasm came on fast and hard. "Tell me what I want to hear, Tali," he commanded. His guttural words shook my body, and my nipples hardened as I screamed what I instinctively knew he wanted to hear.

"Hendrix! Hendrix! Oh shit, baby, I love you. I love you, Hendrix. Fuck, fuck, shit! Oh God," I cried.

"That's right, Thickness. Cum for Daddy, Sexy," he said. The feeling of bliss and heat rolled through me like a tsunami of pleasure as I gushed over his fingers and the table. I could feel my juices running down my slit and on my thighs. I could hear myself babbling and mumbling about how much I wanted him, his dick, his tongue, and whatever else he would give me.

"By the time tonight is over, you won't be able to say my name without following up with I love you. I told you, Thickness, I want you obsessed, and you will be," he promised. I managed to open my eyes, and his honey-brown eyes had darkened. Henny rotated his fingers in my pussy, pressing his thumb against my other hole. I moaned at the contact, and he smiled. I remembered before it scared the hell out of me but now... I was ready for it.

"Don't tease me with that moan, Tali. You weren't ready for it before, but you're going to take this dick right here soon, Tali," Henny said, tapping my hole while twisting his fingers to stretch my pussy. Henny dived back between my thighs and slurped my lips and clit into his mouth. His fingers continued their assault while I came repeatedly, screaming his name. My eyes popped open when that thumb slid into me slightly. "You are so tight, Thickness. I think you'll take me soon."

Henny pulled his hand away from my core and my ass. He turned his head to the side and kissed my inner thighs. I was cum drunk off his administrations and needy for his length to fill me. I wanted him more than I wanted him in the hospital. My nipples were hard, and my core clenched like it was trying to grab onto something. I might have eaten, but my pussy was acting like it was starving, and only one thing would fill it.

Henny scooped me off the table, and I wrapped my legs around his waist.

"I'm still sore, baby," I whispered against his ear. His hands squeezed my ass, and his lips kissed my exposed shoulder. He lay me down on his bed, and I looked up at him. His hands caressed my legs, causing aftershocks throughout my body as he held my gaze. His words replayed through my mind, *'I make sure you stare at me when I push in so deep I make your back bow and your legs shake,'* I realized he was starting that shit right now. He wasn't lying about it, and I could feel his possession claiming me the longer I held his gaze.

*This nigga.*

"You know damn well I would never do anything to hurt you unless I knew the pain would make you cum," he smirked. His words and the glint of his grills had my mind going in every dirty direction. There were plenty of things I wanted him to do to me. My eyes widened, and his smirk turned into a large smile. "I think I might need to take someone to the real *MYTH*," he grunted. I swallowed, knowing about the lower levels through Crescent. I moaned without realizing it, and he chuckled. I licked my lips as I watched him slide his dark jeans and boxer briefs to the floor. Then he took off his black shirt, and my mouth always watered when I saw his smooth dark brown skin and the muscles that covered his body. I bit my lip as his thick chocolate-dipped dick bounced out, curving to the left. My legs fell apart as he climbed over me, ready to give me all ten inches. "You look like you want to suck my dick, Thickness. Is that what you want to do?"

"Yes, I want you in my mouth. I want you to fuck my face like you would fuck my pussy," I panted. Henny's hands never stopped moving because his shirt was over my head and tossed to the floor. My breast sat up and bare. He stared at me while lowering his head to take a nipple into his mouth. I hissed out when he bit down but moaned when he sucked the pain away. I felt the head of his length sliding between my folds, and I almost cried as he pulled back.

"Hang your head over the side of the bed, Tali," he ordered. The honey-brown of his eyes seemed to darken more as he watched me do what he asked. My locs spilled over the edge of the bed, and he stepped forward. His heavy sack was tight, and I wanted to lick and suck them into my mouth. I started believing him about the fruit shit because I wanted to taste his dick like a chocolate-covered banana. I wanted to suck him until his cum was running down my throat.

"Eat this dick, Tali. You like to gag, right? I want you to gag on it, Thickness," he gritted.

My mouth was open, but I widened my eyes at his words because I could still hear the anger in them. Henny was still mad as hell about Tre. I knew I would need to clarify to Tre that our only contact would be about my mother's care, and if he didn't respect my boundaries, I would let Dea handle any interaction. Henny's jaw flexed, and his grills glinted at me in the low light. His dick jumped as he slid between my lips. "Wider, Tali. Open wider for me."

He moved slowly, pulling out and pushing back into my mouth while looking down at me. His hands cradled the sides of my face. His grills flashed each time he pulled back. His hips began to move faster, and his dick slid further and further down my throat.

"Mmm," I moaned. My mouth was full, and the head of his length hit my tonsils, but I didn't gag. I breathed through my nose, taking every inch he would give me.

"I thought I said to gag Tali," Henny said, leaning forward. His large hands gripped my face tighter as he pushed further down my throat. This nigga knew he wasn't small, but I took that shit because I asked for it. I swallowed around him while my hands found my clit. Henny pulled back and pushed back in repeatedly, hitting the back of my throat, and this time I did gag. I gagged so hard I had to suck in air when he pulled back. My fingers were moving, and my hips rose off the bed.

"That's right, Thickness. Breathe through your nose, Tali," he gritted. "Show me how much you can take for me, Sexy."

The bass in his demanding tone had my nipples getting tighter and consumed my thoughts, making my pussy slicker. Henny barely allowed me to catch my breath before his dick was shoved back down my throat. His hands began to massage my neck and shoulders while he thrusted deeply, giving me what I asked for. A whimper escaped my lips when he hit the back of my throat and groaned out my name. "Tali. Fuck Tali," Henny moaned. I felt his dick throb at that moment. His thrusts became faster, harder, and less in rhythm as he roared. "Fuck! Fuck!" I felt his hot seed spill and splash the back of my throat, and I swallowed, loving his taste. My finger never stopped moving while he pumped every last drop of his cum down my throat until it spilled from the sides of my mouth. "Swallow it, Tali," he groaned, breath hitching. He pulled out of my mouth. I could feel the burn from my mouth being stretched, and I loved it. I strained to lick more of him from his tip, but he stepped back, breathing raggedly. My eyes went to his, and I saw the grin across his face as he fisted his length. My eyes dropped lower to see he was already getting hard again.

"Hendrix," I whispered. I licked the corners of my mouth while he watched me pleasure myself. He stepped closer, looking at my mouth as it opened when a small climax hit me. Henny laid his dick on my tongue, and I sucked him inside, letting my tongue roam over his dick as I hollowed out my cheeks. I let the suction of my mouth drive him crazy so he couldn't take it anymore. I wanted my name to fall from his lips again like a prayer.

"Fuck, Tali! Tali, Thickness, shit," he moaned before pulling away.

I stared up at him, and he stood over me. Henny walked around the large bed, and I kept my eyes on him as he climbed onto the bed from the other end. Henny hovered over me before snaking his arms around my waist and pulling me into the middle of the bed. "What did I tell you to say when you screamed my name? Don't let me need to remind you, Tali. I don't see a problem slapping that thick ass," Henny grunted while maneuvering my body beneath his. He pushed my hand away from my clit and placed both of my hands above my head. I couldn't help the satisfied look on my face at the wild possession in his eyes. I think I was slowly going crazy because I liked the look he was giving me. What in the hell was wrong with me? His possessiveness had my body on fire, and I felt my clit throb and my pussy leak juices down my thighs. I knew I had gotten to him just as badly as he was getting to me. Thoughts of him fucking Yasmin or any other bitch had me needing to make sure he thought about nothing but me. His thoughts should be about this mouth and this pussy. Only.

*Yeah, I'm losing it.*

"Obsessed. I can see it in your gray eyes, Thickness—just how I want you to be. Let's see how much crazier I can make you," Henny threatened. I closed my eyes at his words because he knew what he was doing to me. "Look at me!" My eyes snapped open, and he smiled. My heart picked up as he kept a tight grip on my wrists with his one hand. I felt the head of his dick at the entrance of my core. I wiggled, trying to get him inside me.

"Hendrix, please," I moaned, and he stared at me. He licked my lips, and I opened them, letting him take possession of my mouth. He sucked my tongue while rubbing himself through my folds, but not penetrating. I cried every time he bumped my clit with his head. "Hendrix, I love you. Please," I panted. I needed him inside of me.

"Finally, you figured out what you needed to say. Now come ride my dick, Tali," he whispered against my lips. Henny moved and had me sitting up. He positioned himself at the head of the bed. His legs were spread as he fisted his dick, watching me while he stroked his long thick length. Henny only stopped stroking to squeeze the head, rubbing his pre-cum over it before continuing. I slowly crawled up his body, licking every tattoo and his abs until my legs were spread apart, straddling him. He lined up with my core and waited for me. I touched his chest as I slowly sank down on his throbbing dick. I moaned, throwing my head back at the pleasure coursing throughout my body. My pussy was tight and still sore, but the slight pain was nothing compared to the tingling feeling running through me.

"What are you doing to me? How are you doing this?" I asked. I didn't know if I should say it aloud or to myself because I didn't know if I wanted the answer. I felt Henny's hand leave my waist as he rocked into me deeper. His fingers played with my nipples, but soon his other hand moved to wrap around my neck. He brought me forward as he thrust upward, and I felt his tongue against my lips as he squeezed my throat. "Fuck yes. Yes, yes," I moaned against his lips as I circled my hips. I felt my pussy tighten around Henny like a vice when his other hand dropped to my waist and slammed me hard onto him. The sounds of my ass slapping against his thighs made me wetter, if possible.

"It's not me, sexy. It's all you and your obsession. Take your dick like you know how to," Henny whispered. I grinded against him, and he pulled me to him. I opened my eyes, and he was watching me. He smiled at what I knew was my blissed-out expression only had me moving faster. His grip got tighter, and my eyes rolled back from the sensation. He held my hips down and jacked his length up into me.

"Oh, shit. Yes, Hendrix! Hendrix, baby, right there. Hendrix, I-I love-love," I cried as his grip grew tighter. My head spun, and I was pretty sure I stopped breathing as I felt the powerful orgasm rushing from the base of my spine. I rocked my hips faster, chasing the orgasm I knew was coming. "Oh, fuck!" I screamed. Henny growled into my ear as he slammed into my channel harder and deeper.

Henny leaned back against the headboard, and his grip left my throat. Both his hands landed on my ass as he pushed me down harder and faster, making the skin-to-skin contact echo around the room. My ass slapped against him while Henny spread my cheeks apart, using them to slam me down on his long dick. Henny was deep and stretching me out so much that I knew he was making my pussy his home. It would only know his dick and the curve of it when it hit spots no one else ever had. "Hendrix! Oh God, I can't...I can't, please, please, oh God, please, I can't take it," I moaned, but he didn't stop. He was balls deep inside me. My mouth fell open, and I swear drool dribbled out.

"Don't you run from me, Tali! Take your dick, baby. It's what you wanted. You can take it," he demanded.

Henny drove deeper into me, causing my walls to spasm around him. My nails clawed at his chest as I took all of him. Henny leaned closer, and I felt his teeth graze my ear lobe before I heard his deep voice in my ear.

"I want to tie you down, where people can see me fuck you like this. I'll let them watch, but they will never touch you, Tali. I'm going to take you to *MYTH* and show you what you missed for six years," he grunted. My eyes rolled backward at his words, but the knowledge he knew what I wanted and felt comfortable giving it to me had my core clasping around him. "Mmmm, yes, Thickness. You like that idea."

"Shit! Fuck, Got damn! Hendrix! Hendrix! Hendrix, I love you. Please, I need to cum," I cried.

"Fuck, Tali," he panted. Henny lifted me off his length, and the loss of him filling me had me crying out in displeasure. He had me under him in no time, spreading my legs wide. I blinked rapidly as I tried to catch my breath. There wasn't time because Henny was inside of me in a second.

"Damn, Tali. Let Daddy inside, Thickness. I want you to take all this dick. I want you to nut on it, cum all on this dick," he hissed. Henny pulled out to the tip, then sank deeper into my core.

"Oh God, Hendrix! Right there, Daddy. Hendrix," I screamed as I rocked my hips, and he groaned. I dug my nails into his back and knew I would leave marks, but I didn't care.

"That's what I want to hear. Scream for me, Tali."

Hendrix was wild as fuck, but I loved it. He leaned back and moved my legs over his shoulders without breaking his stroke. Henny used my legs over his shoulders to pull me forward as I twerked my ass on his dick. His fast-moving pace would have us both cumming so hard we wouldn't know which way was up.

I thrashed my head from side-to-side as he took me roughly, thoroughly, and possessively. Henny leaned forward, sucking my nipples into his mouth. His tongue moved over my hard nipple, driving me crazy.

"Hen—Hendrix! Yes. Yes, yes," I cried as my body shook. I could feel my pussy tightening around him as he pushed into me deeply. I felt the tears in my eyes building, and I could do nothing when they slid down my cheeks.

"You want more, Thickness?" Henny asked. He leaned over to kiss my face, where the tears left a trail.

"Yes. God, yes," I cried.

I felt his dick harden even more as I tightened around him, and I knew he would fill me to the brim. I wanted to feel his hot cum inside me. I stared into his honey-brown gaze and all thoughts faded as his hand tightened in my locs and pulled.

"I love this pussy, Tali. It's mine. You are mine," he gritted. "Oh fuck!!" Henny grunted as he slammed deeper into my clenching walls.

"Hendrix! Hen-Hen-Hendrix," I moaned, voice going hoarse from screaming for him.

His hips moved in a broken rhythm like when he fucked my mouth. He groaned my name into the crook of my neck. I was dizzy as fuck, and I couldn't keep my eyes from closing at the ecstasy that filled me as I released again, but this time it was with him. Henny fucked me through my orgasm as he kissed my neck, lips, and forehead.

"I've never told anyone other than family that I love them, Tali, but I love you. So make sure you don't get a nigga dead because all of this," he gestured, running a hand over my body before he placed it between my breasts. My heart beat wildly at the intense look in his eyes, and I could see the actual death in his gaze. "All this belongs only to me."

My eyes fell on the four horsemen tattoo with the letters U.C.K. written into the design. I leaned forward, kissing his chest as my core clenched around his softening length. His words affected my body and mind. I pulled back and stared into his eyes while I came again. I was fucking obsessed with a Union City King, and there was no going back.

## CHAPTER FIFTEEN

# HENDRIX 'HENNY' PHARMA

While getting dressed, I stared at Tali, sprawled across our bed fucked to sleep. Her locs covered her face, but the way she lay her ass was poking out, making my dick hard. If I had more time, I would slide back into her tight walls and fill her up again. I knew exactly what I was doing, and I also knew the timing of her cycle. I smirked at that because I knew how it sounded. I didn't want to leave, but it was time to end this shit with Jakobe.

If I knew Ja as I did, I knew it would be a matter of time before he would try to do some fuck shit. He would come at the people I loved first because he was a pussy ass nigga. I gritted my teeth because he knew Tali was in town and how I felt. Jakobe wasn't a dumb nigga, and I could tell he knew what was up that night. If I wasn't trying to fight my pull on Tali that night, his dick wouldn't have been near her. That was my fault for showing too much emotion around a sociopath. He would use every advantage he could and not give a shit about the consequences of it. He wouldn't give a second thought to killing Tali if he knew it would fuck with me.

I left out of the room and went into the kitchen, cutting a piece of cake while Oz stood against the large marble island.

"Why did you have that girl screaming like that, my nigga? Got her professing her love and shit," he chuckled. My eyes narrowed on him because this nigga was eating my fucking cake. He had a wife at home who could cook and bake his big ass anything he wanted. "This shit is fire. I need to get Chef to make this. What's the name of it?"

I stared at his ass for a long minute debating on knocking that fucking plate out of his hand, but then I would need to clean it up. That caused me to look at the dining table because I needed to clean it before we left. I noticed it was clean and could smell the sanitizing solution I used when I breathed.

"Don't worry about how I fuck what's mine, nigga. And don't eat any of my shit. Tali didn't make this for you," I said. "You cleaned?"

"You are all possessive over the cake, and niggas talk about me. But, you damn right I cleaned up. I was not about to wait for your compulsive cleaning ass to finish. We need to bounce now," Oz said, getting serious. Instead of eating my fucking cake, I placed it back into the cake dish and watched as Oz placed his plate in the dishwasher.

"Do we need to get Haze, or is he outside?"

"He should be delivered by the time we get to the vehicles."

"Bet."

Once we got to the parking garage, I saw the blacked-out SUV. Two men stepped out of the truck, and we took their places. I looked in the rearview mirror directly into hate-filled and fearful brown eyes. I laughed as Oz turned the vehicle around for us to head out. The warehouse where Jakobe was keeping his production of *Silk* was right on the outside of

Union City. Close enough to be a fucking problem but far enough that we wouldn't have noticed it. I turned in my seat and smirked at Haze. This nigga thought staying alive was the prize when it was truly death that was the better way out. His arms were tied around his back, his feet were bound together, and the middle seatbelt was secured around his waist. I could tell it was tightened by how it strained whenever he tried to move. I turned back around and faced the windshield, shaking my head.

"What the fuck did y'all do to this nigga? He looks like a prisoner of war or some shit," I questioned.

"Link decided he wanted to visit him. You do know that nigga is still salty about being shot. So since the nigga that shot him is dead, he was the next best thing," Oz chuckled. That actually explained a lot because this nigga looked as though he had been watered-boarded all fucking night long. Not only that but the bruises around his neck were fresh as fuck.

"When you're disloyal, you get whatever the fuck you get. Haze is just lucky that the information he gave us was on point. If this shit goes down like it was supposed to, we could end Jakobe's bitch ass and finish dealing with the rest of our problems," I said. Oz jumped on the I-280, leaving out of Union City. My thoughts shifted back to Tali and the bitch ass nigga Tremont. The hate in his eyes when he walked into that room had my blood pumping, but I also saw he would be a fucking problem. I knew Tali felt as though she could handle him, but I already knew I was going to need to make some shit clear to this nigga before I had to introduce him to what it felt like to be on the table instead of over it.

"Yeah, I need Ja to be put down. I got other shit on my mind like this Ian nigga. You still want to try and do business with a sneaky ass nigga like that."

"Are you just saying that because you think he's related to the Senator? Or because you found that letter with your mother's possessions," I asked. Oz narrowed his eyes but didn't say anything for a long moment. I waited him out because I knew he was trying to separate his feelings from the facts, and the fact was this nigga gave us a heads-up without asking for shit.

"Don't fucking try to analyze me, nigga, but you have a point. Anything attached to that nigga Kenneth, I can't trust. If I didn't know Mala loved that bitch Charles, I would dead that nigga, too," he grunted.

"I didn't think he fucked with his father like that," I said. I knew we would need to dive deeper on that nigga now. I knew from what Mala told me that he wasn't close to his father and mainly associated with his mother and her side of the family. He always had his nose in the air but cared for Mala. She had never said a word otherwise.

"Shantel said that Mala has only met him three times since they've been together. It seems like it's a thing for Kenneth to be a bitch ass father. Still, all that we know about this nigga why do we not know if he had another child?"

"Maybe that's something we need to ask this nigga Ian. I'm sure we will be hearing from him after he had Link's drone shot down," I said.

"This is true," Oz agreed. Oz was quiet momentarily, but I could tell something else was on his mind. "Dea wants to go back to work. She's worried about this fucking charity event and shit. I don't think she's ready for all that," Oz reasoned.

"Did Seyra give her the all-clear?"

"Yeah, and so the fuck what?"

"That's a good thing, Oz. But the more important thing is that she wants to do it. Support her decision. It will make it much easier when you need to put more security measures in place. She won't be able to fight you on it. Don't give her a reason to fight you on that shit. She wants to go back because that's what she does. Dea helps those who can't help themselves. She probably needs to do something to keep her mind occupied. We all will be in attendance at the event anyway. Don't try to hold her back, or that will affect you and her relationship," I said.

"What the fuck? Are you a relationship guru or some shit? You just figured out what love is, my nigga," Oz laughed.

"Fuck you! How the—"

"I spoke to Sanchez earlier, and he had a lot of shit to say."

"Y'all some gossiping ass niggas. Who else was on the phone?"

"Don't worry about all that. You just better donate some big money to this fucking charity. That's all I am saying, my nigga."

Oz laughed and kept laughing every time he looked at me. I was about to pull out my heat, but I wasn't in the mood to crash on this fucking highway. "Nigga," I started, but my phone rang, lighting up my screen. The screen was blank, but I tapped it anyway. "Yo," I answered.

"Nigga, go into the app and listen to this bitch Yasmin. She's with Rodney. The shit is wild because the information I just got on this nigga is blowing me," Link laughed. I could hear the Hemi engine of his truck as he drove along with a choking sound. "Wait until you read the file I received on Rodney Albert Gates. This nigga is wild as fuck, but it explains why he has so much leeway." All I could hear in the background was Faxx laughing his ass off as he choked. I looked at the time, and it was close to one thirty. We had a little time before we all would be in go mode.

"I got you. We are about to listen now," I stated. I looked into the rearview again and smirked. I saw it finally register on Haze's face that he wasn't returning from this shit. Ain't no way we were talking freely around a nigga we would let live. This nigga wasn't stupid, and his muted screams behind that thick piece of tape only made my smirk grow into a smile. I went to the app Link installed on our phones and pulled up the live audio file on Yasmin.

*"Have you found anything on Katrice? How do you know that Dr. Pharma has anything to do with her being missing?"*

*"Are you just dumb, or are you stupid? I told you before who he is and what they do. I do not understand why you can't get that through*

*your head. None of them are good men, Yasmin. But I guess you were
looking through rose-colored glasses because you fucked him. Hendrix
and that nigga Oz probably have your sister slutting herself out from
nigga-to-nigga. You were probably next."*

*"Fuck you, Roe. I guess I was looking through them when I fucked
your whack ass, but I don't hear you saying shit about that!"*

*"Will you get what I need or what? I have a judge ready to sign off on
your paperwork to take over power of attorney for your Auntie Naomi.
It's pretty fucked up that you convinced her that going to the doctor
was pointless when you knew something was wrong. I think that is
fucked up, but to each her own."*

*"I don't give a fuck about that bitch. The only thing I need to do is be
sure to dismiss those doctors and let her ass die the death she should
have had last year."*

*"Fucking cold as shit, Yasmin."*

*"But do you have information on my fucking sister!"*

*"The bitch is probably dead! I saw that nigga Xavier going in and out
of her place of business with Jakobe. Everyone knows U.C.K. is looking
for him, and your sister was fucking both of them niggas. Pretty sure
she got caught up, and trust me, you will never see her again. So, if
you don't want that to be you, then you need to get me what the fuck
I am asking for! Then and only then can you get the fuck out of dodge
before they come for you."*

*"Fuck Roe, that...that can't be true. What the hell does Hendrix have
to do with the Union City Kings?"*

*"Yasmin! He is U.C.K.!"*

We listened for a few minutes, and everything was silent.

*"You're going to get me fucking murdered! What the fuck, Roe! I
planted that software onto those computers and stole money from the
hospital. I forged documents about organ donations and shipments
of pharmaceuticals that have been paid for but never received by the*

hospital. Why the fuck didn't you tell me who he was! Are you fucking kidding me, Roe!"

"You were skimming from the top before I came in on this shit. How do you think I knew to come to you? You're smart, Yasmin but not that fucking smart. If you think Henny won't find out or doesn't know about it, you might be dumber than I thought."

"You know what, I'm done. I did all I could fucking do for you, so just tell me, when will the order be signed?"

"Judge Pasquet will sign the emergency order Friday. That will give you time to do whatever the fuck you need to do before Tali or Shandea can do anything."

"Good. Now, will you at least try and see if you can find anything about Katrice? That's the least that you can do. There is no way she can be dead, just no way."

"I may have a lead on her, but I will need this last thing from you. I won't ask for anything else, and once you do it, we are done. You can do whatever it is that you are going to do and then bounce before shit gets hotter."

"What!"

"You need to check your fucking tone, Yasmin, because I think you forget that you are only in this mess because you were sloppy with covering up the money you were stealing."

"What. Else. Do. You. Want."

"I need you to get all the hospital's information on an employee. It's that easy."

"Who and why?"

"The why isn't important, but the who is Crescent Johnson."

"What the fuck you want to know about that bitch?"

"You know her?"

"And do. She is fucking Henny, let it be told."

*"Oh really? A very interested party called in a favor, and I said I would look into it. I found out where she worked, which is where you come in."*

*"Who is this party."*

*"Better that you don't know. Can you get what I need or not? I need to know where she lives, what she drives, and who else she is around. Find out if she is really fucking Hendrix or not."*

*"That is easy to do. When do you need the information?"*

*"I need to hand it over by—"*

The signal faded and I checked the time, seeing that the chip didn't last as long as we thought. What the fuck was going on with Crescent?

"You know Faxx is about to call—"

My phone rang in my hand, and I hit the screen.

"Fuck! I see the trucks. Henny, we need to handle this Cent situation," Faxx roared before disconnecting. I looked up, seeing the large looming warehouse coming up in the distance. I shoved the phone into the glove box, knowing none of tonight would end well. Whatever Crescent was running from had just caught up with her ass.

"You do realize we are either going to need to kill a DEA Agent or flip him, and I vote to dismember this nigga," Oz stated. He slowed the SUV down and pulled over on the side of the road about a mile away from the facility.

"We will handle it just like we do everything else. Let's get this shit done," I replied. I turned in my seat, and Haze stared back at me wide-eyed as I pulled out my scalpel. "Do you think they will be distracted by a man running toward them with half his face missing?" I asked, glancing at Oz.

"Let's face it. Who wouldn't get distracted?" Oz smirked as Haze screamed.

We watched Haze for a minute while he ran screaming toward the gated building. His hands were tied behind his back, and the blood from his face left a trail on the gravel. Lights began to shine on his figure, and we turned and walked between the buildings to circle around to the door we needed to use to get inside without being seen. I heard the shot, and I knew Haze was put down. Whoever was in charge of security for this warehouse would come to check. Jakobe should be paranoid by now, and hopefully, he would go on full alert. He still wouldn't see shit coming. I wanted him in panic mode. I wanted his little ass operation of selling *Silk* shut the fuck down. This was the shit that killed my brother six years ago. I thought he might have just picked that shit up from someone else. I knew Malcolm was fucking up, and I believed he had fucked around and gone the drug route. When I checked his phone and saw the message, I lost my fucking mind, and that night Union City streets had run red. Malcolm knew he was fucking up, and he knew if he didn't get his shit together, I would be in his shit. He texted Jakobe that night and asked for something to keep him awake. All he wanted to do was study in time to take his exams. All Malcolm asked for was Adderall. There was no confusion between the two because one needed to be injected.

"Link said the drones would drop some surprises from Faxx in thirty minutes. So you know what that means," Oz said in a low tone.

"Of course, he would feel the need to blow something up," I nodded.

We stood to the side of the door. I held a blank keycard up to the reader and waited for it to turn green. Once it did, Oz quickly opened the door, and we entered a small, darkened hall. It let out onto a catwalk, and we could see the entire operation from the raised platform. We knew our people outside were waiting for our signal, but before we could do that, we had to get into the office to shut down the systems keeping the doors closed.

We knew this would be an all-out fight and that most of the people here weren't armed. We approached the end of the hall where the light was spilling out, and we could see the activity of the people Ja had working for him. Most of them had to be illegal and supplied by the Cartel. A lot of the workers weren't from this country from the different languages spoken.

Everyone that was armed was a part of the niggas ridin' with Jakobe. Men were moving crates back and forth, and the women stood at tables lining up pre-filled syringes. Another crew was packaging the syringes into large containers carefully.

I stepped out first, and Oz was behind me, keeping low as we moved quietly across the catwalk, sticking close to the shadow area until we got closer to the door. We ghosted to the door and tried to listen in before knocking that shit down. We didn't know if Jakobe were already here or who would be behind this door, but we could hope. We could hear voices and laughter, but I could tell that neither nigga speaking was Jakobe or anyone I knew. We didn't want to wait any longer, so I turned the knob and charged inside.

Once I opened the door, Oz moved through the opening with his gun raised.

"Shut the fuck up and sit the fuck down!" he roared. I had the door already closed, and I looked out of the small window to see if anyone noticed us or heard us. No one looked our way, so I ensured the room's blinds were tight.

"Who the fuck are you? Do you know who the fuck spot this is?"

Oz had moved to the nigga that spoke and used his Desert Eagle to knock the shit out of him. I was already on the nigga that sat next to the computer and control panel that Link said would cut all the controls.

"I thought I said shut the fuck up, nigga. Where the fuck is Ja?" I questioned. I was already dragging the older man with thin graying hair out of the office chair and pushing him to the floor. He had his hands raised, and I could tell he was shaking. In his head, no one should be able to get inside of here.

"Ahh! Fuck! Y'all niggas fucking up! You're making a mistake," the other nigga gritted.

"You hear that, Oz. We made a fucking mistake," I grunted. My gloves creaked as I held my gun steadily to the man's head while I typed and clicked on the icon that Link said would pull up a window to get me into the system.

"Oz? Who...who the fuck..."

"I said where the fuck is Jakobe, nigga?"

I typed in the password, and the panel door popped open. Just as it did, we hear a walkie going off.

"Lock it down! Pack all it all up and get ready to ship the fuck out! Dex, lock down the office! Get your ass down here and get Morgan out of here. You see a nigga you don't know, shoot first," Jakobe roared. I saw the man on the ground twitch like he was going for the walkie, and I placed a silenced shot to his head. I looked at Oz and saw his jaw tick because it could only mean Kenneth was here. Or was it, Ian? I doubted it was Ian, but I could tell Oz was still skeptical about that nigga. I hadn't met him in person, but when he stared into the camera, the information we had about him and the look in his eye gave me a feeling of, like knows like.

"Dex!" Oz yelled sharply as I moved to the panel and started to flick each switch powering down all the systems.

"What nigga! What the fuck?" he shouted as Oz hit him again across the face.

"I just wanted to be sure I had the right nigga. Get on the fucking walkie and let this nigga know the office is locked down," Oz gritted as he shoved the walkie into his hands. Dex's blood-covered hands fumbled with it at first but grasped it just as Oz lost his patience. "Nigga."

"Yo! Office is being secured. On my way." He said quickly and threw the walkie down like it was on fire. Dex wiped at the gash on his forehead, but blood poured even more.

"Head wounds bleed more, my nigga," I said, closing the panel. Dex looked up, but Oz hit him twice more before he passed out.

"I don't want to waste a bullet on this nigga. Let's move, we got a two-for-one special tonight, and we only have," I said, looking at his watch, "twenty-one more minutes before we all blow the fuck up," he stated.

I moved to the door peeking out of the blinds and not seeing anyone. Oz opened the door just as loud alarm sounds started up. I knew that meant he would now know that we were in the building and whoever we brought with us would be coming. We moved to the end of the catwalk as the entire warehouse went into chaos. Whatever Link had told me to enter had the sprinkler system going off and unlocking and opening the large trucking doors. The warehouse was huge, with crates and boxes stacked up everywhere. People were running around in all directions, but we could see they were all carrying boxes full of *Silk*. It was the drug Jakobe used to kill my brother because he wanted to be more than us. Ja wanted to be the only one on top, but the Cartel still ran him, and that shit would never be us.

We started to take out anyone who got in our way, trying to make our way deeper into the warehouse. We didn't know where Ja was but knew he had to be here somewhere. I could feel the time running out, but I refused to fucking leave until we had this bitch nigga.

"Let's go! Now!"

"This is the reason I didn't need to be here. How the fuck did they get inside, Jakobe?"

"Nigga, you can fucking stay here. That shit will be on you because if they haven't figured out who you are, they will tonight if you don't fucking move."

"After tonight, all this shit is off. I will get someone else to handle the problem, and you can tell the Roja brothers that our deal for them to move shit through this state is off," Kenneth snarled.

I looked at Oz as we came up behind a stack of crates blocking Jakobe and Kenneth from view.

"Ja! We see a way out of here. They got the front covered, but the access road at the back is open," someone yelled.

Oz nodded before checking his clip when suddenly, we heard the sound of gunfire. We ducked behind the crates and saw that two men had rounded the corner. I sucked my teeth before I stood, giving one of them two shots to the chest and one shot to the head. Oz shot the other man in the head as screams and shouts filled the warehouse. We turned simultaneously and focused on getting to Jakobe and Kenneth before they could leave. We fought our way through the warehouse, pushing people out of the way and shooting any nigga that thought to take a shot. I felt a shove on my shoulder as two shots rang out. I slid in the water from the sprinklers and shot back at the men on the catwalk. Oz was aiming in the direction we ran when I saw that nigga. Ja was standing at the other end of the warehouse, waiting for the large door to rise. Ja and Kenneth ducked as Oz shot at them. I heard a roar of pain and knew he hit one of them. I figured it was probably his father by his bare teeth.

"Twelve minutes," Oz shouted.

We started to run toward him, but Ja managed to get to his feet and pulled out his gun. He was with two other niggas, and they all began shooting. We dodged and weaved, trying to get closer because I was not letting this nigga get away. I could see the fear in his eyes as we approached, but he pushed others in front of him as he moved over to Kenneth.

"Fuck! Nigga, fuck it! Stay here and fucking die," Jakobe yelled.

I shot at his ass again, and it missed him by an inch but made him jump back and down to the ground. We never stopped moving as our clothes got soaked, and the increasing exchange of gunfire told me our people were close. Everyone was trying to get the upper hand, but ultimately, it would be us. The entire warehouse was lit up like a Christmas tree with all the gunfire. My eyes are scanning the room, looking for my target. I saw Ja scrambling for his gun that he must have dropped when I almost hit him.

"I'll handle Kenny's ass," Oz said as he reloaded. We were against a turned-over table, and I stood up and shot over it, hitting one of the niggas with Jakobe. Oz stood up as a shot licked off, hitting his arm, but he didn't stop. As my mental clock ticked down, I was leaving Oz to deal with his father while going to Ja.

"Ten minutes!" I called out. I spotted Ja and shot at him as he rolled under a table. He killed my brother. He took the last immediate family I had and then came back like he could take my city. This nigga had the game fucked up. I ain't going to let that happen.

I spotted Ja across the room running, but he turned back, spotting me. I was going at his ass at full speed, not giving a fuck about whoever got in my way. He stopped and threw his head back, his locs waterlogged, but I could see the hate covering his features. Knowing this nigga as I did, he was planning on running. He held onto a duffle bag the entire time we came at him but let his hammer go and left Kenneth behind. Ja started to move toward me, dropping the duffle by a dead body.

Everyone else was still taking on fire or running fucking scared, but it was just me and him now. I could feel the tension leaving my body as he reached behind himself, pulling out another weapon. I shot, and so did he. We both dodged the shots, and I slid behind a large steel table surrounded by packages of syringes filled with Silk.

"Henny! Why can't you just let this shit go, my nigga? You come at me like this city ain't big enough for the both of us," Jakobe chuckled. I ejected my clip and replaced it with another. My internal alarm was screaming that time was damn near out.

"Nigga, you killed my brother, you piece of shit," I said, trying to keep my cool. Ja just laughed at me like the shit was a joke. I knew that he had moved positions, and I listened to figure out where the fuck he would pop up.

"Naw, nigga. I can't help if that little nigga was a junkie. He became a product of these streets you so-called own. That's just life in Union, right?"

I stood up, let off three shots, and he dropped low again. He was trying to circle, but I didn't have time for this bullshit.

"I saw the texts, my nigga. I know what he asked for and what you gave him. It's a little hard to overdose when you can't reach the place it was injected.

"Okay, my nigga damn. Yeah, yeah, I did it. And now I'm gonna fuck your bitch and blow her brains out. Literally."

I was already moving toward him, so when he stood up, I took a shot, but he turned slightly, taking the shot in his shoulder. I could feel myself about to snap, and I didn't even think about it when I used my gun to knock him hard in his jaw. Jakobe had managed to get off a shot, and I could feel the hit somewhere in my abdomen but fuck that. I just charged at him, but he knocked my gun out of my hand just as I kicked his gun away. His punch landed on my chin, but I tipped my head back enough that the force of it was bullshit. I struck back, punching him on the side and to his kidneys. The sound of our fists hitting each other is drowned out by the sound of gunfire and screams. I could feel the adrenaline pumping through my veins when I raised my foot, kicking him in his chest.

I punched Ja's jaw solidly, and he staggered back. I saw an opening and went for it, but he managed to dodge out of the way, kicking a body in front of me. I moved around it while Ja went behind a table, running like a bitch. I raised my foot and kicked the table hard that it crashed into his midsection, and he stumbled. Ja fell to the concrete floor, and I staggered at the pain in my abdomen. I looked down, pulled my blood-soaked shirt away, and felt around for the wound. I applied pressure as I moved to get to Ja, using my other hand to reach into my pocket for my scalpel. I staggered over to him and stood over his body. He glared up at me with empty, dead eyes, but he smiled. Ja managed to grab one of the nearby guns and aim at my chest. I froze, not knowing what to do.

"You always thought you were better than me but look—"

"Nigga, shut the fuck up," I snapped and threw the scalpel at his throat. I saw his eyes widen as a huge explosion sounded, and the warehouse started to crumble.

# CHAPTER SIXTEEN

## LENNOX 'OZ' ANDERSON

I f anyone told me I would pull my father out of a crumbling building, I probably would have introduced them to my *Butcher Shop*. I got Kenny's ass to Milo before returning for Henny. The explosions were starting in the far east of the building, but it was moving rapidly, and when I noticed Henny wasn't out, I knew some shit was wrong. I looked for Jakobe's body, but there was so many and so much debris I wasn't about to stand around and go through each one. That warehouse was about to go up in flames, destroying any traces of Silk or its existence anywhere near our fucking city. I knew that this would have the Cartel really coming at us for fucking with their money. I got the reasoning behind it, but we said one too many times to stay the fuck out of Union City.

"Oz, you need to get him to the *Clinic*! Faxx and I will meet you there," Link shouted. The speakers in the truck seemed loud but brought me out of my thoughts. "Are you holding pressure on it?"

"Nigga, I am fucking driving! I put one of those packs on him before we pulled out. That's about all the time I had after making sure Kenny was locked the fuck down."

"That will help. Did you get hit? Wait, who the fuck is Kenny?"

"I'll be fine," I hissed. "Nigga, Kenneth!"

"Oh shit. You killed Kenny!"

"Nigga. You know the damn plan." I said, turning the wheel sharply, and it pulled at the wound on my arm. It wasn't a big deal, and I could deal with it. I looked into the rearview mirror, ensuring Milo was on my ass. I didn't want my package to be lost in transit. "Who are you calling to help you? Gabe?"

"No, I can't. I need him to deal with the shipments now. I have Faxx picking up your guests that you've requested," Link stated. I knew my brows were in my hairline because if Gabriel wasn't coming, then who else would help with this shit. I was a lot of things, but I didn't know shit about assisting in surgical procedures.

"Then who?"

"I thought about Tali." I raised a brow like he was trippin', but on the other hand, it would be the perfect way for her to see the side of things Shandea had already been a part of. Tali would have to make a choice, and we can find out if she can even handle it.

"Bold move, my nigga. Don't you think she will be too emotional? It's Henny, not you. That's a shot, Link. What about Seyra?"

"Seyra is unavailable right now. Shantel has her at the farm helping with Katrice. It will take them too long to get to the *Clinic*."

"Are you sure about this shit? I know you can patch his ass up, but having Tali assist you is wild."

"Is he dying?"

"From what I can see, it was a through and through, but he's lost a lot of blood."

"I think you and Henny are missing your women's other sides. In the short amount of time they have been here, Dea has been through some major events that would have sent any other woman screaming, and she hasn't broken yet. As for Tali, I guarantee her training will kick in as it did with me. She's a travel nurse meaning she has seen this type of shit before, and when it comes to someone you care about, you will do everything to save them. Will she break later? Absolutely. But if she knows her help is what will save him, she will focus," Link stated. I hated when he had a point. His analytical mind just wouldn't see it going any other way but his way. We couldn't just take him to the hospital, especially when it was so heavily monitored right now, and I knew Henny would want to stay far away from there.

"We need a personal doctor."

"We have a personal doctor," Link said.

"Not when he is the one bleeding out!"

"This is true, but I wasn't talking about Henny. I called Santino home after Dea was attacked."

"Stax! Faxx is going to fucking shoot you for real this time.

"It's his fucking older brother. He needs to work out his problem with him because Stax is just as much a part of us as Faxx. Maybe in a different compacity, but he not far off," Link argued.

"Stax is not that much older, my nigga, but when you're right," I shrugged and then hissed.

"Stax is seven or eight years older than Faxx. Once Faxx talks to him, he will get over it. Stax's time was up anyway. Bringing him and his children home is the best way to go. He can become who the fuck he was supposed to be. Now, we have a doctor. Problem solved."

"What about Tali?"

"I honestly think she should be there to see what this shit is all about. We said no more keeping them in the dark," Link intoned.

The fact that Link foresaw the need for Santino to be pulled away from his beloved hospital in New Kellington said all I needed to know. Things were heating up, and it was time to close ranks. It was a good thing Seyra was home now as well.

"Henny might try to give you a vivisection or some shit when he finds out about this. He wanted Santino to live as normal a life as he could when Keira died. That shit that happened at *VIGOR* broke him when she was caught in the crossfire. You think it's too soon?"

"No, I think he got it together, and maybe now we can figure out what the fuck actually happened that night. It's for his own good either way. I don't want anyone else in his *Clinic* yet. You know how this nigga Henny get and shit," Link stated.

"Fu...fuck both y'all niggas. Where the fuck are we? What happened?"

I looked over at Henny as he pushed himself up in the seat. He coughed and grimaced at the pain.

"We are on the way to the *Clinic*. Twenty minutes out," I said.

"Fuck, did you see Ja? Tell me that nigga is laid out in that warehouse," Henny asked. He leaned forward and opened the glove compartment. Henny grabbed another one of the packs Link insisted we keep on hand. He pulled up his shirt while cracking the pack and shoved it against his back. "Fuck!"

"I barely saw you with all that shit happening. I grabbed your ass, and we stumbled the fuck out of there before that shit went up in flames. If he was in there, that nigga is dead, dead. You good, nigga?"

"I'm fine. I will be fine once I am stitched up. Link! Why did you call Stax? Why the fuck—"

"He was ready, Henny. It was time for his ass to come home. You know it, and I know it. We got too much shit happening for everyone not to be in the same place," Link urged.

"Well, it's on you to mediate between him and Faxx."

"They can mediate them fucking selves. Just hurry the fuck up," Link said before the call disconnected.

"He's an asshole," I said, pressing harder on the gas. My eyes cut to Henny, and his head was leaning on the passenger window.

"He is, and he is going to do what the fuck he wants. Don't be surprised if he isn't picking up Dea and Tali right now."

"What? I wish that nigga would bring my pregnant–"

"Link will force the issue that they need to see it all. He will never endanger either of them, and you know it. But I know where his mind is right now. To him, it's all about them needing to know what is at stake and why they can never become a liability. You know why he will do it, right?"

"Because of Keira. She went to *VIGOR* after he told her not to take her ass down there that night, but it wasn't...she was caught up in the crossfire. A lot of people died that night."

"But if she understood the reasons why we say don't fucking do something, do you think she would have gone? Keira left behind three kids that night because she didn't have all the information. Do you think Dea would have left that day?"

My hands squeezed tightly around the steering wheel as my teeth ground together. I knew what Henny was saying and that he was right.

"Fuck, this...damn," I gritted. Shit was so quiet for so long that I thought it would be easy to bring Dea into this shit and ease her into it. Wrong. Wrong. Wrong.

I didn't say another word as my blood began to simmer at the knowledge that people really wanted to fucking challenge us like this. The simmer turned into anger, then to hate, and onto rage. I kept my eyes on the road but kept glancing back to ensure the truck with my father was behind us. When I stood over him and saw the resentment and hate in his eyes, I wanted to kill him. I wanted to strap his ass down to my table and take small fucking pieces off his body and send them to his bitch ass wife. But instead, I used the butt of my gun and knocked his screaming ass the fuck out. I had better plans for this piece of shit. The warehouse came into view, and knowing what I had been planning for this nigga lifted my mood.

The doors were raising the closer we got, and I didn't need to brake as I entered. This new space was larger than before, and I wondered how long this one had been in the making. This was not a quick move but was already planned out. "Henny!"

I saw him jerk awake, and then the pain crossed his face. I saw Link coming down the stairs with Tali on his heels. I knew if she was here then Dea was somewhere in the building.

"Shit. We here," Henny asked weakly.

"Hendrix," Tali cried before running toward the truck.

"Awe shit, he really did it," Henny grumbled as he repositioned his shirt. He blinked a few times, trying to become more alert, but I knew he wouldn't sell this shit. "Thic...Thickness isss....it's all good. I'm fine," he slurred, opening the door.

"Nigga she can't hear you," I stated before climbing out of the truck. Tali was already at his door before Link or I made it to help her get Henny out.

"What the hell happened? Oh my God. Oz? What the fuck happ–"

"It's all good, Thickness. I'm good," Henny said, holding his wound, but he tilted, and Tali caught him with the help of Link.

"Will all of you move so I can get his ass on a gurney? Tali, is it? I heard that you are a nurse. Is that correct?" I looked up to see Stax pushing a gurney toward us. Anyone looking at him could tell he and Faxx were brothers. They held the same features and the same long thick, ass hair, except Stax kept his pulled up in a fucking man bun. The only noticeable difference was his complexion, especially when they both had their hair in braids. He was darker than Faxx and probably an inch taller than him.

"I am," Tali answered. She helped Link place Henny on the gurney but kept her intense gray eyes on Stax.

"Good. That would be great if you can handle helping me take care of Henny without all the theatrics. It will free up Link to do whatever it is that he actually does."

"I think I can handle it, Mr..."

"Dr. Wellington, but you can call me Santino or Stax. I'm good with either. Let's go," Stax smiled. Henny glared at Stax because he held Tali's hand and smiled at her. Tali stared at him, and I knew she could tell he looked familiar before a smile covered her face.

"That's enough, my nigga. I am bleeding out over here," Henny said, pulling Tali away from Stax.

"Link, let's get him to the room, and we can get set up. Have you dealt with this type of gunshot wound before?"

"I have," Tali said, re-focusing back on Henny as they began pushing the gurney. Link looked over his shoulder to the vehicle that carried the nigga that ruined my fucking chance at a halfway normal life.

"I will bring a gurney back for him. He will need to be stabilized before you start your shit," Link said before they hit a corner. I turned away to face the truck where Milo sat waiting while three of Faxx's team checked the truck. Ace and Echo stepped away from the truck and nodded at me without saying a word. Milo opened the door and stepped out of the truck, looking toward the two men before looking at me.

"Are they A.I.? Because they just don't act...human, my nigga," Milo said, shaking himself. I wanted to laugh because I had asked the same question when I first met them, but I was ready to get things started.

"I wouldn't worry about it. Get Kenny's ass out of the truck, and then help Link get him to wherever he needs to go. Then I want you over to the Vet and help with the shipments," I ordered. I turned away as Link came back out, walking toward me.

"We will get him together, and then you can do what you do. Shandea is sitting in the main conference room."

I nodded and went to where I'd learned exactly who Ian Nevin Lawe really was, but I still had no clue what he had to do with my mother. I stepped inside the room and paused when I heard my mother's voice.

*"Listen to me, Lennox. You must care for your brother as best as possible when I am gone. I have done everything I know to keep you boys safe, but I am always watching over you. If not me, there will always be someone to ensure you both are safe. I don't want you to worry about who your father is, but I want you to know about what he is. Let me tell you how I met him and what he wanted from me..."*

"Lennox?"

I looked at Shandea, and that's when I realized she had paused the video. She wiped her mouth before pushing away from the table. I noticed the small bag of P.B. Bites and the box with my mother's picture beside it.

"Why are you looking at that again?

"Lennox, baby, are you okay? You're bleeding," she said. Shandea stood in front of me and raised my arm. I hissed but knew it couldn't be anything but a flesh wound.

"I'm straight, Dea, but why are you looking at that?" I asked again.

"Straight? Nigga do you see this shit? This needs to be cleaned before you get a damn infection or something. Take me to where I can clean this up. Where is Tali?"

"She's helping with Henny," I said, stopping her movement. "Why are you looking at this again? I thought I put it away?"

Dea stopped and looked at me before leaning to the side to look down the hall, looking like she could see what was happening with Henny. She looked back at me and frowned.

"When you left last night, I couldn't sleep and just kept thinking about what she said in the video. I knew it had to be a clue about how she could obtain all that money. If you can figure that out, what else will you find out," she shrugged. I nodded, understanding what she was trying to do, but I had long since given that shit up.

"It's not something to worry about, Sweetness. Help me clean this up, and then you can meet my father," I said. I glanced at my mother on the large screen before turning away and pulling Dea with me.

After I had cleaned and bandaged my wound, Link insisted I take some antibiotics before continuing with my plans. I stepped into a large room resembling my *Butcher Shop* on a smaller scale. It didn't have the other rooms I had, but this would work if I needed to bring someone here. I raised my brows because they had done a good fucking job. The panel was even on the wall, and I wondered if I had the same tools I did at my spot.

"What is this place?" Dea asked. I pulled her inside with me and walked her over to the wall where a chair and small table sat.

"Listen to me, Dea. You've already seen how I get down but trust me when I tell you that wasn't shit. Even tonight isn't the tip of the iceberg, but it is a lot of what I do. It is how I gain information, make money, and form enemies. Whatever you see or hear stays right here in this room. It doesn't go any further. Not even to Tali," I clarified. Shandea's brows furrowed, and her mouth parted before she closed it. She looked into my eyes, and I could see their confusion before my irritation replaced it.

"So are you telling me you don't trust my sister even after everything?"

"No, it isn't that at all. When it all comes down to it, Tali will have her own shit to carry. She isn't going to need more on top of it, just like you will not either. This is my business, so it means it's our business. You feel me?"

"I think I get it, Lennox. I get it," she nodded. I sat her in the chair and returned the P.B. bites. I knew it wouldn't be blood this time, so she should be straight. Now I can't say she would be able to eat because when this shit started, her mouth will probably be on the fucking floor. She looked over the room and looked over the large table in the middle of it. She looked at the steel chair against the wall and the chains with cuffs hanging beside it. Her eyes fell to the floor, and I could tell she was looking at the hooks where someone's feet could be secured. "What exactly is this place, Lennox, and why the hell am I here?"

"It wasn't my first choice to bring you here, and it was out of my control. But I understand the reason it was done. Remember when you asked to know me? You wanted to know everything, and I said let's start at the beginning."

"Yes."

"Well, we are in the fucking middle now, whether you're ready for it or not. That ring is on your finger because you ain't going nowhere either way," I stated as the doors opened.

"Where the fuck am I? Do you know who the fuck I am? Where is that son of a bitch? Where is he?" Kenny roared. Ace didn't say a word as he brought Kenneth Morgan into the room in a wheelchair.

"Don't anyone here give a shit about who the fuck you are, Kenny," I grunted. I leaned down and kissed Shandea on the lips, snapping her out of her shock. I could tell she knew exactly who this man was, if not who he was to me.

"My name isn't fucking Kenny, little nigga."

"And the polished facade finally drops, and the nigga from the projects of Union City finally appears. What's good, Pops," I said, turning away from Shandea. Ace jerked Kenny out of the wheelchair and threw him into the steel chair. He cuffed him in seconds, and his good leg was chained to the floor.

"What the fuck do you want, money? Acknowledgment or some shit. It can't be money because, from what I know, MYTH does good in the business of selling pussy and dicks," he sneered. His eyes landed on Shandea, raking his dark brown gaze over her. "You selling that pussy since your brother is clearly done with it?" I moved swiftly and knocked the shit out of him. His face went to the side so hard I saw the spit fly out of his mouth. He stared down at the floor for a long minute before slowly turning back to face me. He blinked his eye as his contact slipped out, revealing one light brown and the other so dark a brown that it was almost black.

I heard Shandea suck in a breath, and I knew she really saw it then. He held the same eyes as my brother. It was like staring into the eyes of my twin, except I was now sure this was where we got our fucked up genes. I was in his face in a second, so close to going over to that wall and grabbing my cleaver as I heaved.

"Don't let whatever shit Ja told you to get your fucking tongue cut the fuck out. It won't be so easy to win elections when you can't form fucking words. Go ahead and say something else," I goaded. Kenny clamped his mouth closed and glared at me. "Now, you might think I'm going to kill you because you have been actively trying to take me the fuck out, but that isn't the case. I want to kill you because you killed my fucking mother. You killed my mother and then spread her body parts around her room for us to find."

I punched him in the leg, where I shot him, and smiled as he screamed. "Ahh...ahhh....ahhh...you...you..."

"You think I give a shit about your pain?" I asked, punching him again until I started to see blood. "Oops, my bad nigga you might need more stitches. We don't have that here, right Ace?" I asked, turning to look at the silent man. His full beard twitched, and he raised his thick brows before he smiled.

"Naw, we don't. I got this, though," he said, holding up a knife and lighter.

"Just...just...take me back to that nurse. That's all...all I need," Kenneth stammered as Ace stepped forward. I turned away and looked at Shandea while Ace cut away at his pants to get at the wound. Shandea stared wide-eyed at what was happening, but I noticed her hand was curled into a tight fist. "Ahh! Ahh! Noo...ahhh shit!"

I moved over to Dea while flexing my hand, and she noticed me when I was a few feet away.

"He had your mother killed?" She fumed. "It was him?" she asked, narrowing her gaze.

"It wasn't me! It wasn't me! I didn't have her killed...I didn't...I loved her...I didn't," he gasped. I looked back, and Ace had sealed the wound but used Kenneth's other leg to hold his knife. The blade sank deep into his upper thigh.

"Then who did!" I roared. I didn't know I had left Dea's side until I was in his face. He was lucky to be chained to the wall, or he would have been through it. I gripped his shirt, lifting him from the chair to glare into his eyes.

"The only thing I have been guilty of is trying to get rid of the evidence of our relationship. I didn't...I didn't..."

I dropped him down in the chair, sobbing like a bitch, and looked at Ace. I could feel on a deeper level that this nigga wasn't lying. Ace looked at his watch and then at me.

"And the lie detector test determined he's telling the truth."

"How...how do you...how do you.."

"Does your wife know about us?" I asked, cutting off his stuttering.

Kenneth looked up, hate and fear clouding his gaze.

"Fuck no. I married into money, and if they knew about ya mama or y'all bastards, I wouldn't be where I am today," he seethed. Whether it was true or not, my mother's death had something to do with this nigga, and I would find out what it was. Once I did, I would fucking kill whoever did it and then kill him for putting her in that position. It just wouldn't be before we made use of this nigga.

"Well, that changes everything, Senator Morgan. How do you like the sound of Governor Morgan instead?" I smiled. I always suspected that it wasn't him that did it but because of him, which is what started me down this road of forming a plan.

"Wh-what? Governor...I am not running for..."

"Oh, but you are, Kenny. Wes will be long gone very soon, and you will be our first African American Governor from the great Union City."

"No. No, I won't. I have other endeavors, and I..."

"Nigga, shut the fuck up. I know what you like and the things that sometimes make this limp dick jump. So when I tell you to fucking do something, you will do it. When I tell you to jump, you fucking jump. When I say sit, you sit the fuck down, and when I tell you to scream Hallelujah, you fucking scream it until I say to stop. Now to make sure we understand each other better, let me show you what will bring everything you love crashing and burning to the ground. Because we all know money makes you tick, Kenny, and without money, status, and power, you ain't shit," I said. I looked over my shoulder at Ace, and he moved to open the doors. "You don't know what power is until you fuck with me."

"Holy shit. What the fuck?" Dea blurted.

Shantel's brother Rizyn came through the door and smiled when he spotted the Senator. He went by Jose when working, and it was safer that way. It was easy to let Professor Priscilla Morgan think she got him into *MYTH* and carried the weight in their dynamic, but she had been the target all along. She had always been a part of the plan. I just wasn't sure how I would use her until now. Priscilla came into the room on all fours. She wore a red leather corset and a red leather sensory deprivation zippered eyes and mouth hood with ear pads. I requested that he place Bluetooth earbuds that connected to the watch he was wearing in her ears. She would only be able to hear his voice and his alone. I wanted to be sure that Priscilla could hear nothing at all, even if the hood were removed.

"What the fuck is this?" Kenneth laughed. Rizyn yanked on the leash, and Priscilla hurried inside and continued until she was next to his legs.

"Jose, let me see how well you have trained your sub. I've been hearing good shit about you," I smirked.

"Oz, did you really doubt me?" Rizyn chuckled. He was more at ease around me now, but I didn't miss the trace of concern that crossed his face. I knew that he wasn't expecting this to happen tonight, and I could tell that he didn't want to fuck this up. I wasn't worried because if Shantel thought this was too much for him, she would've pulled him off this job long ago.

"Is this some kind of joke? I knew you were into some sick shit, and you wonder why I never wanted you or your psycho brother," he spat. I turned back to this nigga and missed when Dea had moved. She backhanded Kenneth so hard his bottom lip split from the diamond on her finger.

"He didn't need you then, and he damn sure doesn't need you now. Think about that before you open your fucking mouth to speak to him again," Shandea sneered. She was shaking, and I reached out to lower her hand, pulling her to me.

"Don't dirty your hands with a nigga like him, Sweetness. Shitty ass people like him are hard to wash off," I grunted. My dick was hard as fuck, and if this nigga or his wife weren't in this room, I would have fucked her pretty ass against this wall. "Jose," I said, looking over my shoulder. He lightly touched the top of her head before sliding his palm over her leather-covered cheek. He unzipped her mouth, and she breathed deeply while moaning his name.

"Who is your MASTER."

"Sir, you are my master."

"Am I a good master to you?"

"Yes," she moaned. But she quickly replied again, "Yes, Sir, you are the best master."

"I'm displeased with you."

She whined but closed her mouth and lowered her body to the floor. She bowed low to his feet, waiting for his command or punishment. He was good. "Tell me your name!"

Priscilla jumped, and she quickly sat upright, breathing heavily.

"Priscilla Daphne Morgan, your loyal and willing servant, Sir," she panted. "Have I—"

"Shut up!" Rizyn shouted before reaching down and zipping her mouth closed.

"No. No. No, no, no, no...this...no, you can't do this...how..."

Rizyn used the leather leash and gave Priscilla ten hard slaps on each ass cheek and the backs of her legs. I turned away but nodded at Rizyn to leave before looking back at the stunned Kenny. I held out the hand that wasn't holding Dea, and Ace placed pictures in my hand. I turned over the first photo showing his lovely wife naked and tied to their bed as Jose fucked the shit out of her. I dropped that one to the floor, and the next one nearly caused him to choke on his tongue.

It was a picture of him being breastfed by none other than my mother.

"You will run for Governor, and you will win. You will do what I say when I say it because you will be U.C.K.'s fucking puppet. Now tell me everything I need to know about your son Ian."

"Ian? My son was a decorated hero and died in service of his country. And that was about the only good thing he's done for the family. Why?"

Dea stiffened in my arms, but she stayed quiet while we watched his bitch ass begin to cry. Ace moved around me and punched him in the ribs causing him to double over in pain as he choked.

"You aren't the one asking questions. Puppets don't talk. They get their strings pulled," Ace gritted. Ace stepped back, and I smiled at his pain, fear, and torment.

"Interesting. Now tell me what the fuck you have going on about the Cartel and what all you know about Alex Tilderman."

# CHAPTER SEVENTEEN

## SHANDEA 'DEA' SAUNDERS

I didn't know what exactly to feel when I woke up this morning. I was still battling with being kidnapped and assaulted and finding out I was pregnant with twins but lost one because of the incident. Then last night happened, and I can't unsee everything that happened. Sitting in that room staring at Lennox confronting his father was an entirely different person from who I knew. This was the same man in the club that night that I hadn't seen since, but I could tell he felt more himself when conducting '*business*' as he called it.

I didn't know what fright and shock were until Link appeared in our penthouse out of nowhere, telling me I needed to get dressed. All I got was shit went down tonight, and Oz will need you there, and we would need to pick up Tali. When I asked what had happened, all I got was Henny had been shot and needed treatment. Suffice it to say I didn't even question it and just did what he ordered. I also found it strange that I wasn't afraid at all by his presence or how he just fucking appeared out of nowhere like a damn ninja.

I typed a few emails and spoke with a few children, but I was taking it easy on my first day back. I could tell Lennox wanted me to stay home for a little longer, but I couldn't. Not only was I going crazy in the house, but I knew the longer I stayed away only gave the kids I was trying to help more reasons not to trust anyone. They all had abandonment issues, and I wasn't about to add to them. I looked up when I heard a knock on my office door and smiled at Cara as she slipped into my office.

"Hey girl, I know you are only working a half day today, but I wanted to review a few things about the charity event with you. We usually hold it at the Grand Vista Hall, and we have many local donors that attend, but this year we have six more donors added to the list that will be attending. This has never happened before and could really give us what we need to help our kids," she smiled.

"Really? I know Miranda is ecstatic about it. Do you know who they are?" I asked. I was getting excited about it as well. The money would go a long way to help the forgotten children of Union City.

"All I know is she keeps going on and on about everything being perfect because 'Mr. Kennedy will be attending,' and he is the top donor to the cause," she said, using air quotes.

My stomach dropped, and I felt sick when I heard that name. What the fuck was his problem? I knew Lennox had pulled this man up once, so I hoped this was not about me.

"Oh, oh really? I thought he never came to these sorts of events?" I laughed. I turned to face my computer and pulled up my email so I could let Miranda's ass know I wouldn't be there.

"Normally, he doesn't, but this year he all but insisted that he attends. From what I heard, he was so taken aback by everything and 'you' that he has added another twenty thousand dollars to his already generous gift of one hundred thousand dollars. So whatever good shit you said, please keep it up. This will keep our doors open for at least two years," Cara sighed.

I smiled tightly while exiting out of my email. There was no way that I couldn't show up now. He seemed like he would be the type to pull the donation on some bullshit or never donate again.

"That is great. Is there anything that I need to help with?"

Whether Lennox knew or not his ass would be fucking going that night. I didn't care if he donated as himself or anonymously. I just needed him there as my fiancé because I refused to get caught up with Elliot's ass. I had a flashback of the first time Lennox and I had sex. The man in the other building stood there watching us as Lennox fucked me so good I knew that was the night I conceived. I didn't know who Elliot was and didn't care while he got his nut until he showed up at my job. Mr. Kennedy's side remarks in the conversation bordered on indecent and made me feel uncomfortable. I knew Lennox had pulled him up about me, but I would need to tell him that he was here and would be attending this event.

"I don't think so. I think everything is taken care of, but Miranda did say she would like you there greeting the donors when they arrive since you made such a great impression."

"Of course she does," I laughed. Cara laughed before looking at her watch. "I guess you are about to get out of here. Does that rock on your finger have anything to do with it, or are you still not feeling well?" Cara raised her brows, and looked down at my left hand.

"A little of both, actually, but I am finished catching up with my cases. So I am going to get out of here," I smiled. Cara waved before she exited my office while I powered down my computer. I felt so weird and out of place now after all that had happened, but I couldn't lie and say I didn't miss those crazy ass kids. My phone buzzed, and I saw Tali's name flashing when I looked at it.

"Hey girl, hey," I answered. I sat back in my office chair with a smirk on my face because I could tell Tali was just as stuck as I was in Union City.

"Hey, are you still at work?"

"Yes, but I was about to leave for the day. Why, what's up?"

"I know that we need to have a sit-down and 'share' some things, but it's just one thing I need to know," she said. My body tensed because of some things I couldn't share. There was some shit we did not need to be saying over the phone. Hell, I knew that much.

"Is whatever it is okay to…" I let the question linger, and she scoffed.

"Man fuck the other stuff, Dea. Did you know your man bought the bank that owned Mama's loan? Did you know all her medical bills were paid for and not by the grants and shit we filled out. I was going to wait until we saw each other, but this shit was burning a hole in my soul," she shrieked. I would be surprised if I hadn't known Lennox, but I wondered what took so long.

"No. No, I didn't know that until now. But honestly, Tali, are you surprised?"

She was quiet for a minute, and I heard a beeping noise in the background.

"No, I'm not, but it was still like, what the hell? Everything is like, what the hell? I'm coming over when I get off," she whined.

"No, come over tomorrow. Dr. McQueen is coming for a home check-up, and Lennox will be out doing whatever it is he does. Bring Crescent so we can talk," I said, standing.

"Fine, I guess," she sighed.

"Stop being dramatic. You act like it's weeks away, and just to give you a heads-up, the meeting about Mama is on a Saturday. We are both off, so it seemed like the best time. I'll forward you the email," I said.

"Great," she sighed again. "Did I tell you he knew that Tre was texting me?"

"What!"

"Yass bissh, this is why we need a face-to-face. I miss your face," she giggled.

"Bissh, I literally just saw you a few hours ago. I think Henny's crazy is rubbing off on your ass," I laughed. I picked up my purse, looking around to ensure I wasn't leaving anything.

"Stranger things have happened before. But fine, I need to do some actual work, so I'll let you go," Tali said.

"She ain't doing shit," Sanchez shouted in the background.

"Shut up and sign your dang instructions," Tali laughed before disconnecting the call. I dropped my phone in my purse and stepped out of my office. I closed and locked the door before turning around and heading up front to let Cara know that I was gone.

"I'm looking for Shandea Saunders. Could you tell her that, Ro...oh, never mind. Here she is," he smiled. I glanced at Cara, and she frowned, but I smiled. I pulled Rodney over toward the office sitting area out of earshot. His gaze traveled up and down my body, causing me to feel disgusting. I folded my arms across my chest, leaning my head to the side.

"What do you need, Rodney?"

His eyes narrowed on my hand, and I fought the urge to fidget under his intense glare. I blew out a breath and widened my eyes. "What do you want, Rodney? I'm leaving for the day. So what can I do for you?"

Rodney moved so fast that I didn't have time to pull my hand away before he grasped it.

"What the fuck is this? Are you fucking kidding me, Shandea?" he shouted. I saw Cara look up with a frown, and I shook my head. I yanked my hand away from Rodney and glared at him.

"Lower your fucking voice. This is where I work. If you can't respect that, you need to leave. I really don't see why you are here or looking for me anyway," I gritted.

"You're marrying that nigga, Dea? I didn't think you could be this fucking stupid, but I can see I'm wrong. How could you fuck with that nigga? Do you know he is the prime suspect in the case of your missing cousin? Do you know witnesses saw people from his club running up into her house and dragging her out? That's the type of man you like?"

I laughed. I laughed hard as I shook my head at him.

"Why are you here, Rodney? Because clearly, it isn't about Katrice because she is home. My sister is the one who put out the missing person's report for her, not her own sister. So what are you saying? You sound crazy as shit. So what is this really about?"

"Do you even know the niggas that you are associating with? Do you?"

"Goodbye, Rodney. I have entertained your bullshit long enough. Please, do not return here again, or I will file a harassment complaint," I snapped. I turned to walk away, but he reached out, gripping my arm tightly. I was jerked to a halt, and I turned to face him when I saw two men walking through the doors. I knew they were looking for me because I told them I would leave early today.

"Where is the Senator?"

"Get. Your. Hands. Off of. Me."

I held his stare. I could see the anger on his face, and I saw the moment he noticed Lennox's men walking toward us.

"Where the fuck is Kenneth Morgan?"

Rodney let my arm go when I twisted sharply and turned to face him. I adjusted the strap of my purse and raised a brow at him.

"How the fuck should I know where a sitting Senator is or isn't. I didn't know a Senator was missing. A lot of people have been going missing lately. Maybe you and your boys should actually solve some crimes instead of harassing young black women," I said.

"You're playing a dangerous game, Shandea, and I won't be there to help you when you get fucked over," Rodney gritted through clenched teeth.

"Well, I think things for me will work out smooth as silk," I smiled. I turned away and could feel Rodney's eyes drilling into my back. Why would he come here asking questions? What exactly did he fucking want?

Did he expect me to slip up or believe his shit? One thing was for sure, Lennox was right when he said people would come at me from every direction to fuck us over.

I got into my car and headed over to *MYTH*, figuring I would just meet Lennox there instead of going home. I didn't even call him about the Roe shit because I was sure his boys had already snitched to this nigga that someone had touched me. I knew he could only get into the building because of his badge. Lennox had shared the information about Rodney and him being a DEA Agent trying to take U.C.K. down. I wondered if it had to do with what happened six years ago, but if it did, that is some petty ass bullshit. Rodney wasn't a saint, and I knew that shit all too well.

It didn't take long to get to *MYTH*, and instead of parking, I pulled right up to the front. Someone peeled away from the door to come and take my car when I got out and stood up. I wiped a hand over my houndstooth print skirt, ensuring I didn't have peanut butter crumbs. I had run out of my P.B. bites and tried to get the last bit in my mouth when the light turned green. Lennox was already going to talk shit about my breath. He didn't need to find the evidence.

"What's up, Ms. Dea."

I looked up and smiled at Jaycen while fixing my bag on my shoulder.

"Hey, Jaycen. Not working at the Emerald today?"

"Naw, you know we gotta switch out the rotation occasionally," Jaycen chuckled.

"I understand. It was good to see you," I smiled. I felt surreal inside the club because it looked so different from the night we came. When I entered the club floor area, I saw Lennox leaning against the bar, rolling a cigar between his fingers. He'd stop smoking them when I almost took his head off, but he still had a habit of rolling them through his fingers, which I loved. It was just something about the smell of an unlit cigar. I loved it, or the baby loved it. I approached him when his head turned my way, pinning me with his cognac eyes.

"Why the fuck was another nigga touching you, Shandea?"

I was already expecting his line of questioning, but I didn't expect him to be waiting down here. I just shrugged at him because what could I say? I broke his hold on me, and it wasn't like the shit was welcomed.

"I handled it," I said, strolling up to him. He leaned down, kissing my lips, and I felt a hand go under my curls and squeeze the back of my neck. Lennox sat the cigar down and placed his other hand over my stomach, something he just started doing lately.

"I was just reading the file we got on Rodney. I want to use his ass to my advantage and remind him that he is a bitch and needs to stay in his place."

"You don't need to insult dogs, Lennox."

"Funny. Let's take this meet and greet to my office, Sweetness. I still have work to complete and a meeting with my people in a while. You don't need to stay if you don't want to," he said, letting me go. Lennox turned around and took my hand, leading me to a bank of elevators that led to the floor where his offices were held.

"I'm okay. I'll wait for you today. I honestly came because I really wanted to see exactly what the hell you be doing here," I said. Lennox held up a card, the elevators opened, and he pulled me inside.

"If you want to see some freaky shit, just say so, Shandea," he smirked. I faced him and stepped closer as I grabbed his blood-red tie. I ran a hand up his muscled chest that I could feel through his white dress shirt. His dark gray designer suit fit him so well that I wanted to find out who he had made them so I could buy more in the colors I wanted to see him in. Lennox didn't move, and I appreciated it because I was still not mentally all there. But I couldn't deny my love for him and the love that he had for me.

"Is that what your meetings are about? Some freaky shit?"

"I call them lessons, and they can get nasty," he groaned. I pressed up against him, and I could feel how hard he was for me. "You about to get fucked, Dea, and I just told you I had shit to do. Keep playing with me, and you will be the fucking lesson," he gritted. I bit down on my lips as moisture pooled in my panties. That day at the hospital just wasn't enough, even though his tongue had me climaxing a minimum of four times. It was like he and Faxx were in some kind of pussy eating contest, and I don't think Crescent nor I gave a fuck about who won. Lennox reached up, pulled my lips from my teeth, and licked into my mouth. The elevators dinged, but I was lost in how he sucked on my tongue. Lennox's hand held my head in place as he took what he wanted from me.

"Jesus, Boss, can't you do this shit somewhere, like in one of the hundred rooms downstairs or in your freaking office," Shantel gagged. I opened my eyes wide and tried to pull away, but Lennox wasn't finished. His eyes were open and staring behind me while his hand grabbed my ass. I moaned. "Dear God, come on! Get off. I need to be somewhere," Shantel groaned. Lennox pulled back and chuckled before spinning me around.

"Hi, Shantel," I smiled.

"Hey, girl. Did you get a spanking as well? I took my punishment like a bad bitch, which was worth it. I wish I could have killed Katrice, but there is always tomorrow," she smirked.

"Who punished you? You didn't do anything wrong," I said.

"Don't listen to Shantel's spoiled ass, and why the fuck are you wearing my damn clothes?" Lennox shouted. Shantel leaned to the side, effectively holding the doors open.

"I am not spoiled, and I told you I like how they feel. Now move, nigga," Shantel frowned. She did look cute in the overly large tan and green custom-made sweatsuit and white Nikes. It looked comfortable. But I couldn't help but notice the red strap of something under it.

"And where the fuck are you going?" Lennox questioned.

"I am a whole grown-ass woman. I have a job requiring me to do shit for four grown-ass men. Now get out of the way," she snapped. Lennox pushed me forward as they bickered until the elevator closed.

"I should pull up her tracker. I don't trust her," Lennox grunted. I waved to Dominque before closing his office door.

"What?" I laughed.

"She's up to something. I know her sneaky ass. She fucking somebody," he said, sucking his teeth.

"That's her business," I huffed.

"Her business is my business."

"Leave that girl alone. I don't know how she deals with all of y'all cock blocking her. Let that girl live, damn," I said. I sat on the edge of his desk in front of him before he pulled me into his lap. He opened his laptop, and then his phone rang.

"Oz," he answered while typing in his password.

"I got your message. You need the passkey?"

"Link, why would you send me a file and then not the fucking password? What fuck are doing? You're over here trippin' and shit. I know how y'all crazy niggas be," Lennox said. I sat in his lap as he pulled up his email.

"Fuck you. I did it so you would need to call me when you had to open it," he informed. "I need to be on the phone when you see it."

"Nigga, give me the fucking code," Lennox insisted. I watched as he pulled up the email in question and then clicked the play button, entering the code provided by Link. A video came up, and it was of the same fucking chick Nia. I frowned automatically, stiffening until I saw Sam pacing the living room while she wiped her face. Oz turned the volume up, and I almost choked when she stood up, revealing a baby bump.

"Oh shit," I whispered.

"Exactly. That wasn't in that fucking video now, was it?"

"Shut up! What did she say?"

Lennox started the video over and turned up the volume more.

*"It's not his baby, Sam! I've been trying to fucking tell you this shit for weeks, but you were fucking ignoring me. I knew my going through with my plan hurt you, but when it got down to it, I couldn't. I couldn't do it, and I wasn't even going to continue until I found out that I really was pregnant. And I knew for sure that it wasn't Wes's child. I did the test. This baby is yours," Nia confirmed.*

*"What the fuck, Nia? Why didn't you say anything? Why didn't you tell Oz about this shit? Not only will he be mad as fuck, but this nigga liable to fucking kill me."*

*"Oz will not kill you. I can fuck whoever I want."*

*"Not when you took on a job! What the fuck! I don't think he would have given a shit if you told him about the possibility, but you kept it from him," Sam shouted.*

*"Because I wanted to tell you first, nigga! I wanted to tell you about it first, but you would never give me a chance or try and hear me out. Did you think I wanted to fuck up a good lick? No, I didn't, but I ain't mad about it. Wes don't give a fuck or want anything to do with this child. There ain't nothing but positives in this situation."*

*He sighed. Nia moved over to Sam, rubbing a palm up his chest and leaning into him.*

*"If this nigga chop my hand off, you will need to feed two people instead of one," he chuckled.*

*"I will have no problem taking care of you, Samier. Now, how about you feed my pussy this dick. I missed you, baby," she purred. Nia pulled Sam to the couch, and he sat down, pushing his pants down.*

*"Sit on it, then. Let me feel that wet ass pussy."*

*Nia removed the thin dress and dropped it to the floor before straddling him. She groaned as she began to bounce on his dick.*

"Oh, my God. Wait, who the fuck is that?" I pointed. Lennox leaned forward, rubbing his temples. "Is that Damari?"

"It is," Lennox grunted. I watched, transfixed, as Damari walked into the house and dropped whatever he was carrying to walk around the couch as Sam bounced Nia on his dick. My eyes widened as he unbuckled his belt when he got to the back of the couch where Nia was facing.

*"I see y'all worked this shit out."*

*"Pregnant pussy is some good pussy, my nigga. Especially when it's my seed in there," Sam moaned.*

*"Oh shit, yes, baby, harder," Nia moaned. Damari stroked his dick and gripped Nia's braids.*

*"So you're having his baby, Nia? After you have this baby, you're going to have mine, right? Ain't that right, Nia," he gritted. Nia moaned as his grip tightened, and her eyes rolled back.*

*"Yes. Yes, Daddy. Anything, Daddy, I will have your baby, I promise," Nia cried.*

*"Good. Now swallow this dick like a good girl."*

Lennox slowly lowered the laptop screen as Link laughed over the phone.

"Nigga! I did not see this shit coming at all. How did you not know they were fucking?"

"You mean all of them? Damn, I would've thought Sam was the dom in the situationship," I laughed with Link.

"That's what I said! Damari gives pretty boy vibes, but obviously, we got it wrong," Link chuckled.

"Fucking bullshit. I should beat the shit out of all their asses, but this one is on Nia. She should have opened her mouth before now. We could have been ahead of the game. I'll handle it, my nigga," Lennox sighed.

"Bet. Dea! Are you cooking tonight? I wanna–"

Lennox ended the call, disconnecting Link while I laughed. This chick Nia was wild as fuck, and I still wasn't sure if I ever wanted to meet the girl.

"Get up for a minute, Sweetness. I need to go over a few things before I need to teach my people how things are done. Tell me what Rodney had to say," Lennox demanded. I smirked because I could hear the aggravation in his voice, and at least it wasn't directed toward me. I kissed his lips, stood up, moved over to the office chair in front of his desk, and dropped down. I pulled out my phone to go through emails while I told him about Roe's dumbass.

I finished telling him about the thinly veiled threat that I would be slutted out next and how I was fucking stupid when the doors to Lennox's office slammed open. I turned in my seat and saw a frantic Dominique shouting to stop at the tall, brown-skinned woman standing at least six feet without heels. The woman rocked the fuck out a faded glory cut with streaks of purple through it. She wore a black genie baby jumpsuit that showed her long, toned legs and the fact that she didn't need to wear a bra.

"Oz! Did you miss me, zaddy," she moaned, throwing herself in my man's lap. "I couldn't wait to get back here to ride this big dick, zaddy," she smiled and then looked at me. "Who is this? A new one to train? Tell her to wait outside, or she can watch. She might learn something," she purred.

The bitch moved so fast that it took a minute for it all to catch up with me. I stood up so quickly that the chair flew backward, but I wasn't the only one. Lennox stood up, effectively dropping the bitch to the floor.

"I know you are fucking lying! How many more bitches are about to walk in here, Oz? I need to ensure I will have enough bullets," I spat.

## CHAPTER EIGHTEEN

# LENNOX 'OZ' ANDERSON

T he way Dea looked with her eyes flashing and the words coming out of her mouth had my dick hard as fuck.

"Mr. Anderson, I apologize. I tried to stop her, but she wouldn't listen," Dominique huffed. Nique glared at Zanaya on the floor before looking at me with a smirk.

"It's all good. Thank you," I said through clenched teeth.

How and why the fuck was Zanaya here? I didn't know she was coming, but her ass won't leave after this stunt. "What the fuck are you doing here, Nya?" I asked, walking around my desk and leaving her to pick herself up off the floor. Even if Dea wasn't in here, she knew, like everyone else, not to burst into my office.

"Oz? What the hell?" Nya scoffed. I was sure the runway model wasn't used to this type of treatment, but I wasn't any other nigga, and she knew that shit. That was on her. The fact she believed she had some right to me was hilarious. We fucked whenever she was in town from time-to-time, but that was it, and it had never been any more to it than that. She ain't never rolled up in here like this before, so I can only believe she knew Shandea was here.

"What the fuck, Lennox? You know what...I...I'm going to go home. I don't even feel like dealing with funky ass bitches today. She's lucky I have more than just myself to look after." Dea's light brown eyes scanned over me and then shot to Nya.

"What the fuck are you talking about? We've had this conversation, and we will not keep having it. I gave that shit a pass because of everything that went down, Dea, but please keep pushing with this leaving shit," I threatened.

I stood before her as she pinched her lips together, trying not to speak. My dick was hard as shit when Dea got jealous, but I didn't need anything crazy going through her mind. I already knew that she was taking things step-by-step, and this shit could set her back. Dea's old insecurities wouldn't disappear regardless of how much we have moved forward. Fucking with those bum ass niggas fucked up her mindset, but I blamed myself because I should have dragged her back here as soon as I realized she had run.

"Back the fuck up, Lennox. I don't even feel like dealing with the bullshit. Get your slut buckets in order," she said.

"Slut? Hunny, I don't know who you are, but let's not get it twisted. We have been fucking longer than you have been around." I kept my eyes on Dea. I didn't give a fuck about Nya and her bullshit. Dea and I were conversing, but her light brown eyes narrowed slightly. I watched as her jaw clenched tightly. Her eyes moved from me and landed on Nya.

"You just let random ass bitches sit on you like that? When I'm here, will I have to always be on guard for one of these women thinking they can fucking touch you? She's lucky right now I don't beat her fucking ass, but by her looks, she seems like she might bring in top dollar."

"Sweetness, you are starting to sound like me, a little possessive with a good business-first mindset. That's a dangerous game you're playing," I said, my lips curving in a smirk.

"Because you belong to me," Shandea proclaimed.

"Yeah, but I saw it in your eyes before you could hide it."

"What the hell are you talking about?"

"Oz! What the hell is this? Why are you ignoring me?" Zanaya screamed. My patience was ending, but I needed to make Dea aware of what I was referring to.

"Zanaya! Get the fuck out," I commanded. I never looked away from my wife while Zanaya mumbled under her breath. Shantel would need to have a conversation with her because if I did, she would be liable to be taken to *FANCY PLANTS*. I knew she rolled up in here on purpose. Everyone here knew about Dea, and I was damn sure Nya got the word while she was in Paris. Yes, she was one of my exclusive Escorts that only worked with the rich and powerful in different countries, but the money she brought in didn't mean shit when it came to Shandea. When the door closed, Dea rolled her eyes and tried to move away, but I grabbed her arm. I pulled her back, leaned my head to the side, and studied her.

"What are you talking about?" Shandea asked.

"You didn't even realize it. That shit happened in a matter of seconds, and your first instinct was I was fucking her. Your second was to run. I saw it, Dea, so don't fucking lie," I stated.

"So what if it was? You run a fucking escort service, Lennox. Yes, I know we are together, and you are mine, but they don't! They don't know that because if they did, she wouldn't have brought her high dollar-priced ass in here and sat in your lap like she does it on a daily basis. So yes, I thought it. And?"

"That's what you think? You believe I haven't done enough for my employees to understand where you stand in my life?" I asked. My hand was wrapped around her throat now, and I could feel her swallow thickly as she trembled slightly.

"Clearly not," she said, raising her brows.

"Trust me, niggas know what's up, and if they don't, they will. Everyone, including you, will know when I'm fucking finished here today," I declared. I pulled Dea forward and crushed our lips together, knowing damn well Nya had returned. My eyes were open, and I could tell she could see how close she was to losing her life. I licked Dea's bottom lip before licking back into her mouth, making her moan. Shandea opened wider to me, and her arms came under my suit jacket and around my waist.

Her body pressed tightly against me, and her lips pressed firmly against mine. I slipped my tongue inside, licking the roof of her mouth, and she gasped slightly. I pressed closer so she could feel the length of my body and my dick. I kept a hand on her neck, massaging lightly while I gripped her ass and pushed her closer while claiming every corner of her mouth. I let my large hand roam along the length of her body, but soon returned to that ass. I broke the kiss when I knew I had her where I wanted her to be. I knew Shandea, and I knew her pussy was wet as fuck for me right now. I broke the kiss, and a mix of a growl and a groan made me chuckle. Dea was blinking, but I could tell she noticed my cold gaze as I stared behind her.

"I told you to get the fuck out, but since you're here, let everyone know there is a meeting session on sublevel three. Once this is done, Zanaya, I think you will need re-education. I'm sure Shantel will be pleased."

"Shantel? Where is Nia? I don't think I need to see Shantel–"

"Now!"

Nya tripped over her feet to get out the door. I looked back down at Shandea and flexed my hand around her throat.

"Maybe I should let you handle your business," she whispered.

"Oh naw, Sweetness. It's about time I help you get rid of those insecurities you have, because I am not the other niggas. You do remember how Crescent had to take her punishment?"

Dea panted slightly, and her pupils dilated as she stared at me.

"Yes."

"Well, it's your turn. You will gain two things from this, Sweetness. The knowledge that everyone here in this building today will know who the fuck you are and what you mean to me. And the second is realizing who this pretty little pussy belongs to," I rasped against her ear as I roughly pulled her to me by the neck. Shandea moaned when I licked the shell of her ear before spinning her around.

"Lennox, I don't..."

"Nope, too late. I'm about to fuck all your insecurities about us right out of your body. Let's go, Sweetness."

Before leaving my office, I sent Shantel a quick text, letting her know she would need to deal with Zanaya. It didn't look like she would return to modeling anytime soon. I held Shandea's hand as I pulled her to the elevators at the back of my office. I typed in a code and silently waited while we descended into *MYTH*. The elevator stopped on sublevel three, and the doors opened to a hallway lined with rooms on each side. At the end of this hall was a large room where I held special shows or sessions. I stepped into the room and looked at Trenton, who stood holding a tablet. If Shantel was my right hand, then Trenton was hers. He was efficient, so once we entered, he closed the doors and stood before them.

"Trenton, make sure you take notes of this session," I ordered. I looked at Dea, and I could see the 'what the fuck' in her eyes. The people that were in this room weren't like the partying club workers up top. Everyone was in different attire, from leather to chains to full-body latex. We even had some in masks who stood together in a corner.

"Is this where the Black Wolf be?" Dea whispered. My steps faltered because how the fuck did she know about him? I looked to my left where the niggas in masks stood. A few wore wolf masks, but nothing like what the Black Wolf would wear.

"How about I won't ask you how you know about that," I answered. Dea squeezed her lips shut as I dragged her to the raised stage. In the middle of the stage was a dais that sat covered in black velvet. Bindings hung from it at every angle.

"What the fuck?" Dea panted, but I said nothing. I turned around and looked over the people that were present today. I knew Trenton would take the notes, so what I said would be relayed to others.

"I want you all to watch me closely. I will personally show you how to punish a sub who doesn't trust in her dom. What do you do when their insecurities lead them? How do we show them who they belong to so those insecurities no longer matter?"

Shandea's eyes scanned the room. The lust filled them as she saw all eyes were on her. I could also see the apprehension, but the beat of her pulse in her throat and the lick of her lips told me all I needed to know. They were watching closely and carefully. Most of the men there were already hard as fuck, but they knew the deal. Everyone in this room knew who the fuck Shandea was, but I had to prove to her that she was no secret. Shandea moaned shamelessly when she felt my wet, hot tongue lick her neck. "Which one of them needs to understand who the fuck you are?" I whispered into her ear. I wanted her to own up to who was making her feel less than what she was. She knew better, but showing Dea I didn't give a shit about Zanaya would make her get over this shit faster. Zanaya and her feelings were nothing more than collateral damage to me. I stared at Nya, and I could see the hate and submission in her posture because she knew she'd fucked up.

Dea shook as my hands slid along her body, and I let my hand circle her neck and made her face Zanaya. "Fuck her. I told you people would do anything, and you can't let them in, Sweetness," I whispered against her ear. I pulled Dea behind the dais, where she could still be seen but not fully. Both my hands rested on her breast while I grinded my length against her ass, and she moaned. When I teased her nipples with my finger, her glossy lips were slightly parted from all the pleasure. Dea was sinking into a haze of pleasure, but I knew she hadn't done something like this on this large scale.

"What have I told you, Sweetness? How often do I need to tell you I am not those other niggas?" I asked. I pulled slightly on her curly hair, gathering it into my fist and gripping tightly. I pulled her head back, and it caused her chest to stick out, making her relax her head on my chest.

"You don't...you don't need to tell me anymore."

"What!"

"You don't need to tell me anymore, Lennox," she moaned. I let one of my hands slip from her breast and down her sides to pull up her skirt. I gathered the material up until her ass was showing to me. I smacked her ass before using my feet to move hers apart.

"Show me your pussy, Shandea."

She gasped lightly when my fingers found the split after she removed her panties. I didn't make it easy for her to do, and the more she struggled, the more she moved against my dick.

"Fuck," she moaned.

"Good, you understand now," I said as I rubbed her clit, my fingers following rhymical movements, and I let my speed increase as I rubbed.

"Fuck, Lennox, shit," Dea moaned as her hips moved. Her eyes closed, but I pulled her hair slightly, and they snapped open. Lust filled her gaze, and I could tell the pleasure made her dizzy. "Oh God," she moaned. Dea was dripping wet right now, and the watchful eyes of the people in the room were making it even worse. I knew she liked it by the way her thighs shifted every time I moved her head from side-to-side. Dea bit her lip, and I knew she was getting closer. I loosened my grip on her hair, and her head dropped low. I noticed she was close to cumming, so I increased the movement. Dea squeezed her eyes shut as she climbed closer to her climax. I let her hair go completely and gripped her jaw. I raised her head slowly, and she opened her eyes.

"Don't cum," I ordered.

"Please," she begged, but I let my hands slowly slip out of her wet core.

"Nope. I asked you to trust me, but you doubted me, even if it was for a second. We not doing that shit, Sweetness," I said, raising my fingers to my mouth. I licked her juices from them, savoring the taste of her pussy as she watched me.

"Lennox," she cried.

"You want to cum, Sweetness?"

"Yes, yes, please. Fuck me," she panted.

"Keep your head up and eyes open, Dea," I demanded. I pushed her onto the velvet dais.

I removed my suit jacket and dropped it to the floor. I loosened my tie and used the thin piece of clothing to bind her hands behind her back.

When I was done, I pulled her by the material. She jolted up, and her ass pushed out.

"Ahh! Ahh, shit, fuck," she moaned when I slapped her ass simultaneously. Dea's breaths came faster as her juices slid between her folds and down her legs.

"I will let you cum. Do you trust what I say?

"Yes!"

"You should have the first time," I said.

I unbuttoned my white shirt, took it off, and let my pants and boxers fall to the floor. I slid the head of my dick between her cheeks. I held on to the tie but used my other hand to spread her ass open. I let my length rub through her juices. Dea moaned, jerking, trying to make me push back so I could slip inside. My dick nudged at her entrance as she moaned and cried for me to fuck her. Shandea knew normally I would be deep in her pussy by now, but she had to know. I was already mad that Rodney touched her, but that doubt in her eyes was it. I can't have that. Not with all the shit I knew we would need to deal with in this life.

"Please..."

"Please, what?" I pushed in slowly.

"Please...fuck me. I'm sorry, Lennox...I know you...I have always trusted you."

I pulled her back to me. Her eyes looked into the crowd, but she couldn't see them through the lust. She was on edge and ready to cum as she squirmed. I pushed inside her core in one stroke. "Fuck, yes, yes, please, Daddy, please, fuck," she moaned. My other hand skimmed around her waist and found her pussy. I sought out her clit, rubbing her juices as she panted. I watched her face, and her eyes rolled back when I used the tie to pull her down on my dick. Dea's ass slapped against my thighs.

"Keep your eyes open. You like it when they watch, Sweetness, so watch them watch you," I grunted in her ear. Her core clenched around me, spasming as I pushed in deeper. I rotated my hips, and Dea screamed. She began to push back, trying to chase the orgasm that was building in the base of her spine. I bent my knees, driving up into her tight sheath while gripping one cheek, spreading it apart, and buried my shaft deep inside. I pulled back, thrusting in slowly until she started to shake. Her legs began to tremble as she moaned. I felt her juices sliding down my length and coating my balls. I slammed back inside, thinking that Sam's bitch ass was right. Pregnant pussy was some good pussy.

"Lean forward, Dea, and stand up on your toes. Throw that shit back on your dick, Sweetness. Let me see you take it, Dea," I grunted. I began to move faster, pumping in and out, pushing her further and further on her toes. I let her ass go, wrapped an arm around her waist, and slapped her clit.

"Fuck Lennox."

"That's right. I wanna be so deep in this pussy you only remember my name," I gritted. I circled my hips as she pushed back. I stepped closer, forcing her to lean further onto the dais as I ground my dick into her hot, slick core.

"Only Lennox," she panted. "Please, Lennox, I need to cum."

"I tell you when to cum, Shandea. You want to cum all over this dick, Dea?"

"Yes, yes," she screamed. "Ah...ah..." she gasped. I pulled out, and she groaned. "Oz," she whimpered, and I laughed.

"Oh, it's Oz now. Is that who you want, Shandea?"

"Baby, please, just fuck me," she begged. I pushed back in, and she arched up, trying to suck in a deep breath. "Ri...rig...right there," she heaved. Dea bit down on her lip as her eyes blinked like she was drugged. "I...harder, right there. Oh, shit, I'm going to cum–"

"I'm always Lennox to you, Shandea. That's what you scream while I beat this pussy up."

"Oh God, yes, Lennox," she cried and clenched around me. She was close, but it wasn't time for her to cum.

"Did I tell you to cum yet?" I asked in a rough voice. "You must have forgotten that this is a punishment. Naw, Sweetness, you don't get to cum yet. Stop trying to sneak, or you won't cum at all."

I pulled back out, stepped back, and flipped her over. I gripped her waist and sat her on the dais. Her hands were behind her back, and they kept her body raised. I put my arms under her legs and pulled her to the edge. I pushed back inside, and she clenched around me. I let one leg go and leaned on the table, driving into her tight pussy.

"Ahh...shit, yes, yes," she moaned. I let my fingers slide between her slit and flicked the bundle of nerves that sent her into a full-body shock.

"Don't cum!" I yelled again, stopping immediately.

Dea's body was already semi-convulsing as she jerked forward, and her eyes dropped in disappointment and anger.

"I need it. I need you," Dea said between moans.

"What did you say?"

"I need you...just you. I want you to fuck me so hard I'll crawl up these walls."

I fisted her hair, pulling on it slightly, making her head fall backward to look at who was watching. I think she forgot because as soon as she saw them, her core clenched, sucking me deeper as she licked her lips.

I pulled Dea forward, slamming her on my dick hard like I knew she liked it. Her cries and moans grew louder. Shandea trembled slightly, but I kept rubbing the head of my dick over the ridges at the top of her core, causing her to convulse. Her clit pulsed, and her legs wrapped around my waist as she rode me from the bottom.

"You want to cum. You better take your dick. Own that dick, Sweetness."

I slammed my length harder inside her pussy as her warm sheath tightened around me. Her pussy gripped my dick like a vice trying to milk every last drop of nut I had in my body. I groaned as my orgasm started in my toes and rushed up, causing my thrusts to get wilder. Dea's eyes closed, and she closed her mouth to prevent her from asking if she could cum.

"Cum." I ordered, and her body convulsed as a wave of pleasure shot through us both. I felt her pussy quake as her climax hit, and she moaned from the back of her throat.

"Oh fuck! Lennox, Lennox, Oh my God," she screamed as her legs gave out, falling from around my waist. I thrust two more times before I filled her to the brim, and I felt my cum leaking out of her wet heat. My dick was still shoved deep in her pussy as I looked up and stared directly at Zanaya.

"And this is how your sub will know who is in charge, or my case, my wife," I said before looking down at Shandea's sore but beautiful body. Her breathing was ragged, but I felt hard again when she opened her eyes and licked her lips.

"What about using that next time?"

I turned around only to see the bondage cross.

"I hope you're ready to take this dick again, Sweetness, because you're playing with me now."

I would have Shandea on that cross after the pregnancy. She had no idea what she was asking for, but she would learn.

## CHAPTER NINETEEN

# HENDRIX 'HENNY' PHARMA

Tali sat on my desk between my legs, unbuttoning my shirt to look over the dressing covering my wound. She was fussing at me, but it wasn't the first or last time I would get shot.

"You should've stayed home, Hendrix. You're crazy for coming in here today. You have to be in pain," Tali frowned. Her pink scrub pants pulled across her thick thighs, distracting me from the email I was sending.

"Naw, pain is relative. I'm good, Thickness," I said, rubbing my hand up her leg. She came down to have lunch with me and change my dressing while we reviewed her mother's care plan.

"If you say so. You can't be doing too much, Hendrix, while this is healing. You need to take it easy. You can now, right? He's...Ja is gone?"

I breathed out a sigh because I wasn't entirely sure, and I didn't like that shit. I always wanted to be sure when I put a nigga down, they weren't getting back up. I knew Tali was worried, but I refused to lie to her about it, either. Until I knew for certain Ja was dead, she still needed to keep her guard up and be on the lookout for this nigga.

"I want to tell you yes, but I didn't see the light in his eyes fade. But I know if he isn't, this nigga is low. He was hurt worse than I was, Sexy. Don't worry about me. I'm good," I said, pulling her forward.

"Did I or did I not say you need to be careful?"

"Who is the doctor in this room?"

"Me when it comes to making sure you do what YOUR doctor told you to," she smirked. "You know, Dr. Stax," she sighed with a smile. I couldn't stand that pretty ass nigga. Stax always had women falling over him. I narrowed my eyes at her, and she tried to move. I wrapped an arm around her waist, pulling her forward.

"Don't play with me, Tali. You like that nigga?"

"Stop! I can't...I'm not. You so aggy," she laughed. I let her finish the wound dressing, and when she was done buttoning my shirt, I clicked the email reply from Tremont.

Dr. Pharma,
I would like nothing more than to meet with you and the board at their earliest convenience. I have already taken the necessary steps to have one called for your unprofessional behavior. I do believe this is in the best interest of all parties. Please limit all contact with me to a strictly professional standpoint.
Dr. Ignacio Tremont

I leaned back in my chair and smirked at the email. The fact that this nigga thinks he knew Tali's best interests had me. Who the fuck did this nigga think he was to make such an assumption? I could already tell this nigga wouldn't get the picture. Tali was right about one thing, this nigga was a petty muthafucka. Running to the board because he was jealous like a bitch. I leaned my neck from side-to-side, cracking it. I knew he would approach Tali on some bullshit, but I would let her handle it. Because if I did it, I was liable to shove that nigga down the elevator shaft. She just better not let this nigga touch her like they still had some kind of connection.

"What's wrong with you?" she asked. Tali leaned back, and I looked up into her narrowed marble-gray eyes.

"I'm good, but ya boy is not," I said, tipping my chin. She looked at the screen with a frown.

"My boy? What the hell are you talking about? No—" She twisted around fully, and her foot hit the carpet, and I held my hand out to steady her. "I know you are fucking lying right now!"

"He will come and talk to you, Tali. Just don't let him fucking touch you. I don't know what kind of shit that nigga was on, but I don't like how you start to think after you are around him or have had any contact with him," I stated.

"How would you know my thoughts about anything about him?" She turned back to me slowly and folded her arms across her chest.

"We're not doing this," I said, pulling her arms down. "You know damn well what I am talking about because it's the reason why you were acting out of pocket right after we fucked in Sanchez's room," I said.

"You know I don't care about having sex in front of him. It wasn't like it was the first time," she scoffed. "Let me get back to work. Cent was already mad at me because I left her in the computer training room and came down here. Then Faxx showed up, and she thinks I set it all up," she giggled.

I gripped her wrist tighter so she couldn't pull away and raised a brow.

"It's not about having sex in front of Sanchez. That was the problem. It was asking that nigga to basically cum for you. That's what you said, right? That's what you wanted?" I studied Tali as her eyes widened before a mask settled over her face, and she began to close down. "No. Nope, fix your fucking face. Did I say I had a problem with it? Aren't I the one who told you to ask for what you wanted? I already told you what I wanted to do, so what's the difference," I imparted.

"Why are you bringing this up? Shouldn't you be worried about this meeting and what it could mean for the hospital?"

"Don't deflect, Tali."

I waited her out as she stared at me before looking away.

"I didn't want to deal with the aftermath of it and what you would have to say about it. Or probably more how you would look at me," she stated. I stared at her as her words ran through my mind. Emotions were a far-reaching concept for me, but I understood what she was saying if I didn't understand how she felt. I wouldn't give a shit what anyone else thought, but that was where we were different.

"I don't give a fuck what you want to do, watch, or experience as long as I am the only man touching you. As long as you know, everything from these locs to your pretty ass toes belongs to me. You can do you and go off, Thickness. Because when it's all said and done, the shit I am going to do to you once I heal up will make what we got started to look like a G-rated movie," I insinuated. I jerked her wrists forward and reached up to the back of her neck, pulling her to my lips.

"Mmmm, Henny, you know I don't have time for this," she whispered against my lips.

I took my time licking her bottom lip until she parted them for me. I dipped my tongue into her warm mouth, and she groaned. I sucked on her tongue while massaging her neck. I let her wrist go, and my hand dropped to the small tie holding her scrub pants up. Then there was a knock, and the door opened.

"Dr. Pharma, what is this!" Yasmin complained loudly. Tali jumped and tried to pull away from me, but I still held her neck. I kept her lips on mine as Yasmin watched. "What the fuck?"

My gaze moved to Stephanie, who smirked at Yasmin before turning around to her computer. She let this shit happen on purpose, but I didn't give a fuck. Yasmin's hard brown eyes stayed trained on me when I pulled away from Tali. I moved my hand from her pants, mad as fuck that I was that close to her slick heat. I let Tali go and leaned back into my chair as Tali hopped off my desk, doing her best to fix her clothes before turning to face her cousin, or was it, sister?

"What can I help you with, Ms. James?" I asked. Yasmin's gaze left mine when Tali turned to face her and then grew heated.

"Can we speak about this in private?"

"Anything you need to say to me can be said in front of Tali. She is your family and holds a stake in this company," I added. Yasmin's jaw clenched forcibly, and Tali shifted her weight at the knowledge. I planned to let her know once she signed on at the Women's Center, but...

"What the fuck is this? And if it is what I think it is, you cannot do this! I will sue you for harassment and—"

"Close the fucking door, Yasmin, and let's talk about all the fucking money you stole from me."

Yasmin's head snapped to me as her eyes widened at what I had said. She turned around to leave the office, but Stephanie stood in her way, bringing her up short.

"Get the fuck out of my way," Yasmin said, trying to push by Stephanie. Everyone always said that Shantel got her mean streak or fighting skills after the incident, which left her permanently scarred, but those people didn't know Stephanie.

"Bitch, back the fuck up and go have your meeting you couldn't wait to have, remember."

"Bitch," Yasmin roared and pushed Stephanie out of her way. Tali was about to move, but I caught her arm, shaking my head. Stephanie moved so quickly that I didn't see the punch to Yasmin's chest but instead saw her stumble backward further into my office.

"This bitch will dog walk your dollar store weave around this fucking waiting area. Now own up to your shit and take a fucking seat," Stephanie seethed. Yasmin could barely breathe, and Stephanie turned her cold gaze to me.

"Thank you," I smirked.

"Let me lock up the outer area while you have this little meeting. Oh, and Tali, please ensure he brings you to our family dinner. We all will be in attendance, and attendance is mandatory, Hendrix," she smiled. I kept my mouth closed because I already knew Auntie was about to pull weight, but it was time anyway. It wasn't like Tali was leaving Union City or my fucking life.

"We will see you there, Mrs. Stephanie," Tali smiled.

"I like this one, Hendrix," she sneered in Yasmin's direction before closing the door. I pushed up from my chair, removed my glasses, and rubbed my eyes.

"Now, the amount of pain you will receive from me, Yasmin, will depend on how much money of mine you will recover. Because if you can't, I will remove a finger for each bogus transaction you made," I snarled.

Yasmin coughed as she gasped, trying to take in air. I could feel Tali at my back as I moved closer to where Yasmin was leaning against the wall. Yasmin pushed herself away from the wall as if she could actually get away from me. She looked around the room like someone was about to jump out and help her escape.

"You...you can't do this. You... you!" She looked at Tali with fearful and hateful eyes. "I'm family, and you let him threaten me like this? It's getting heated," she stammered.

"Family? Bitch, please."

"Your little code word for 'help' in that heated statement ain't going to mean shit when no one is listening."

Yasmin's gaze went wild, but as I approached her, she went for what she knew best, and that was making herself the victim.

"Just like your damn mama, bitch! Fucking your sister's dicks," she sneered. "All we wanted was the family y'all had! That's it," Yasmin whined. I stepped quickly and was in front of Yasmin before she could move around the couch. I pressed her up against the wall with one hand. The blunt tips of my fingers dug into the flesh of her throat.

"Hendrix, I don't give a shit what she is saying. She can't get what you asked for if she's dead. Get what you need and get this bitch out of here," Tali waved. I smiled at Yasmin because what Tali didn't know about Yasmin and Katrice was what they had planned for their Mama.

"Remember when I told you that your mother is now a part of my family?"

Yes, Hendrix," she answered. Her small hand was on my shoulder, and I blinked, realizing I was squeezing the fuck out of Yasmin's throat. I eased up slightly, and she breathed as her hand weakly clawed at my forearm.

"Do me a favor and grab the phone that is next to the laptop. Click the icon with a dove and hit the first recording you see. I waited as Tali did what I told her to do. I held Yasmin against the wall fighting the urge to slam her bitch ass into it until she lost consciousness. Tali held up the phone and hit the screen.

*"Will you get what I need or what? I have a judge ready to sign off on your paperwork to take over power of attorney for your Auntie Naomi. It's pretty fucked up that you convinced her that going to the doctor was pointless when you knew something was wrong. I think that's fucked up, but to each her own."*

*"I don't give a fuck about that bitch. The only thing I need to do is be sure to dismiss those doctors and let her ass die the death she should have had last year."*

*"Fucking cold as shit, Yasmin."*

*"But do you have information on my fucking sister!"*

Tali stopped the recording, and the fire in her gray eyes told me all I needed to know. Yasmin wasn't walking out of this room alive. She was dead walking.

"Henny, get the information you need, and then I have a favor," she gritted.

"What do you need, Thickness?"

"I've always wanted to assist in open heart surgery. Do you have one coming up?"

I looked Yasmin over as her eyes grew three times their normal size.

"Wh..wha..what! No, no you...Tali...Tali...wait, just wait," she heaved.

"There is always someone in need of an organ donation, especially for heart transplant patients."

I didn't know if Tali was serious or if she was just trying to fuck with Yasmin's head. But when I turned my head to face her, I saw her eyes scream that she would do anything to protect those she cared about. Tali not only wanted Yasmin dead, but she wanted to assist me in doing so.

"Are you sure about this, Tali? I can handle this myself."

"It's your *Clinic*, Hendrix. I wanted to see it all. If you prefer, we can take her bitch ass to the stalls where Katrice took an extended vacay," Tali scoffed, but when her gray eyes met mine, my dick throbbed and jumped. Obsessed. I had become obsessed that night, but now she had become my absolute obsession. I turned back to Yasmin and leaned in closer to her face.

"I want every dime you stole from me transferred into accounts under the name Rodney Gates."

Yasmin knew the smile and the dead look in my eyes told her all she needed to know. She'd just fucked up, and now she was about to find out.

Tali glared at Yasmin for another hour, but I could also see the hurt, sadness, and disgust on her face. Luckily she was only in for the day for computer training, not on the floor. I could tell she was becoming more agitated whenever Yasmin glanced my way. Before she moved to leave and go back to work, she stared at Yasmin on a laptop that connected with Link and pulled me down to kiss her. I felt like she had it in her head to fuck the shit out of me in front of Yasmin, but she pulled back.

"If she does anything but keep her fingers on the fucking keys, I will break her damn neck," I stated, hoping that would calm her growing unease. I knew she didn't want me and her in the same space because I'd fucked her, but I didn't want Yasmin. Tali knew this shit.

"Oh my God," Yasmin cried. Her hands shook at my words, but her fingers never stopped moving. I guess Tali's eyes were bugged out of her head at the casual statement, but I've said worse shit.

"I know...okay, hold up," she put up a hand before looking at the ceiling. "You do understand how crazy that statement is, right? It's not that you don't know how crazy you are?"

I laughed, and it caused Yasmin to jump slightly. Tali raised her brows at me, waiting on my answer.

"What the fuck do you think? I used to kill small animals or some shit. I'm not crazy, Tali. I'm fucking insane, but I manage it and bend it to my will. Yes, I know how what I said might sound crazy to others, but tell me, did it settle something inside you knowing I would do that, or are you uncomfortable?"

"If I was uncomfortable about it, would you stop? Would you give this shit up, or is it something you gotta do?"

I thought about what she was asking and knowing the true answer. I knew I didn't want to do it because it was not necessarily a want but a necessity. It has to be done.

"This is what I need to do, not only for me, but for my brothers and others close to us. If anything in that life makes you uncomfortable, I will go out of my way so you will never come into contact with it again. You want Dr. Pharma, that's who I will be for you. I don't change for anyone, and I do what the fuck I want to. But for you, Tali, I will be everything you need," I said. Tali's brows pulled together, and she looked away. I didn't want to lie to her and say I would stop because that was impossible. "What do—"

"No, no, just no. I told you I wanted to know all of your personalities and meant it. I don't want one side of you. I want it all. If she touches you, though, Hendrix, I'm calling Shantel and Mala. Then we will take her ass to the farm," Tali sucked her teeth.

She stood on her tiptoes and kissed me before spinning around. I watched as her thick ass swayed toward the door. Tali's flawless espresso skin and long locs had me curling my hand into a fist because I wanted to drag her ass back and bend her over my desk. Tali walked out, chatting with Stephanie before the door closed. I knew Stephanie was telling Tali all about our dinners at Link's parents' home. This month was about to be something else with her and Dea attending. My gaze slid to Yasmin, who had tears rolling down her face as we discussed the meaninglessness of her life.

"So...so you all did take my sister? But... you sent her back. Why? Why kill me, Hendrix?" she questioned. I clenched my jaw and let a tight smile cross my face.

"Katrice's time is limited, but she will serve a purpose later. As for you, bitch, there isn't enough shit you could do to save yourself. The only thing keeping it painless for you is me not telling Tali or Dea how you intentionally kept their mother ill until you found out she was dying. So if you want it to be quick and painless, I suggest you shut the fuck up."

I glanced at the screen when she sucked in a breath and saw Link's face in the corner as he watched her work. I could see a question he wanted to ask in his eyes, but knew it wasn't the time. I already knew what it was, and the answer was no. I would tell Tali and Dea about what this bitch was doing to their mother, but now wasn't the time. We needed her to set up herself and that nigga Roe in the process. Then I had an idea. "Yasmin, I would like for you to create another account. I want you to shift two million of that money into an offshore account. Make sure when you create the account the owner of it is Dr. Ignacio Tremont."

"This nigga is wild! Shit, this will be one of the best board meetings we've ever had," Link chuckled.

I agreed, since this was the only meeting we've ever technically had. The only wild card was the eighth member. I had to have the shares open publicly for a while before closing it. We bought up all the shares, but someone purchased two percent before we could. They have remained a silent board member since it was formed, but replied to Tremont's request for an in-person meeting. Even Link couldn't pull up information besides the Neveena-Sonny Memorial company name. It was strange because that was where my mother and father were buried. It was also where Oz's mother was laid to rest. I frowned, thinking about the name and the letter Dea found with his mother's picture. *SONNY*.

"I...I'm finished. Wh...what else do you need? Whatever you think I said or did, Rodney made me do it. He has some kind of vendetta against U.CCC.K," she whispered that last part. Link leaned back in his chair and narrowed his dark eyes on Yasmin. I walked forward and sat at my desk in front of her.

"Did she do everything correctly?"

"She was slow as fuck and slightly sloppy, which is probably how she was caught in the first place. It's sad that she's sexy as fuck, and has some brains, but is a piece of shit. I will take care of the rest before I leave for the farm. I had a few card counters today," Link smirked.

"Bet."

I reached out and slowly closed the laptop while watching Yasmin. She swallowed thickly and licked her lips. "Who the fuck said anything about U.C.K.?"

Yasmin began to fidget as she smoothed down her off-white short-sleeved fitted dress. Her large chest moved up and down rapidly as her eyes bounced between mine. Yasmin grew up in this city, and I knew damn well she knew the name. No one in Union City could walk around ignorant of who ran shit. They just didn't know who we were.

"I...I...Hendrix, I didn't mean anything. It was just something Rodney said and..."

"Yasmin."

Yasmin closed her mouth and stared at me. I could tell she saw the same thing she saw in my gaze when she brought her ass to my office that day when Aunt Vanessa called her out. "Place both palms on the desk."

"Oh shit. Oh my God, please, please, please," she murmured but did what she was told.

"Do you know that Tali will be my wife and the mother of my children one day?"

"I...I..."

"Shut. Up," I knew that I asked her a question that she felt the need to answer, but I wanted her off kilter. She closed it and just shook her head confused. "Then you realize that you were trying to kill my soon-to-be mother-in-law. You were actively trying to kill the woman that gave birth to Tali."

Yasmin stopped nodding as her eyes darted around. I wasn't sure what she thought she would find, but it wasn't there. "I refuse to do the same to you since you're family and all," I shrugged as she relaxed slightly. "So I decided to go ahead and make that appointment for you. I know a family that will be so happy with the heart you will be donating," I smiled.

"Wha...what?"

I reached out faster than she could see and grabbed the back of her head. I slammed her forehead into the desk three times in rapid secession. Her head slumped forward, and she fell heavily onto the desk. I stood up and walked to my door, opening it to see Stephanie on the phone.

"Hold on, girl. This crazy ass nigga looking at me," she whispered. "Dr. Hendrix, how can I help you?"

I blinked at her ass because she wasn't talking to anybody but my Auntie.

"Call Faxx's clean-up crew. Someone needs to be delivered to the *Clinic* for an appointment," I said, stepping back into my office.

"Ohhh girl, that bitch finally headed to fucking Hell! Bougie ass bitch."

# CHAPTER TWENTY

## TALI SAUNDERS

I wanted to see Mama before I left today, so once I completed my assigned yearly health assessments that Union Memorial required us to take, even if we were travel nurses, I stretched and stood up. I wanted to return to Henny's office and beat the shit out of that bitch Yasmin. I still couldn't believe the urge and feeling that came over me. How could she want to do some shit like that to her aunt? I didn't give a fuck about what my daddy did or didn't do, my mother never treated either her or Katrice differently. I almost turned back because I saw the wince of pain on his face when he stood up. Henny never noticed I didn't sleep the rest of the night because I watched him. I could see the pain etched on his face every time he moved in bed.

I was hoping nothing else would go down and he could relax. I told him we didn't need to go to the charity event and that Dea would understand, but he shook his head in the negative. He looked at me, touching my cheek like he was apologizing. *'I can't show weakness, Tali. You never know who's watching,'* and all I could do was nod my understanding. I did get it, but damn, he was in pain no matter how he tried to hide it.

"You good? I still have a few more to do, but I'll be done before you clock out. I can meet you over at Dea's," Crescent said. She was still mad that I left her with Faxx earlier, but I knew she loved when he showed up.

"Girl, bye, I'll wait. I want to see Mama anyway. Are you still ducking out on Faxx today? I don't know why you just don't drive the rental he got for you?"

Crescent crossed her arms and raised a brow. She tilted her head to the side, making her side-swept blond and brown cornrows pool onto the computer keyboard.

"I know you can't think that is a rental. Fransisco is not slick at all. I am not taking or driving shit he's bought me. I will drive when he returns my shit or when I buy a new one," she snapped.

"You're trippin' Crescent, but do you. You always talking about me and Dea, but now look at you," I smirked. "Cuffed up with a U.C.K. hitta," I laughed. Crescent widened her eyes and looked around the empty room before calming down and shooting me the finger.

"Bye, Tali," she said, waving me off.

"Don't do that! You love me."

"And do, but you still get on my last nerve," she sighed.

Her phone buzzed on the desk, and she froze when she looked at the screen. She turned off the screen without answering or declining the call. I frowned because I knew it wasn't Faxx. Even when he'd call, she would answer, rolling her eyes. From what I saw, she had never let his calls go unanswered whenever I was around. I pushed the computer chair under the desk and approached her station. Crescent sat staring at the computer for two minutes, and that was it for me.

"Cent, what the hell is going on with you?" I asked. I leaned over and clicked the multiple-choice answer so she could move onto the next test.

"Hey! I knew the answer, Tali. Damn," she jumped.

"Crescent Johnson Pharma! What the fuck is up with you?" I asked again. She looked up at me, trying not to smile, but she started to laugh. I raised both brows and waited for her to spit the shit out. "You know all the shit I've been through and what's happening now. But I still don't know anything about you, Cent—nothing about your past or family. Or tell me why you've been so jumpy lately. Whatever it is, you can talk to me. You know that, right?"

Crescent looked up at me and smiled, nodding her head.

"I know, I know it's just...it's just hard to trust people. And yes, I know our situation is a little different since my work hubby is my boss, but it's hard for me. Give me a little more time?" She sighed. "I promise we can sit down and talk about everything. I just..."

"It's cool, Cent. We are here, okay? Whatever it is, we will have your back on it. If I need to beat somebody down, I will do it. On God," I said, tapping a nail on the table.

"Chile, please, if your ass ain't knocked up and shit. The way y'all be going at it, I don't know. Sanchez told me all about your nasty ass," she sang.

"Bitch, fuck you," I laughed. "See why you are gossiping with this ninja. You could have gotten the tea from me. He's not going to tell you all about that thang thang he workin' with," I hummed.

"What! Oh, shit, tell me. Tell me all about zaddy Sanchez," she clapped.

"Nope! You gotta wait now. Since you are talking behind my back," I said, backing away. I turned around and jogged out of the room, but not before I felt something hit my back. I turned around, saw a balled-up piece of paper, and fell out.

"Fuck you, Tali. I'm going to tell my man how you're acting," she shot back. I waved and went to the elevator, glad I could at least take that alarmed look off her face.

I made my way to the elevators and jumped on, preparing myself to see my mother. I never wanted her to see me worried or upset, especially with everything she was dealing with. I got off, entered her room, and sat beside her bed. She was asleep, but I didn't care as long as I was with her. I knew this new treatment schedule was harder on her body, so I wasn't about to wake her. I sat back, thinking over everything, and those bitches came to mind again. I just couldn't understand the shit. How the hell could you, as a human, do some shit like that? I was angry but had second thoughts about taking a life like that. I looked at my Mama, and it seemed to fade away. They were willing to let my mother die to have a payday. I shook my head, and the thoughts of strapping that bitch down and stabbing her seemed to cool my blood. My eyes widened, and I shook my head, pulling out my phone.

**Tali:** *I think your psycho tendencies are rubbing off on me. Can a person catch crazy?*

**Henny:** *As a professional crazy is most definitely contagious. Do you need a prescription?*

**Tali:** *Yes! What is the medication?*

**Henny:** *This Dick! Unfortunately, it has to be administered in the buttocks. It can hurt a little, but not for long.*

I crossed my legs as moisture coated my panties. I felt my core heat up and grow slick at his message. Why I had never allowed anyone else to take my anal virginity, I didn't know. I never forgot what he said six years ago about it, and it was almost like he claimed it. Yeah, I was definitely catching what he got.

**Hendrix:** *Scared? I can talk you through it.*
**Tali:** *What if I just decided to keep the craziness instead?*

I waited while I watched the chat bubbles. They stopped and then started again.

**Hendrix:** *Tali, you will still take all this dick either way.*
**Tali:** *Why it always gotta come down to sex lol?*
**Henny:** *What's really going on, Sweetness? Are you having second thoughts?*
**Tali:** *About?*
**Hendrix:** *Your first surgical experience.*
**Tali:** *Yes and then no. I'm not used to my thoughts wandering down that path.*
**Hendrix:** *Tell me what you want. What do you want to happen?*

My head snapped up when the door opened, and Tre walked inside, holding his tablet. He looked up, and his eyes swept over me before holding my stare.

"Tali, I am glad you're here. Your mother's treatment is going as expected. The meeting tomorrow will mostly be about the next course of action."

"Oh, yes, okay, that sounds great. We have questions and concerns about it, but I can wait until the meeting. I'd rather Shandea be here when I ask," I smiled.

"Perfect. It's always best for all family parties to be involved in the decisions."

I was so glad he decided not to bring up the other day. My phone lit up, and I saw Henny sending a question mark. Tre walked closer, and I hit the button, turning the screen off. He looked down at my phone and then moved over to Mama. While he checked her over, I unlocked my phone to answer Henny.

**Tali:** *I don't know. We can talk about it later. I'm okay.*

**Hendrix:** *Are you sure? I can call it a day, and we can go home and discuss it. Everything happened fast, and it could have been the heat of the moment.*

**Tali:** *...*

"Tali, can we speak outside for a moment? I don't want to wake her. She's had a long day," Tre stated. He didn't wait on an answer as he moved to the door. Regardless of how Tre acted, he was an exceptional doctor. I got up, stuck my phone in my pocket, and followed him outside the door. I closed it and turned toward him. Tre promptly grabbed my elbow and pulled me toward an equipment room.

"What the fuck are you doing?" I hissed. I jerked my arm back, but he was stronger. His grip tightened, and he pulled me through the door. "What the hell is wrong with you?" I gasped when I spun around. I pushed him in his chest, and he stumbled back slightly before catching himself.

"What is wrong with me? What the fuck is wrong with you? Jumping from doctor to doctor, I see. No wonder we were never going to work out. You don't know how to stop while you're ahead," he scolded.

"Nigga what?"

Tre shook his head and curled his lip up like he was staring at trash.

"Speak like a grown woman, Tali. You got me out here looking like a fucking idiot in this hospital. How many men are you sleeping with here? Is it one, two, or is it three? Because I see you laughing with that light-skinned security guard. How long are you going to keep spreading your legs for everyone?"

I knew my mouth was open, and my brows had to be in my hairline. I didn't know I had moved until I heard the echo of the slap bounce off the walls.

"Fuck you, Ignacio. I didn't ask you to come here, you chose to come here, and I hoped it was to help a patient in need. Not to worry about who I am and who I am not having sex with. It didn't seem to be a problem when I was fucking you, so why now?"

Tre clenched his jaw and his hands as he narrowed his eyes at me.

"Is Pharma the type of man that you want? You just let a 'Nigga' fuck you in your place of employment and a patient's room?"

"What the fuck are you talking about?" I frowned at him because how the hell did he know that? I knew Henny and Sanchez would never say anything about that day to him. So how did he know? Tre smirked as he looked me over. My chest was heaving, and I felt myself shaking.

"Oh. Hendrix didn't tell you?"

"Tell me what?"

"Dr. Pharma, didn't inform you that I walked in the room while his dick was shoved down your throat?"

My eyes widened because he hadn't. But why the fuck would he be in Sanchez's room in the first place? What I did and didn't do was none of his business.

"Don't look so shocked, Tali. You liked it. By the sounds, you loved that shit. Is that what you want? You want it quick and dirty right here?" He gestured to the equipment room. I pulled back at his vicious attack on me. The hypocrisy of his words floored the hell out of me because we had sex in his office. I looked down and saw the large bulge in his suit pants and slowly raised my gaze to his. He licked his lips before he sighed. "I don't want to argue about this. I know he was probably taking advantage of you, Tali. You can't take the hood out of that kind of people," he chuckled.

"You don't know shit. You don't know a fucking thing about me even though we spent a year together. I spent one night with Hendrix six years ago, and he knew more about how to please me than you did when I fucking coached you how to. You can talk shit about me and what I like all damn day, but what you won't do is say shit about Hendrix. You don't know him or me. If handling my mother's case will be too difficult for you, we can find another qualified doctor. We are not together and will never be together again. If you can handle it, then the only words you need to say to me are about my mother, and that is it," I snapped. I was in his face, and he stared at me with his thick brows raised at my words. I pushed his shoulder to move him out of the way of the door.

"He's really gotten into your head. With the things you like, Tali, he will never take you seriously. At least I was willing to settle. All he wanted was another round and couldn't even take you off the job to do it. Can't take the hood out of some 'niggas' right," he scoffed.

"If we were on the streets, Tre, I would show you what hood looks like because I see you forgot I grew up a product in Union City streets. Don't test me, Tre, and stay the fuck away from me."

I opened the door, but I was looking over my shoulder at his shaking head. "Trust me, you don't want the problems I come with," I swore. I turned around and widened the door, and ran into Hendrix. "Henny," I squeaked. The hardness in his eyes as he stared over my head spelled RedRum! *Murder.* "It's all good. I handled it," I said, touching his chest. He reached up, grabbed it, and held it to his chest before pushing me back inside the equipment room. He stepped around me but never let my hand go. He would drag me if I didn't move, so I followed. Tre raised his head as he looked Henny over and grimaced. Then Henny chuckled. The shit was dark, deadly, and cold.

"Let me explain something to you, Tre. If you ever look at, touch, or approach Tali again, I will ensure you can no longer perform another surgery. If you love your career, walk the fuck away," Hendrix threatened.

"You are the one that needs to be worried about practicing anywhere ever again, Pharma. Not after we finish with our meeting," Tre snorted. I didn't know how I ever convinced myself he could ever be a replacement for Henny.

"Nigga, if you think I am talking about you losing your license or job, you are a fucking idiot." Henny stepped closer, but Tre stood there. However, I could see his expression change because he had no clue what Henny meant. What else was there if not losing your position? "This...this hood nigga will make sure those hands that make you money won't even be able to pick up a spoon to feed yourself. Do. Not. Fuck. With. Me. I will see you at the meeting, my nigga," Henny vowed. He turned around and pulled me through the door.

After all that shit with Tre, Henny was surprisingly chill about it. He said what he said and then told me he would come over to Oz's when he finished for the day. Now I was watching Dea move around the living room, trying to find a smell that no one else could smell.

"Are y'all sure you can't smell that? I don't want my house stinking when this doctor gets here," she said. I only smelled the roast she was making because I wanted that with some mashed potatoes and roasted carrots. Crescent raised her brows at me and shook her head.

"Dea, is it the food? Smell the oven," Cent laughed. It was all but a minute before we heard gagging. We both jumped up and ran to the kitchen. Dea was over the trash can dry heaving.

"Oh my God, I think the meat is bad," she cried. The girl had been so emotional since we got here. I looked at Crescent before moving to my sister and taking her into my arms.

Crescent went to the fridge and grabbed her fruit salad and a jar of peanut butter. I took her back to the couch before going around the room and lighting scented candles.

"Here you go, mommy. Take your mind off the smell with some fruit," Cent smiled. Dea perked up, grabbed the bowl from Crescent, and stuck a piece of watermelon in her mouth.

"Mmm, oh my gosh, this shit is good. Cent, can you get me the grilled chicken out of the fridge, please," Dea asked. I returned, sat on the couch, and waited for Cent to return. Crescent sat the meat down with a scowl on her face. I bit my lip and tried not to gag as Dea stuck a spoon of peanut butter in her mouth and then rolled up the meat and chewed.

"Okay, okay, I'm good now. So Henny didn't kill our doctor. That's progress," she chewed.

"The fact you got my Dr. Sexy acting out of character on the job is wild. But let's talk about the good shit. I wanna know all about Sanchez and if he's slanging," Crescent laughed.

"Yass, bissh, I need to know," Dea giggled.

I shook my head just as the ding sounded at the door. It opened, and the guard let in Dr. McQueen. She was pretty as hell with a bomb-ass pixie cut that showed off her high cheekbones. She smiled at us, and her chestnut brown skin glowed as she came forward. The way Dea spoke about her, she seemed larger than life, but she was no taller than me. Her large expressive brown eyes made her seem like a Bratz doll with curves. She was dressed down but still made it look like she was stepping onto a stage. The dusty pink lace strap off the shoulder sweater hugged her chest just right, and she rocked it with a pair of light-washed jeans.

"Hello, hello, ladies."

"Hey Seyra, these are my sisters Tali and Crescent," Dea said, sticking more of the chicken into her mouth. I saw the slight widening of Crescent's eyes before she blinked rapidly.

"Hello, it's good to meet you all."

"It's great to meet you as well. We will get out of your way so you can do your thing," I said.

"Girl, oh please, Dea is doing well. I just want to check some vitals and draw some blood. You all can continue like I am not here," she laughed.

We waited a few minutes as Seyra asked Dea a few questions and confirmed that, yes, she was still pregnant. She also told us that Shandea was almost eight weeks along. Ever since I found out Dea was pregnant, I had a question at the back of my mind as to how. When she had the accident with my father, they told us it was all but impossible for her ever to be able to carry. I was sure that Seyra told her all of this the day she was discharged, but it felt like Shandea didn't think it was real. She needed to hear it again, and I understood.

"Dr. McQueen, I have a quick question," I interjected.

"Sure, but it's just Seyra," she smiled.

"Sorry," I laughed. "Can you explain to me why they would tell us that Dea was unable to get pregnant?"

She looked at me and then Dea for a long moment before she sighed.

"Honestly, I don't know. Looking at her chart and when I examined her, the only reason I can come up with is that there was so much trauma that was a possibility. But time heals, and miracles happen," she smiled.

I nodded and caught Dea wiping away a tear, so I changed the subject while Seyra checked her pressure.

"Well, anywho, let me finish about Sanchez. When I was asked what I wanted, I asked to see. I was like, that is what I want to see and for him to...to let go," I finished. Dea choked, and Crescent moved forward.

"And! Get to the real shit, bissh," Crescent rushed.

"Ahh, ladies, full disclosure. I don't need you to tiptoe around me. I've known U.C.K. since college. I am pretty sure nothing you say will shock me," she quipped.

"Really? Lennox didn't tell me that," Dea said.

"Probably because I haven't been in Union City for years now. I came back for you, Ms. Saunders. If it weren't for all of them, I might have never been able to be the doctor I am today. So when they call, you answer," she smirked.

I looked at Dea, and she shrugged at me. Crescent just waved her hands around like let's get on with the story.

"Well, okay then. Let me run it back so you know what is happening," I stated. I started from the Tre mess and then when Henny took my ass in Sanchez's room.

"So you're telling me you asked him to masturbate for you, and he did it?" Crescent asked.

"Yes! He hesitated for a minute, but when he pulled his pajama pants down under his balls, the thickest dick just fell out. When I say thick, I mean that shit was like Sprite can soda mouth challenge. Can you make a sprite can disappear in your mouth? That's what I mean. Girl! That thang was like a bat, and it would have broken something. I don't know how he ain't tipping over 'cause that thing got to be heavy," I said. Crescent's mouth was half open, and Dea licked her lips, speechless.

"So, so you're saying it was thick Yeti cup thick but short," Seyra asked. I sat back, licking my lips and shaking my head.

"Nawl, naw, I ain't say that, Doc. He had to be eight inches at least. And the way his hips moved, he learned what he was doing," I grinned.

"Shit, is he just okay looking because you can't be packing all that and be sexy as hell," she quizzed.

"Girl, have you met any of them for real?" Crescent joked.

"Yes, but I ain't never have sex with any of them. It is most definitely not like that whatsoever," she said, shaking her head.

"Well, you know how Lennox, Henny, Link, and Faxx look, right? You're not blind even though it's not like that," I said.

"Tali is right Seyra. They all are lip biting and panty wetting—"

"I get it! I get it! Yes, they are, but we are talking about this Sanchez," she coaxed.

"Girl, he is hard nipple pinching, sexy. That boy is fine as fuck, and if someone didn't insert themselves in my life, I probably would have tried to hit that," Crescent laughed. "He's fine as fuck and a good dude. Now we know he's hiding the Loch Ness Monster with his half-blind ass," Crescent hummed, and we all started laughing.

"Damn!" Seyra shivered.

"You know he asked me to help him out for a few days now that he is home. I'm supposed to go over there Monday," Crescent smirked.

"Bitch, Faxx will really shoot your ass this time," Dea laughed.

"Fuck him. He is not my man. If I want to help a friend while also checking out his larger-than-life dick, then I will," she shrugged.

"Yeah, aight!" Me and Dea laughed.

"Wait. Why does he need help? Is he really sick or something?"

"Oh, damn, I forgot you don't know him. No, and yes. But he had eye surgery to restore his sight," I explained.

"Oh, I see. I mean, I only have one patient at the moment. I could probably find the time to help him out," Seyra shrugged. She wasn't looking at us as she cleaned up the tape and needle from taking Shandea's blood. We all stared at her and waited until she looked up at us. "What?" she smirked.

"Don't even try to 'what' the situation," Crescent giggled. Seyra rolled her eyes and got up to dispose of her trash. When she came back and sat down, we all looked at her. I looked up and saw the door open and figured it was Oz or a guard.

"I just want to help. I have medical experience," she shrugged. I tried to catch her eyes, but she thought I was trying to get her to spit it out. She rolled her eyes and pressed her thighs together. "Fine, fine! I wanna see Sanchez's monster dick!" Seyra gushed. "See it, stroke it, and possibly try and fit it in."

"Seyra!" I hissed. Crescent's mouth was on the floor, and Dea slowly turned to look over the back of the couch.

"Why is it that every time I come home, y'all talking about some nigga dick?" Oz questioned. "And Seyra, I expected more—"

"Naw, naw, Oz, let her finish. I wanna know what she plans on doing to my little man," Sanchez said, licking the corner of his mouth. Henny stared at me, pointing two fingers in my direction.

"Little! Apparently, we know that is a lie," Cent guffawed.

"Oh, so Crescent hasn't learned her lesson yet. Don't get your little friend's eyesight taken away so soon," Faxx assured.

"Fransisco, wh...where did you come from?" Crescent choked as she stood up.

"It's all good, Faxx. Crescent is fucking around," Sanchez stated and moved toward the couch. I stood from where I was seated, grabbing my purse as Seyra turned to face Sanchez. I saw her eyes travel over his well-defined body, and she licked her lips. She finally got to his eyes and gave him a smile.

"Got damn, shit, ah, yeah. Yes, I'm available for house calls at any time. All the time," Seyra panted.

## CHAPTER TWENTY-ONE

# CRESCENT 'CENT' JOHNSON

I stood in my bathroom mirror, looking at myself as I applied gloss to my lips. Shandea hit me in the chest when she introduced me as her sister. I know Tali saw the happiness on my face. I knew she was right that I needed to talk to her about all this shit. I just didn't want to get her or Dea pulled into my bullshit. I never thought I would end up on the radar of the Union City Kings either, but I have, and now I was caught up.

*Boom Boom Boom*

I turned around and frowned at the banging on my door. I wasn't sure if it was one of the neighbor's friends getting the wrong door because I wasn't expecting anyone.

"Don't be banging on my damn door," I shouted. I swung it open, expecting to see a random nigga looking for the chick in the apartment above me. "Wh...what are you doing here?" I asked Faxx. I was looking around, but no one was in the hall. Whenever he picked me up, I was lucky no one could see his ass through the tint. Unlike Dr. Sexy, the others were suspected of being a part of U.C.K. I did not need that noise where I lived.

"If you were home where you're supposed to be, I wouldn't be here," Faxx taunted me while eyeing me up and down. His dark brown gaze traveled my body before returning to my eyes. I grabbed him by the shirt and pulled him through the door.

"Get in here before someone sees you. Why are you here, Fransisco," I asked, closing the door.

"Because you need a ride to this little lunch since you won't drive your car. How else will you get there?"

"Bus, nigga. That is how people travel when they lack transportation," I scoffed. I stepped around him, but he caught my arm, pulling me back.

"That's true, *Mi Amor*, but you have a car, and since you're acting like a brat, I have to pick you up. Because I know damn well another nigga isn't," Faxx warned. His thumb rubbed my skin, causing my body to heat while my mind drifted to that fucking mango. When he called me my love in a slight accent, my body moved closer to him unknowingly.

"I don't take cars or larger gifts from men, Faxx. I...I just can't," I uttered.

"So tell me why? Why won't you do it? Because it isn't like you can't."

I knew what he wanted, but I still wasn't ready to reveal my secrets and soul. I knew him, but I didn't truly know him. It was the same way with Roman. I trusted him so quickly and gave him every part of me and look where I was now. In a shitty ass apartment hiding from a nigga I stole from because he turned out to be a piece of shit. I wouldn't repeat my past mistakes and wouldn't drag Faxx or anyone else into my shit.

"It doesn't matter why I can't because it's my choice not to," I answered.

"Then it's my choice to pick you up and take you where you need to be. I will pick you up and put you in my truck, Cent," he threatened. My breath hitched at the memory of him lifting me and laying me out on that table. It was effortless and surprised me again because not many can lift my plus-sized body. There weren't many that I trusted to attempt it. Faxx stepped closer to me, raising my chin so I could meet his eyes. "You keep licking your lips like that, *Mi Amor,* and I will put them to use. You look good enough to eat right now, but I don't want to be late. I just need you to remember you," he said, touching my temple, "are mine, and so is the rest of this body," he went on. His finger left my temple, and his hand traveled down the length of my body. It wasn't a soft caress but a firm claiming kind that had my panties wet.

"You can't just walk into my life and think you will own me, Fransisco," I whispered. His lips were so close to mine that I could feel their softness. The leather and gunmetal scent clouded my thoughts when he was this close to me.

"Crescent, I don't need to think I will own you. After you held that gun to my head and let me taste that juicy pussy, baby, I already possessed you," he murmured. His tongue came out, and he licked my lips before pushing inside, and I opened them like before. It didn't matter how I tried not to like this light-skinned fool, he was pushing his way into my life, into my heart. I had no compunction about knowing I got off on *crazy*, and Fransisco was as wild as they came. Faxx pulled away, taking his heat and his drugging kiss, away from me, causing a shiver through my body. "Are you wet for me, Cent? Is that pussy calling for Papi," he asked.

My heart pounded, and I thought that shit would leap out of my chest. I licked my lips, and his dark gaze stared me down, waiting on my answer.

"Ye...yes," I gasped. I felt his hand sliding up my bare thigh, moving my dress's fabric out of the way.

"Yes, what?" Faxx said harsher.

"Yes, Papi," I moaned. His finger traced a line over my panties and up my slit. I could feel his dick pressed against me, and my pussy clenched.

"Good girl. Now let's go to lunch. I want to sit and eat, knowing my pussy awaits Papi's tongue. That's your punishment tonight since you won't tell me what you're hiding from me," he smirked.

I opened my mouth to say fuck you, but he grabbed my hand and pulled me to the door. *What the fuck does he know? Faxx is acting like he already knows some shit, but he shouldn't. Would he still be here if he knew what I had done? Will he trust me after knowing?* I pushed the thoughts away because no one in Union City should know what I ran from in Clapton. I grabbed my purse and phone from the counter before he yanked my arm out of the damn socket.

"Keep pulling me like this. I will shoot you for real," I threatened.

"*Mi Amor*, you are just making my dick harder and my obsession with you stronger."

Faxx didn't bring the sexy as fuck Audi today, but I wasn't mad. I loved climbing into his blacked-out Grand Wagoneer. The shit was sexy as hell, and it felt like you were sitting on large couches instead of car seats. It was huge, and the seats' leather was soft as butter. I could sit in this SUV all day like it was a second home.

We pulled up to Emerald, and I looked around. I had only been able to come here once but never returned because the shit was expensive. It wasn't like I couldn't afford it, but I refused to spend that money. I was supposed to be Roman's possession, but I left him. Everything concerning me was his, from how he put it, and I left. It was bullshit, and I finally refused to play his games, and took the money, fucking up his investment into a new business. I didn't know that until I got word of a deal falling apart because of that money. So instead of staying in Clapton, I ran here. I ran back home to Union City.

Roman wasn't just chasing me for taking his money. He was also chasing me because I was his money-maker. I think whatever he was doing had something to do with U.C.K. They could take it as I stole from them if that was true. Would they even listen to my side of things? I see their fun sides, but after these past few weeks, none of this was all fun and games. These niggas didn't play when it came to loyalty or their money.

"Let's go, Cent," Faxx said, stepping out of the truck. The valet opened my door, and a cute man helped me out of the vehicle. He quickly dropped my hand when Faxx came around the car. I didn't get how his eyes could be so hot or almost scolding when looking at me, but when they landed on others, they were cold as a dead body.

"What's this lunch all about, and why am I here?" I asked.

"It's a pre-game before the charity event. I have a dress being delivered for you to wear," he said, scanning the area.

"A dress? Wait a minute. I never said anything about attending this thing."

"So you're not going to support your friend? That's not like you at all," he raised his brows.

"Of course I am, but I don't need you buying me shit."

Faxx raised a brow at me and widened his eyes.

"But you will wear it for me, right?" He looked so pitiful and hopeful. What could I say?

"Yes, Fransisco," I sighed, and his expression changed instantly. *I've been played!*

"Thought so," he smirked. I followed him into the beautiful restaurant that was covered in shades of cream and emerald. It definitely was named after its looks.

"Mr. Wellington, welcome back. Will you be dining alone or—"

"Our party should already be inside. Thank you, Veronica," Faxx said.

His stride never stopped, and I would have felt slightly out of place if he wasn't wearing a pair of black cargo pants and a black long-sleeved fitted shirt. The one gold cross earring in his ear was his only accessory except for a matte black watch. I swear I couldn't tell if it told a time or what, but he never took it off. None of them actually wore things flashy the way Roman and his crew did. But what they did wear made a statement of what they were. All of their clothes were designer, even when they were understated. They screamed RICH as fuck. What people didn't realize was, they were crazy as fuck as well. Everyone sitting at the tables were dressed elegantly compared to my navy blue and black sweater dress and thigh-high knee boots. I should've planned my outfit better, but I chilled the hell out when I saw Tali and Dea. They were dressed as similar as I was.

"Why are you so nervous, *Mi Amor*? It's just family here," Fransisco whispered in my ear. Dr. Sexy looked up and smiled at me before he stood up. Link and Oz noticed and did the same while Faxx pulled out my chair.

I couldn't wrap my mind around how gentlemanly they could be and then turn around and stab someone in the neck. I sat down smiling, feeling more at home than I had since my grandmother died.

"Dr. Sexy, how are you feeling? Is Tali taking care of you correctly? I don't need my work hubby all fucked up in the game," I laughed. When I was with Faxx alone, it was like I became putty in his hands. But being around others allowed me to mess with him. I felt my chair rise a few inches off the floor. It settled back in place, but now I was so close to Faxx that I might as well sit in his lap.

"I'm good, Cent. I will let you know, though," Henny smirked. I peeked over at Faxx, and he squinted at Henny before a large arm draped over the back of my chair. I felt it when Faxx leaned closer to my ear, his lips brushing against the shell.

"You like fucking with me, don't you? You think messing with me is a joke, Cent?"

I sucked in a breath when I felt the cold steel of his gun sliding up my leg. My core pulsated, and my clit throbbed at the contact.

"Cent! You're coming to the event, right? I really need all y'all there. I do not want to be cornered by that Elliot dude. He's creepy as hell," Dea said, then bit her tongue. I could barely breathe when the gun barrel ran over my panties and along my folds. "Ye...yes...I am coming...I'm coming to the event. I wouldn't miss it," I stammered. I saw Oz turn to look at Dea with a frown, but she just kept her eyes forward, picking out the foods she wanted to eat. Shantel turned her head to me because she was the closest, and smirked.

"I think Cent is coming in more ways than one," she laughed before raising her hand for a waiter.

"Shut up, Shantel," I gritted. I felt Faxx's nose running up my neck as I tried and failed to move away.

"Keep that plump ass still before I sit you in my lap. If I do that, nothing will stop me from fucking you right here in the middle of this restaurant," he warned.

"You wouldn't dare do some insane shit like that," I hissed.

"Crescent, I've told you before I've been diagnosed as insane, and you like that shit," he stated while using the gun to tap my sensitive clit.

"Fuck," I moaned softly. I shook my head, trying to think straight, but it was hard. "No...no, you said they told you...you have antisocial personality disorder. It doesn't make you insane, just...different," I said. I felt his lips on my cheeks and Link's raised brow.

"Dea! What the fuck do you mean he came to see you at work? When? You know what? We can talk about this shit later. He is not approaching shit while I am there. I'll deal with his ass after your event, baby, because I warned his ass," Oz grunted. He leaned back in his chair, pulling Dea with him. She stuck some kind of food combination of fish, a peanut butter sauce with a tomato in her mouth. Ewww.

"Baby, it's not that big of a deal. He didn't try anything with me. Here, try this," she said. She held up the fish covered in the peanut butter sauce to his mouth. His face was priceless. We all held disgusted looks, but he opened his mouth anyway. That was true love because I would not!

"It's not bad. I guess Chef can make anything taste good," he grunted. "But that nigga is done," he chewed. Dea rolled her eyes and continued to eat her nasty ass concoctions. My heart was still pounding, and I prayed when I stood up that my juices wouldn't run down my legs.

I felt the gun leave my skin, and my head cleared while my heart slowed to a normal pace. I could still see it in his lap as he tapped the hammer against his knee. I swallowed and turned to Shantel as she ordered a round of shots for us and a non-alcoholic strawberry daiquiri for Shandea.

"Yass, Shantel! I am trying to turn up before this stuffy ass event. Is Seyra joining us?" Tali asked.

I caught the looks between the men before Henny smiled. His grills flashed in the light like he was a different person. Now I understood when he told me in the VIP that it was just Henny. It was because Dr. Pharma wasn't present. Shit. I felt myself shaking slightly because even though I liked a little crazy, I'd just found myself in a pool full of psychos who didn't mind drowning you.

"Oh, she will be there, Thickness. We all will."

He smiled, and then it slowly faded. I followed his line of sight. Apparently, everyone else did as well. I felt Faxx stiffen, and the arm over my shoulder pulled me closer. I blinked, and so did everyone else, other than Shantel. She was on her phone, looking at it with wide eyes. She began typing frantically, but I had to look at the man approaching us. There was something about him that drew all attention to him. His presence seemed to suck in the rest of the air that was left for us peons after Link, Faxx, Henny, and Oz took the rest.

My gaze traveled over thick thighs, which were muscle through the fitted suit pants. My eyes perused further up to the silver belt buckle and up his chest. You could tell he was hard as a rock under that shirt. He carried his suit jacket in his arms, and by how his shirt covered him, you knew it was custom tailored to fit him. I met his eyes and sucked in a breath when his hazel-green eye looked me over. The other was covered in a patch, but he reminded me of the character Davis MacLean. His shoulders were huge, though, like he could've played a contact sport. The temp fade, paired with the low-top haircut and the black and gray weaving through it, made him look like a whole daddy snack. I never knew the salt and pepper look would make my mouth water.

"Goddamn…" I whispered. At least, I thought I did because he heard me and smiled. His white teeth were perfect, like the goatee covering his face and smooth dark caramel skin. Shantel stopped texting, realizing everyone was quiet, and raised her head, setting her phone aside.

"Who in the hell is that? Jesus lawd," Tali mouthed to me. Henny leaned forward as the man stood behind Shantel and smiled at everyone.

"Well, I see I am in time for the family lunch date. Are you not letting your older brother join you, Lennox?"

My head whipped to Oz, and he stared at this man with different emotions playing on his face.

"Sure, if only to get some fucking answers," Oz stated. The man took the seat next to Shantel, sliding it closer to her, and she stiffened. Oz's eyes tracked the movement, and his glare landed on Shantel. Link looked shocked and then curiously at the man, before looking at Henny.

"Wasn't his eye brown before and the patch on the opposite eye?" Link asked.

The man looked at Link and smiled, but his gaze turned back to Oz. I could've been seeing things because I swore it softened when looking at him. BROTHER. Oh shit. I looked at Dea. Her eyes were wide, but she bit her lip as she checked him out.

"We can get to all the questions and answers soon. How about we get down to business since your messes are all but cleaned up now? Is that still something all of you are interested in?"

Henny studied the man for a second and looked at Oz. There was a quick glance, and I could tell that a conversation just happened right before us. Faxx finally moved and leaned across me with his hand out.

"It is an honor and pleasure to meet you, Rogue. I never thought this day would happen," Faxx smiled. I did a full slow pan to him. He looked like a kid at Disney World seeing Mickey Mouse for the first time from the excited expression on his face.

"No, it's a pleasure to meet you, Sandstorm. I've heard great things about you and your team. But you can call me Ian," he said, shaking Faxx's hand. He had an arm across the back of Shantel's chair as he reached across her. I looked wide-eyed at Faxx because I honestly had no clue what he did or used to do. *Who the fuck is Sandstorm?*

Ian pulled back but never removed his arm from the back of Shantel's chair. He turned to look at Oz and Henny, waiting on their answer. Oz leaned forward, placing his hands on the table, eyeing Ian with a frown.

"I have two questions before we do any kind of business, brothers or not, because I don't trust you. Him," he said, tipping his head toward Henny, "he's got that feelin' like you're one of us, and him I trust. So before we accept doing any kind of business, I need to know something," Oz insisted.

I heard the intake of breath coming from Shantel, and when I shifted my gaze to look at her, I saw Ian's other hand lightly rubbing her thigh. She looked at me, and I could see the slight panic and lust she was trying to hide from the others.

"Okay, I don't see a problem with that," Ian mused.

"What the fuck do you have to do with my mother? And why in the hell does your father think you are dead?" Oz asked. His jaw was clenched, and his hands were in fists as he stared at Ian. It was like all of us were holding our breath, waiting for him to answer the question. From what I knew from Shandea, Oz's mother was murdered, and Oz still didn't know who did it. He couldn't think it was his brother, could he? Then again, Xavier was crazy as fuck, so there was that.

"It was in my best interest to let my bastard of a father think I was dead so I could do what was asked of me. After my mother died under suspicious circumstances, I knew my father couldn't be trusted. He had been seeing his current wife, and she was the one who helped get him to reach his current level. Do I think he killed my mother? I do not. But whoever did it is close to him. They're moving things behind the scenes to further an agenda. He isn't innocent by far. It's just he didn't pull the trigger, so to speak.

"Another larger force was at play in my father's career. He doesn't question it. I was a leftover of an old life that couldn't take him further in his political life. He got remarried, and that's when I learned about my brother Charles. I was treated secondhand, stepped on, and belittled, but I knew I just had to hold on. My father began his usual ways again, so I followed him. I found out my father was seeing a woman who looked similar to my mother. So I followed her another day, and when I did, I was shocked. I found two boys who looked just like my father, and I knew then how he would treat you. Just another product of the street he was 'slumming' in. And one of them had our eyes. Once I found that out, I knew he wouldn't care for either of you. It would ruin his image if it were to get out. So, I made it a point to get to know your mother and told her about my mother. I told her he would never want her children. It was just her he wanted," Ian stated.

I looked around and saw a frown on Oz's face. Henny leaned forward listening intently, but Shantel sat stiffly beside me.

"I was leaving for the military, but I ensured that you both would have the life you deserved. My mother's family had money, but she held no power in the life Kenneth wanted. He never knew just how much or how wrong he was about the power behind the name Lawe. But in the end, my mother made sure I inherited it all. Where do you think that money came from that you have? Still, no matter how much I looked, followed, or stalked, I couldn't figure out who wanted my father in these positions. But I knew his infatuation with Sonny was getting out of hand. Becoming too public would damage his career. I had a feeling that something would happen."

Oz shifted ever so slightly and looked toward Henny. I watched as Dea placed a hand over his, and they looked eyes like they were both asking the same question about the money.

"Are you the reason why Link had such a hard time tracing that money back to anyone?" Henny asked with a frown.

"Yes, and what do you mean something bad would happen? How did you know that it would happen?" Oz grumbled. The table was silent, looking at Ian like he had all the answers the crew had been looking for, for years. If he had this much on them, had he looked into me?

"Yes, I didn't need anyone finding out where that money came from. It helped me remain in the shadows to do what I needed to do. I will get to why I thought something was coming," Ian stated with a shake of his head. Shantel slowly turned toward him, waiting with interest in what else he had to say.

"Aight, bet," Henny said, waving for him to continue.

"So I went back to Sonny, begging her to go. I was still a kid at eighteen trying to explain what was coming. I couldn't physically do anything yet. I could feel it coming like a bad storm, but I was leaving soon. I told Sonny it would be a matter of time before his enemies or some unforeseen bullshit would come to her door. I couldn't hear about losing my little brothers, and I refused. I told her to leave Union City, and then it was time for me to leave. Before I went into basic training, I sent a short letter telling her that I would watch out for you and your brother, and I meant it. I knew I needed to ensure you wouldn't worry about anything once you were of age. I told Sonny to make a video for y'all explaining everything so you know she never would abandon y'all, just in case. I was in the military with so much money that I didn't know what to do. I placed the money in a trust and set it up how she wanted it done. I wished she'd listened, but she stayed because my father loved her, and she felt like she had him under control."

The frown on Ian's face told me he wished he had done more, but I knew from personal experience that you can't make people do what they don't want. Sonny apparently wasn't ready, and it cost her her life. Ian sighed with a shake of his head but pushed on with his story.

"Over the years, we spoke about this at length, and she began to admit to strange calls, visitors, and random cars driving by her house. That was the exact thing that happened to my mother. I told her it was time and knew I had to return, get my brothers, and protect them because my father wouldn't claim them if something happened. I was finally coming back home, and that's when I got the news. It happened again. A woman was found dead and dismembered. Her children found her. I returned home and confronted my father, telling him he was the common denominator. I told him to take care of his children, and he laughed. It was bitter, and he said things happened when they needed to. Those bastards would be next. I needed to dig deeper and do what I promised. The only way to do that was to become a ghost. I had the skills and wanted to kill him right there, but I knew it was best just to leave. He could and would be used. Then I decided it was time to let that life go as Ian Morgan and I became Ian Nevin Lawe. That allowed me to watch over you both as I promised Sonny while building a network and wealth. With us together, nothing can come at us. And whoever is behind our mothers' murders will be dealt with," he finished.

We all sat silently, watching and waiting for what Oz had to say. He leaned back, but I didn't miss his quick glance at Henny. Hendrix cleared his throat and rubbed at his goatee.

"So, business. What is up for offer?"

Ian looked at Oz for a long moment before facing Henny.

"We integrate all our businesses and expand. If we are together, we can take Clapton and Del Mar, making it U.C.K. territory. My thought for our legit businesses is that combining will be the easiest. All I need is someone who knows the inside and outs of your business to merge us as one fully. I think Ms. Waters would do. She can...become my personal assistant. Isn't that right, Shantel? I mean, since you have infiltrated my offices already," he insinuated.

"No! Absolutely not! Fuck no," Oz shouted. Ian raised his brows, but we all turned when Shantel stood up, almost knocking the chair over.

"Oz! I will do it. It's fine. I can handle his business as well as ours. End of discussion," Shantel panted.

"I told you to stay away, Shantel. I told you not to pursue this. You don't—"

"Lennox, I can handle it. I got it, Boss," she said as her gaze traveled to each of them before she turned and rushed out of the restaurant.

"I take it that this is a deal," Ian smiled, but his eye watched Shantel until she rounded the corner out of sight. I felt Faxx lean closer to my ear as Henny and Ian began to talk while Oz glared. Link was quiet, studying Ian like a unicorn and wanting to know his secrets. I was deeper than before with them and knew I couldn't turn back. I shouldn't be here or hearing any of this, but they trusted me. Fuck.

"So when will you tell me all about this Roman nigga?" Faxx grunted in my ear. My entire body tensed, and I knew everything was about to come crashing down around me.

# CHAPTER TWENTY-ONE

## SHANDEA 'DEA' SAUNDERS

The Boys and Girls Club employees had been planning this charity event for weeks, and everything was perfectly in place. The decorations were up, the food was ready, and the guests were starting to arrive. I was excited to see everything come together and to raise money for a good cause. I had no clue the guys had come together as four of the five donors until Lennox told me. He also shared that Kenneth was the fifth and contributed to this great cause.

"So, is he going to show up?" I smiled to cover my words. Lennox was at my side looking sexy as shit in his Champagne Oro Lucentezza Ciottoli double-breasted waistcoat with a white dress shirt under it. The champagne suit pants molded to him as a perfect fit because it was made only for him. The color set off his dark skin tone and made his eyes seem like they were on fire. My champagne off-the-shoulder paired cocktail dress matched his swag perfectly. I almost choked when I was told how much they individually donated. It was millions. Miranda looked at me like '*what the fuck*', but I couldn't miss the excitement in her eyes of how much cash was about to flow. Miranda pulled me aside and offered me the job permanently, saying there was an open seat as a center director over other social workers. Miranda wasn't too subtle when she told me we would work closely to manage this money. I could tell she wasn't clueless of who Oz was. The question of 'isn't he the owner of *MYTH*' was a dead giveaway. I politely told her he was just another business owner with his hands in many areas.

"Oh, he will be here, and when he comes, he will be announcing that he is running for Governor," Lennox stated. His eyes never stopped scanning the crowd, and I wondered if he was uncomfortable or on edge.

"Baby, are you okay? You don't need to stay here if this is not your scene," I said, getting closer to him.

I was so glad that his scent didn't turn my stomach, and I praised our baby for that because I loved it. Lennox looked down at me as he rubbed his beard. I still worried about the wound on his shoulder, but he proved to me that he was good before we left. He picked me up with one hand and fucked me against the wall by the front door before we left. My legs still shook from the memory of it.

"Sweetness, I'm good. I just like to watch my surroundings," Lennox smiled. He leaned down and kissed my lips. I could also see how his knowledge of Ian was still fucking with him. I knew that relationship would take some time, but we had time.

"Okay, I will mingle a little more with the others. I don't think creepy ass Elliot is coming. We are nearing the end of the event," I said, patting his chest. I was glad because I knew Lennox would have probably tried to kill this dude.

"Don't go too far. I see Kenny's ass, so let me handle that," Lennox instructed.

I smiled at him and moved through the crowd, greeting and thanking everyone who came out. It had been a success, and I was so happy for once in my life. My mother would be okay. I had a family, a job I loved, and the man I always wanted. The baby completed my circle. I finally reached Tali, Hendrix, Link, Faxx, and Crescent. I hugged both Tali and Crescent. I kissed Hendrix, Link, and Faxx four times for their incredible donations.

"We got you. You're our baby sister, so of course," Link said, hugging me. He wasn't one for many words or emotions, so it surprised me, and I cried. "Ahh shit. Hormones," he chuckled, pulling me back into his arms. I heard someone hitting a glass calling for our attention.

"It's time. Let's go support our brother," Hendrix said. His smile was gone, and they all moved to stand behind Lennox as he stood beside Kenneth. I told Tali and Crescent I still needed to make my rounds. I hugged them both and continued through the crowd while Kenneth spoke.

*Ladies and gentlemen,*
*I am honored to stand before you today to announce my candidacy for governor of this great state. As many of you know, I was born and raised in Union City, and it is with great pride and humility that I offer myself as a candidate to lead this state forward.*
*Growing up in Union City, I saw firsthand working families' struggles. My parents worked hard to make ends meet and taught me the value of hard work and perseverance. I also learned the importance of giving back to the community, so I am thrilled to kick off my campaign with this charity event.*
*This event is a wonderful opportunity to unite as a community and support those in need. It reminds us that we are all in this together and must work together to build a better future for ourselves and our children.*

*As governor, I will be committed to creating opportunities for all our citizens, regardless of their background or circumstance. I believe that we can build a state where everyone has the chance to succeed and where we can all be proud to call home.*

*I look forward to meeting with all of you in the coming months and sharing my vision for this state and Union City. Together, we can build a brighter future for ourselves and our families. Thank you.*

As this bastard spoke, I moved around through the crowd until I started to feel uneasy. Elliot was here. I knew his ass was here by the crawling sensation along my skin. I had clarified that I wasn't interested, and Lennox had already shown his displeasure. But he didn't seem to get the hint. I tried my best to avoid him, but he followed me through the crowd. The event was packed, and I knew my guards probably couldn't even see me. They were at every entrance, so how did this idiot even make it inside?

People were starting to eye me like I was crazy, and I didn't want to ruin the event. So I stopped and smiled while clapping at Kenneth's bullshit. I ignored him and focused on everything else but him. But every time I turned around, there he was. It was like he could smell me in the crowd. It didn't matter where I moved. He found me and would stay a few feet away. He licked his lips, and I saw the slight bulge in his pants. I rolled my eyes, increasingly frustrated, when I saw him heading toward me again. I tried to move away quickly, but he caught up to me. I was between a hallway and the stage where Lennox spoke to Kenneth.

"Hey, Shandea," he said with a smile.

"Elliot, I really don't want to talk right now," I replied, trying to sound polite but firm.

"Why not? We could have a great time together," he said, leaning closer. "You like having great times, don't you?"

"How did you even get inside?" I fumed.

"I've been here before it started. I've been watching you all night with him. You've been teasing me, but now it's my turn," he said, eyes roaming my body.

I grimaced in his direction and turned to walk away. I felt his hand on my shoulder, and he jerked me backward into the hallway. I turned around, pissed the fuck off, and pushed him away from me.

"I have a fiancé, Elliot. I'm not interested. Trust me and walk the fuck away," I said, trying to back away.

The look in his eye was one of possession and entitlement. He didn't seem to give a shit about my words because to him, apparently, what I wanted didn't matter.

"Little girl, you should feel privileged that I want anything to do with you. As much as I give to this place and these people, you're giving me what you freely showed me will continue the money I push into this place. Do you want to be the cause of the club to lose its biggest donor?"

He hadn't realized that he was no longer the biggest donor, and even if he were, I still wouldn't give a shit. I moved before I knew it and slapped the fuck out of him. I knew it hurt, but I saw the rage cross his face. I tried to move, but he grabbed my bare upper arm and squeezed so tightly I knew it would leave bruises on my light skin.

"Get the fuck off of me," I hissed. Elliot pulled me through a closed door and threw me into the middle of the room. I steadied myself on my heels and turned around to face him.

"You've been teasing me and showing me that little cunt, and you think I wouldn't come for it. Your little boy doesn't know who the fuck I am, Ms. Saunders," he grunted.

"I don't give a fuck what you think. Get the fuck out of my way," I shouted. I went to push him, and he stopped me. I raised my knee to hit him in the balls, but he twisted. I didn't stop there, and my fist flew across his cheek. Then I felt the slap across my face, and rage filled me.

"Some of you women need a little more discipline than others. You will learn as my sub," he informed.

I heard the door open, and Lennox rushed inside. He looked around the room, and then his eyes met mine. He saw the look on my face, and his eyes darkened. They went almost black, reminding me of Xavier. His jaw clenched as he walked towards me. I could see the anger and murderous rage in his eyes. As Lennox got closer, Elliot finally seemed to notice him.

"Oh, and here he is. Coming to threaten me again?" Elliot asked, looking at Lennox. I was relieved that Lennox was finally here. But I was also afraid that a dead body was about to be at my first charity event. Lennox walked up until he was on Elliot. He was all in his space, and I could tell Elliot was beginning to get uncomfortable. I think Elliot began to notice the death in Lennox's glare.

"She told you to leave her alone. I told you to leave her the fuck alone, but here you are fucking up her night. Naw, I can't have that shit, and I can't have another man obsessing over my wife. Here is a secret, I've killed every man that has thought about claiming my wife. I killed every single one of them."

"You...you can't threaten me this way. I have connections, and I golf with the chief of police every Sunday," he scoffed.

"And he told me that you take a trip on your yacht around this time every year. So it won't be suspicious when you don't fucking return," Lennox grunted. My eyes were wide at his knowledge of his life, but I shouldn't have been surprised.

"How...how...do you..." Elliot stuttered.

Before I knew it, Lennox had him by the shirt and began to pound his fist into his face. I was horrified, watching Lennox beat this man so badly that his face began to look like ground beef. I felt tears in my eyes at how he was ruining his beautiful suit and realized I was losing it. I had no remorse for Elliot or guilt about his death. I was worried about a damn suit! Lennox pulled back, breathing heavily while standing over Elliot's body.

"Are you good, Sweetness?" he asked, stepping closer to me. He reached out to touch my face but pulled back, seeing the blood on his hands. I moved, reaching into his inside pocket, and pulled out a handkerchief. He took it, wiping his hands as clean as he could get them.

"I'm fine, baby. Are you okay?" I asked. Lennox pulled out a phone and typed in a message. He pocketed it and moved closer to me,

"He touched you? Did he hurt you?"

"He did touch me, but I'm good baby. How are we going to clean this up and you," I asked, looking him over. Blood covered the front of him and stained his white shirt. He looked himself over before turning his dark gaze to the floor.

"I'll take his hand before we roll him off his boat," he seethed. Lennox turned back to me and moved forward as the doors opened and men entered. I kept my eyes on him when my back hit the wall.

"I'm putting your suit here, Wiz. We will take the body to the *Shop* for now as requested."

"Bet. Close the door when y'all are done," he ordered.

Whatever was happening behind him faded to the background as I stared into his eyes. They began to lighten to his usual color. I licked my lips, and his eyes moved to the motion.

"We need to get back so I can help bring this event to a close," I panted.

"Naw, I need you to help me out of these clothes. Start with my pants," he demanded. I swallowed as I slowly slid down the wall and to my knees. I knew we needed to discuss what had just happened, but I wanted him in my mouth. Fuck the event. It was over anyway.

## CHAPTER TWENTY-THREE

## TALI SAUNDERS

I enjoyed mingling with people and gaining contacts interested in the Women's Center at my sister's charity event that I wasn't sure I would've had fun at. Hendrix seemed like an entirely different person around these upper-class people, and it was interesting how they all wanted his attention. Then I realized we were in this class of people, and my hands started to shake. It was the same way with Faxx and Link as they moved through the crowd. Dea had already rushed off to finish her rounds, probably talking more people into spending more money. She looked so happy that she was glowing. That made me so happy that I couldn't believe I had never wanted to return to Union City.

"You will get used to it, Tali. Keep doing what you're doing, and you will have them eating out of your hands," he whispered against my ear. I had my long locs swept up off my shoulders, leaving my neck bare.

"I don't know about getting used to it. Dea has this shit down, but me? I don't know," I said. Hendrix laughed and pulled away to speak to someone who wanted his attention. I felt Crescent come up on my side, and I turned to face her. She looked beautiful in a pale pink A-Line princess satin ruffle one-shoulder sleeveless floor-length dress. The split up the thigh was hot as hell, but elegant. Faxx watched her the entire time, no matter where she moved in the room.

"How the hell do they fit in so well with these people? I feel so out of freaking place it isn't funny. I shouldn't be here," she muttered.

"Girl, stop. I know exactly what you mean because I feel the same way, but I'm told we need to get used to it. This is a part of their world, just like the other stuff," I said. I smiled at a passing guest, and Crescent frowned.

"Hendrix is just a work hubby, Tali. This is not my scene," she stated. I turned to her, giving her my full attention like she was trippin'. "What?" she frowned.

"Bissh, you know what. I don't understand why you are running away from Faxx. When it came to me and Dea, you had all this shit to say, but now look at you. That man wants, wants you, and he doesn't seem to have trouble proving it, either. What is up, Cent?"

Crescent looked everywhere but at me for a minute and sighed.

"Fuck, fucking shit, you're right. It's just...it's a lot. Can we talk about this over the weekend? I...I just need to prepare myself and work through some things," she finished. Her eyes raised to mine, and I held them, seeing her terror. I wanted to demand her to talk now, but I knew she could shut down on me if I did. I wasn't sure if the fear was of talking about the problem or if it was someone that she feared talking about.

"I can do that. But Cent, we are seriously having this conversation. Whatever is going on, we can figure it out," I said. I pulled Crescent into my arms and hugged her tight. I saw Faxx watching us over her shoulder, and a frown crossed his face. His attention was caught, though, by a man with ice-blue eyes, and they got into a heated conversation. I pulled back and saw the unshed tears in her eyes but a smile.

"I promise. No more stalling," Crescent said. I pulled her with me as I spoke with more and more people as the event began to come to an end. It was a beautiful evening, and the atmosphere was lively. Crescent began to have fun and started to interact more with the people. We were having a deep conversation about mental health in the black community with one of the leaders of the Department of Health when Hendrix caught my eye. He nodded for me to come to him, so I excused myself and whispered to Cent I would be back. I weaved my way through the crowd and went to Hendrix's side. He took my hand and pulled me close to him. He leaned down, kissing the side of my neck before placing his lips on my ear.

"Seyra is here, but I want you to listen," he chuckled lightly.

"Okay...what are y'all up to?"

"Just...pay attention," he said quietly. I raised my brows while sipping my wine as Seyra walked toward us. I immediately noticed she wasn't looking at us but at the man standing slightly before us, speaking to a few people. I frowned, noticing it was Kenneth, and knew it would be some shit. I saw when he noticed Seyra and quickly ended his conversation to stare at her. She wore a gorgeous rose gold high split dress that hit the floor with a sweetheart neckline. The short sleeves hugged her arms, but the color brought out her brown skin tone with flecks of gold.

"Congratulations Senator, this seems like a different move for you," Seyra smiled. She held out her hand, and Kenneth took it, kissing the back of it as he stared at her in amazement.

"You look so familiar to me, lovely. Have I had the pleasure of meeting you before Mrs..."

"Doctor. Dr. Seyra McQueen," she corrected but then stepped closer to him. I heard him suck in a breath as her large breasts pushed against his chest. "But you can call me Mistress."

"Ex...excuse me," Kenneth rasped.

"Shut up. You heard what I said, Kenneth. Now, after this event is over, I will need you to call me, but before that, you need to make an OFFERING to me. I'll even let you know what I need. I want an apartment in a high-rise, and not just any apartment, but a penthouse in the middle of downtown. I also want the deed in my name and handed to me before you even consider contacting me. I will let you figure out how to get it done. After that, I will see what I can do for you."

Her tone was hard, almost harsh, but I saw him shiver, and his chest stopped moving.

"I...I don't know who you think you are, but..."

"Shut. Up. All I want to hear from my bitch is yes, Ma'am, or yes, MISTRESS."

"How...who..."

"You will be a little bitch to me until I can make you my good little boy," she sneered and then smacked his dick. Hard. I almost spit my wine out of my mouth when his eyes rolled back, then snapped open and looked down. I followed his gaze, and he looked at the lump in his pants as if he'd never seen it before. Seyra had already stepped back, and his head came up with a look of astonishment. She held out a card with a raised brow but looked away, uninterested in whether he took it. Kenneth grabbed the card quickly from her fingertips and moved closer, trying to keep his voice low.

"I will become your best little boy, Mistress," he panted.

"See that you do."

Seyra walked away, disappearing into the crowd like she was never there. I turned to Hendrix, and he bit down on his lip before pulling me away.

"Nigga, what the fuck was that?" I hissed. I tried and failed to hold the laugh, but it slipped out.

"It's our insurance policy at play."

"No, no, what exactly just happened?"

"Oh, that was just a little financial domination kink, and it helps that she resembles Lennox's mother a little," he said under his breath.

I raised my brows, vowing to look that shit up because that seemed like a good ass business to be in. I drank the last of my wine as people filtered over to speak with Hendrix again. I placed my empty glass on a tray coming by when that third glass hit me. I had to get to the restroom quickly. I leaned into Hendrix, and he stopped his conversation to give me his attention.

"I'll be right back," I said, nodding to the bathrooms. Hendrix nodded, and I excused myself and went through the crowd to get to the outer area where the restrooms were located. I sighed when I saw no line as the cool air hit my skin. The ballroom was slightly stuffy because there were so many people. I stepped into the private one-stall bathroom to relieve myself. I barely recognized myself as I stared into the mirror while washing my hands. I was usually in scrubs or at home lounging around in jeans and a tee shirt. I only dressed up when we were going out. Shandea had burst into the apartment with a huge smile, holding bags.

She had a dress bag and another bag that I guessed held shoes. I rolled my eyes at her, but she dismissed me and ordered me into the room to try on the gown she picked out. Looking at myself, I had to say it was perfect, and the color told me who bought it. I was sure his only stipulation in the dress was the burgundy color. The princess sleeveless, off-the-shoulder asymmetrical applique organza dress showed my curves off in a way Hendrix had difficulty letting me leave the damn house. It was damn near an order to leave on the dress and the nude heels when we got back home so he could fuck me while wearing them. I laughed because I was ready to skip the damn event so we could stay and do that, but this was Dea's night. I stepped out of the restroom and left the small corridor when a hand spun me around. I was smiling because I knew it was Henny, and he was about to do some wild shit.

But my smile dropped when I saw him. Jakobe. The man that shot Hendrix and the man Hendrix warned me might not be dead. I tried to move away from him as quickly as possible, but he grabbed me by the arm before I could get far.

"Where do you think you're going, Tali?" he said, his voice laced with venom. His hand wrapped around my mouth, firmly covering it as I tried to scream.

I tried to pull away from him, but he was too strong. He dragged me back down the hallway, away from the party and everyone else. Jakobe took me to a secluded part of the venue, and I knew I was in trouble. I slapped at his arm and tried to stab him in the foot using my heel. Once he got me through the doors, he removed his hand and wrapped it around my neck. "Shut the fuck up, Tali," he growled into my ear.

"Ja, Jakobe let me go. Let me go! You don't...you don't want to do this," I tried to reason with him, but he wasn't interested in listening.

"You think you're so smart, don't you? You think that psycho ass nigga gives a fuck about you?" he said, sneering at me. "You thought you could just walk around safely in this type of life? No matter how he tries to dress it up for you, this is still the streets. And now you, along with that nigga will become a product of them. Another dead body to bury in Union City."

I could feel the fear rising in my chest, but I refused to let it overwhelm me. I had to fight back. I struggled against him, trying to break free, but he held tight.

"You know he is going to kill you. You aren't shit without Henny. Is that why you are acting like a hurt little bitch?" I gasped. His grip tightened, and I used my nails to claw at him.

"You don't know shit," he said against my cheek. His long locs tickled my collarbone, making a shiver roll over my body. He was too close, like a snake ready to attack. "You like that? Like it when I'm close to you? I remember how you loved sucking my dick. How about I recreate that night, and this time I can fuck your brains out before I blow them all over these pretty floors."

I was beginning to panic because I knew this nigga would do exactly what he said that he would. I was determined to escape him, no matter what it took. He was not about to rape and kill me for Henny to find. I raised my foot and stabbed down as hard as I could into his foot. I raised my arms and jammed my elbows back into his chest, hoping I hit wherever Henny shot him. "Fuck! Fuck!" Ja roared, but his grip loosened, and he stumbled back, giving me a chance to run.

I took off as fast as I could, but I heard him chasing after me. I didn't know what else he could be capable of, but I knew I had to keep moving. I could hear his footsteps getting closer and closer, and then I heard the sound of a gun being cocked.

"No more running, Tali Ho," he grunted.

I stopped and slowly turned around just to see him pointing the gun at me. I froze, not knowing what to do. I was terrified. I held my hands up just as his finger flexed. But then, out of nowhere, I felt a shove, knocking me down. I heard the two loud shots and saw Crescent get hit. She pushed me out of the way, and the next thing I knew, she had been shot instead. I watched in horror as she fell to the ground.

"No! No! Noooo," I screamed. I was in shock, unable to move. I couldn't believe what had just happened. Everything sped up in real-time, and I crawled toward her body. I heard someone shouting, but I couldn't determine who it was. "Crescent! Crescent!" I cried. I couldn't help but feel guilty – if Jakobe hadn't seen me, Crescent wouldn't have been hurt.

"Tali! Tali! Snap out of it and hold this!" I heard Henny's voice, pulling me back from the edge I was standing on. Crescent. I had to save her. I snatched the shirt from him and put it over her wound.

"Tali, I got that nigga," she coughed.

"Bissh, shut up!"

She coughed again and closed her eyes until I screamed at her to open them. She stared at me, and I could hear someone wheezing and gasping. While holding pressure to her chest to stop the blood flow, I turned around and saw Henny standing over Jakobe with a gun to his forehead.

"It was always your fate to become a product of these streets. Fuck you, Jakobe," Henny condemned before he unloaded his clip into Ja's head. I knew then I couldn't ever let my guard down, not even for a moment. I turned back and looked down with a smile at Crescent, but she had stopped breathing.

"Hendrix!"

## CHAPTER TWENTY-FOUR

## HENDRIX 'HENNY' PHARMA

It had been three weeks. Three long fucking weeks before we could have the board meeting with Tremont's bitch ass. I was still sore, so I needed those weeks to heal, even though I didn't want to admit it. If Stax hadn't been there, I didn't know if I would have survived Crescent's surgery that night. When I saw all that blood covering her, and heard Tali screaming, I damn near lost my mind. That could have been Tali lying there, but Crescent took the bullet. It didn't make anything better because Cent was still lying there dying.

Faxx came in and lost it, shooting Jakobe so many times there was no way anyone could identify the body. He had started to slip into blackness, like when we discovered Cece had a rare heart defect at birth. I had to pull him back because he would be no good to anyone in that state, and many people would die if we couldn't rein him in. So, I made the same promise to him as I did before Cece's surgery.

*SHE WILL LIVE, OR I WILL TAKE HER BACK FROM DEATH ITSELF.*

That promise reined in his rage enough for us to get her out of there and to the *Clinic*. Link had a sixth sense knowing shit was about to pop off because having Stax beside me for the surgery was a miracle sent straight from God. Eight hours and twenty-three minutes later, we all sat beside Crescent, waiting for her to wake up. Now that she was healed enough to go home, we all felt like we could breathe. It was no way I would let Faxx lose whatever it was that they were building together or my work wife. So, I pushed off the meeting until Crescent was discharged. I told his ass he didn't need to be here today, but he assured me it was fine because Crescent had therapy today, and Tali was staying with her at his house. I shook my head because I knew Crescent was out of there, his home, as soon as she was on her feet. Faxx wasn't concerned about it, though, and brushed me off.

I pulled into the parking lot and hopped out, mentally preparing myself for the day because I was ready to attend tonight's appointment with Yasmin. I thought Tali would have backed out, but I was wrong. She decided that Yasmin had done too much and would continue to do it. It still hurt her to say the words because it was still her family, regardless of anything. I suggested she sit it out, but she insisted on being there. After her decision, I confessed to her the extent of what Yasmin and Katrice had been doing, and she was ready to attempt the surgery on her own.

I didn't want the rest of what was done to sway her decision because it would have been out of anger. It was fine with me to tell her since she had time to think it over and decide what to do. But I needed her to know everything. I didn't expect the 'fuck it, let me do it' or for Shandea to ask for a pair of scrubs. Without prompting, Yasmin spilled everything she knew or what she had done to Mrs. Naomi and how it all started six months before her going into the hospital. Tali and Dea blamed themselves for not being there for their mother. They sat down and spoke with Mrs. Naomi to ask what was happening while they weren't there. Mrs. Naomi had been doing just fine until the sisters decided they wanted to '*help*' more. It started as doing house chores, grocery shopping, and taking her to appointments. Then they started to cook her meals, saying she needed to eat better foods to care for her health. Naomi hadn't known her nieces were slowly poisoning her with lithium pills that they crushed into her food. Before she decided to go into the hospital, they had a lawyer set up to come out and have her sign power of attorney, but it didn't happen. Naomi's pastor convinced her to go and get checked out since she's been sick lately. That was the only reason why we found the cancer, and luckily, we did. It was a lot of devious shit, but the kicker was it was Naomi's sister's idea. The Judge, ready to sign off on a power of attorney, had no knowledge but had been contacted by Rodney. He'd been lying his ass off, but his time was coming with the info we had on him.

That news had both sisters livid, but Oz assured them it would all be handled in time.

It was no longer an obsession between Tali and me. After all this, it just became a full-on shared psychotic disorder. I wasn't sure if that was a good thing or a bad thing at the moment. I had Stephanie make us an appointment with Faxx's therapist as well. At this point, we all were going to be seeing Dr. Malone. She was about to be busier than ever before since she technically only had two patients. I told Link it would be best if we all made an appointment with the therapist, including my cousin Kreed when he came home.

I entered the building using the back halls, but instead of going to my office, I made a different turn to get to the meeting rooms. I smirked, opening the door to the same conference room we used for Crescent's meeting with that bitch, Pamela. Link, Oz, and Faxx sat at the table looking over a folder, and I moved to take my seat at the opposite head of the table from Oz.

"How's my work wife doing?" I opened the folder, trying not to laugh. I heard something heavy hit the table and peeked to see Faxx watching me.

"I love you like a brother Henny, but keep fucking around about Cent. I will blow up that new Bentayga," he dared. Link choked, and Oz smiled before unbuttoning his suit jacket.

"Okay, but seriously, how is she?" I asked. My joking had subsided because I was upset by what happened and felt it was my fault.

"She's doing good. Cece is being really gentle with her, so taking care of MY wife is helping in my life in more ways than one," he shrugged.

"My baby is always gentle with the things she cares about. As long as it doesn't talk bad about her daddy, uncles, or aunties, she's good," I said, looking away quickly. Then I frowned. Would we need to watch Oz's kid the same way? I hoped it skipped a generation or something.

"I got a call from Justice this morning, and I spoke to Kreed," Link said. I raised my head to give him my attention because that bastard didn't call me. It was probably because I was recovering, and Link had been handling most of the shit lately with Oz.

"Did they give him a date yet?" I asked. It had been almost 11 years since he took that charge for me. There wasn't enough I could do to make up for all the time he'd lost, but Kreed disagreed with me every time. Taking out the one person who tormented him and his sisters was payment enough. I sent my little cousins to the best schools and ensured they had everything they wanted and needed. I did everything I could do for Kreed while he served my time. Now it was time for him to come home.

"They did. He will be released in three months. His other news concerns Yung D-Mar, or Princeton, not being the bitch we thought he was. Kreed believes we can use him if we are considering the merger with Ian," Link said, looking at each of us. We all turned to look at Oz, and he drummed his fingers on the wooden table.

"I've spoken with him at length about a few things, and I don't see a reason why we can't. As always, Henny's intuition about niggas except Jakobe is right," Oz said.

"First off, I told all of y'all he and Xavier were the same, but I didn't see them going down this path. Maybe I was too close to them," I sighed. We all turned when the door opened, and Aunt Vanessa, Stephanie, and Stax walked into the room. Faxx sucked his teeth and threw himself back into the chair when his brother sat beside him.

"You going to get your shit together, Fransisco, and put your heat away. This is a business meeting," Stax chided. We all watched as Faxx muttered under his breath but put his gun away. Stax raised a brow but said nothing else, leaning back in his chair.

"Well, where is this doctor? I have places to be today," Vanessa asked. Before I could reply, there was a knock, and the door opened, revealing Dr. Tremont.

I felt my anticipation at seeing that pompous bitch beg for his job and his life rise to new levels when he looked around the meeting room. The evidence I created against him was too strong for Dr. Tremont to get out of the embezzlement scheme.

Dr. Tremont sat at the head of the table closest to Oz, dressed impeccably in a tailored suit. He smiled at me as he sat, but I could see the confusion in his eyes. He knew something was up, and I could tell he was nervous when I smirked at him.

I took a deep breath and cleared my throat. "Dr. Tremont, I have some evidence that I'd like to discuss with you." I pulled a stack of papers from the folders Link had provided and slid them down to him. Aunt Vanessa, who sat on the other side of him, stopped the papers and placed them in front of him.

Dr. Tremont's eyes widened as he glanced through the documents.

"What is the meaning of this, Hendrix?" he asked, voice shaking.

"I think you know exactly what it means," I replied, my voice steady. "You've been embezzling money from the hospitals you've worked at, for years, and now this one. I have proof."

Ignacio's face paled if that was possible for his skin tone. He seemed almost gray as he realized the gravity of the situation. "This...this...is bullshit! He did this! We are here to discuss the unprofessional conduct I witnessed inside of a patient's room! He..." Tremont pointed at me, "he was having sexual relations with a staff member. I truly believe he was using his authority over her and who knows how many others it has been. I demand his job!"

"Hendrix, is this true?" Vanessa asked. Ignacio smiled, leaning back into the leather chair while all eyes landed on me. I rotated my neck and took a deep breath.

"Aunt Vanessa let's not pretend like you weren't in the kitchen of the Emerald on a counter when I walked in one day," I retorted. Stephanie started to laugh, and Vanessa fixed her collar rolling her eyes. I never took my eyes off Tremont. His frown at my words made me smile.

"What the fuck is going on here?" He fumed. He tried to stand, but Oz's hand slammed onto his shoulder hard.

"Sit the fuck down nigga," Oz ordered. Tremont fell back into the chair, looking around the table as fear crept into his eyes.

"See, just like I told Tali when she was worried about you and your petty ass shit, I am the mutha fuckin' board. This is my hospital, and I do what the fuck I want when I want in it. This is our fucking city. Do you feel what I am saying to you?" I stood up, walking toward him, when the door opened again. Ian walked in, and I wasn't surprised. It only made sense that it would be him that was the silent partner.

"I apologize for being late. I was...tied up. What have I missed?"

"Help me. You're an international board member, correct? These...these people..."

"These people are about to give you an offer that would be in your best interest to accept. Because if I need to get involved, you will not like your body's condition when I am through with you," Ian said. He moved and took a seat next to Stephanie and kissed her hand.

"I like him," she smiled.

"What do you want from me?" he asked, desperation creeping into his voice.

"I want you to keep quiet about everything you know about me," I said firmly. "And I want you to stay away from Tali. She's mine now, and I won't tolerate your interference."

Dr. Tremont's eyes narrowed, and I could see the anger bubbling beneath the surface.

"You can't do this, Hendrix," he spat. "You won't threaten me."

My eyes locked on his. "Oh, but I can," I said softly. "And I will. You have a choice to make, Dr. Tremont. Either you keep quiet and stay the fuck away from Tali, or I expose you for the fraud you are. The third option is I put you on the fucking table and slowly take a piece of you away until there is nothing left. I don't want to do that because you are an exceptional black doctor, but if you keep fucking playing with me, I will kill you and not give a shit about it. You don't know me nigga, and trust me, you don't want to know any of us."

There was a tense silence in the room as Dr. Tremont considered his options. I saw the slight shaking in his hands that he tried to hide under the table.

"He's taking too long," Faxx snapped and stood. He had a gun with a silencer attached to Tremont's forehead. The smell of urine hit the room as he cried out.

"Fine," he said through gritted teeth. The tears leaked from his eyes at the fear filling his body.

"He's a bitch," Vanessa said, standing.

"I'll keep quiet and stay away from Tali. But... I want to leave, Hendrix. I...I can't...I...."

I smiled coldly. "Oh, you want to leave. Naw, big man, your contract is for two years, and I paid you quite well for your expertise. Do your fucking job, and you can walk away from all this at the end but always remember what I have on you, Tre. And remember that I will not hesitate in destroying your legacy or taking your fucking life," I warned. "But for now, we have a company to run. You're dismissed. Oh, try not to let yourself overthink and call the police. You'll never make it to testify, now get the fuck out."

Faxx turned the gun around and smashed him in his nose, breaking it.

"Ahh! Ahh shit," he cried.

"I would have broken your hands, but we pay you to use those, not to sit around on disability leave," Faxx chuckled.

I couldn't help but feel a sense of satisfaction at watching Dr. Tremont trip over his feet to get the hell out of the room. But I also knew I had to be careful because niggas like him liked to be stupid.

"I will keep someone on him," Ian said as he put his phone away.

"Bet. Now it's about time for my two o'clock appointment," I said. Everyone else stood, and we all filed out of the conference room like it was just another meeting completed for the day. I didn't want to kill that nigga, but if he tested my limited patience, he would end up just like the rest.

Tali stood next to me while we stared down at the table with a conscious Yasmin looking back at us. Cliff was my first test subject, with a drug I created, and it worked very well. Yasmin was still very aware of what was happening, but I strengthened it this time so she couldn't move.

"Are you ready for this, Tali?" I asked.

"Tali...Tali...please...you don't..."

"You did this to yourself, Yasmin. It will be okay. You won't feel anything," Tali said, looking at me.

"Scalpel," I said, holding my hand out. Tali placed it in my hand as tears ran down Yasmin's cheeks. I leaned over to ensure she saw the scalpel while I placed it on her skin.

"You won't feel anything, Yas, not at first anyway," Tali said as I began her first assisted surgical procedure.

Everything went smoothly, and someone received a perfectly healthy heart today. Tali and I walked toward the car, and she was extremely quiet.

"Are you okay, Thickness?" I asked, stopping her from walking. She sighed but looked up at me, biting her lip.

"I think that's my problem. I'm fine," she admitted.

"Well, what else is it?" I asked because I knew there was more. I could feel it.

"What's next?"

I raised my brows because this was not what I expected at all. It could be maybe it hasn't hit her yet, but we would take it a day at a time.

"It's time to meet the family officially. We're going to dinner," I said, taking her hand and leading her to the car.

"You believe we are ready for that step?"

"I would have pulled an Oz and slipped a ring on your finger this morning, but something tells me you are going to focus on the new Women's Center for a while, and that is fine with me," I smirked. Tali stopped, and I looked down at her.

"Am I wrong?" I asked. Tali stood on her tip-toes and kissed me.

"Naw, you know me better than I thought you would be able to. I didn't think this was where I would be six years ago, but I wouldn't want it any other way. I love you, Hendrix," Tali confessed. I dropped her hand and wrapped my arms around her waist. I let my hands drift down to her thick ass and squeezed.

"Thickness, you are my sweetest obsession, and I hope you will understand that you will be completely consumed by the love I have for you. There is no going back, Tali," I declared. I stared into her marble gray eyes, waiting to see the fear or apprehension, but she smiled.

"I guess there is no need for me ever to scream PLATINUM," she said, pulling me closer to crush her lips against mine.

## MALIKITA 'MALA' SAMUELS

F inally, being back home around my family relieved pressure from my chest that I didn't know was there. Of course, I spoke to all of them often, but it wasn't the same as being with or near them. All of them may be crazy as shit, but I loved them and wouldn't trade them for anything in the world. It was suffice to say I would do or endure anything for all of them. I parked my car in front of a modest two-story home in the suburbs five minutes outside of Union City. I found it wild that Mrs. Laverne and Mr. Elijah didn't want to move out of their middle-class neighborhood or leave the house they raised Link and Kina. I loved everything about Kina and her craziness, but her smarts sold it. I swear that girl was smarter than her brother, and Link was smart as hell. He was sexy too, but he got on my last fucking nerve.

I immediately felt guilty and looked down at the diamond glittering on my finger. I sighed, opening my door and getting out of the car. The driveway was full, and I could tell everyone and their mama was in attendance tonight. The last family dinner was postponed because of the charity event shooting, so I knew this one was about to be lit. I walked up to the house, still debating what I wanted to do. I needed a job because there was no way I could sit in that house all day and night. I was so tired of this existence I was living, but you had to do what you had to do in this life. I heard a horn and saw Shantel pulling up and parking behind me. I waited on the steps until she ran up and hugged me. Shantel was never this expressive if it wasn't me or anyone from the crew, which was rare as hell.

"Why are you so happy this evening? Have you found another person to enslave?" I smirked. She punched my arm and reached out to hit the doorbell.

"Finally ready to admit you wanna pull on Link's locs?" She retorted.

"Bissh, really," I said, holding up my hand.

"Bitch, please tell me where he at," Shantel said, looking around and then behind the bushes. "Because he ain't here, and you don't even like the nigga," she hissed.

"He...he had a meeting this evening and..."

"Blah, blah, blah, blah, just say he ain't want to be here around your peoples," she grumbled. She wasn't lying because he didn't want to be here. But it wasn't just about my people but about the neighborhood. It wasn't the...the right income range he wanted to be seen associating with, which was stupid to me because they had more or as much money as his family. The door opened, saving me from having to answer Shantel, and I screamed when I saw Kina standing there.

"Shantel! Mala! Oh my gosh, I missed y'all so much! Please hurry up and come in because all of them idiots keep drilling me about having a boyfriend. The triplets didn't come with Uncle Stax, so I have no one in my corner. I'm damn near eighteen, and they are still in my business," she huffed, pulling us inside. The idiots were Henny, Oz, Link, and Stax when we entered the dining room. I noticed that Faxx, Cece, and Crescent weren't there, but I understood why. I was sure Mrs. Laverne was fixing them huge ass plates for one of us to take them later.

"Hey!" Shantel and I said in unison before taking our seats after kissing Mr. Elijah on his cheek. We hugged Mrs. Laverne, and I kissed my mother and Aunt Stephanie before sitting down. The dinner table was set with fancy dishes and silverware, as the aroma of delicious food wafted through the air. The only open seat was next to Link, and he looked... agitated.

"What's your problem, Kyte?" I asked, looking over the dishes as everyone talked. Tali and Dea waved at me but were engrossed in conversing with my mother and Aunt Stephanie.

"I know damn well I told your ass to stop calling me that, Kita," he said under his breath. I screwed up my face because I hated that name. Charles used that name, and it grated on my nerves. Link knew that shit but loved to mess with me.

"Well, Lakyn, what the hell is your problem? You are sitting there with your face all ugly and shit. Shouldn't you be happy about your baby sister being home and getting ready for college? Your three best friends finally stopped being fuck boys?" I asked. "Or is it because you're so into those computers you don't know how to talk to real girls to get one, so you're jealous," I hissed. His dark eyes moved from his plate and over to me, pinning me to the chair. I swallowed reflexively as they narrowed on me and shakily reached out and picked up my wine glass. His dark brown eyes always did something to me, and tonight was no different. I squeezed my thighs together as my core heated up. It felt like his eyes burned my skin as he stared at me. I was wet and horny as fuck, and I couldn't do this shit anymore. I would talk to Shantel after dinner before I could talk myself out of it. I knew I was being childish with Link, but it was always this way with us. Being an adult now didn't change a damn thing. I saw his mother's worried looks and wanted him to snap out of it.

"Keep fucking with me, Mala, and I will forget whose little cousin you are," he said in barely a whisper. I thought I was about to cum on myself right at the table until Mrs. Laverne turned to us.

"Link! What is the problem, son," Mrs. Laverne smiled. She could see that her son wasn't his usual quiet self. He was even more silent than normal.

I watched Link raise his glass to take a sip of his wine. He placed the glass back down on the table with a grimace.

"I can't keep running this casino without a manager," he complained. "I need someone who knows the business and can handle the day-to-day operations. I can't keep worrying about the shi...stuff happening on the floor while dealing with other business."

Everyone around the table quieted down as he spoke. I looked around and saw the concern on Henny, Oz, and Stax's faces. I had been out of the loop, so I needed to catch up on what the hell was happening.

"We understand, dear. We're happy to help in any way we can," Mrs. Laverne tried to soothe him.

"I know, Mother. I need someone who knows what they're doing. Someone like me, and there aren't many like that who I can trust with my business," Link gritted. His mother stood up, and his father put his fork down, giving him his attention. He was so freaking spoiled it wasn't funny, but if one of us had this same conversation, we would get the same treatment. Mr. Elijah clapped his hands before holding up his finger like he had a great idea. I took another sip of wine and listened.

"Well, what about Mala? She's been working in the business industry for years. She could help you out," Mr. Elijah said, folding his hands.

"Yeah, big head! Mala is a GOAT. She can take any business and run that ish like a well-oiled machine," Kina said, snapping her fingers. I choked on my wine, and my mother patted my back beside me.

"Wha...what? I... ah..."

"Elijah, that is a wonderful idea. You know Mala is looking for something different now that she is home. Who else would be better suited for the position? She knows the business end of it, and also, we won't need to worry about people in our other business," my mother said. I looked up and found Shantel staring at me with wide eyes before her eyes dropped to her phone. What the fuck was she doing? This is a crisis situation right now, and she is all in that damn phone. I can't work with him.

Link scowled. I knew he didn't like me and tolerated me at best. I was sure he didn't want me near his business, and I didn't think it would be a good idea anyway.

"No way. She's not qualified. And besides, I don't want to mix business with...family."

"Nig—Link, we are all family. What are you talking about? You know damn well Mala is overly qualified to do it," Henny said. He was always looking out, but this time, I just needed him to shut the fuck up.

"Link, we're just trying to help. Mala is a smart and capable woman. Maybe you should give her a chance because you can not keep running yourself ragged. It would be best to have someone on the floor who can handle the problems that arise. Mala is perfect," Mr. Elijah stated. Link shook his head.

"Absolutely not. I don't want her involved."

The tension at the table grew thicker, and I was getting mad even though I knew this was not a good look for me.

"What's the problem, Kyte? You act like I can't run circles around you and your team. You know me and how I work, so quit with the bull crap. I can handle your little casino," I chuckled. I could feel his eyes on me like he was lasering a brand on me.

"Link, Mala is right, and your refusal isn't getting us anywhere. You need someone to help you with the casino, and we want to support you. Maybe it's time to put your personal feelings aside and think about what's best for the business," Mrs. Laverne said.

Link glared at me, but he knew she was right. Just like I knew I shouldn't have opened my mouth. He took a deep breath before shaking his head no.

"Lakyn Kyte Moore! Malikita will be coming to work for you until you hire someone else. The decision is final. Now fix your damn face, and get it together, and stop acting like a child. Act like the man I raised you to be," Mr. Elijah announced. No one, not Oz, Henny, Faxx, Stax, or Link, would ever say a word to that man. He was like a father to all of us, and when he said this is what will happen, that's what it was.

"Fine," he said through gritted teeth.

"What!"

"Yes, Father, you're correct in your hypothesis about the situation," Link stated quickly. I would have laughed out loud if I didn't know he wouldn't turn his stern glare on me.

"Okay then. And Mala, no back talk on the job. This is a professional situation, and everything is high stakes. You know what this entails and how the other side of life can creep into regular business. So be prepared," Elijah said.

"Yes, sir," I said quickly.

"Shantel put that phone down and eat your food," he ordered.

"Yes, sir," Shantel said, looking at her plate.

"Shantel, you have been on your phone a lot. Mind telling us what you were doing before arriving at this dinner?" Oz bit out.

"I-I had to handle the Katrice situation. You know, reorient her to her new role," Shantel stammered uncomfortably.

I frowned at Shantel because I could tell that was not the entire truth and by the way Oz narrowed his gaze on her he could tell as well. Now just wasn't the time to grill her about it.

"Laverne, where did you find him? I need me a take charge kinda man of my own," Stephanie laughed, taking the heat off of her daughter. Everyone chuckled as all eyes went back to Link.

"I'll talk to you later, Mala, if you're interested. But if things heat up, it's on you to handle," he stated.

"I can handle myself, Link," I nodded.

"That's all we ask, dear. Now let's enjoy the rest of this meal," Mrs. Laverne smiled. Kina bit her lip so she wouldn't laugh, and I kicked her under the table. They always had a way of making us feel like scolded children when we were grown as shit. I didn't understand how knowing what they knew about their son and us. They made it all seem so...normal.

The rest of the dinner passed in relative silence, with only the clinking of silverware and the occasional grunt or sigh breaking the stillness. Link was still fuming, but he knew he had to do what was best for the casino and his peace of mind. Regardless of how much he couldn't stand me, he knew I was U.C.K. for life, and that was that. I held the same horsemen tattoo as the rest of them, so there was no getting out, even if I wanted to.

As the meal ended and the plates were cleared away, I stood, excusing myself to call Charles to check in. I went into the small bathroom upstairs and pulled out my phone. Four missed calls. Shit.

*"Charles, I..."*

*"How long will you be Kita?"*

*"Dinner just finished, and you know they like to do dessert and a few family games before we leave."*

*"Are you somewhere else? Are you where you are supposed to be, Kita?"*

*"Charles, I asked you to join me, and you declined. I am always where I say I am. I only have enough gas to get here and back home."*

*"How long?"*

*"A few more hours. The same time, as usual, Charles."*

The line disconnected, and I sighed. I screamed silently before I took in a breath. I would have killed him years ago if I could've, but it was impossible. I fixed my skirt and shirt before opening the door and stepping out. I ran into a hard chest, and my immediate reaction was to twist out of reach and bring my forearm up and into someone's throat, but I was slammed against the wall instead.

"What the fuck are you doing, Mala?" Link gritted in my face. His long locs fell forward as he held me against the wall without effort. His body pressed against mine, and I could feel every inch of him, including his hard length pressing against my stomach.

"My bad. It was...wasn't...it wasn't intentional. I...I...I was caught off guard," I panted. His brows furrowed, and his eyes darkened to almost black. He pressed closer, looking into my eyes.

"Is someone hurting you, Mala?"

I swallowed, trying to get some moisture in my throat and wondering if he heard what I was saying on the phone. I was already wet, and my core was screaming at me. He was too close. Too fucking close. I had to say something to make him move.

"And if they were? What are you going to do? Hack them to death or something? I'm good," I said, pushing forward. Link sucked his teeth and slammed me back against the wall holding me in place with a hand at the base of my throat. He was harder than before, and I was so close to just sliding down this wall and taking him in my mouth.

"One of these days, your mouth is going to get you fucked up and tied down," he whispered. His lips were at my ear, and his warm breath tickled the side of my neck.

"Link! We're ready! Hurry up so I can beat your tail," Kina yelled.

"I'm coming, you little punk," Link replied. He turned his head back to me, his dark eyes scanning my body. God only knew what he was looking for before he let me go. "You should be nicer to your new boss Malikita. You may not like the punishments when you fuck up around me," he threatened, turning away and leaving me shaking.

Fuck.

Shantel and I managed to play one round of games before I said I had to go. She followed me, wondering what the hell was going on. Once we were outside, I turned on her and knew she saw the desperation in my eyes.

"What the hell is going on, Mala? Are you okay?" she asked, concerned.

"I want my birthday present early."

"What? It's...it's like a month away," she questioned.

"So! I will owe you or do whatever you ask when you need me to."

"How? You don't even control your own money, which is wild, but to each its own," she shrugged.

"Shantel!"

"Okay, okay, what is it? I will do whatever. What do you want?" She asked, concerned.

"Take me to *MYTH*."

"What?"

"I want the Black Wolf to take my virginity. I can't take it anymore. I was ready to get on my knees in that house and suck Link's dick an hour ago. I can't do this anymore," I cringed.

"Charles..."

"Fuck Charles. That is not why...it doesn't matter. I need to do this and on my terms Shantel. I know you understand that. He has dictated everything else in my life just about. I need this."

"Then just fucking leave his whack ass. It's not like you can't," she said.

"Shantel, do this for me."

"But the Black Wolf? Are you sure? He's...he isn't anything to play with. Bitches go dumb and stupid after fucking him and you...you're a vir..."

"Shantel! Will you do this for me or not? You should understand where I am coming from. This is my decision," I retorted.

Shantel stared at me for a long minute before cursing.

"Fuck! Fuck, fuck, fuck, come on," she said, dragging me to her truck. "I had a damn re-education session tonight, but I will do it tomorrow because you're my sis. You can't wear that either, and you must wear a mask. It's policy," she said, driving off.

It wasn't long before I was in the lower levels of *MYTH*. Shantel had me dressed in a black leather corset that had no bottoms. I almost lost my nerve, but there would be no way I could work around Link being horny as shit. I had to have someone to buss it down so well that he wouldn't be a thought.

"Thank you for this," I said.

"Don't thank me yet, bissh," she said. She held up her phone to my face. "Now, repeat after me. I asked my best friend to give me the Black Wolf as a birthday present even after her objections," she said. People wearing everything from nothing to a full-body catsuit walked by.

"Are you serious?"

"Dead ass, now say it, or we can turn around," she said. I could tell she was serious, so I repeated her words, and once she finished, she put the phone away. "Well, no turning back. Let's go," she said, dragging me through a door. The room was damn near empty, with nothing but a platform in the center of it that was raised from the floor. The room was a deep red, almost black, with inset lights on the walls that changed between a soft white and red. The floors were covered in thick black carpet, and on one side of the room were rows and rows of different styles of paddles, whips, cuffs, and ropes. That's when I noticed two men in each corner with a masquerade-style mask shaped like a wolf.

"Wha—"

"Get up there and place your feet on those footrests. Hurry, it's almost time," she grumbled. I rushed over to the platform, glad I gave myself no time to turn back. I climbed up and did what she said.

"You will be here?"

"Unfortunately, yes," she sighed. I heard a door open, and my body began to shake from the cool breeze that entered the room. All I could see was a tall, dark figure moving toward me. The mask covering my face had me feeling relieved because this was embarrassing as hell. I was laid out like a damn offering to a man they called the Black Wolf. I must be crazy. Thank God Oz, Henny, and Link were still at the house. Today was the only time I could get away with this.

"Who do we have tonight?"

His voice was deep and melodic. The timber of it vibrated through my body and straight to my clit.

"The birthday girl," Shantel answered. I jumped when warm, strong hands caressed my bare legs and my inner thighs all the way to my pulsing clit. The black wolf mask covered his entire face leaving only black holes for eyes. The black cloak covered his body, and all you could see was his unusually long thick dick that already had pre-cum at the tip. The head was wide, and I almost cried at the thought of it pushing inside of me. But that was what I wanted. What I needed to happen. I licked my lips, and he growled like a fucking wolf.

"That will be your name tonight. I will call you Birthday Girl, and you can call me Mr. Wolf."

"Yes, Sir, Mr. Wolf," I moaned. I could feel the heat rolling off him while he stood between my thighs.

"Say that again. I liked it," he gritted. The bass in his voice had my nipples standing to attention and begging for his mouth.

"Mm...Mr. Wolf," I gasped when his hand pinched my hardened nipple

"Mmmm, okay, Birthday Girl. Tell me your safe word," he ordered. He pushed my legs farther apart while massaging my clit. I stared into the black pits on his mask, and it was like he stared into my soul.

"Ahh...I...ahh," I stammered. I felt a slap to my clit, and I couldn't help the moan that escaped or the shock of it feeling so fucking delicious.

"Tell. Me. Your. Safe. Word."

The growl of each word had the cream from my core dripping from my folds. I couldn't stop the moan or the memory of Link pressing me up against the wall from flashing in my mind. He was always who I wanted, but I would never be able to have him. I had to have one thing for myself: The Black Wolf. Damn, the consequences!

"K...K...Kyte."

Until Next Time

# Dear Reader

**Thank You For Reading!**
***Product of the Street is a series that will span at least five books.
My epilogues are not used to give you a happily-ever-after ending.
They are used to progress the story's plot and develop characters in
this universe. Product of the Street is a series; every character will
still be a part of the storyline, and you will always see how their
relationships progress. Those of you that have read my paranormal
series already know. Once this series concludes, you will have an
epilogue telling the futures of each character. I hope you stick along
for the ride and know that just because the story moves on does not
mean it is the end of the story for your favorite character.***
I would love to hear from you, so please consider joining the
Product Of the Street book group on Facebook!
http://www.fb://group/558629379526942?ref=share&mibextid=NSM
WBT
**I Hope You're Ready For Book Three! Date TBA**

# About The Author

E. Bowser is an author of Paranormal Romance, Fantasy, Urban, and Horror Fiction. She writes whatever stories her imagination can conceive. E. Bowser has always wanted to write a story that people would like to read and would fall in love with the characters. She loves when readers give their feedback so she can make her next book better. E. Bowser loves to read herself and takes great pleasure in doing so whenever she has the chance. E. Bowser started writing short stories about life, anything horror or paranormal, when she was in middle school and still has not stopped.

E. Bowser has been an independent self-published author since 2015 and has no plans to stop as long as her characters keep talking.

Thank you for reading. I hope you enjoy the series so far! Please review. I love them, or feel free to contact me on Facebook, Twitter, Instagram, good reads, book bub, or through my website. Thank you again for reading, and keep looking for more Deadly Secrets series, The Rayne Pack series Spin-off, Dream Walker, and Product Of The Street Union City Series!

*Follow or contact me at the links below to see what is coming up next!*

*www.ebowserbooks.com*

*www.facebook.com/authorE.Bowser*

*https://www.bookbub.com/authors/e-bowser*

https://www.goodreads.com/ebowser

# Books By The Author

**Deadly Secrets Brothers That Bite Books 1-5**

The Deadly Secrets is an exciting series focused on Taria, Michael Quinn, and LaToya are friends and lovers fighting against evil forces.

Deadly Secrets Awakening Book 1

Deadly Secrets Revealed Book 2

Deadly Secrets Consequences Book 3

Deadly Secrets Consequences Book 4

Deadly Secrets Royalty Book 5

## Deadly Secrets Novellas/Novelettes

This collection of stories will give you a glimpse into the lives of Taria, Michael, LaToya, and Quinn, along with many others. Sit back and fall back into the paranormal world of Deadly Secrets.

Desires of the Harvest Moon

Twice Marked Witches and Wolves

Rise of the Phoenix

A Vampire and His Alpha Mate

A Hunter Touched My Soul

Brothers That Bite Chronicles Volume 1

Trick Or Treat The Babysitters From Hell: Deadly Secrets Halloween

Rescued By Fire: Gio & Selena's Story

Scorched By Desire: Sire & Lydia's Story

Trick Or Treat A Night From Hell: Deadly Secrets Halloween

## The Crown Series Books 1-3 On-Going series

This series would be best read if you start with Deadly Secrets Series Brothers That Bite books 1-5 and other novellas.

Taria, LaToya, Michael, and Quinn are back together again in Deadly Secrets Hunters Regin: The Crown Series. Taria Cross was turned into a Vampire by Michael Vaughn, and she became his Queen. Not only does she have to figure out this new part of her life, but she is a Hunter as well, and that is a whole other list of duties.

Deadly Secrets Hunters Reign Book 1

Their Sirenian Queen Deadly Secrets Story

Deadly Secrets A Vampires Temptation Book 2

Deadly Secrets When Queens Are Crowned Book 3

Twice Marked A True Alpha And His Witch Deadly Secrets Story

Shades Of Passion Deadly Secrets Story Book 1

## The Rayne Pack Series On-Going

Follow the Rayne Brothers as they find their Mates and fight the forces of evil. See how Dax, Max, Malic, Alex, Jarod, and Thomas fight for those they love while being attacked on all sides.

An Alpha's Claim Book 1

Submission To An Alpha Book 2

## Dream Walker: Visions of the Dead On-Going Series.

What if you had the ability to see things before, they happened? Saw a zombie outbreak unfold before your very eyes? Could you embrace visions of the dead coming back to life? For Kaylee, who has been chosen to receive this gift, these visions are the beginning of a nightmare.

Dream Walker: Visions of the Dead Book 1

Dream Walker: Visions of the Dead Book 2

Dream Walker: Visions of the Dead Book 3

Dream Walker: Visions of the Dead Novella (Collection of short stories)

## Product Of The Street: Union City On-Going Series.

In a single night, soul ties were created that bonded these two couples in ways they'd never planned or imagined. But will betrayal, jealousy, and death make them second guess their connections being destiny or tear them apart? ***This book contains explicit language, graphic violence, and strong sexual content. It is intended for adults.***

Product Of The Street: Union City Book 1
Product Of The Street: Union City Book 2
Product Of The Street: Union City Book 3 (TBA)